A BOOK OF THE EFILU LEGACY

DRAGON'S HEIR

Glenn Parris

THE EFILU LEGACY: DRAGON'S HEIR: THE ARCHAEOLOGIST'S TALE
Copyright © 2021 Glenn Parris. All rights reserved.

Published by Outland Entertainment LLC
3119 Gillham Road
Kansas City, MO 64109

Founder/Creative Director: Jeremy D. Mohler
Editor-in-Chief: Alana Joli Abbott

ISBN: 978-1-954255-26-5
EBOOK ISBN: 978-1-954255-24-1
Worldwide Rights
Created in the United States of America

Editor: Alana Joli Abbott
Copy editor: Scott Colby
Proofreader: Bessie Mazur
Cover Illustration: Mike Hamlett
Cover Design: Jeremy D. Mohler
Interior Layout: Mikael Brodu

Visit **outlandentertainment.com** to see more, or follow us on our Facebook Page **facebook.com/outlandentertainment/**

The wall of Law, long standing as surrogate for justice, offered stability impervious to change. Its fortification shines as an Efilu triumph for all to see. Still, walls are peculiar things. They keep the unwanted out while constructing a perfect prison for their creators. The Efilu forged their barrier around a treasury of sins, a weightless burden until the debt comes due. Sixty-five million years have yet to wash the Exodus's taint from the Alum. Atonement, inexorable, painful, and righteous, must reunite all the children of Fitu. For the Alum renders one inevitable constant in the universe... change.

Prophecy of Dragon

— TABLE OF CONTENTS —

PRELUDE
— THE KEEPERS' GAMBIT —

Sun rays breached an indigo horizon off coastal Maine. As night retreated westward from the morning's assault, cold light failed to thaw the lingering frost. Sorensen's Tavern played errant haven to the lonely port of call jutting defiantly over Howard Cove. Brackish waters lapped barnacled piles underpinning the pier. The rickety establishment seemed to sway, humble and mostly unwanted—but then that was the point. An ordinary day at an out of the way watering hole, prowled by wayward seamen and petty criminals.

Its opened window admitted a fresh breeze, cleansing the stench of spilled beer and sour sweat wafting from the walls, tables, and floor. The whole pub seemed to doze as it recuperated from a good rabble-rousing the night before. For two enigmatic patrons, inconspicuous would not suffice. They needed to be ignored.

A one-eyed sailor sulked at the window, peering absently past his moored ship to the ocean beyond. *How many more "ordinary days" are left?* His eye found the mirror behind the bar, and he considered the ordinary reflection therein. The old man mused.

It could be so nice to be a Nelky. To Blend! Completely unseen by human eyes.

"I heard that." A woman's voice chided him, so feeble as to affect a willful sotto voce. Settled in on his blindside, this woman, who appeared of Chinese extraction, nursed a teacup, freshly poured full and nested in a matching saucer, its contents yet too hot to drink. "—And it's *Melkyz* now, I hear." The very portrait of patience and sagacity, the frail figure pinched the cup handle delicately. The woman's bearing cast an air of seniority relative to her companion's.

"They're coming." The old mariner half turned toward her and winced. He snugged his moth-eaten skullcap down and warmed his hands around the steaming mug of coffee he'd set on the bar.

"Why so surprised?" asked the Chinese woman. Thin and hunchbacked, with a deep, wrinkled countenance, she perched on the seat next to him as she spoke. "We knew our diaspora would return one day." Steam rose from her tea, fogging a glass eye, as she lifted the cup to her lips. "Fortunately, we have prepared."

"Yes, we were wise to keep the Exodus Corridor clear," the sailor remarked, peering out toward the harbor. He brushed his patch down securely over his empty eye socket, one he had never bothered to fill with a prosthesis.

"Remember who we're dealing with!" The old woman's words were lost as the foghorn shook her slight frame on the stool. The horizon remained blue and clear as far north, east, and south as one could see. An intimate, telepathic query confirmed that neither she nor her companion had permitted fog to roll in this morning. She returned her attention, and one good eye, to her confidante, meeting his monocular gaze with intensity.

"Yes. We know what their response will be if they find we've been guiding Fitu's fate," the sailor said aloud when the lighthouse had finished its sound test.

The barkeep worked his way to their end of the countertop, wiping down the beer-stained wood as he hobbled. He was fat and bald, but had both his natural eyes. He gave a casual good-morning nod to the sailor, ignoring the old woman and what appeared to be idle chatter between them.

Unforced anonymity. No psychic tracks. The elderly pair remained silent for long moments until the portly man finished his brief chore and limped on his way. Here, away from the ears, eyes, and minds of any who might expose them, they could afford to contrive their plans in the old ways, casually and out loud in the midst of chaos. The two abettors indulged in delicious recklessness.

"Remnant Efilu technologies have been restored to pristine working order with marvelous creativity." She allowed herself the smallest crease of a smile. "We must waste no time in clearing the museum. We can't leave any traces of how we directed Jing—human—evolution."

Layers of grime stained the sailor's weathered face with accents of sienna deep into the wrinkles flanking his mouth. "What of our poor children?" the old man asked, displaying the first hint of any compassion between them. "We can't save them all."

"Nestled in the Exodus Corridor and powered up, our Jing Pen museum is sure to be detected when the Efilu return," he said. "We must fold the edges of space-time around the remnant technology."

She tilted her head and gazed fondly at the barkeep stacking glasses at the end of the room. "How elegantly we engineered our Toys," she preened with more than a hint of pride. "Hewn from sterile clay, we've fashioned the Jing Pen to play gods to our precious Jing, shepherding a Humanity that now stands, an independent swell of fire and water in *their* image and *ours*."

"And our fingerprints are all over them, too," the old man retorted.

"Yes, on the Toys, but not on our Jing," she said, her assertion rich with maternal ferocity. "We can demonstrate that the Alom crests in them without our help! What has happened once can happen again. The One venture nears fruition. Not even psychic geniuses of the Efilu Realm can *Turn* them—and that with only sixty-five million years of work." The crone frowned. "The Jing Pen shall be Humanity's last line of defense if the Alom flows turbulent and war comes."

"War?" the sailor spoke in a husky whisper through gritted teeth. "War is a contest between equals. You boast of Toys wielding sixty-five-million-year-old technology." He huffed. "Antiques. Our highland friend fears the One Experiment is on the verge of failure, at best. At worst, the Greater Society will elect to end us all."

The matron peered sympathetically at the bartender. "The cerebral inhibition lobules will protect these Jing, but the poor creatures cannot engage in intimate discourse with one another— not the surface-dwellers, anyway."

"Gray matter enrichment tricks." The sailor's face sagged. "Their only advantage is that the psychic inhibition field will silence *all* parties, Efilu and mammal alike. We can only hope our long-gone kindred will be baffled by the loss of innate contact long enough to make mistakes."

The dowager gazed into the distance with firm resolution, raised her cup again, and decreed softly, "Cut ties with the Masons, the Illuminati, and all regional secret societies. They're on their own now." She concluded the conversation with grim, tight lips. Then she finished her tea.

Part 1

A PLAGUE OF TYGERS AND DRAGONS

THE SEAT OF POWER

Tiest, a world fashioned around a gas giant to be the Efilu capital.
It rotates stellar dimensions with purpose:
Bedrock to Alom, The River of Fate.
To nourish vast, massive, ever thirsty roots.
Tree of Ages engineered in turn to cradle an ancient city.
Not so small a place, and visible from high orbit.
This citadel serves as Seat of Power, The Round Table.
One Realm, One People, One Future.
This Eminent Domain, an elaborate monument to Efilu hubris.
An apparition,
endowed with a mystique,
and worshipped as a God.

Chapter One
— THE ARCHAEOLOGIST —

A pool of glistening gray rippled in its pedestaled basin, the gloom of the dais broken only by a solitary lamp. The vessel's shell, adorned with runes inscribed and embossed upon it, lay centered on the altar. A male figure, small compared to many of his spectators, crept out of the darkness, bearing a precious relic central to the rite.

As eldest meg of the Melkyz House of Kemith, the duty fell to the son of the dead. He raised his burden above his head, offered a silent invocation, then unwrapped the disarticulated members. Well versed in the ceremony, even profound grief did not distract the Kemithi heir apparent. He performed the revival as it had been executed time and again through millions of generations with traditional verbal chants in the Common tongue. Only discipline kept him from projecting thoughts of overwhelming grief for all to hear. The intimate, psychic projection universally employed among the species of Efilu for ages, strangely felt now too personal to share.

The power to animate the argent-jet flecked syrup, as if driven by the Alom's Fire of Life, was small consolation, given the subject.

The staging ritual culminated in the immersion of severed hands, tethered together like a pair of gloves by thick nerve fibers. Upon completion of his grim chore, the orphaned minister retreated into silent shadows. Again, he reverted to archaic verbal expression in a paradox of intimacy. The title, *Ati,* dying on his lips, he suppressed the accompanying *goodbye mother.*

Once submerged in the mercurial nectar, cold digits of still-supple flesh writhed, delicate and nearly alive. Fingers contracted, then reached out of the bowl as they spawned Vit Na's Animem— her lifetime's memory incarnate. Wrought from shimmering nano-synthetic silt, Vit Na Iku coalesced. An innocent witness, conjured to lifeless substance, knelt incomplete at the behest of the living.

Her audience settled into their seats, eager to learn details omitted from the mind-numbing records presented by the *ReQam*'s surviving crew. The mission log fully examined, though informative, satisfied not one council member. The leaders of the Efilu Greater Society, guided by laws too long held to abandon, beckoned the shadow to give her testimony. Judgement of this heir to Fitu required profound knowledge in this place where direct, intimate communication was impossible. To decide the destiny of Man, the Efilu needed more.

Instantly upon becoming sensible, Vit Na recognized the hallowed Hall of the Round Table. A spotlight highlighted her form as she rose to her feet, half-formed eye sockets already searching her surroundings. Once again, she was on Tiest, capital world of the vast Efilu Realm. Tiest, where the end began.

"Greetings, Surrogate Major," the First Impressor formally hailed her return, telepathically projecting the ritual recitation. "Speak you now on behalf of these mammalian claimants' merit."

The realization of why she was here and what was required weighed heavily on her, even during her reconstitution. Her techni-crafted ghost would perform as Surrogate Major on behalf of this mammalian claimant's virtue. As a newly formed Animem, she projected the Iku oath of submission: "I rise to serve."

The ship's entire surviving crew had been dismissed, save High Commander Tur, who remained silent in the shadows, struggling against deep waves of emotions. Vit Na's revenant beauty begged his touch again. Still, his heart ached as he watched the perfect, familiar stranger. Her dark eyes locked with Tur's for a long moment of recognition, then reluctantly focused on the authors of the technology that had summoned her.

Drawing a deep breath, more out of habit than necessity, the avatar stretched phantom limb and tail. Finally, taking on the balance of her vital features, the Animem, Vit Na Iku, spoke one mind to many at the Council's command.

"I was never a prophet. The gift of prescience would have rewritten my fate were I so. These fur-mites, as we came to deride the hairy creatures ages ago, are no longer mere vermin. All evidence indicates that they are indeed descended from those little mammals we left behind during the Exodus. Whether they are natural, extant Jing or genetically engineered Jing Pen is contention for another time. I will proceed from the premise that they are Jing—banal mammalian children of Fitu."

"Turtle-spit." The anonymous telepathic expletive intimately pierced the minds of every other member of the Council in the darkened chamber.

Vit Na Iku continued without pausing. "I anticipated your objections, though I can neither hear nor address them, so bear with me, please." She paced the dais with all the grace and poise that characterized her life as the tenacious spotlight followed her.

An audible murmur underscored the telepathic protests to the Animem's suggestion, but the soul-recording was not interrupted again.

"By our reckoning, sixty-five million years is time enough for a group of species—even mammalian species—with sufficiently advanced traits to evolve, to fill vacant niches. Some of them filled ours. The society we encountered, Humanity, now calls our Fitu 'Earth' by way of record. The key question is: do they rise to the required level of Efilu standards?"

Again, came the lone intimate mental projection: "Granted, these milk-suckers might develop sentience, even language, maybe even some rudimentary semblance of intimate communication—but gain higher awareness of the Alom stream and recognize their place in it? Never!"

"Still, they seemed to have compensated for this failing with single-species dominance, among other adaptations," the Animem continued. "We doubted that mammals could have survived the aftermath of the fragment impact when our ancestors determined that *we* could not.

"Tur and his executive staff postulated that many saprophytes and arthropods could have survived on decaying organic matter—a simple, but stable food network for small creatures. Perhaps mammals cannibalized one another, supplementing with grubs and fungi. This has been documented in cases of Jing famine on our worlds."

"They are ALL our worlds!" the dissenter interrupted again with authority, shocked that anyone could consider it otherwise projected along with the words.

Vit Na continued her report, unperturbed. "This could have sustained a diminished population until the sun emerged from its wintery sleep. The blanket of soot and cloud would have begun to clear the atmosphere in a few hundred years, allowing plant seeds to germinate again.

"These biped Jing descendants have become wickedly cunning," Vit Na Iku's thought projection almost hissed. "These…Humans. There are traces of the Keepers throughout this Jing empire, at least by inference, so we do suspect their handiwork. As far as we can tell, however, they played no direct part in this mammalian evolution or engineering scheme."

A thought rose from the dark. "Could this evolutionary mimicry be natural?"

"They could never have survived the end of the world," drawled another mind-voice, his silhouette hidden among steely, wooden arches of the crowded hall.

"Who knows?" Vit Na shrugged. "The Si Tyen Keepers specialized in the impossible. We do know this: The Quatal had no part in the administration of the Poison. We vanquished an alien race for treachery that was not theirs. Maybe the toxin's effect of mental dulling clouded our judgement. Maybe we just wanted the alien presence of the Quatal gone. The truth is so much more complicated; we conclude that the Poison was likely visited upon us from within our own ranks."

At this, the discord among the Council became a clammer of minds, but Vit Na pressed on.

"I'm just an archeologist," she projected. "One who should never have embarked on this venture, I might add. The Greater Society's collective animated memory extends well before our departure from Fitu. We still have maps and city specifications that predate the Exodus. The crew of the *ReQam* should have *known* where to look for clean, yellow algae. What of value could I contribute?" Vit Na Iku paused, as if waiting for an answer that she could not perceive. The Animem spoke again. "As it turns out, only this: the Alom must have preordained my presence for a singular purpose—to convey an intricate knowledge of human events such as no other Efilu could. As Saymon once said, 'Even the most humble of souls may be venerated, if the Alom's currents so favor.'

"How pretentious I've always considered that proverb. Never was it my intention to make the name 'Vit Na of Kemith' an embarrassment to our family. I'm sorry... 'Vit Na Iku.'"

Tur interrupted, "It's easy to forget that she's no longer among the living, from the perspective of this psychic maelstrom of input. My fellow crewmates assisted her in organizing her thoughts, hence this incongruous Animem image perspective. There was simply no time for a finer-tooled solution. Some kind of Jing interference, we suspect. May the surviving House of Kemith forgive this offense."

After a nod to the mission commander, the First Impressor urged with a calming psychic tone, "Please continue, Iku."

"What we discovered about the little furry vermin, now known as Humans, is of paramount importance," Vit Na said. "Besides the absence of intimate senses, down pelts, or tails, they have come to resemble us in most disturbing ways. They mimic our architecture and even our political structure. Without legacy artifacts from us as templates, how could this be without the tutelage of the Keepers? Ceremonial images of Si Tyen are found worldwide, inscribed with runes pronounced 'Dragon' in the dominant tongue." She vocalized the word phonetically for all to hear, the first words spoken aloud among them.

"'Dragon?'" an incredulous voice asked aloud in accompaniment to his intimate query. "Did you mean to say—'Dragon,' Iku?"

"Yes, the very name of the self-same Tyen who declined rescue at the time of the Exodus—a most damaging indictment, to be certain. If Dragon's Keepers of the Faith cult were in any way involved, we may be compelled to destroy the Jing Pen and scorch the planet. But if not..." She paused to allow the historic significance of sponsorship duty to settle over the Council. Through the haze of Animem perception, a statuesque, winged figure loomed, motionless in the shadows. Vit Na Iku could not name him, yet she knew him somehow. Even in death, she feared him, but she had an oath to fulfill.

"As we all know, what happened once, could happen again...or before."

A thought rose from murmured objections. "Are you implying that this cognate Jing branch of the Alom may have been left behind during the Exodus?" The notion hung in the air, repugnant to all present.

"Possibly," she said. "We may be obliged to invite the Jing into the Efilu Realm. They could qualify as a Lesser Society of their own; their scant numbers barely amount to six billion. Hardly a political threat to even the smallest society."

An undercurrent of protest rose again as Vit Na Iku, endearingly reminiscent of her legacy, gestured for calm. "I can only guess at the dispute breaking out among you, my sage Council-meren, but this dilemma is born of our own negligence. We have made precious few changes to our laws in sixty-five million years.

"Ironically, the Jing have a word that they use to describe a person or organization that has become obsolete or fails to remain competitive. They call them 'dinosaurs.' Coincidentally, this is also the word they use to describe fossil remains of wild animals and livestock from our time on Fitu. Their prevailing belief is that *we* all died in the wake of the fragment impact. They credit their survival to their own resourcefulness and superior genetic traits."

As if sensing the stunned silence in the room, Vit Na Iku hesitated a beat before projecting, "If we're not careful, their words will become prophetic."

The Iku visage sat on her haunches as she whisked her gaze across the room she observed only through the lens of death. The cogent portion of her testimony concluded, Vit Na spoke directly one last time. "For security purposes, I hereby impart my Animem to the Greater Society Council. In so doing, I realize my family may never see this most personal of all chronicles. Rest assured that High Commander Tur is not guilty of any coercion in this decision. This terminal choice was mine alone."

Tur shifted uncomfortably on his haunches, but kept his thoughts to himself.

"Note that there is a coded segment herein." Somehow, her eyes found his. "As is my right, access to this portion of the Animem shall be restricted to Tur for the duration of his lifespan. The content is of a purely personal nature and of no significance to anyone else. Please convey my regrets to Clan Kemith."

Her son glared briefly at Tur then bowed his head in acceptance of his mother's final wishes. A violation of traditional intimacy, the entire council would now experience her life as she saw, heard and felt it, a privilege usually reserved for the immediate family and select clan.

Vit Na Iku announced, "Prepare to initiate sequence! Begin."

Chapter Two

— DANCE OF PASSION —

My entire brood was on our home grounds for an educational retreat. As Mater of our small house, I should have been there to guide the lessons. I delegated that responsibility to one of my eldest sons. I was unable to attend due to a previous family commitment: to study—actually, to re-study—a replica of hieroglyphs in the catacombs beneath the Round Table.

It was a wonderful trip. The whole text in question had been studied interminably, but someone is always raising answered questions from the dead. You know how it is. At any rate, it did make my job that much easier. I had so little groundwork to do that the task was no burden at all.

Everyone knew the condition of the Keepers at the time of the Exodus. Most of them were so demented from starvation that they themselves didn't know what they were writing about. Endless gibberish about Toy-making.

As one of a very few qualified archeologists in the quadrant, I was asked to render my interpretation of these writings. My family had already volunteered my services. I could not refuse.

The assignment, for which I had been allotted a week, took less than three days. How could any obligation be this easy? And timely! I was secretly grateful for a little break from the responsibilities of parenting.

Tiest, as the seat of power of the Efilu Realm, was a magnificent world. They sent me to the source to compare the reproduction with the original Si Tyen writings. I had never been there before. A retextured gas giant, its surface area rivaled that of a small star, yet its gravity fraction was only 1.031 of standard.

The landscaping was artful, even from orbit. Various species of grasses and trees formed geometric patterns with artificially defined edges, subtle enough in design that its form would remain forever pristine, unlike a cheap sand painting, subject to blurring winds spread across the planet. That heavy-handed approach went over satisfactorily on smaller worlds, but on Tiest, it would just display common taste on a grand scale.

Tiest's polar cap was impressively marked by the Forest of Feelings. The worldscape as a whole was a work of art, but the forest was a crowning masterpiece. A home to the psychic echoes of generations of Si Tyen philosophers, the formation appeared as a circle bisected by a sine wave, into a deep green semicircle above and an ashen silhouette below. Great twin lakes dotted the centers of opposing teardrops, chasing each other in the swirl. The wider consensus, of course, epitomized the cross-section of our DNA molecule, the mirage infinitely extrapolating skyward toward the future and rooted deeply in our past, streams of fire and water. The Alom—the River of Life and Fate.

I'd arrived at a fortuitous moment. For three hours out of every seven years, Tiest eclipsed the distant red giant, the Blood Star, obscuring its brighter yellow companion. As the reflection of brilliant yellow returned, it lit the rim of the northern pole, revealing the Tyelaj.

The Tyelaj—a double image, an abstracted rendering of an adult Tyen in fetal position, one oversized wing gracefully spread to form the upper arc of a circle. In the glow of the Blood Star, blazing vapors curled out of a half-opened mouth and under the body to form the lower arc, the far wing all but invisible through it.

It was said that those graced by the apparition of the Tyelaj were endowed with a touch of Si Tyen mystique for life—a myth that did not justify traveling during such intense radiation of stellar flares in the gravity well created between the two large celestial bodies. I've always believed the legend to be no more than an excuse for foolish planning, actually. What a spectacle to behold, though!

Central Port Exchange usually shut down traffic during this period. The captain of my transport would probably be demoted, at least, for getting us caught in the solar storm. Still, I had had all the cubs I planned to have, so what did I care about a splash of radiation? After the storm passed, we were allowed to dock, while port medical personnel efficiently administered routine treatment to the passengers for the radiation exposure.

I made my way without escort through the throng traveling from the celestial port to the capital. Security processed all newcomers. No exceptions for nobility, I learned. The Wilkyz Exchange official—more than twice my size—brought up an out-of-date image of me, stooped down, and compared it with my person. The image showed fewer characters in my torso tattoos and a mane-style I hadn't worn in five years, but no substantial changes in stance or gait.

The Wilkyz guard traced my image, lingering long enough over every curve of my figure to rile me. Even without overt projection, his manner revealed a desire to reach down and stroke my back. Most Wilkyz had that urge; soft, slick Melkyz down beckoned their touch and always sent their serotonin levels soaring. As well as that disgusting ear fetish.

He reluctantly dismissed me when he gauged the ice in my glare. To prompt that crass commoner to address me as *Ati* Vit Na would have reduced me to the depths of his caste. In parting, I flicked my ear at him, incensed, but he just hummed with private pleasure. I felt violated–Wilkyz found pointed ears erotic and all but irresistible.

Upon arrival at my family's private carriage, a fetching pilot acknowledged my credentials and properly saluted, "Ati." He politely projected his name, but I must confess I wasn't listening, and I didn't ask him to repeat it. A member of a humble Melkyz subspecies I had never encountered, he moved with a lean, alluring smoothness and ushered me to my cabin. Leering at his predatory bearing, I decided I liked his patches. I made no secret of lust for his sturdy, marbled physique. Why should I?

Having seen to my comfort, the pilot managed to demur my approving gaze before retreating to the control chamber. I inspected the accommodations. Everything seemed to be in order.

The cabin's wall-mirror reflected my visage, and I gave it a spin. From every angle, it revealed a travel-weary specter in need of grooming. I shimmied up against the wall brush to tidy my back and tail, then slicked my solid black mane about my scalp. I noted how thick it had grown with age. Smoothing the delicate transition follicles to a matted finish along the rim of a glabrous face, I then raked a wisp of mane away from my forehead for an accent.

Yearning fingers traced the gentle features I inherited from my mother. I missed her. The mirrored image highlighted the fact that I tended to wear softer, iridescent cosmetic tones at eye and brow these days. Streaking lashes and brows wisped with vivid colors seemed so juvenile at my age.

Maturity.

Rich, red lip dye matched my body runes. The coordination achieved more of a fashion statement, rather than the social status it signified. I've always been a little embarrassed by those elite blood tattoos; the obligatory symbols denoted rank among the ruling class of Clan Kemith. I imagine everyone deals with her station in her own way. I never understood why it had always been so difficult for me.

We descended to International City Plaza from low orbit. The commercial hub served its thirty million residents comfortably as a buffer to those inter-societal legislators and their aids. The representative councilors bore the burden of governing the two trillion souls that formed hundreds of disparate societies of the Efilu Realm. Representatives of over four hundred enlightened species teemed the bustling city streets. The secure port buzzed with urgent traffic as shuttles embarked for the Round Table.

A broad-based plateau rose from the geographic center of the vast savanna. Atop the mound, one could make out a few details of the Round Table even at this distance. The seat of Efilu power would play host to my ultimate assignment. The Round Table represented the pinnacle of civilization—but the swell of my spirit lay in a more primitive direction.

A brief detour to see an old friend would come first. I chartered an ornithic ferry to carry me to my destination. By nature, the Windriders only landed at their home nests. The artificial lifeforms carried elite patrons on cross-country treks, but only to a hover-halt for designated debarkation. Unscheduled stops were still relatively easy to insert into the program without getting into trouble with Windrider owners. One objective proved an especially popular deviation. The centerpiece of Tiest, that theriac, Eye of the Tyelaj, attracted more pilgrims than did the Round Table itself.

The less-trafficked Blind Eye of the Tyelaj hid deep in the Forest of Feelings, the perfect place to make up for lost time with Tur. We had known each other for over twenty years, but family and clan responsibilities had kept us apart; it seemed like ages since I had last seen him. I had time to reminisce as the mindless Windrider carried me northward. This one only slowed enough where I indicated to allow me to safely leap off into a preselected clearing.

My grand soldier had arrived before me and selected a strategic position to survey the glade. He looked pensive—I guess that's how I'd describe it; statuesque, motionless, or on guard would also fit the observation. So Wari always looked that way in unfamiliar surroundings. Tur was as big as I remembered, big even for a So Wari: broad, thick shoulders, arms as big around as tree trunks. Such a sharp contrast to my own kind. Legs like great pillars held him as steady as a fortress; armored plates along his spine flapped absently as he basked, patiently waiting in the heat of the day. Wide, deep-set eyes seemed to glow as they scanned the infrared spectrum from shadowed sockets. Long ears stretched out horizontally, changing orientation periodically to detect any soft sounds from many angles that might be out of place, or sudden shifts in air current that might represent the silent movement of a foe.

I recognized this So Wari preoccupation with stalking predators as the evolutionary trait it was, as well as being the reason they had survived their extinct So Beni progenitors. Tur's short-cropped pelt and green-brown marbled plumage were worn loosely in a neat, conservative fashion. That was deception. That finely creased coat could fuse from matted pile into nearly impervious, gleaming armor in the merest instant. How I loved the sensation of my retracted claws gently caressing that nap.

Somehow, seeing Tur in that pose struck me as funny. All at once I felt an explosion of joy and freedom. I felt like a cub again…and cubs like to play.

I hollered as I sprang at his feet. His initial start was genuine, but when he recognized me, the quality of his laughter told me he had missed me in kind. I assumed my most threatening warning posture while holding back further laughter. Tur must have caught the spirit of the moment because he turned and fled, still laughing, his usual military façade dropped.

My dear friend frolicked into the forest like a shath fleeing its hunter—me. A ridiculous sight it would have been, had there been anyone else to see it: a five-hundred-pound Melkyz chasing a nine-ton So Wari warrior! The game was so silly that neither of us could seem to stop.

Burning off the tension of the "civilized world," we must have roamed for one finger of a koridyme into the forest. Our little "hunt" exercised instincts that had lain dormant within us for most of our adult lives. It was exhilarating. My heart was pounding in my ears, my nerves on edge, nose full of Tur's scent. His searching gaze was authentic, confirming the effectiveness of my invisibility. It felt good to *Blend* into the surrounding glade. It felt...basic!

"Can we dispense with the preliminary drivel?" The impatient speaker in the shadows projected the command toward the Animem without consensus from the Council. "Just show us the inflection points of this dark tributary to the Alom. We have minds of our own. We don't need treacle from dead meren."

Tur rumbled as he projected his warning to the council member. "Respect for the Dead, please."

"We still need to understand why she was sent," another voice said. "There's got to be a reason. They were obviously *synesprit* during life. This is not coincidence. Keep some of the personal content in the account. Let's see more."

Tur grudgingly nodded approval for the less intrusive editorial approach as they watched.

With that, the self-aware perspective melted away as Vit Na was swept deep into the stream of her Animem. The remainder played as a recording of events supplemented by internal motives and insights as demanded by the Council. The images, sounds, smells, and textures drew back to directly interface with each Council participant.

They watched the balance of Vit Na's shortened life play out before them where she had left off. Vit Na became the huntress as the Council became part of her circumambience, present yet invisible in every way to her world.

She stalked Tur. Knowing the So Wari's combat prowess and hypervigilance, Vit Na realized a predator of her size was the one in danger. If she sprang on him unexpectedly, his reflexes could take over before his intellect could check them. She might go from a long-absent friend to a pleasant memory in an instant. This element of danger added to the chase deliciously.

Vit Na made a conscious effort to override her own instincts and track him from an upwind vantage. He would be much less likely to apply deadly force in a defensive maneuver if his nostrils were full of her familiar scent.

Just as Tur entered the clearing beneath a rocky bluff, she struck. Vit Na moved like lightning; outstretched foreclaw first caught his well-armored back, the downward stroke propelling her past him. Twirling her lean, muscular body, she brought her feet to bear against a hardwood tree to rebound toward her quarry.

She struck his midsection with all the force she could muster. Tur, still playing along, pretended that she'd actually knocked him off-balance and rolled backwards a full 360 degrees on his tail. Breaking the action with a foot, he came to a complete stop in a defensive warrior posture, his massive arms raised as if to fend off a formidable attack.

Vit Na braced momentarily, then bounded toward him in apparently reckless abandon, spinning in midair just as her whip-like tail came into range of his abdomen. It blurred into motion, delivering three powerful blows to solar plexus, spleen, and finally the muscular area of Tur's thick neck. Lesser quarry would be easily felled by such an assault.

Tur feigned collapse, but he was unable to contain his laughter. Mildly out of breath, Vit Na stood triumphantly over her beloved prey while Tur—not even winded—lay there on the soft humus, still laughing. They rested until Vit Na caught her breath, then they talked.

"Tell the truth; you really couldn't see me?" she asked.

"You tread like a shadow and stalk like a dream—terribly close, yet always out of reach."

She arched a perfectly trimmed eyebrow. "And my attack?"

"You were a symphony of lashing wind, battering hail, and biting rain, all at once," he said as he reached up and clasped her waist in his hands. "But now I have you, the dream made flesh." After a gentle shake, he relaxed his grip and ran the fleshy fold of his thumb along the softness of her pelt. Stroking upward, he indulged the merest caress of her pointed ears. The way he caught her apical tufts between fingertips set them twitching in rhythm with his touch. After so many years apart, they remained *synesprit*.

"It's so good to see you, Tur." Vit Na shook dust and leaves out of her pelt, then knelt, relaxing on his chest. "It's like no time has passed at all."

Tur raised an eyebrow without projecting an accompanying thought.

"Of course, I have a couple dozen children now. My clan has prospered thanks to our work, Tur. Kemith shath are prized livestock, now fetching top prices on a thousand worlds."

Tur nodded, closed-lipped. Vit Na immediately recognized the reference to flesh-eating as a *faux pas*. So Wari were herbivorous. The marketing of meat never played well with pachysons. "Our own Yhm Vel assumed the mantle of Grand Mater Familia years ago."

"That explains the meteoric Melkyz success," Tur commented, ignoring the predaceous reference. "Seems your society is into everything these days. You must be very proud to have a Mater Familia from your own clan ascend to Grand Mater. Who rules your clan now?"

Vit Na took a gracious bow as answer.

"Ah, now I am impressed!" He lifted Vit Na off his chest and set her softly on the forest floor.

"It's only an interim appointment," Vit Na said. "The Elders are vetting the last two candidates. They may have already selected a replacement for me...if I'm lucky."

"They may surprise you and choose wisely." He crinkled his chin. "Unfortunately, politicians tend to have short memories."

"They still talk about you single-handedly saving the shath herds, Tur."

He remembered. A slow virus localized to the hypothalamus had been the putative agent. Similar plagues had been known since before the Efilu left Fitu, but autopsies of the affected animals revealed nothing.

"Your chattels have had no anorexic relapses since those days?"

"None," Vit Na said absolutely. "As I remember, your specialty was bodybuilding for undersized So Wari sentries. Neuro-stimulation processes for warriors with muscle failure, wasn't it?"

He further remembered that a young Vit Na had been assigned to help select the most specific virulent vector to distribute the remedial phage.

"The process is still in use," she said, her thoughts full of praise for Tur, rather than pride for herself.

The fresh, new archeologist had distinguished herself by locating and cloning a variety of leech that was suitable for the task, one that had the added expedience of being both easily visible and removable. Tur remembered how taken he'd been with her ingenuity.

He came out of his reverie only to realize that Vit Na had changed subjects. Her conversation drifted from common projection to hushed, intimate tones as if to avoid being overheard.

"Discussing the shortcomings of one's mates is frowned upon among my people, but comparing the scion of one mate with that of another—well, that's expressly taboo," she said, reminding him of Melkyz custom. "Yet it's become glaringly obvious that my most recent brood is...inferior."

She frowned in reflection. "It's not only intellect they lack, it's judgement, instinct, enthusiasm, aggression. They aren't bad enough to be classified as developmentally delayed, but they're certainly dull," she sighed. "It's a relief to finally get it out in the open."

It had been a real source of frustration to her for some time. She half expected a sympathetic response from Tur, but he'd slipped back into silence.

For the first time, Vit Na noticed the paradox of their respective characters. Most Melkyz were individuals of few words, solitary souls. The So Wari, by contrast, were social creatures, a bit more garrulous. The differences between them traced back to their respective pre-Efilu roots: solo hunter versus herd society.

Tur stood, took several paces toward the trees, and stared into the shadows. He half turned back toward Vit Na and spoke more freely than he could to any of his own kind.

"There are weak ones in our herds, too," he said. "It's not just size. It's attitude. Careless, even stupid meren are rising to positions of prominence. What really doesn't make sense is that they're born to reputable lineages, pedigrees that have consistently produced great leaders for ages. What's more, they are breeding like vermin."

"That's it!" Something had been nagging at Vit Na for months, but she had never quite hooked her claw on it. "The younger clan members have been spawning off-season. Bad enough for a meg to rut at whim, but worse for meren to bear fruit of such union. The families of Wilkyz traders showed similar patterns..." She fell silent.

This was a passing observation to her, but Tur had obviously spent considerable time mulling it over. "Vansar behavior has also been eccentric." He looked at Vit Na. "To your point, doesn't it bother you that at least four different species we've noticed between us have demonstrated significant flaws in their gene pools of late?"

"It's a known phenomenon, Tur," she deflected. "Every so often, most species, intelligent or not, develop groups of traits that are liabilities, usually as a result of intentional selective breeding. The burden of tolerance becomes critical with a periodicity of eighty thousand years or so, at which point there must be either a purge of flawed genes or extinction. It's healthy in the long run."

Tur leveled his gaze at her. "Yes, but have you ever heard of a time when more than two societies reached the nadir of that incompetence simultaneously?" He paused as he watched her ponder the rhetorical question.

"Have you discussed this with anyone yet?" she asked after a moment.

"No, of course not. I didn't realize until now that the problem extended beyond my people and the Vansar."

Vit Na thought gravely to herself, *Four species that we know of...* She saw that what had begun as venting frustrations of family problems was expanding into a social malady. She could tell by his eyes that he couldn't let it go. She needed a diversion.

Opportunity is where you find it, Vit Na mused as she peered into the mouth of a large cave. Its upper fringe, draped in furry moss, appeared to be large enough to accommodate even Tur's bulk.

Perhaps I can coax him into a little exploring, she thought as she dashed recklessly into its depths. She wasn't sure if it was her manipulation that distracted her friend or his need for a lightening

of the spirit—a heavy lift, the foregoing escapades notwithstanding. After all, the prevailing credence was that So Wari don't
play. Vit Na brightened as Tur's head emerged behind her through
the cavern's inner mouth.

The cavern was much larger than its modest opening suggested.
As Tur made his way up to Vit Na's level from the entry, he stopped
and smiled. Vit Na was standing in ankle-deep water beneath a
natural fountain, her thirst nearly quenched. Tur's gaze followed
the runoff away from the vestibule.

The stream broadened and slowed before extending into the
distance under the great vault's dim light. Bands of sunlight
streamed through apertures in the ceiling, dappling the surface
of the lagoon. As their eyes became accustomed to the gloom,
the chamber took on an unexpected beauty. Scant but brilliant
shards of light diffused throughout the cavern as they reflected
off the walls and watery surfaces. Bright flowers abounded in a
vibrant assortment of colors, some floating in the pool, adding to
its serenity.

The stalactites were enmeshed in a tangle of vines, which bore
succulent fruits almost as varied and fragrant as the flowers below
them. Somehow the aroma of the place seemed to pleasantly
contrast the dankness of its first impression.

The couple seemed to realize their hunger in unison. Tur's lunch
was easy; the large fruits were quick pickings and remarkably
sweet for wild fare. The fish, on the other hand, were fast, a good
challenge for Vit Na's agility. She used her tail to herd them toward
the shallower side of the pool. The simple task of asphyxiating
her game by removing them from the water was confounded by a
miscalculation on her part.

The fish were also carnivorous, likely living on crustaceans
and hatchling crocodilians. Vit Na found their sharp little teeth
sinking into her feet and tail deep enough to irritate, but not
enough to draw blood. After several failed attempts to subdue her

prey, she discovered that a single claw pressed into the soft, fleshy protuberance just behind the gill caused instant paralysis and death for the fish.

"That's more like it. I was beginning to think they were going to have me for lunch instead of the of the other way around," she sighed.

"Could have been worse," Tur laughed. "You might have tumbled into a nest of fur-mites. I hear there are carnivorous species in the deep forest."

Vit Na shuddered and narrowed an eye at him. "Are you serious?"

She peered into the shadows, wary of Tur's milk-suckling vermin, then cleaned the remainder of the clinging little nibblers from her legs and tail. Her hunger got the best of her as she split one open and ate the flesh without preparation. Vit Na found the flavor unusual but quite pleasing. This newly-found delicacy, she decided, was best savored raw. Her hunger was sated after forty or fifty pounds of fish.

Tur had finished eating while she was engaged in catching her meal. He sat and watched with a touch of revulsion. Herbivores always experienced mixed emotions when watching predators feed. It was tolerable to witness the demise of dumb animals, but never pleasant. Washing the sticky fruit residue from his hands proved to be an effective diversion from Vit Na's ravenous exploits.

Vit Na was beautiful in the dim lighting of the cavern. Her fluffy black down, neatly clipped in contrast to her closely cropped midriff, rendered a trendy hourglass shape and glimmered with droplets of moisture from her fishing efforts.

During the quiet digestion of their meals, Vit Na detected a dry, cool breeze coming from the direction opposite their entrance.

"So, the cavern is really a tunnel," she said. Pressing the playful mood that had prevailed for most of the short morning, she urged Tur on toward the hidden exit.

The cavern reopened onto a cliff. A natural path, apparently formed by the course of the stream fed by the lake water that had either dried up or changed course, led away from the outlet. This little mystery was solved by a glance over the edge.

The water had eroded through the bedrock of the cave floor and spilled out the side of the cliff face. The dried riverbed path beckoned them down the hill—but the thought of hiking that trail was swept from the couple's minds as they beheld the sight above them.

A lone Tyen, engaged in what could only be the legendary Dance of Fire, was boldly framed against the tranquil welkin beyond. A violet cloud of abisund spores wisped and whirled for its collective life.

In hot pursuit, the lithe, graceful figure of the Tyen expelled its crimson vapor to bind the spores and draw them into its hungry gullet for digestion.

"The last reported sighting of a Tyen Dance was over eighteen years ago," Vit Na whispered to Tur. "There are so few of them these days."

"Legends are most deeply rooted where facts are scarce," Tur remarked with similar awe. "It is said that the Tyen mate for life. Each couple produces only one offspring. They're said to be immortal, living partly in the spiritual world and partly in the physical world, endowed with omniscience and the ultimate wisdom of the Alom."

"I've read a little about their physiology. An electromagnetic charge lends the Tyen lighter-than-air buoyancy, which is all but depleted by the consumption of the abisund spores," she marveled.

"Natural enemies. Tralkyz used to hunt them for sport. Our intelligence sources say they overcame that disadvantage after feeding long ago." Tur was well briefed.

"No other enlightened member society is as enigmatic as the Tyen." Vit Na's thought projection became wistful in stunned admiration.

Tur looked down to draw Vit Na's attention. "No witness of a Tralkyz/Tyen encounter has described a Tralkyz success in thousands of years. The Tralkyz would never discuss the matter with outsiders, despite their braggadocio—or perhaps because of it. One on one, the Si Tyen are considered invincible."

"The very basis of the Tyelaj was to endow the capital world of Tiest with Tyen-like invincibility and shroud its leadership in heavenly wisdom. Ordinary meren charged with governing trillions need an air of the divine. The Council treats the so-called Children of Dragon like fanatics, yet exploits that mystique for their own gain." Vit Na wondered what effect the Tyelaj exposure had on her fate. "The myth falls short. Truth be known the Tyen, as a whole, are as flawed as any people."

"Certainly, they were among the most intelligent of the Higher Societies." Tur sounded as if he wanted to argue the point. "Their fluid-crystal systems form the foundation of Animem and gel integration technology. There seems to be divinity in their blood somewhere."

Vit Na frowned at her friend's superstition. "From what I know, their social structure is limited, and their numbers are falling off, presumably due to some genetic flaw perpetuating infertility. Many an epidemiologist predicts Tyen extinction in the foreseeable future," she said. "If the Tyen truly are prescient, they seem unnaturally accepting of the end of their time in the sun."

"Yes, I know: 'An eternal night approaches for the noble dreamers,'" Tur quoted from an ancient poem, reminding Vit Na how long that prediction had been in the offing.

Tur's thoughts were a maelstrom of emotions as he watched the Dance. Time nearly stood still. The So Wari watched, motionless. "So beautiful!"

Yet so disturbing. Reminiscent of a hunt, the Dance upset Tur. Intellectually he knew the abisund spores were flora, not fauna. The Tyen were technically herbivores—hence the nomenclature *Si Tyen*—but the desperate struggle lent a sense of fright. Prey fleeing predator.

"Very confusing. Perhaps it's best for the So Wari psyche that the Tyen Dance of Fire is so seldom seen."

Tur's thoughts rang hollow in Vit Na's mind. She stood enthralled by the spectacle for all the reasons that perturbed Tur, her head bobbing and weaving in consonance with every swoop, soar, and dive of the venerable meg. Tyen philosophy was highly revered in the super-hunter societies of the Melkyz, Wilkyz, and Alkyz. Whatever the Tralkyz thought of Tyen teachings, they kept their opinions discreetly to themselves.

"The abisund quarry is a marvel in itself, isn't it?" Vit Na projected hushed thought tones to Tur. "They're actually a semi-conscious collection of spores. Each generates just enough of an electromagnetic charge to accelerate to twice standard gravity, a bit more when directed at less than eighty degrees."

"I know, Vit Na." Tur's revulsion was showing. "I read, too."

As if he had said nothing, Vit Na lectured on, "They coalesce into these clouds, essentially becoming intangible to large grazing animals, even to avian feeders. Swarms of insects bent on savoring their nectar are discouraged by a nasty little electrical discharge." She laughed.

"Personally, I've never seen them before. So Wari don't even have these recordings in our Animem database." He shook his head and heaved almost imperceptibly. "Just scattered footnotes. But seeing this chase live, the 'behavior' of the abisund suggests the presence of a rudimentary neuro-system, even a consciousness." Tur tried to avert his eyes from the sight.

"I understand the parent flower, by contrast, is quite bitter in taste." Vit Na recognized his revulsion for what it was and went on: "Low in nutritional value and widely found in the most inconvenient grazing places." She cast her gaze downward, away from the spectacle in the sky, and back to Tur.

Tur, amused as Vit Na took on her maternal teaching persona, simply listened to the lecture. "The collective organism could be thought of as having a backward life cycle, with intelligence, high energy, and maximum mobility characterizing the immature stage and reproduction occurring briefly at the end of an extended childhood.

"The Tyen solution to this unique defense was ingenious," she said, gushing. "Over the millennia since the Exodus, the Tyen developed their salivary glands to ionize digestive enzymes and organic acids. The exhaled mist binds to the charged spores, immobilizing them. A low-level bioelectromagnetic field tuned to attract digestive vapor back into the mouth is generated in the gut, pulling the spore-enriched vapor back in for complete digestion."

Tur seemed to recover his intestinal constitution as she talked him through what soared above them. "A Tyen should only have to feed this way three or four times a year. Still, there is the question of the postprandial heaviness that forces an almost immediate landing after the Dance. They must expend a lot of energy chasing 'that which cannot be touched' through the sky. We know they have more economical alternatives to this feeding ritual, but it appears to be some kind of Tyen rite of passage."

"Tyen tended to build dens in mountaintops and cliff faces," Tur projected as softly as if the Tyen were within range of the conversation. "Si Tyen wings are really overdeveloped dorsal plates, much like ours. The homology led to very powerful erector platys muscles but, unlike true avians, their bodies evolved more for downward gliding than sustained flying." Tur caught on to the psychology.

That's it, Tur, rationalize the analogy back to its non-carnivorous nature. Vit Na nearly cheered him.

He continued: "So, they build up a subdermal electron cloud which, when excited and allowed to expand like a balloon, effectively decreases their corporeal density to less than that of the air around them."

"That is so, until after they've fed," Vit Na said. "The digestion of the abisund spores temporarily drains the electron field, forcing the individual to land and regenerate the charge. I have just *got* to see how they overcome this weakness."

She hunkered down in anticipation, but Tur motioned for her to exercise caution.

This was the time of the Tyge. In the shadows of the Dance of Fire, a pack of Tralkyz hunters known as Tygers would be near. Distant cousins to Vit Na's own Melkyz, the Tralkyz were the second largest of all the super hunters and arguably the deadliest. They were always attracted by the Dance of Fire and would stalk a sighted Tyen through the forest below for several fingers of a koridyme. When a Si Tyen landed, there was always combat—a Tyge. When on the trail of a Tyen, Tralkyz hunting parties were always at least thirty strong and formidable.

Tralkyz were built much like larger versions of the Wilkyz and proportionately more muscular. Second only to the Alkyz in size, their soot-gray coats were accented by tufts of red-orange plumage spreading from behind their ears. During a nocturnal hunt, the quarry would find itself surrounded by ghostly, low-pitched moans.

The crimson tufts were incandescent and gave the appearance of eyes of much larger hunters. Fear made many victims panic—often the first of a series of final mistakes. The hunt for a Tyen was special, though. For Tralkyz, the Tyge was transformative. It merited the selection of only the best Tralkyz Tygers.

The Tyen always landed near water, or so the legend went. Battles took place partially in the natural world, partially in the supernatural world, the rest veiled in mystery few other Efilu eyes ever saw. If they did, they never lived to tell about it. The Tralkyz were ravenous after such an encounter, capable and cunning enough to devour any innocent bystander so foolish as to be in the wrong place at the wrong time.

This unusual and violent ritual was respected by the Greater Society for ancient reasons that were largely forgotten. The Tralkyz never involved others or destroyed property in these affairs, so no other member society had a legitimate qualm. The Tyen themselves had never lodged a complaint.

The Tyen, although reclusive and often eccentric, were not reckless. True to form, this old one had selected a battleground near the river. And true to the legends, a pack of Tygers waited.

As he alighted in the clearing staked out by the pack, a mysterious fog issued seemingly from the forest floor itself. The eerie haze was gray-white, not the crimson of the Tyen vapor. As it floated past the Tralkyz nostrils, their anxiety faded. The gas was innocuous; the Tygers would still be able to attack.

Tralkyz surrounded the lone Tyen and paired off for the assault. The leader was distinguished by his greater size, the two guards at his flanks his seconds. The Tyen locked eyes with the leader, ignoring the remainder of the pack.

Vit Na began to move, oblivious to Tur and his warnings. The blood rush had consumed her, as it did many predaceous peoples, making her mesmerized by the combat unfolding before her eyes. She glided down the mountain path as surely as if she had done so a thousand times before. Tur was less sure but, afraid for his companion, he followed close behind, as stealthily as he could. Taking up position beside the blood drunk Vit Na, Tur forced her catatonic body into a crouch. A thicket of brush provided them cover.

A lone figure stood motionless in the center of the clearing, the Tralkyz Tygers nowhere to be seen. Only now were the voyeurs close enough to see the noble warrior's true splendor.

The Tyen stood some thirty feet tall, but somehow seemed taller. With its deep-set eyes and extended jaws accented by tufts of downy fibers at the chin and cheeks, the visage was reminiscent of a lean, powerful So Wari.

The eerie light filtering through the heavy forest ceiling shone more like moonbeams than sun. The illumination in the fog created a halo effect about the Tyen, like a bolt of lightning in still life.

The moment was viscous with tension; only the mist seemed to fidget restlessly at the great one's feet. Neither of the spectators realized that the Tyen was surrounded by the pack until the leader roared his challenge.

Tralkyz chiefs were half again as large as their followers— adolescent hormone surges and pharmaceutical manipulation, not genetics. A twenty-five-foot mass of heavy thew was flanked by two barely-less-menacing lieutenants, each crouched in a threatening posture. The stance was mirrored by the eighteen pairs of Tralkyz maulers surrounding the Tyen.

The lone warrior shifted his gaze to meet the gleaming eyes of the lead Tyger as if the others didn't exist. Tyen mores held a wayward leader culpable for the actions of those in his charge. The Tyen's wings spread wide in warning, then retracted back slowly for true combat again, motionlessly inviting the pack's advance.

Two pairs attempted to blindside their quarry, and the leader's lieutenants waited until the Tyen's attention was drawn to the movement before attempting a strike of their own.

The distraction was at best too brief, but more accurately nonexistent. Action that could only be described as physical music flowed with the rhythm of the assault. Tyen defensive claws sliced through the throats of the first two as another limb launched the second duo with ballistic force at a third pair. The sickening crack at impact heralded the departure of three souls from this plane. The fourth assailant would gratefully rise again in several minutes with a dislocated shoulder and a few fractured ribs. The ease of the maneuver gave the remaining Tygers pause, but their leader was undaunted.

This chief knew that tactic!

The Tyen could put attackers at a disadvantage by offering them the offensive until they recklessly lost their patience. *The patience of the Tralkyz was like a puddle; that of the Tyen, like a sea.* Tur recalled the proverb and saw now that it was indeed based in truth. The pack exploded into action from every direction. So Wari military training stressed one principle above all else when faced with a Tralkyz adversary: no matter the size of the group, Tralkyz always attacked in pairs. The rate of attacks was accelerated such that the tactic was lost on the inexperienced observer.

The Tyen's fighting style now mesmerized Tur as well as Vit Na. The So Wari were widely regarded as the masters of the martial arts in unarmed combat, but this bout astounded even Tur!

"The Tyen fights not with six appendages, but with nine," Tur observed, his thought tone razor-tight at Vit Na.

The Tyen's leg, arm, and tail technique was the best he had ever seen, but the use of the head and neck was stunning. There was no biting—that would be considered savage among herbivorous beings—but feinting and butting of opponents off-balance, only to strike a deadly blow with one of its seven natural weapons, was well within limitations of couth. The Tyen's final pair of martial tools were the most surprising of all.

Their bony "wings" were always believed to be a hindrance in Si Tyen ground combat, recessed to the spine in the retracted position for protection. This was not the case at all. The Tyen wielded them as swords, slicing or bludgeoning opponents left and right. And such efficiency! Nearly every blow either killed or maimed only one member of paired Tygers. The psychological effect of the tactic soon took its toll as single Tralkyz became confused and disoriented as loners. This was not cowardice; they were trained from birth to fight as partners. The Tralkyz leader signaled quarter and assessed his losses, then measured the Tyen carefully.

Again, he was motionless. A hint of a smirk at his lips, blood dripping from his claws, the Tyen had not a scratch on him.

He's not even breathing heavily! Tur noticed.

This, too, was a clever ruse to hide his fatigue, but it was working—the Tyger chief looked about the clearing for a body count. Fifteen casualties, incapable of combat. Most of them would not survive the week's end, even with attention to their wounds. Those still standing bravely maintained combat stance, but they also felt the effects of the pummeling they themselves had received.

The Tralkyz leader knew that to signal a second attack would cost him another seven or eight meren, with no guarantee of victory.

Too expensive. Tur found himself assessing reengagement in silent proxy for the Tralkyz leader.

The Tyger chief acknowledged defeat to the Tyen and ordered the bearing of casualties back to their city for treatment or interment, never taking his eyes off the triumphant warrior. That disturbing, grim smile on the Tyen's face saluted a worthy Tyge's end as the battered troop marched proudly back into the forest. Somehow, a sense of approval was conveyed in that smile.

Perhaps a lesson well learned, Tur thought. He inhaled deeply in reflection. Fully armored up, a well-trained So Wari soldier in his prime might survive such a face off. Tur wouldn't have wagered that a crippled Tyger would find a way to deal him a mortal blow in parting for his efforts. After all these weren't just Tralkyz, these were Tygers: As Tralkyz went, these meren were the best at their best. Despite distant kinship, So Wari weren't Si Tyen. Although the confrontation between So Wari and Tralkyz warriors might promise a furious battle, a Tyge it would not be.

As the last trace of the Tralkyz Tygers faded into the forest, Vit Na surprised herself with her first coherent thought: *they're remarkably civilized in defeat.*

She suddenly noticed Tur staring at her with a puzzled expression. Before she could assure Tur that she was fine, a splash in the nearby stream interrupted his obvious question. As they turned to investigate the sound, a gaze of unnatural intensity captured their attention.

The Tyen was still there in the clearing. His eyes locked with Vit Na's. The inexplicable sense of danger was so overwhelming she dared not turn to confirm that it was shared by Tur, already tensed for combat.

So focused was she that the backdrop of the forest itself faded to nothingness in the shadow of the Tyen's presence. Mere moments seemed an eternity as she struggled to remain still. Was it her imagination? Did the winged knight truly see her, or did he merely peer into the darkness of the thicket, wary of a hidden threat?

Just when she thought she could stay still no longer, the Tyen disappeared without a trace. No rustling of bushes, no flapping of wings—simply gone. A second splash distracted them as they realized that, despite remaining motionless, their orientation had shifted fifty degrees to face the stream. The serpentine head bobbing in the water strengthened the legendary connection of the creatures with the Tyen Dance of Fire.

Even with such intimate involvement, neither she nor Tur could confirm the myth of Tyen–serpent transmorphism. Bewildered, Vit Na turned to her companion, only to see his head strangely cocked to one side, as if listening to urgent thoughts.

After a moment of listening herself, she spoke, "Tur?"

His demeanor promptly changed. He was calm and all business as he commanded, "We must go."

Puzzled, she asked, "Where?"

"To offer our services," he said. "There is a need."

Chapter Three
— EXPOSÉ —

"**E**volution is interesting, isn't it?" Vit Na looked up at Tur. The So Wari diplomatic skyship carried them in silence, but for her pontification and the external sounds trailing hundreds of body lengths behind the craft that now swept urgently toward its destination. The transition of the landscape from the wilderness to suburban was no more than a blur at this speed. "I mean, from an archeological standpoint."

He seemed distant. She continued to try to draw his attention. "Initially, the term 'Round Table' applied to the actual great table in the hall of the So Beni rulers."

Tur continued to stare below them. Vit Na caressed his arm and went on: "At the time of the Pact, it was referred to as the Hall of the Round Table." Her history lesson falling on deaf ears, Vit Na's monologue became more of a distraction to take her own mind from the matter at hand. "All records dating from the Exodus show the Round Table to include the table, the hall, and the surrounding superstructure. Now, of course, it's taken for granted that the Round Table includes all of that and the plateau it rests on, power towers and all." She laughed nervously.

Tur seemed to have settled into grim contemplation. Sound roared into the passenger chamber as the transport began its deceleration. Vit Na was sure it had maxed out on velocity. They would arrive back at the Round Table long before sunset. It had taken her more than five times that long to get to the polar forest this morning.

What could possibly merit such haste? she wondered.

The ship had met them right where they stood in the clearing of the Tyen encounter. *The pilot had been sent for both of us—even called us by name,* she considered. These facts indicated the highest priority. *And he addressed Tur as "my commander,"* Vit Na observed, repeating it guardedly in her mind. *"My commander" this far from his world? What are we caught up in?*

Her heartbeat quickened as she realized the most disturbing observation. *Tur! How had he gleaned the goings-on of a secured meeting from over a dyme away? Unless someone was tracking his whereabouts from the beginning, only Tur could have summoned the transport—that's level four communications. Furthermore, his personal field of influence couldn't possibly extend so far—that was reserved for level five intimate communications. No So species possesses better than very superficial level three communication skills, and even that must be induced in the most gifted and best trained individuals.*

Tur, although very intelligent, had never displayed such talent. Vit Na looked at his solemn form.

Is he wrestling the same concerns in his own mind? And why is he shutting me out?

Rault, the Round Table's security chief, reviewed his agents' intelligence reports for a third time. He had been at it all night. It wasn't that he didn't understand them; he was a quick study. He simply couldn't understand the "why" or the "who" of it all. Rault's office consisted of a gelatinous chamber nestled in one of myriad pruned stumps eternally laid raw from the great tree. Powered by the energy flowing through the cut ends of its xylem/phloem network, the parasitic apparatus inflated into a vessel to serve its master's every need. The roughly cube-shaped structure took on the convention of a generous office. The security chief reduced the room's dimensions and sealed it before expanding the gelcon display. Rault was cautious, even for a So Wari.

Here in the maximum security of the Round Table itself, Rault had installed modifications for added secrecy. The So Wari, the hereditary custodians of the Round Table since the So Beni extinction, had local jurisdiction of the ancient city-palace, but formation of the Council precluded the maintenance of independent intelligence organizations. Most of the Lesser Societies adhered to this rule. The So Wari did not.

He subdued the lighting and dampened the acoustics to focus his mind. Rault considered every conceivable facet of the raw data. It was his extraordinary talent for radial thinking that had recommended him to the So Wari covert surveillance organization in the first place. Discretion and attention to detail accounted for rapid promotion to the Inner Circle—the secret cabal that reported directly to the So Wari Supreme, Meeth. Ninety-seven years of loyal service and friendship kept him from saying no to Meeth, even when it needed to be said.

The assistant commander maintained a rank two full levels below his appropriate station to avert attention from his activities. "Meren below the rank of commander seldom merit surveillance," Meeth had told him. Rault often found himself in position to observe situations without revealing intent.

Rault's focus first detected the aberrant behavioral pattern. At least fifteen Lesser Societies showed signs of mental, psychic, and emotional deterioration. Extinction or civil war was imminent in all but three of those.

He described this observation to Meeth as "unprecedented and certainly not accidental." Remarkable notions by any So Wari, but shocking coming from Rault, known for reserved discourse when reporting preliminary findings.

Why was I so candid? Rault thought. *Fuel to an obsessive mind. The investigation should have been turned over to Council Intelligence— where it belonged. The expression on Meeth's face told me his intentions were otherwise.* He shook his head. *I should have run then.*

Rault had known Meeth long enough to know when he was about to break with the traditional path of united Efilu transparency. Sitting on information like this carried risks. Very high risks. Meeth had convinced him that there was far more to this than natural selection bias. There was conspiracy afoot—conspiracy that threatened the future of the So Wari people.

Genetic plague, Rault thought. *Treachery. That's the trouble with insightful pareidolia—is it perception of a reality that no one else sees or intense paranoia?* Again, he mused, *I should have run.*

Rault did not have enough information to make a decision, but the potential threat could not be ignored.

Could a faction of a Lesser Society be involved in polygenocide? It makes no sense! The Council would surely eradicate the entire species for such a conspiracy. No one would take such a risk. Even the Lesser Society of origin would struggle to crush such a plot once it was uncovered.

Therefore, by this reasoning, the culprit must be an outsider.

In the sixty-five million years since the Exodus from Fitu, the Efilu had encountered only four intelligent alien species. Of those, they had been in direct conflict with only one: *the Quatal.*

Their near-spherical forms, deformable into pseudopodia, gave them the advantage of shape-shifting. By virtue of these sturdy, dendritic appendages, they built rambling cities, bridges, and tunnel systems throughout their worlds. Collective formations of propulsive pods had conveyed them between neighboring planets for centuries. They had no need to develop tools until they encountered the Efilu.

When they witnessed the Efilu fluid-crystal spacecrafts, they became...ambitious. They found that they could roughly duplicate the metamorphic Efilu technology with local resources. The essential constituents were in short supply on their home worlds; ergo, expansion!

The Efilu–Quatal conflict had ended nearly one hundred years ago. The Quatal, finding themselves hopelessly outmatched by staggering Efilu forces, had withdrawn from the disputed region within six months—hardly worth noting historically, were it not for the alien factor. The Quatal had been restricted to a single three-satellite star system, and no further incursions had been attempted.

Perhaps, until now, Rault thought.

Rault had sent four of his best agents secretly into the field in search of Quatal traces. Those four, plus a fifth—Moc, a young female warrior who came highly recommended—were the maximum requisite number suitable to investigate the anomalies without arousing suspicion.

Rault had briefed each one individually, delicately, revealing motives on a strictly need-to-know basis. No two operatives were given the same limited scraps of information. They had been out for just over a day and a half standard when the siege began.

A silent alarm went off in Rault's concealed office. He immediately shut down every database and analytic paradigm, prepared for permanent erasure at his signal. He exited the room quietly, collapsed it behind him, and walked briskly through the corridors to the public levels where he could already hear the ruckus.

The sound of security shields disintegrating impelled him to quicken his pace. Only his military discipline prevented panic when he saw ruptured security barriers at several outer portals and unconscious So Wari guards on the floor beside the outstretched wing of a dead Vansar. An Alkyz meg lay in a corner, motionless.

He hesitated just long enough to examine one of his own fallen sentries. *No signs of trauma, respiration shallow, no detectable neurotoxins on the mucus membranes or in the air—neurodisruptors! But they're illegal, except—* He looked up and down the corridor. *Oh, no–NO!*

The trail of immobilized bodies led straight to the command center.

Rault now found himself running through the ancient halls. He forced his way through several damaged containment doors only to arrive in a disturbingly occupied command chamber. Before him, his twelve remaining guards, the five So Wari on monitor duty, and Moc were all in the custody of Greater Society security.

The officer in charge was unmistakable. Weyef, the vigilant Council Intelligence Chief, exerted her authority smoothly. "Who is the ranking officer here?" Weyef asked tensely.

The Vansar mer was tall and slender with wings retracted. Physically, her species was at a disadvantage in the relative confines of the Hall, but this mer projected a somber air of power that gave even the mighty So Wari pause.

"I am," Rault answered. As her attention shifted, he introduced himself with his public assignment. "Rault, intercession commander of this installation."

Weyef stood at eye level with Rault, her wing plumes fanned out to give the impression of a broader back. She gazed at the So Wari through a pair of huge, luminous Vansar eyes. A luxurious mane of orange-red feathers with golden highlights dominated her crown. The soft fronds hung loosely from her scalp to her hip, where they were neatly tied in a short binding braid. The plumes toward the front of her head swept down and forward. Even as the gentle strands seemed to move with a life of their own, caressing her face and forehead, such stunning beauty deceived no one. This mer was a force to be reckoned with by any threat to the Council.

"I would like to hear more about this 'epidemiological study of Quatal landing sites.'"

Rault winced. *Please, by the wisdom of Saymon, tell me that Moc didn't try to sell such an idiotic lie. Quatal landing sites...on Tiest?!* That would have raised suspicion from anyone over fifty years old. Anyone over one hundred twenty would have scoffed outright at the notion.

Rault looked at the Vansar security chief. The set of her wings told him that her intellect was offended. *The Quatal had never come close to Tiest, much less successfully landed here.*

She clasped Moc's shoulder. "This one claims to be completing a survey started eighty years ago by the So Wari xenobiology department," Weyef said skeptically.

Rault reconsidered the setup. *Given So Wari obsessive/compulsive tendencies, the story seems feasible so far. What gave Moc away?*

He affected a bewildered expression as he looked from captive to captor. He was pleased that Moc's thoughts were inscrutable and just as confounded that Weyef displayed at least equal discipline. All the while he hid his own thoughts: *How much do they know? Were the others caught as well?*

Rault's number-one priority now was damage control. He had nearly completed the secret code to erase the file when a presence—more like a force of nature than an individual—stormed into the chamber.

"What transpires here?" A demand, not a question, bellowed by Meeth.

Weyef's initial reaction was part flinch, part flight reaction. The So Wari Supreme, leader of the most powerful Lesser Society and Premier of the Realm, was known to nearly all by reputation, if not in person. Meeth's presence, and the power he represented, terrified both Rault and Weyef equally.

Before the startled avian warlord could respond, Car Hom, Alkyz delegate emeritus, entered the chamber from the portal opposite Meeth's entry. Car Hom held almost matching repute.

"Yes, what *is* going on, Meeth?" The question had a perceptibly softer tone to it.

Meeth's demeanor did not betray his relief to see an old friend among Moc's accusers. Rault knew Meeth and Car Hom went back many years. The society of the Alkyz represented the largest of the super-hunter species. Powerfully muscled lower body and tail tapered to sleek, agile upper body. Long, thick arms extending from strong broad shoulders contrasted with the meg's advanced years. The sharp forearm plumage was slicked back, and all claws retracted, inconspicuous as lethal weaponry. His face was pleasant and his thoughts calm, but that only served to magnify Meeth's agitation.

"I come into *my* hold only to be greeted by a multinational invasion force? The entire plateau will be surrounded by So Wari defense forces in moments. Drop your weapons and start explaining this nonsense, *now.*"

Meeth is half bluffing. Rault kept the thought private. It was true that the Round Table had already been surrounded by So Wari forces, but Meeth knew only too well what the assault was about, and he knew it might be about to cost him his life.

"Meeth, you surely recognize this 'multinational force' as Greater Society Security and Council Intelligence," Weyef said and dropped her hands from her hips to her sides.

No more needed to be said. They all knew that Council edicts superseded even the commands of Lesser Society rulers, no matter how powerful they were.

Weyef spoke again: "Your agent, Moc, was caught in a bad lie."

"A *bad* lie?" Meeth demanded.

"She was caught," Weyef shrugged. "In my opinion, that made the lie bad. I find the novelty of the act interesting. We haven't investigated a *lie* in centuries."

Rault suspected that Meeth had to admire Weyef's directness, even under these circumstances.

"Our interrogations reveal that you have a secret intelligence network," she said to Meeth. "This is no surprise and, by itself, does not merit this intervention. However, we have also discovered that, for some time now, you have been in possession of evidence that several peoples have been at immediate risk of decline, if not extinction. Concealing this kind of information represents a major transgression." She paused, looked Meeth squarely in the eye, and said, "How do you explain this?"

A moot question. No explanation would assuage the wrath of the Council at large when the allegations of internal espionage surfaced, especially not with implicit sabotage of this magnitude.

Rault could already see by Car Hom's posture that he recognized the direction of discourse and its requisite conclusion.

"I, for one, am in the dark," Car Hom confessed. "Exactly what is known, by whom, and for how long has that knowledge been available?"

Clearly annoyed at the distraction, Weyef reasserted her position. "Meeth knows, Council Intelligence knows, and I know. Although you are welcomed at these deliberations, by virtue of past service on the Council, Car Hom of Alkyz, you cannot interfere with these proceedings."

"Deliberations," Car Hom repeated slowly and softly. "As you have just indicated, the indictment of a Lesser Society leader should be a formal Council matter and not a criminal interrogation. Therefore, the proper setting for this process is the full Diet of Tiest held in Round Table chamber itself. The entire congregation must be summoned and assembled before any action can be executed." The clever old Alkyz had effected a stay of pronouncement against his troubled friend, if only for the moment.

Yet he was no longer the final word of the Alkyz Confederacy. Car Hom had yielded leadership of the Alkyz delegation to Yaw Daor, mostly because the younger meg had shown such outstanding administrative talent and ambition. A perfect opportunity for a middle-aged meg to retire from active politics. Yaw had been the Alkyz advisor for sixty years now, and Rault trusted him implicitly. *At least the Alkyz voice would speak fairly on this matter.*

All the while, Rault had been searching for answers to the questions everyone else was dancing around. *Whoever or whatever is behind this "plague" has operatives on Tiest, and in high places. And just how did they overcome our security measures? They have specifically targeted Meeth. My new recruit is on the ground, but too far away to help.*

Again, Rault considered the erasure sequence to his files on the lower level. *It could backfire, and there will be no turning back if it does. Tur will have no intelligence to start with. No time. No way out for our sovereign, unless...*

During the discussion, attention had shifted away from the So Wari network, away from Rault and Moc.

Rault made eye contact with her, but he dared not project a thought. *If Moc is as good as her reputation, she'll read intent without thoughts.*

"This has gone too far!" Moc declared.

Everyone in the room turned toward her.

"The investigation was a family matter. I used my position at Hall Security to gain access to Council Intelligence files—information I believed would explain the developmental deficits in my family. When I discovered that the So Wari were not the only people so affected, I began to look for a factor common to all."

"Be careful, young one," Weyef said. "Thoughts expressed here in open forum cannot be unsaid."

Moc hesitated just long enough to acknowledge the advisory of her rights before continuing. "By single-handedly discovering a danger to the Greater Society, I would have advanced my standing in the clan further than seventy years of work in the intersociety service could have done for me. Now I have jeopardized my entire family!"

Ambition—a nice flourish, Rault thought to himself. He considered her lie as she feigned regret. *The story is internally consistent and feasible. The motive for confession at this moment was perfectly timed. Realistic. She is good!* Rault silently held his breath as he awaited the reaction of the inquisitor.

"This is very serious, Moc. If the facts bear out, you may be facing a penalty more severe than you know."

Weyef had taken the bait! Now to guide the follow-through. "As local commander, I will take custody of the prisoner and—"

"This is now a GS security matter. You have no authority here, Rault," Weyef admonished. Pointing at Meeth and Moc, she said to a subordinate, "Take them into custody."

Not off the claw yet! Rault thought grimly to himself.

As they were led to the Table chamber, Rault reminded himself of the fallen So Wari guards in the corridor. *Unarmed and surprised, they were still able to mount a formidable defense against superior forces. The dead GS squad members attested to that.* He was proud that he had chosen and trained them so well. *I will always honor their sacrifice.*

Rault's reverie was interrupted as his liege's tail brushed his toes in passing. A subtle call for attention. They had been marched to the Council chamber, Meeth escorted to the head of the Round Table by Greater Society security officers, where he was respectfully seated. Rault could not hide his shock as he gazed at the assemblage of delegates. The thirty high societies' envoys comprising the Diet of Tiest flanked by four hundred lower society delegates settled in the chamber, every chair filled.

The entirety of the Council, already seated at the Round Table—waiting.

Rault's mind went into radial thought mode. Forcing all the data collected by his team, deductively reasoning through Weyef's actions and conclusions, and calculating the motives behind the events into a coherent analysis was accomplished in microseconds. All the while, Rault still appeared focused on the Council Intelligence Chief's words and instructions.

This was all planned by someone. Someone even more careful than Meeth. Someone who was scared. Whoever they are, they want Meeth out of the way—and badly.

Rault's mind raced as he desperately filtered out the extraneous goings-on. *Tur will need an updated file to walk him through this new development.*

Rault needed to decide which delegate or delegates weren't listening to the evidence being presented.

Our perpetrator has already decided how this little exhibition will end. They would be indifferent to the argument, no matter how convincing. Rault focused intently. *Moc's testimony will be thrown out, of course. Her conviction would not serve the conspirator's interests. Council Intelligence may be just a pawn here, but if it is a willing party?* Rault shuddered visibly.

Slijay, the Council Intelligence Coordinator, intoned unctuous Sulenz projections. "The overwhelming evidence indicates that there is indeed a So Wari secret intelligence network, which has been collecting data for months, showing trends in physical and mental illnesses among several species. Documented cases of intrasocietal feuding, acts of perversion, even homicides are numerous. Personal gain at the expense of regional ruin with no remorse or sense of responsibility is evident on a multi-stellar scale. Such weakness would certainly be disastrous.

"Although Moc was the first to be captured, she does not have the talent, the experience, or the resources to conduct a research project this extensive. She is covering for her superior."

"Is that fact or conjecture?" Yaw Daor, speaking for the Alkyz Confederacy, questioned the Sulenz.

"Circumstantial evidence," Slijay answered. "Her story does not reel out. The study in question was closed after completion eighty years ago."

He couldn't know that! Rault thought. *Only a So Wari Elder of that clan could have known the details of an obscure study like that. There would be no reason to dig it up. Without already knowing its content, there should have been no cause for suspicion. The only other way...*

It came to him all at once: *Level four psychics.*

It was the only way to discern the duplicity of Moc's statement. *Only knowing that her truth was false would have prompted anyone to investigate such pointless trivia. The culprit then had to implant in the minds of the investigative team the idea to look in enough places to reveal the security measures that we had put so carefully in place.*

Still, they didn't seem to know all—a credit to the superb defensive psychic training of Rault's forces. Rault found himself subconsciously reanalyzing the available data in this new light. *Who among the Efilu possess level four intimate communications skills?*

The Si Tyen, of course—but they are so aloof, above political aspirations, Rault considered as time ran short. *The Kini Tod? Too timid. They don't have the gonads to execute this kind of scheme.*

Thea, the Ironde speaker, continued, "This Council finds the confessed not guilty of the crime she claims."

Rault did not allow himself to become distracted by the machinations of this tribunal. *The Notex? No. They are much more direct. They also lack the patience to carry out so intricate a plot.* Rault's mind swept forward through the possibilities. *Ejtok are limited to such communications within a single family unit.* He shook his head imperceptibly to himself. *Too easily traced.*

"...Further, we find that the intelligence network, regardless of who is running it, is most likely responsible directly to Meeth."

Time was running out; they were closing their jaws around Meeth's throat.

That was the extent of the species with...

The moment of radial epiphany rolled through Rault like a tsunami. *Induced psyches!*

"Moc is free to go."

Someone with limited psychic ability is using technology to induce and coordinate latent psychic geniuses to an artificially advanced level of performance. The asset may not even know he is being manipulated.

With blunt Ironde candor, Thea concluded, "Meeth, as delegate and So Wari Supreme, you alone are hereby declared guilty of suppressing vital information. This violates the fundamental spirit of the Pact and disrupts the integrity of the Greater Society."

There was no time left. Rault knew what he had to do.

"The punishment is immediate: death by—"

Rault bolted out of his position beside Meeth and raced to the portal on the far side of the chamber, knowing full well that he would be stopped before he could reach it. Rault made an ostentatious move to trigger the erasure sequence he had been toying with on his left arm as the three Vansar security sergeants seized him. As they tried to restrain him, Rault tossed the big avian on his left arm across the table. At the same time, he deftly unfastened the device from his arm, so it would appear to be thrown accidentally in the same direction.

The Sulenz delegate shrieked a thought across the chamber: "Stop him!"

Two Alkyz guards moved to restrain him.

Rault reckoned along the same lines of conjecture as he struggled. *It would take at least level three psychics to start with, but there are at least fifteen suspect species in the complement of the Greater Society. The question now becomes: Who is greedy and arrogant enough to even attempt a selective purge?*

Five security officers now held Rault's struggling form firmly.

Now the final ploy! Rault was still thinking covertly, but simultaneously he revealed a lightly cloaked thought.

"...hidden files," the Sulenz delegate projected to the Council attendees. "On a lower level! Quickly, seize that control device." As Slijay pointed, several meren scrambled for the bait Rault had thrown them.

Rault, apparently apprehended in the act of treason, confessed freely to his sovereign in open Council. "I knew that after you were executed, GS security would seize all records." He mounted an informative plea of forgiveness for his crimes to Meeth. "They would have eventually traced the coverup to me. I have forgone promotions to conceal my schemes for years. The only way to protect myself and my family was to erase any connection between myself and this scandal. If there was nothing to be found after you were dead, they would stop looking and I would be safe. I just didn't want to be implicated. I don't want to die," Rault begged at Meeth's feet. "I beg you, spare my family."

With no more than a glance, Rault sensed that Meeth was at once profoundly impressed by his brave maneuver and touched by his loyalty. Rault knew full well that such a conviction meant death not only to himself, but to his immediate family as well.

Meeth had no choice but to play along and—

The Sulenz delegate, Slijay, declared, "I want him thoroughly interrogated by Council Intelligence."

Even I won't long withstand the mind-probing of Ironde agents, Rault knew. He broke away from his captors and ran straight at Car Hom. *Surely, Meeth's oldest friend will do the right thing when the time comes.* Rault pinned all his hopes on that loyalty. That friendship. *The execution of a traitor to Meeth, regardless of Council orders.*

The So Wari fearlessly allowed Car Hom to grip his neck in the ensuing struggle. The two souls closest to Meeth exchanged a last glance as Car Hom hoisted Rault erect, still gripping the fugitive's neck tightly.

The final revelation came to Rault simultaneous with the snap of his own spine:

The Ironde and the Sulenz!

The thought floated away from him as the blood flow to his brain was interrupted. The urgency of that last thought was lost in the narcosis of carbon dioxide backwash from paralyzed lungs. Rault's mind faded to a peaceful darkness.

Chapter Four

— VISTA —

Meeth stood before the oriel in his private chambers. The setting sun painted his coat a vibrant collage of colors, contrasting its normally subdued earth tones and his sober mood. This same sun that burned his mind with the image of his best friend slaying his closest confidante, now glowed contrite with soothing, soft, orange hues, struggling to erase the wound. Aged green and blue spinal plates, exaggerated in Meeth's silhouette looming against the far wall, twitched restively.

The features of Meeth's face seemed even darker than the long shadows on the wall. The lines in his brow and the corners of his mouth completed the grim, eerie portrait. Eyes open, yet blind to the great expanse of plains past his own reflection, Meeth's thoughts roiled. His mind fixated on the events of that afternoon. The "who" and "why" still eluded him, in spite of the heavy wage paid. The whole sordid affair had seemed to last forever, but in actuality the midafternoon siege was over well before sundown.

Even here, secure in his most private offices, he could not afford to show the smallest hint of grief for his fallen comrade. *If Rault learned anything significant, he carried the secrets to the mound with him,* Meeth regretted.

A "traitor" could not be allowed to contribute his Animem to their Tarn, no matter the circumstances, and the pooled knowledge and experience Rault ferried with him to the Alom was an immeasurable loss to his herd. Meeth knew some of Rault's meren, but he could not select one of them as a replacement. Not yet. Some in Council Intelligence were not completely convinced that the So Wari Supreme had played no part in the incident. Meeth had to assume that he would be carefully watched.

For the first time in his one-hundred-sixty-year reign, Meeth was without an independent intelligence network. *I feel like I'm going into battle shaved clean.*

"Justice has been served." Frustration melted into anger as the thoughts Slijay expressed came to mind again. The Sulenz seemed a bit too satisfied with the outcome.

Satisfied? Meeth seethed. *Perhaps relieved.*

Memories continued to flow. He remembered Thea's vulgar Ironde habit of patting one on the back during narrative. Most thought the Ironde did it because the gesture could not be reciprocated, in light of their coats of razor-sharp spines. Thea's gesture grated on Meeth more than the sentiment itself.

"Feels good to be alive, eh?" the Ironde leader had said. Thea was shoulder height next to Meeth. Beautiful snow-white Ironde plumes stood erect on his body. The untrimmed down gave the appearance of a soft puffy flower, but petting that pelt could cost a digit. Even an armored So Wari could sustain a cut or two if careless. The weathered, dark gray skin of Thea's face was nearly raw. Wrinkles fanned out around eyes and mouth, more a reflection of Ironde heritage than age. He had looked at Rault's body and shrugged broad, stocky shoulders. "What do you think, Meeth?"

Meeth had resisted the urge to clench either his fists or his teeth and simply said, "Justice." The vow was taken as commentary on Rault's execution.

"Cowardly scum," Thea's aide commented out of turn. Then she asked, "Your clan?"

Social skills of a tree Jing. Meeth wanted to growl at her but resisted the urge. Thea himself had recognized the insult. He dismissed the mer and apologized for the comment. His condolence reminded Meeth of the sensitivity that eighty years' service on the Council had fostered.

Just when his faith in Efilu nature was on the mend, Weyef had joined the growing ranks of those who couldn't help saying exactly the wrong thing.

"I assume you have some recording devices in place, Meeth?" she'd asked in whispered thought tones. "Might it be possible to"—Weyef looked around abashedly—"obtain a personal copy? For review, of course. I must make a full report, and I don't want to miss any details."

Meeth had known that the residual Blood Rush still held Weyef on an obvious high. *Any recording provided to her will certainly be available on the Vansar black market by month's end.*

"A good kill," she had declared. "Bloodless, though."

That didn't matter. Meeth knew the mixed feelings many predators held in check. Intellectually, they truly abhorred violence as much as any, but the blood lust ran deep. A recording of an earnest kill of a worthy adversary was quite valuable.

This weakness is what kept Weyef from the Vansar seat on the Diet, Meeth realized. He found himself comparing her with the Vansar head of state. *Neph would have had more self-control.*

The hiss of a Kas Pen brought Meeth out of his reverie in time to see the beast's coils embracing the struggling form of an herbivorous tree mammal on the floor of his office. The fur-mite had ventured in through the open window. The succulent fruit it had filched rolled silently from its hands as it tried to loosen the serpent's death grip.

Meeth reached for the fallen fruit and replaced it in the bowl. He balanced the melon atop the assorted bounty overfilling the dish as he heard the little ribs crack. The gaping jaws of the ophidian dislocated to accommodate the limp animal. Unlike most So Wari, Meeth didn't wince at the death and consumption of prey by his Kas Pen.

At once, Meeth realized how long he had kept Tur waiting. He felt no guilt about the impropriety. He signaled his secretary to admit Tur to the outer office.

Now this! Meeth groaned. *This virtually unknown meg enters the picture. Governor of a quadrant in Porew cluster. Where the hell is that?*

He well knew Porew, home of a major industrial center and military command training base. On that scale, Meeth realized this Tur was distinguished. But here it was another story—Meeth's story—and the last thing the So Wari Supreme needed now was another distraction.

Weyef had already questioned Tur and learned nothing she did not already know. She had delivered a succinct but detailed report to Meeth promptly. The Dance of Fire account had been reduced to no more than a footnote. *They'll all be winding their necks for months to please me.*

Many on the Council were embarrassed by the near blunder of executing a leading delegate and monarch of a High Society on so few facts. Many, but not all.

Meeth decided to use the prevailing situation to his full advantage. He reviewed Weyef's report. *It's good, but Rault would have turned it upside down and backward to reveal something she had missed.* Meeth grudgingly gave her due credit. *It's an earnest effort, in any circumstance.*

Weyef, impressed with Tur's deductions and assessment of the situation, wanted him included in the investigating team.

She had properly requested Meeth's consent, however, before enlisting Tur's aid. This bolstered Meeth's confidence that she was trustworthy.

Meeth himself was unimpressed with the dossier on Tur. Still, Weyef had insisted that Meeth grant him this audience before the impending session of the Council. The So Wari Supreme found Tur's unsolicited insights into the "Poison Scandal" aggravating, and he all but ignored the extraordinary nature of the feat itself. He concluded, on his own and without Rault's vast resources, that the impairment impact on four species was more than noteworthy.

Could be no more than excellent deductive skills, but what if... Meeth pondered for a moment. *Such extraordinary psychic talent! He could be dangerous. Too dangerous.*

Tur was convinced Meeth intentionally kept him standing outside the closed door just long enough to cause him embarrassment from passers-by in the outer offices. Despite the obvious sleight, Tur would never let the Supreme see him seethe.

The heavy doors slid open, exposing an opulent office. Meeth stood behind the gel console. The desk construct currently doubled as a reception table as the doors rolled open to reveal a stoic Tur. Meeth appraised him in a cursory fashion, yet still Tur remained respectfully at attention.

"What are you doing here?" Meeth asked.

Tur's reply, devoid of emotion, was simple. "I came to help."

"Your help is not wanted."

"It's *necessary*," Tur stated tersely.

"Who do you think you are?" Meeth paused imperceptibly before answering for his guest. "You're no one! You can't begin to grasp the political nuances at play here. You come in here spouting what you *think* you know about plagues, conspiracies, and aliens and you'll ruin our already tenuous standing among the other High Societies."

He's on the verge of an eruption, Tur thought. Tur strained to keep his composure. *No one* spoke to him this way—not even the Supreme Leader of the So Wari people! Tur was on the brink of getting physical with the older meg, but he thought better of it. That would be a fatal mistake.

To distract himself from the dressing-down, Tur allowed his eyes to roam across the ancient artifacts along the walls and ceiling. There were few objects on the floor, he noted.

"You have already focused undue attention on me." Meeth continued his tirade more civilly. "There is some speculation that you seek to reestablish a secret espionage operation. You can stop wasting my time with your embarrassing delusions of grandeur. I have no use for you."

Now, a furious Tur leveled his gaze directly at Meeth. "Let's talk about embarrassment for a moment, shall we? Rault surmised that there was genetic tampering going on that involved several peoples. Fine. But he was too inept to report his findings to the proper authorities without bungling the effort, and he got himself killed."

They faced each other across the table, a mere head length apart, ears outstretched openly antagonistic. Their palms lay flat on the solid gel surface, arms vertically locked, supporting the two meren like the columns of two opposing siege-mecha about to launch toward one another. Tur decided not to reveal his communications with Rault before his death, given his leader's current attitude.

Meeth moved suddenly. Tur responded to what he instinctively saw as a threat just in time to catch his balance. His pelt smoothed into dense armor. Reflex. The gel console, which had been serving as the table, melted to sol state from underneath their hands and began to envelope them from the floor up.

Tur was momentarily intrigued by the density of the incon-spicuous device as it filled the confines of the office. The console resettled into gel state as a comfortable fore chair grew between Meeth's feet. A much less comfortable chair-construct shot abruptly upward beneath Tur. It clutched him in place as he tried to withdraw from its crude curvature.

His pinnate plumes still folded into tight glistening mail, Tur braced to break the grip of the gelatinous extension when Meeth waved him back with a gentle hand gesture. There would be no violence. The chair's edges softened.

"The official report said that Rault was conducting an inde-pendent investigation for his own purposes," Meeth tossed the statement out like juicy, ripe fruit and then waited silently. Would Tur seize it?

Tur refrained from couching the expected query and remained silent, as if he sensed that something had changed here. The physical differences were obvious but nonetheless striking; it was the strange shift in mood that was confusing.

With his peripheral vision, Tur examined the "new" interior of the room. The ancient office had an austere charm suited to the So Wari Supreme. Soft pulses of red, orange, and violet light emanated toward the center of the parlor, and murals of dynamic fluids decorated the walls all around. Beautifully textured patterns shifted on the wall surfaces separating the displays. Luxuriously styled pedestals supporting replicas of large potted flowers and ferns now littered the floor. The gentle motion of the fronds somehow enhanced the illusion that the three-dimensional dioramas surrounding them actually defined the parameters of the gel cell.

The open design was meant to be relaxing, but the soft colored lights intersected to form a stern, white field enveloping the personal spaces of the two occupants of the salon. The harshness of the light hid nothing, reminding Tur that he was still under Meeth's scrutiny.

He wants something, Tur thought. *What?*

Presently, Tur filled the room with a deep, rich chuckle that percolated up from the bottom of his heart. "How much of your mind do you wish me to read?" He stared Meeth squarely in the eye, having a little fun at his sovereign's expense.

Not missing a beat, Meeth responded, "It's not *my* mind I'm interested in your reading. I believe we have enemies in or around the Council. We could use a level 3 in our court."

We, Tur thought, controlling his exuberance at being taken into the So Wari Supreme's confidence. *He may be employing the ruling persona's "we," for all I know.* Tur suspected this wasn't the case, but it helped him maintain his composure.

"Then you don't believe the Quatal are acting alone either?" Tur asked.

Meeth drew his head closer to Tur. "I'm not sure the Quatal are involved at all."

Tur was taken aback by this revelation, but he said nothing, deciding to hear Meeth out.

"The Quatal do have machines capable of transporting them here. That's true. But to do it without being detected by our surveillance posts? Impossible!"

Tur thought it through slowly before speaking. "How do you account for the Quatal traces found at multiple sites and verified by Rault's own people, as well as Council Security?"

"How were they confirmed?" Meeth demanded, his newfound patience now intense.

"The usual way." Tur stood now, clasped his hands behind his back, and paced slowly as he described the methodology. "Foreign protein scans, analysis of enzymes for known Quatal products: sulfur, iodine, silicone ratios, and concentrations in micro-samples of secretions. These findings in the setting of the appropriate magnetic resonant disturbance are quite unique."

Meeth listened, then offered, "Most forensic scientists would know just what to look for, I would imagine."

"Of cour—" A look of consternation traversed Tur's face as he realized how long it had taken for him to see the obvious. Suddenly the insults hurled at him moments ago seemed a little less trifling. "If one knows what will be searched for, one also knows what to plant," Tur concluded grudgingly.

A sudden bruit disrupted their confrontation as the cell reverberated around them.

Meeth asked, "What now?"

Meeth's secretary indicated that his next appointment had arrived.

"Damn." Meeth *could* keep the next appointment waiting, but he realized that spending an inordinate amount of time with this Tur would look suspicious. He shifted the gel apparatus back to its original form and induced a holographic display of the outer chamber.

His secretary was chatting with Fath, who waited patiently for admittance. Meeth said nothing, but his eyes told Tur to remain at ease and silent. A brief gesture triggered the ancient doors to open.

Fath entered, already delivering his report. "I have fully interrogated Moc."

The newcomer eyed Tur inquisitively.

"And?" Meeth prompted, apparently paying no more attention to Tur than to a familiar piece of furniture. Fath's momentary distraction by Tur's presence ceased with a curt nod in the latter's direction.

"The 'family matter' story was a hoax, as we suspected. She now admits to protecting Rault."

Not very well, though, Meeth thought to himself. "Did she admit this to Council Security?"

"No. She adheres to the story that Rault had assisted her in her personal endeavor for reasons of his own." Again, Fath was momentarily distracted, this time by the bulge in the belly of the Kas Pen curled up in the corner. Fath swallowed uncomfortably.

"No disciplinary action against either Moc or her family," Meeth decreed. "As far as I am concerned, there has been no crime. I do, however, want a full gene probe performed on her before the sun rises." Then, to both meren, Meeth announced, "Dismissed."

Tur rose casually from his relaxed position, but Fath wasted no time in leaving.

As he reached the doors, Meeth called out, "Fath." He waited until the security meg returned his full attention to his superior. "Don't go out of your way to make the probe... comfortable. Understood?"

Fath acknowledged the order and resumed his exit forthwith, passing the previous guest in the doorway. Tur manually closed the doors to the office as he left and watched the lights in the chamber dim.

Chapter Five
— A SEASON IN HELL —

Dead!"

"Ol, it makes sense to first find out if—"

"I said DEAD!" Ol Ygar simultaneously projected and screamed his sentiment. The Tralkyz delegate was adamant to the exclusion of reason. "I don't want to discuss it with them in a civilized manner. I don't want to torture a confession out of them. I don't even want to listen to them squeal as they die agonizing deaths. I want them erased from existence! Not an egg, not a scent, not even funeral ashes will remain. I will personally wipe out every memory of them for all time."

The Council chamber was silent. Ol Ygar stood alone at the table, the rank and file of the Council all staring silently at him after his tirade. The sergeants at arms, now flanking him, gently urged him to take his seat. Ol hung his head in embarrassment and noted the bulging veins in his temple reflected in his workstation. His hands shook. Ol Ygar sat wearily as Yaw Daor spoke.

"As I was saying, I think it prudent to extract as much information from the Quatal scientific community as possible, see how extensive this 'Poisoning' is. So far, we know it at least includes golden algae. Suppose it has also spread to grasses, common flowers—"

"Unlikely." Slijay the Sulenz delegate opened the symposium's discussion, his opinion expressed with uncharacteristic calm in the wake of the Tralkyz harangue. "Their intent is now obvious: they wanted to minimize the risk of being prematurely discovered. The more levels they tainted, the greater the chance of discovery. Algae are the sole common link to the various food systems. Destroy the algae and you have effectively destroyed the entire Efilu civilization and its supporting biospheres."

The Ironde chief, Thea, objected. "That's an exaggeration, isn't it? I mean, we certainly cannot allow a threat to any member society, but truth be known, fewer than five percent of the Lesser Societies are at risk here."

"The Alom flows through all of us as it flows through each of us," the Roog, Shem Ris, commented from his water-filled corpuscle. Skin retracted from fins to reveal oversized hands on stubby arms. Vestigial feet flapped around to maintain position as he righted himself.

The Ironde spoke reasonably, "Yes, I appreciate the spiritual implications, but—"

"We are not talking about spiritual jeopardy," Neph interrupted Thea without apology. Obviously disturbed by the information, the Vansar ruler shared her own analysis. "Every animal life form derives an essential portion of its neuroendocrine milieu from the interaction with algae nucleic acid–protein domains. The high-energy system is so complex that our scientists don't fully understand it to this day." Vansar neurobiologists were surpassed only by Roog and Sulenz in sophistication, and all among the Council knew it.

"There must be some way of synthesizing a substitute." Thea looked around at his colleagues, his alarm growing at the delay in response.

"Our bioengineering consortium is working on that as we speak, but the defect is so... fundamental," Evem Ta the Wilkyz answered, speaking for the first time. "We may not be able to synthesize it in large enough quantities." In answer to the Vansar's pessimism, he added, "It's not just a simple genetic omission or substitution. This peculiar nucleotide sequence could permanently alter the neural synapses it contacts, actually rewriting the DNA to a new 'sense.' Eventually, one would end up with various parts of the brain and central nervous system that could no longer talk to each other."

"Elegant in its own way," Sund Kai, the Mit Kiam delegate, observed, then queried with her typical practicality, "How will this toxicity manifest itself?"

Evem Ta looked to Slijay to respond.

"Difficulty in concentration and logical thinking at first, with progressive dementia," the Sulenz delegate explained. "In many cases, paresis and seizure activity."

There was silence again. A sound mind and neuropsychic faculties were paramount to every Lesser Society.

Thea again reached for hope. "The Realm is so vast; I can't believe that all the algae are tainted."

"The actual field statistics are still pending, but sample data thus far does not look promising." Neph's head hung low.

"How 'not promising?'" Sund Kai pressed.

Evem Ta answered, "Dismal."

Meeth had been watching the exchange of information for patterns. *Nothing yet*, he thought to himself. Then he spoke, and the communal projections of the assemblage fell silent.

"The Kini Tod and Gen Rost have come up with an interesting approach that I initially thought too dangerous," Meeth interjected. "This discussion has changed my mind."

All eyes focused on the demonstration display projecting from Meeth's workstation.

"Their recommendation is for the use of another 'poison' of our own design." Against an undercurrent of dissenting thoughts. Meeth went on. "The idea is to delay the degradation and excretion of nucleic acids. The interruption of the natural cycle of nucleotide clearance would keep them in contact with the synaptic microenvironment until they begin to break down in several months. The stagnation will eventually cause malaise, anorexia, and neuromuscular irritability, but there would be no permanent damage. As it stands now, only three percent of the total sentient population has been directly exposed. We can now identify the affected algae, as well as any contaminated food products, and isolate them."

"We need a definitive solution to this predicament," Sund Kai objected. "A few months is not a long time, Meeth. Let's make sure we get this right."

Meeth found it unsettling that Sund Kai could be so cool and rational under the circumstances. *"Predicament?" We face mass extinction!*

"The Poison now has a defined origin and dispersion rate," Meeth said, making up the plan even as he shared it with the congregation. "We have to look in the most remote corners of the Realm, even—no, *especially*—in failed world projects. Planets that never got beyond the second stage of fitu-forming. With any luck, we will find some genetic remnants of the necessary organisms."

"Unlikely," Evem Ta said. "Those worlds were abandoned because there was some fundamental incompatibility with carbon-based life."

"Don't you mean Efilu life?" Yaw Daor objected.

"No," Evem Ta insisted. "I mean any carbon-based life. Remember, we utilize even hostile planets and worldlets to their fullest potential." Evem Ta's tone revealed a hint of pride. "Those celestial failures were not near-misses; they were outright disasters."

Meeth barely hid his disappointment. Before he could speak, Thea preempted him. "We have nothing else to lose by searching at this point. Meeth, if you wish to proceed with the second phase of your plan, you have Ironde support."

Murmured thought projections echoed Thea's sentiments.

Meeth struggled to obscure his second agenda. *I must determine for sure what part the Quatal play in all of this—if any.*

He knew that something akin to the Blood Rush was boiling in herbivorous and predaceous peoples alike. There could be no negotiation to spare the Quatal. Any attempt at that and the Council would turn on him in a heartbeat. He could not even be certain his own society would stand with him. Ultimately, sacrificing the Quatal would be less disturbing to him than ordering the execution of his friend Rault's family. Meeth knew he had to take advantage of this mob mentality and the way it interfered with logical thinking. A desperate idea came to him.

"The Quatal have made a fatal mistake. They have repeated their Threat to Life. This, in the wake of the generous mercy we showed them in the first conflict, adds insult to the injury! There can be no question; they have chosen not to live in the same universe with the Efilu." He paused for effect. "So be it, then. They shall not live!"

A piercing demand from Slijay cut through the wave of zeal consuming the throng. "Specifics!"

Meeth rolled on. "A tenfold energy match for the entire Quatal system will be calculated. The Roogs will see to the details. The Melkyz will send their best strategist to lead a maximum-grade assault against them."

"A threefold match should be enough to ensure complete—"

Meeth cut off the anonymous voice of reason reaching through the chaos. "We will have their *total* annihilation! Any glimmer of Quatal existence must be extinguished."

Meeth stilled his mind momentarily to sense any suspicious under-thoughts from the group.

Still nothing.

"We'll maneuver the three surveillance posts to the far side of the Quatal system. The trio will be sufficient to block any attempt of flight or distress summons." Meeth projected, then thought to himself, *Distress summons! To whom? They'll be all alone in this one.*

For the first time, Meeth noticed the Si Tyen delegate in the back of the crowd. *Timon just silently watches, as the Tyen are given to do of late.* A dolorous countenance defined the Tyen's face. *How will High Tyen Chybon respond to Timon's report?* Meeth wondered.

"Wait!" Slijay protested. "The Quatal don't even know we're aware of their plot, yet. Moving those listening stations is sure to raise their suspicions, perhaps even alarm."

Meeth turned deliberately to Slijay. "They have dealt a death blow to some of us right here on the capitol world. I'd venture to say *we* don't know what *they* know or don't know."

Slijay said no more. It struck Meeth that the Sulenz ambassador had been unusually vocal during this Council session.

"The stations will shut down except for life support and grade-zero propulsion," Meeth explained. "Timing is everything here." He drew them all in with a gesture. Projecting a real-time image of the Quatal system, Meeth indicated the turbulent solar activity. "Our blockade will move into position under cover of the solar flares. They will be completely invisible to any telemetry sensors. The storm will reach its peak before this night is over. We must make our move now!"

If the Quatal are half as intelligent as I think they are, this will be the perfect opportunity to slip past our spy network, Meeth thought. *Maybe they have been doing so all along.* The notion that a few explorers, perhaps even a few colonies, may have secretly gotten through inspired him somehow. The Quatal were remarkably adaptable. *It would be a shame to see such a brilliant civilization extinguished over a matter that didn't even concern them.*

A grim thought intruded into Meeth's speculation. *If we don't find a way out of this predicament, the Quatal may be the only ones left to write our epitaph. The choices we're driven to make against our best judgement in these days. Mob mentality—I thought we had risen above this.*

Meeth cautioned himself about careless thoughts; at least one other in the Council chamber was as cool and calculating as he.

The nuclear fires burned brightly in their wide orbits around the Quatal star system—a short-lived tribute to brave Quatal defense forces. The desperate tactics were ingenious, even by Melkyz standards.

The Quatal were, of course, hopelessly outmatched.

It's nearly sunrise on Tiest now, Moc thought, observing Nar Quy, the mission commander, in wry amusement. *Rare to see a Melkyz annoyed.*

"Pilot, keep the formation tight." The commander projected embarrassment at Quatal resistance encountered by his strike force, though Moc accepted the hasty deployment had not put the Efilu at their best advantage. *Rault should have piloted this vessel. I'm only here because my lie was better than his. Or less valuable to catch.*

Still... *Amazing,* Moc thought. *This is epic battle. Who'd have thought that the Quatal forces could be so... innovative!*

Nar Quy was so perturbed, Moc could hear the edge of his private thoughts; he nearly broadcast them for all to hear. It didn't matter to Nar Quy that he had lost only twelve out of the twenty-five hundred ships he commanded. It also didn't matter to him that he sent fifty billion Quatal souls to oblivion in the cold void of interstellar space. By Roog estimates, that represented more than half the entire population of this alien civilization. What did matter to Nar Quy was that he completed his task: erase everything Quatal from existence. Nar Quy pressed the assault, his ships carelessly passing the miniature stars born of the power cores of the ruined enemy fleet.

Moc concealed her own thoughts. *Our advance squads already ravaged the three worlds of the star system. Bombardment has ruptured the tectonic plates. What more can we do to these people?*

The view field displayed smoky atmospheres now studded with flashes of volcanic eruptions, twinkling jewels of death on charcoal-gray blankets. All defensive activity had ceased. The main body of the Efilu task force moved into position.

Almost before Nar Quy gave the order, the dissection of the charred planetary bodies commenced. Moc read his feelings as if he were muttering them aloud. Nar Quy felt somehow cheated that he could not hear or smell the carnage he inflicted on the alien worlds. The intervening void somehow smothered the Blood Rush, diminishing his satisfaction.

Moc adjusted telemetrics for her commander. The holographic magnification brought the battle almost into her lap. Like yolk welling up through cracks in an egg, the lava flows connected the volcanic fires. The planetary rotation spun shards and huge fragments of the disintegrating worlds away from their axes. A wave of Efilu vessels had been assigned to atomize the newly formed meteors as they dispersed from their centers of gravity. The destruction wrought on the worlds of the Quatal continued until the expanse stretched free of all but smoke and dust.

"The station commanders are checking in with confirmations that the Quatal evacuation effort has been obliterated," Moc said, receiving communications from the edge of the star system and summarizing the collective reports. "Refugees consisted of mainly germinal centers, a few mentors, and livestock with nutrient rations. No survivors. All debris pulverized."

"Acknowledge the reports, Moc," Nar Quy said with calm resolve. "Order the outposts to withdraw to a safe distance."

Moc watched Nar Quy frown at the retreating scavenger sorties still vaporizing the scattered ice asteroids. *He knows full well such miniscule celestial bodies cannot support life at all. His sub-commanders are just venting pent-up angst at the Quatal skyscape.* Moc kept her thoughts tight as she piloted the flagship through the burning carnage. *Nar Quy barely hides that he shares their frustration.*

The solar flares died down as the Melkyz-led Efilu taskforce extinguished all native life in the star system.

Upon reaching optimum range, Moc acknowledged then transmitted Nar Quy's executive order for all ships to focus their main weapons on the star itself. The debris of the dead fleet had been winking out of existence as the last of the subatomic reactions consumed them. A line of Rid Sadox—the "Star Crushers"—moved into position.

"The Sadox have not been deployed in hundreds of thousands of years," Nar Quy remarked distantly to Moc, then winced.

There it is! Now he remembers we don't feel the same quickening in the kill as super hunters. Moc coordinated inexperienced meren directing the arcane operations under Nar Quy's command. *He narrates the details as if reciting poetry.*

"The type-3 Sekwoy reaction will reach out to compress antiprotons into a near-planetary mass, smaller than a beady Sulenz eyeball." Nar Quy toothed a predatory grin. "This is the reverse process to our main propulsion process.

"Take note, Moc. Neither you nor generations of your descendants may ever see this weapon in use again. Together these powerful vessels will rend a tear in the fabric of space-time that will open at the center of the Quatal sun. There the antimatter mass will draw the core of the star into the singularity. Watch how the energy of collision will not escape the growing gravimetric forces."

It's as if the dying star is reaching out to stroke her children with a last anguished caress before implosion. Moc watched in revulsion. *Just gathering them close to her celestial bosom.*

Nar Quy continued absently. "The star will shine dully for several months, perhaps even a year, before regressing to a dim glowing ember, its nuclear fuel spent."

"What a waste," Moc loosed a candid thought.

"Did I invite commentary?" Nar Quy snapped. "They were Poison incarnate. Malignancy like that has to be excised with wide margins." Then in a softer tone, he said, "Moc, sometimes there is greater value in sterilization than recycling."

The statement lingered in Moc's mind. *Sterilization. Why, then, do I feel more soiled now than when we left Tiest?*

Chapter Six
— HOME SEARCH —

The afternoon shadow of the Round Table loomed westward, consuming a sun-drenched patch of grass. Meeth hadn't been on a picnic in the open savanna like this in decades. Fragrant fresh citrus fruit tasted intoxicatingly sweet, the air, warm and exhilarating. The solitude soothed his soul. Hustle and bustle of life on the capitol seemed mercifully distant.

Meeth closed his eyes as he chewed. Images of So Wari heavy equipment and construction activity came to mind unbidden. His people had prospered with an intersocietal trade surplus in manufactured building shells.

Not as esthetically popular as Wilkyz styling, but much more sturdy, more durable, he mused with pride. *Factory bases for the industry of other lesser societies.* Wan Tuk and Kini Tod gel-core design quality matched that of any other production lines.

Meeth hadn't thought of how specialized nearly every member society had become in reputation: Melkyz interstellar security vessels, Vansar telemetric technology, Roog communication systems, Sulenz wildlife management systems. All interactive, but no longer interdependent. The fragility of that former schema had been made manifest at the end of the Golden Age. Contemporary wisdom demanded that all societies maintain the means of independent existence.

When news of this crisis reaches the general public, there will be social upheaval, Meeth fretted. *Alkyz diplomatic skills will certainly be tested in the aftermath of that revelation. It will inaugurate a new balance of influence among Lesser Societies. The So Wari chair-seating on the Diet of Tiest could be upended. Energy storage and transfer enterprises will be of premium importance. The Ironde could be in position to dominate the entire economy of the Efilu Realm.*

A disturbing truth became obvious to him. *Worse, their vulgarity would likely alienate them from most of the higher societies. The Greater Society could seethe into civil war.*

A flap of wing passing overhead yanked him to vigilance. *A pterosaur passing this close to the city?*

Meeth's left ear twitched imperceptibly, then stiffened. He listened intently for a moment, long So Wari ears stiffening, then protruding from the sides of his head like horns, but he heard nothing. Waiting for a threat to get within hearing range, even with the advantage of So Wari stereoaudiometry, could prove fatal. He focused on the grass around him.

Insects.

He actively discerned their collective life force, comparing it qualitatively with what he'd registered moments ago within his personal sphere.

Fewer!

Something was driving them away. Bugs should have been attracted by the scent of the fruit. But still Meeth heard and smelled nothing.

One hundred and fifty million years of adaptive evolution is not easily blunted. Meeth could almost taste the danger, but he knew that panic would play right into the trap. He leisurely reached for a fresh piece of fruit, scanning the horizon as he did so.

A breeze carried organic scents from that direction. *Insects and mammals—fading, though,* Meeth concluded. *Flight.*

The threat was behind him. As he sat to enjoy his snack, he subtly braced to snap to the coming ambush armed.

He had already examined the landscape in his photographic memory and formulated battle options when the lunge came. Razor-sharp cowlicks of plumage raked impotently across a mailed neck as Meeth deftly evaded a tail cast to ensnare his feet. Meeth's own tail launched the assailant into the grass in front of him.

Car Hom recovered and countered with another offensive, seemingly before touching the ground. Meeth was caught by this attack and suffered several shallow cuts from the lightning-fast hands and clawed feet. The Alkyz Death Grip was slipped thrice with no significant injury.

The adversaries circled one another warily.

Stalemate.

Meeth stood silently, watching his determined friend in confusion.

Without dropping his guard, Car Hom asked, "Why did Rault sacrifice himself in the Hall the other day?"

"Rault was a coward and a traitor," said Meeth slowly, eyes narrowing. "Are you with his cause?"

"Yes!" came the answer with no hesitation. Car Hom dropped his guard as he spoke. "You can drop the charade, Meeth. If I cannot eliminate a meg of your years, I should never have been able to best Rault so easily."

"Your prowess is legen—"

"Stop!" the Alkyz aggressor interrupted. "I fully expected to be defeated, maybe crippled in that scuffle. I wanted no more than to hold him at bay until reinforcements were available." Car Hom leaned forward. "But *no* So Wari would leave himself open at such a critical moment in battle as Rault did. Not unless he was presenting a show for an audience."

So, legendary Alkyz arrogance yields to wisdom, Meeth thought with relief. *And cunning to friendship.*

"Does anyone else know?" Meeth asked, caution in his tone.

"Of course not. This was my first opportunity to speak with you alone. You weren't where you were supposed to be." Car Hom smiled. "Very sloppy, I thought. I had to decide if you were beginning to weaken or if you were up to something."

"Did you think I was getting old?" Meeth asked.

"Age is a toll the Alom extracts from we who endure the future." Car Hom recited the adage with sincerity.

Meeth smiled and dropped his guard, then responded with the traditional salutation of combat survived: "You honor and strengthen the So Wari people. Rault was a great but necessary loss. Something is going on, Car. Something I don't understand. We are at a distinct disadvantage here."

Car Hom sat on his haunches, catching his breath.

Meeth seized the advantage. "They burned him without retrieving his Animem, Car. They burned him and every secret he dug up. This goes beyond breach of tradition or even respect. This goes to agency of our foes."

Car Hom considered Meeth's thoughts before projecting his own with a change of subject. "The Ironde have come up with a foolproof solution today."

"Oh?" Meeth noted the hint of cynicism in his tone.

"They're taking samples of cerebral spinal fluid from uncontaminated individuals, now that we can identify them. They're running them through a modified polymerase chain reaction sequencer and plan to construct a series of retroviruses to rewrite the altered sequences."

"Keep plugging them in until they get a functional algae strain again," the So Wari said as he sat, too. "Elegantly simple in its mechanics. Typically Ironde. Do you think it will work?" Meeth wanted an answer. Despite his suspicions, there was a logic to the Ironde's experiment, and in that, there might be hope.

"No," came Car Hom's grim response, "but it's a wholehearted attempt just the same."

Meeth stood and paced as he ruminated on the subject, then spoke softly. "Our only chance is to feign complete ignorance."

"All well and good to avoid discovery, but what are we to do about crushing this alleged plot?"

Damn, Meeth thought. *'Alleged' plot!* Car Hom was with him, but not totally convinced.

The liability of the So Wari's hypervigilant reputation in this age of complacency had surfaced yet again, and Meeth was out of time. Above all, he needed to convince *this* ally. It came down to a leap of faith.

"Here is what we will do..."

Vit Na seemed to wrestle with the very air in the room. She didn't know what was going on, but she sensed the intensity of chicanery around her and could not manage to keep still. She had already made short work of her archeology assignment and transmitted her report to the client. Now the lot of her dear friend consumed her.

Tur hasn't contacted me in days.

She paced. The dignitary lodgings, situated in the lush garden district adjoined by parks, museums, restaurants, and entertainment, boasted luxury of the sort obviously meant to placate its residents—and its more dubious guests. After a brief, exploratory walk, she assessed the resort environment. The junket simply sharpened her perspective through a well-gilded veil of deception.

Privileged standing in her society had, in many ways, blunted the seduction of hedonism. Free access to all, but communications in the southern sector of the Round Table frustrated her further because of her accommodations rather than despite them.

It seems some guests can correspond selectively with the outer world, Vit Na brooded. *I'm sure outgoing communications are being censored, albeit subtly.* She laughed to herself without humor. *Incoming tidings are probably being monitored, too.*

It occurred to her that she had not received confirmation of her report's transmission from her client. Vit Na seethed at being held completely incommunicado without explanation.

Melkyz didn't believe in the concept of the "inescapable trap." There was always a way out. She decided to indulge in the apartment's lavish bathing chamber as she considered her options.

Nice, she thought as she dipped her tail in soothing waters. *But this tiered pool is a bit excessive, especially for a So Beni, So Wari or any other So construct.*

Grudgingly, she admitted to being pleased with the warm southern exposure offered by the tri-level apartments. An ornate table next to the pool held intricately crafted flasks. Vit Na reached for one, uncapped the fluted neck and sniffed. As she inspected the other vessels, she read the runes on their seals and smiled. *Assorted Mit Kiam emollients. These don't come cheap.* It occurred to her: *These luxuries were designed for Melkyz tastes.* She peered back at the tubs.

A leisurely dip might prove distracting though, she thought.

Vit Na eased into the upper pool and bathed quietly, reviewing the boundaries of her confines. As she swam the steamy waters, she pondered the possible motives for her sequestration.

It can't be the content of my report. That project had to be of the least interest to anyone with a pulse, she thought. *Surely, I'm being observed for the company I've kept.* Again, her mind drifted to Tur. *He's being manipulated. To what end, I don't know. Nuk!* she cursed. *He'll go over a cliff for duty.*

The sun glared brightly through the large, decorative transom above the sunken parlor's portal. Incandescent reflections gleamed in the suds clinging to her jet-colored pelt. Precious secretions along her plumage matched the index of refraction to the air around her. Her means of invisibility, now floating there in the vat, washed away.

Vit Na's apprehension mounted as she realized the loss of the aniline-enriched oils to the warm water's shampoo. She promptly spilled her body over the edge of the upper pool into the cooler anointment of the lower tier. Those soothing bath oils made her more comfortable but did not restore her *Blending* capability. There was no immediate threat, but with her primary defense system temporarily incapacitated, she felt suddenly vulnerable.

The sunlight had just taken the chill out of the waters. She submerged in the cool basin to restore her body temperature and rinse the scented emollients through her downy pillage.

She emerged from the water and stepped through the aquaphilic containment plain. As the water-stripping effect quickened a shiver rippling through her body, she calculated how long she would be unable to *Blend* again.

Why did that thought cross my mind? Vit Na paused and considered the temporary loss of her species' main stealth measures. The security factor of the Round Table, as a So Wari stronghold, stood absolute.

A shudder caught her by surprise. Exiting the bathing area, completely dry, she made her way toward the sleeping chamber. Her mind wandered back to the handsome Melkyz pilot who had flown her to City Plaza days earlier. She caressed her shoulder with a Sharu massage hold and felt it relax. The maneuver served its function. The tension slid down off her lithe arm to fall into nothingness between delicate interlacing fingertips.

Perhaps he has made his way to the Round Table by now, she thought. If not, she could always order someone similar from the entertainment district. Perhaps working through her carnal urges would clear her mind. Vit Na reached for the gel console on her way to the sleeping chamber and summoned the concierge. "Do you have sindech on your menu?"

He displayed gourmet choices from a dozen restaurants and suggested a menu that might please her most. The concierge graciously offered to call a transit vehicle for her.

"No, thank you. Bring it to my quarters, life-warm with a nice garnish. I'll be dining in tonight."

"Why Tur?" Car Hom's final question still echoed after he had listened to Meeth's stratagem in total.

Meeth could have given his friend any one of a dozen sound and legitimate reasons for placing Tur in command of this clandestine expedition to Fitu. He was intelligent but could follow orders. He was creative but would remain focused. Tur was born to lead but was not overly ambitious. The So Wari commander had the necessary experience documented to justify Tur's appointment as team leader.

Above all—and this was the very point Meeth's own skepticism could not overcome—he trusted Tur. A dubious enough trust for Meeth, safely on Tiest, but he was sending Car Hom off to parts unknown, subordinate to this brash young meg.

The matter was settled with respect to the staff selection arrangements: Tur could select the personnel, subject to the Alkyz's approval. Effectively, each conscript crew candidate received an immediate nod or rejection, no time for debate between the two executives. Meeth scrolled through the candidates. He tapped a finger on a Melkyz archeologist. *What's an archeologist doing among the senior staff finalists? Our Animem Tarns go back beyond the Exodus.* He stroked his chin as he considered. *Who put her under diplomatic confinement? She's not in the Melkyz clandestine community structure.*

The threat did come from within, but he seriously doubted a Melkyz part in the plot. They're smart, really smart, but they were totally committed to finding the Poison. The official search would prove futile, Meeth was sure of it. His own private search was an even riskier venture than Rault's failed investigation. Meeth provided for a crew of two hundred and fifty, although he hoped they wouldn't take that many.

How many good meren will I get killed this time? Meeth had to protect them the best he could. His thoughts returned to the Melkyz archeologist. *Who released her? Not Yhm Vel.* The Melkyz Mater Familia was also Kemithi. If she had intervene, he'd have never heard the end of it. *And Tur doesn't have the authority…yet.*

He could waste no more time on inconsequential details. Meeth set the launch for dawn. The *ReQam* would serve well. An old-time survey ship, Meeth had seen to its reconstruction personally. A few surprises were added for the curious in case the ship was stopped in transit… and he had a good feeling about Tur and Car Hom. The *ReQam* waited quietly under the inland sea for departure.

As Meeth looked out over the expanse of moonlit savanna from his office, he remembered his father's final meal with the family. Corp had been ill for many months. Wasted by starvation and emaciated by consumption, he lay dying.

The painful cancer had spread to most major organs in his body, but still he hung on. Pain had etched a permanent furrow in his brow, but he endured it.

A lifetime of leadership and sacrifice had prepared him for nothing else, Meeth realized.

It was forbidden to bring more than water to the ill. Corp's strength had worked to his disadvantage under a law designed to eliminate weakness.

In the privacy of his death chamber, Corp dropped the façade of courage and fortitude he put forth for his herd and issued soft moans of agony.

As a cub, Meeth had once witnessed a moment of his father's despair, unseen by Corp or family. He remembered being demoralized by the patriarch's cowardice. Meeth was torn by guilt watching his once-powerful father waste away. Corp's loyal family stood by helplessly, sharing his anguish.

Putting on that farce of dignity, all the while begging for death in the emptiness of his misery.

In the final days, the family could stand it no more. Under the pretext of collecting the Animem, the whole family smuggled small bits of Corp's favorite foods to him one night.

Yet, to waste food on the dying... Meeth wrung his hands. *How can I ever honor any of my kin knowing such shame?*

The worn shell of a So Wari chief had bitten weakly of each offering from his family, the food falling from his mouth, unchewed.

Corp had explained it to Meeth after that last supper: "Laws have held our peoples together in peace for eons. Sometimes, though, there is no merit in blind obedience to the law. We create them to preserve our strengths and protect us from our weakness. It often takes a lifetime to realize that our very strengths are so often our weaknesses, as much as surviving our weaknesses gives rise to our strengths. Fairness, patience, mercy, generosity—all contribute to the strength of our civilization. When decisions are made, they are guided by the body of the law, but executed in the spirit of justice. That justice is what is truly important. It preserves us, no matter the adversity."

Words. Corp had abandoned the province and his family, left them leaderless. Meeth remembered thinking that his father had lied for the first time since he had known him. *He left me! Such craven weakness, giving up like that. After all, pain and hunger were only feelings. What did they matter when the mind and soul were needed? To make such absurd excuses—an insult!*

Corp ate next to nothing that night, but oh, how he savored those last meager morsels, Meeth now remembered.

His father hadn't seen the following dawn.

Now Meeth was skirting the law and he knew it. *Am I just making excuses, as once my father did, or am I doing what has to be done?*

The Great Council's search effort is fruitless. Meeth knew they would find nothing. *The architects of this catastrophe have surely seen to that. We must get a step ahead of them.*

He had to approach the dilemma from a desperate angle. One no sane individual would entertain.

Surrounded by enemies, the only safe recourse is to feign ignorance and play along. His thoughts turned guarded and somber. *With my most trusted ally away, no one will be here to shield me when the storm crests.*

If I make another mistake, I'll be done. He allowed himself a solitary moment of self-pity. *There will be no requiem for me.*

Chapter Seven
— BACKTRACK —

"This is Tur, commander of the geological survey vessel *ReQam*." He answered the hail with ears erect, tips turned up. Silvery nanosynthetic silt vaporized and the mist congealed into the holographic image of the guard ship's command center. Tur in turn allowed the other to see his own ship's bridge.

The amenable Melkyz officer eyed him long and carefully.

Tur stood easily erect in his usual stoic manner. He surmised that this patrol ship sub-commander was the relief officer on duty. This one was too tentative to be the ship's commander, but Tur suspected the senior officers were Melkyz as well. That called for prudence.

I knew a geology ship lurking along the outskirts of the Realm would raise a few questions, Tur thought. *Meeth knew it too, damn him.*

Likely this Melkyz officer, Desq Ja, was trying to decide whether to awaken his superior officer over this minor irregularity. Tur didn't relish the notion of matching wits with a Melkyz strategist.

The young meg deliberated for a long time before speaking. "If you don't mind me saying so, you're out a little far for such an old ship, commander. You haven't had any propulsion or navigation problems, have you?" The query was more than appropriately polite.

"No," Tur projected. "We are quite aware of our position and course, Des Qua." No elaboration on the mission. Deliberate mispronunciation of the name sowed Tur's first seed of umbrage.

"A craft like that is... well, obsolete," the Melkyz officer said.

That observation is painfully obvious, but the concern is valid, Tur thought.

The survey-class vessel was shaped much like a spiral mollusk shell. The neutral configuration was ideal for burrowing when necessary. It was the last of such ships, built over five hundred years ago; few engineers would even recognize the technical configuration of some of its parts.

"We are the outermost patrol ship in this sector. Were you to suffer a malfunction, it would be unlikely that you'd get a timely response to a distress call. You could become stuck out here for months if you are lucky, years if you aren't."

Tur shrugged casually, but said nothing. Desq Ja sincerely wished to help. Not easy while suffering the indignities heaped on by an unabashedly brusque So Wari mining captain. Tur's nonchalance was pushing this Melkyz officer. Tur had always been good at reading people, and he had this one down to a toe. He knew he was getting under the sub-commander's skin with his not-so-subtle contempt for the inquiry.

"Commander," said Desq Ja firmly, "your vessel's outer markings are dull, almost indistinguishable, even at this distance. We almost passed you by. Our secondary telemetry systems are detecting mid-range EM emissions from your power core. Your propulsion efficiency can't be more than forty-seven percent of optimum."

A touch of arrogance in his thought projection, Tur said, "I have engineered certain modifications in the drive section to more than compensate for the losses, Sub-commander... Disc Jay, is it?"

"Desq Ja!" The exasperated correction came after the second solecism of his name. "Adding two additional Sekwoy generators to the stock drive is a dangerous 'modification,' Commander. Creating a type-1 Sekwoy reaction to boost the propulsive generator might get your ship to the tipping point, but it doesn't stop the power leakage. Check your Pitkor equation. It just adds radiation to be spilled." Desq Ja was almost pleading. "The rate of loss will probably increa—"

"Are you authorized to probe ships on private business without notification or consent, Sub-commander?" Tur affected indignation.

His patience worn thin, Desq Ja explained, *"Passive* telemetry reveals much to a *seasoned* commander. There are few ways to get that kind of energy emission out of a ship of that design and age short of completely gutting it and replacing the endoskeleton and visceral structures." The spiral/counterspiral design was well known as the basic structure of geologic science vessels, a design model over four centuries retired from service. "But I know that could not have been done because of the prohibitive cost involved," Desq Ja said.

Good. He knows So Wari frugality well, Tur thought. *He'll also know how some low-class So Wari are given to callous disregard for the feelings of small-statured peoples.*

"The blur in your communicated image as well as the loss of background definition, in spite of our efforts to enhance them both, betrays the EM field buildup." Desq Ja's ire finally erupted in explicit contempt to the scrap pile's commander.

Tur responded, "When you become a *full* commander, you'll probably understand that skill can make up for the inconvenient lack of technological luxuries." He casually looked back at his navigation crew, out of the offended Melkyz officer's field of view, as a final jibe.

Tur heard Desq Ja's projection, unfiltered. *Ah, finally! This Melkyz sub-commander has wound his neck long enough trying to help an "incompetent, arrogant So Wari and his foolish crew." If I want to risk losing our two hundred souls in the depths of interstellar space, he'll let me.*

Officially, everything was in order. There was no imminent danger, and assistance had been refused. *He'll bury the log entry in the milieu of insignificant passing observations made on his watch,* Tur mulled. *Details not included. It's what I would do at this point.*

Tur imagined Desq Ja almost wishing the *ReQam*'s commander would rot in space with a death grin frozen on his ungrateful face.

Tur waited until the security ship was well out of scanning range before resuming full dampened power. The EM field dissipated from the command center. The *ReQam*'s state-of-the-art propulsion system returned to active status. The delicate balance at "Pitkor's tipping point" of matter/energy transition was a necessary first step to reaching zero mass. Only then could the *ReQam* accomplish the complex Sekwoy type-2 rift reaction without crushing the ship and crew into a singularity. Drawn inexorably into the lingering fold, the crew evaded the time dilation effect and navigated to normal space deep beyond the distant void.

No specific orders had been issued to Tur or Car Hom regarding divulgence of the grand scale upgrades in the craft's interior, but it was obvious by the incongruous exterior that this information was to be shared on a need-to-know basis.

No doubt Meeth is covering his hindquarters in case the mission goes sour. Tur wasn't sure he liked that, although he respected the tactic. He had decided to protect his own tail by not actually "lying" about the true modifications himself. *It will be tough to prove me guilty of anything except vulgar behavior.*

Tur rested on his haunches, ruminating. He looked up to see Car Hom with his arms folded in front of him, nodding his approval.

The So Wari affected a facial expression akin to a vague frown, then rose to leave the command center.

Car Hom gave Tur a light pat on the back as the commander passed. Tur ignored the silent accolade and continued to his office with a curt gesture for Car Hom to follow him.

Vit Na sat off to one side of the chamber, her back against a wall, and surveyed the contexture of the keel. *Professional comforts, but not luxury.*

The *ReQam* provided less of a contrast to the quarters Tur had liberated her from on Tiest than she expected. The other department heads and section chiefs were murmuring about the haphazard setup and lack of organization. Their apprehension indicated how ill-prepared they all felt.

The Tralkyz, Bo Tep, seemed animated, yet somehow the most relaxed of the group. Vit Na felt uncomfortable around Tralkyz. The more relaxed they appeared, the more uneasy she became.

Head of Acquisitions, she thought as she watched him. Vit Na shuddered at the thought of him "acquiring" anything from her.

Tralkyz had a notorious reputation for being unnecessarily vicious. Worst of all, they had no fear or reservations regarding personal injury or loss. No enemy or situation intimidated them. It was said that if a Tralkyz lost both legs in combat, he would chase his conqueror on his hands and tail.

A chilling legend to frighten cubs, but obviously exaggerated. Vit Na peered at Bo Tep. *Perhaps not so obvious in this very close chamber.*

This one was reputedly tougher than most, but she found herself staring at him anyway.

Where do I know him from? she wondered.

The executive officer was due any time now, and most of the department heads scrambled to organize their staff assignments. Car Hom would want reports immediately available upon arrival in the briefing room. The room went completely silent as the portal melted away to reveal Tur, flanked to the right by Car Hom.

The room remained open to the hall as Tur gruffly projected, "Level seven and above."

Car Hom made a short, silent gesture for all nonessential personnel to leave. The remaining senior staff fidgeted restlessly. No aides or support staff to help them through this meeting. The door almost caught the tail of the last individual to leave as it closed.

——————⟨ ● ⟩——————

"Outside the Realm?" Vit Na watched Kellis, the Head of Geotechnics, gape around the room. She would see if everyone else was taking the news as incredulously as she did.

Kellis, on the verge of casting an objection, held her thought. Only then did Vit Na realized the only other mind-voice haunting the room was Bo Tep's snickering. Tur and Car Hom stared impatiently at Kellis's fluster. The Tan Barr mer's broad, armored shoulders sagged slightly in embarrassment. She found the courage to proceed more delicately.

"I'm sorry for being a little thickheaded, Tur, but what is the purpose of going outside? If we are to look for uncontaminated algae specimens, we're not going to find any in unexplored space." Kellis gained confidence as she couched the question more thoughtfully.

Car Hom waited for the nod from Tur before speaking. "We are not heading for unexplored sectors."

Bo Tep quipped, "But you just said outside the Realm. To me, that means going where no one else has gone. What are we doing, going in circles?"

A stern look from Car Hom failed to check the Tralkyz's casual manner.

"The *ReQam* will retrace the path of the Exodus as far as necessary to find algae remnants. Our thinking is that all the known worlds have been or will inevitably be contaminated." Tur said no more on the subject. "For security reasons, this information goes no farther than this room for now. There will be a briefing for grade three and up upon arrival at our final destination."

Tur stepped toward Bo Tep. His proximity and intensity spread ripples of dread throughout the room. It was clear that the next inappropriate thought Bo Tep issued would be his last. So Wari suffered no fools.

Tur was caught off guard when the silence was broken not by Bo Tep but by Doh. The short Kini Tod scientist was the only staff member who seemed truly thrilled to be there. "We are going all the way back to Fitu, then?"

Vit Na rolled her eyes in exasperation. The Kini Tod's obsession with the mystery of the Keepers wore everyone's patience thin. Groans from others in the chamber echoed her sentiments.

With uncharacteristic patience, Tur responded, "It won't be necessary to go that far. We've made numerous colonies between the current boundaries of the Realm and Fitu. We are certain to find appropriate specimens in the ruins of those abandoned colonies."

"Unless someone has beaten us to them," Bo Tep added somberly, without his characteristic sarcasm.

Tur and Car Hom shared an uncomfortable acknowledgment of Bo Tep's insight.

This Tralkyz is a thinker, Vit Na observed, shifting full attention to the scoundrel, *suspiciously quiet and attentive. Doesn't fit their profile.*

Tur went on, trying to ignore for the moment the unexpected Tralkyz support. "We have been inconspicuous so far. I believe we have escaped notice."

"Except that of the last patrol ship," Bo Tep said, more in Tralkyz nature.

"That was handled adequately," Tur remarked.

Nothing more from Bo Tep, Vit Na observed, *but he has made his point.*

"I want every department up and running within the next three days. My apologies for the haphazard departure." Before any questions could be asked, Tur turned and moved to the exit with Car Hom three head lengths behind him. The remaining staff looked at one another's puzzled faces.

Ikara, one of the other lead scientists, spoke with resignation in deference to the tasks at hand. "We all have a lot to do." The Denmar mer's rich sienna coat rippled along a serene, statuesque frame like fluid clay. Ikara's fatigue, apparent only in the drag of her black-tipped tail, played quiet contrast to her calm posture. "I'll be in Xenobiology setting up my staff if anyone needs me." She hesitated for a moment to allow spontaneous consultation in the hopes of avoiding the inevitable interruptions later.

But none came. *No such luck*, Vit Na thought.

Ikara hugged her own tail once in frustration, then left. The others soon followed suit.

Vit Na felt a chill run up her tail as Bo Tep prowled to her side.

"What would Tur have done if he hadn't gotten that ship to leave the way it did?" he asked softly.

An interesting question, Vit Na had to admit. She thought about it, then answered, "Probably impress the ship into subordination. He has that authority as High Commander."

The Head of Acquisitions was persistent. "What if the other commander had *questioned* Tur's authority? Under the circumstances, that wouldn't have been unreasonable, and he'd have been within *his* rights."

Vit Na's apprehension continued to rise. "I don't know," she said unconvincingly.

"Yes, I think you do. I've heard you two have been very close— *synesprit*, in fact."

The earnest urgency in his face deserved an answer. "If they didn't comply with the conscription order, he would have destroyed their ship and every hand with it." She found herself returning his resolute gaze.

"I had to know," Bo Tep answered her unspoken question with more compassion than she had thought possible.

She found her anxiety returning. *I'll have to tell Tur about this conversation, and Bo Tep knows it.* As she watched him drift down the corridor, her tension again melted away and she felt as if she had just helped a close friend. *Odd that the thought's not more disturbing.*

"How did you come to select Bo Tep, anyway?" Tur asked.

"He is an accomplished leader and very well thought of in the Tralkyz community," Car Hom responded matter-of-factly.

"The traits that the Tralkyz find commendable, most of us find deplorable," Tur pointed out. "I thought for a moment I was going to have to kill him on the spot."

"Yes, I noticed that."

"And?" Tur demanded.

Car Hom just shrugged in response.

Tur, now irate, declared, "That should have been your responsibility, *Commander.*"

Experience and patience allowed Car Hom to recognize the disciplinary tactic for what it was, and he took no personal offense. "I don't execute my staff or personnel for *attitude* when making suitable observations." No "Commander" followed the response. Car Hom returned Tur's angry glare with no hostility or malice of his own.

Presently, Tur relaxed and swept his ears back against his scalp. "You're right, of course. Still, he did seem out of character for a moment there, did he not?"

Again, a shrug was Car Hom's sole response.

This line of conjecture was going nowhere, Tur decided, and he changed subjects. "Departmental organization and assignments seem to be moving forward." He waited for Car Hom to chime in.

Silent acknowledgment.

"I've been especially impressed with Loz," Tur opined. "He has retrieved ancient maps of the Exodus Corridor and is already coordinating with the liaison offices of the respective departments to be consulted."

"I think the whole organization is solid and capable." Car Hom was not petty and offered his personnel assessments forthright. "We did a good job in the selection process, if I do say so myself."

Reflecting for a moment, he then offered unsolicited advice. "If I may make a comment, Commander?" Car Hom did not await permission. "This ship is not staffed solely with So Wari warriors, and no amount of discipline or intimidation will make them react as such. They simply cannot be as regimented."

"And?" Tur probed.

"I just think this group's diversity could be used to considerable advantage, given enough freedom to express themselves."

Tur nodded slowly, recognizing his point without agreeing. "And should I have any... misgivings about a staff member's performance?"

"Then I am at your disposal," Car Hom stated with So Wari–like clarity.

"I'll keep that in mind," the High Commander said. Tur chewed a puzzling question. "I'm curious. Why did Meeth name this ship the *ReQam*? I don't know this word."

Car Hom didn't answer the question immediately. After a moment, he said to Tur, "It translates as 'Salvation' in the old common tongue."

Tur instantly searched his cache of Animems from his training days. "Why dub a ship with a word from a dead language? What does salvation mean in this context?"

"Strange concept," Car Hom said. "The notion describes a neutral party's effort to remove a person or persons from danger or imminent threat."

Tur asked. "By a 'person or persons,' you mean prey? Why would one with no blood in the fight, no qualms with either party, make such an investment? That makes no sense."

"Hence the word was obscure even before the language became obsolete," Car Hom responded, thinning patience barely showing. "Meeth didn't change the name when he commenced the overhaul, he just kept the decommissioned vessel's name and registration. Discretion, I presume. On to more pressing matters. I've scheduled an executive meeting."

"When will you assemble them?" Tur asked, dropping the idle pursuit of ship's history.

"A level seven staff meeting is scheduled to begin in—well, actually, right about now. If you will excuse me." Car Hom rose and exited the executive suite, crossing the promenade garden to the chief of staff's office, adjacent to the conference room.

Tur allowed himself a reluctant smile. Car Hom had stood his ground without disrespect. *Meeth chose well.* He realized that assessment could be extended to include the *ReQam's* commander, too. Then he busied himself reviewing the preliminary reports from the defined sections in each department.

Car Hom presided over the meeting. Archeology was the fifth department to report.

Vit Na appears unsure of herself, almost timid, he observed. *Nonetheless, her particular department is one of the best organized. She even constructed a display of the surface of Fitu, including ruined cities at the time of the Return and the most likely continental drift pattern over the ensuing sixty-five million years.*

Car Hom's appreciation of her talents deepened when he saw the surprise on Kellis's face at the display.

Accurate! And without help from Geotechnics. He almost chuckled out loud. *Tur feels as uncomfortable as he'll allow himself to be about Vit Na heading a department under his command, but she's easily the best-suited to the task.*

The meeting adjourned on schedule.

"Talented, I'll say that for her." Bo Tep appeared at Car Hom's side, sharing his opinion unsolicited. "She's also the only crew member on board of noble birth."

"You're a chief, Bo Tep. None would ever provoke a Tralkyz with two seconds by his side." Car Hom indicated the absence of Tralkyz guards.

Bo Tep showed no signs of intimidation and projected challenge. "What are you trying to say, cousin?"

"There's bound to be some resentment toward her." Car Hom smiled a closed lip expression and projected his response narrowly for Bo Tep's mind only. "But the others are professionals. They'll get over it."

"Faster than she will, I'll bet," Bo Tep proposed in parting, nodding to the executive officer before disappearing about his own business.

Watching the Head of Acquisitions depart, Car Hom signaled Devit to his side. An accomplished analyst, the Ironde's unorthodox appointment as weapons master had been Tur's call. The staff dispersed at different tempos in the microgravity outside the meeting room. Professional conferences turned casual as the chief of staff and weapons master conversed.

"I thought the remainder of the staff meeting was amusingly satisfying," Car Hom said as he looked down at Devit for his take on the meeting. "No one gave an unsatisfactory presentation. In fact, the vast majority were brilliant. Especially well prepared was the Acquisitions department."

"Yes. Contingency trees were well thought out, the choice of consultants well-researched and integrated. The only presentations that were lackluster were the ones that should have been so," Devit noted. "Nutrition and Waste Management, and Medical are mere formalities." The Ironde added a dismissive gesture.

"The minor department heads rightfully avoided wasting time making showy presentations," Car Hom said conversationally. "Quick, to the point, and over before anyone got bored. Quite a feat of restraint. The mission is vitally important, yes, but I expect it to be drearily routine. Supplies are more than adequate as the passengers are mostly young, healthy, and free of the Poison."

"The only concerns pertaining to the Medical department are about the anticipated effects of the counteragent if the mission runs too long," Devit observed. He watched for Car Hom's response to his assessment.

"You've got that right, Devit," Car Hom declared, then thought privately, *The last thing we need on a crucial, So Wari–led mission is irritability and carelessness.*

Car Hom also knew in the back of his mind that there was no proof positive that the Poison had been screened out, with all the subterfuge in play back on the capital. When the personnel traffic thinned, Car Hom's tone took on a more serious tenor, and he projected narrow thoughts for only Devit to heed. "The Medical department will act as a silent sentry for signs of infection." Car Hom caught Devit's eyes. "You can keep that to yourself, can't you, Devit?"

"Of course, sir," came the weapons master's answer, equally discreet.

"Good meg." Car Hom acknowledged the contract, clasped his hands behind his back, and ambled down the hall.

Car Hom thought of Brajay, the Sulenz medical officer. The Sulenz, whether deservedly or not, had the reputation for run-on thoughts. *Can I depend on him to confidentially monitor Tur for deterioration?*

With the group dismissed, Car Hom realized his hunger. He spied Vit Na floating leisurely toward her quarters and matched his pace to the archeologist's. Large people preferred walking the halls except when hurried. Gently propelled by personal sphere of influence, her glide dragged to a halt as she turned an inquisitive face to the *ReQam*'s executive officer. Intent on extending an invitation to dine with him tonight, Car Hom faltered. The impropriety of the request might engender ill feelings toward her from the other department heads. The offer died in its inkling.

I'd better eat alone tonight, he decided.

Car Hom answered her unspoken question by saying simply, "Nice work."

She nodded an awkward "Thank you," then carried on her way.

As he watched her retreat to her quarters, he allowed himself a private assessment of the young archeologist.

Most impressive.

Part 2

EMINENT DOMAIN

— HOME AGAIN —

The voyage has been long, the arrival, unexpected.
Quantum energy, gone. *ReQam*, ablaze.
Losing its fight with gravity.
Atmospheric drag.
The Old One returns and watches from on high.
Greenery. Life. The Garden world, revived.
He calls in intimate communion.
The echo is lonely and unanswered.
For Man has no voice.
The Old One looks away from Man.
Again, He speaks.
This time, to the sea—hoping for answers.
Intimate Voices spring forth.
"Who speaks for the Sea?" Old One asks.
"The Skeewii; Whale, Dolphin, Seal, Otters.
Who calls to us?"
"I, the Old One."
A chorus of Skeewii voices return clear and strong,
"Where do you come from?"
The Old One answers, "Here, and beyond."
A wise dolphin speaks,

"Eons ago, we saw corpses of great ones in decay on the ocean floor.

We know not from whence they came."

Old One says, "They died… After," then asks,

"Why so brief the collective memory?"

The Skeewii do not understand—or remember.

The Old One notes, "All other land creatures seem to fear Man."

"We parted ways with Man, Skeewii to the Sea Below, they to the Sea Above."

Dolphin says, "Man seldom communicates with the sea."

Seal, "They strut as apex beasts of both seas."

Whale, "Until, they enter our Sea Below."

Otter, "These humans lack intimate communication skills.

Build cities, build walls, soil rivers.

Man has no concept of the Equality of other.

The humans poison the boundary between the Seas."

Whale declares, "Most of us avoid humans."

Saddened by Man's ignorance, Whale clarifies,

"Rarely do humans reciprocate with food, or valuable services when aided."

Otter laments, "Instead, they hunt us."

"But," Seal curls his nose and says, "we are waiting."

"Waiting for what?" asks the Old One.

Dolphin answers, "The final apocalypse that Mankind will visit upon himself."

"We will reclaim the depths, then the shallows."

In a chorus from the deep, "Then the Sea Above, Below, and Between."

Then all were silent.

Old One understood. "The Children of Dragon have been busy."

— Interlude —

THE LORD, THE CRONE, AND THE SAILOR

A storm-brewed British countryside surrendered two wayward voyagers to the castle entrance. The butler greeted the wind-tossed pair with a single blench at their arrival, but of course, the butler was only human. The servant escorted crusty sailor and pruned carline alike to the appointed chamber and announced them. Upon receiving the visitants, the squire of the manor dismissed Cyril and waited for the steward, his duty done, to close the heavy oak door. The host waited for the click of the latch before speaking to the guests.

"Winter approaches." The noble adjusted his silk robe and squatted at the great stone fireplace as he stoked the flame. His unlikely company sat side by side on the cool leather sofa.

"They are on their way," the Chinese woman spoke first, her voice little more than a rasp.

"You mean to say they are nearly here," the sailor corrected. "They've entered the Corridor!"

The patrician used no names. Not here, not among his own. It would have undermined the colloquial intimacy of dialogue despite its mundane, verbal nature. He sat down in the matching wing chair and adjusted a monocle over his good eye. "They are not close," he said, his voice strong and adamant, "but their arrival is now imminent."

Each of the three sighted eyes surveyed the room as if for some hidden bastion of strength. All lingered on the crest over the mantle as they scanned. Nothing unique to the uninitiated; many family coats of arms bore the symbol of the dragon somewhere in the design.

"Are there no Si Tyen among the ship's complement?" the lord asked.

The old mariner hesitated a beat, as if consulting with some arcane source, then responded, "None."

"The Tyger is on board, though, is he not?" the host asked.

"That, at least, is confirmed," the sailor intoned. "Oddly enough, the Tralkyz is not the random variable."

"The Melkyz and the Notex are the elements that we cannot see." The Chinese woman peered into the near distance. "The streams of the Alom whose courses we may not know." She turned to her companions. "Only time will tell. Time, and the Alom."

Chapter Eight
— FALSE HOPE —

C ar Hom absently rubbed a nearly full belly. He had finished the bulk of the well-seasoned sindech and prepared to stretch out on his divan to savor the last few sweet morsels spanning the fish's ribs. Ripples in the portal barrier indicated the presence of a visitor. The door opened to reveal Tur.

"May I help you, Commander?"

"I've disturbed you." Tur had an inquisitive look on his face, trying to disguise disgust at the last remains of the grilled fish. "I'll just come back when you're done."

"No need," Car Hom replied. "I've more than dined sufficiently."

Tur still looked hesitant. "Sorry to interrupt your meal."

"It's all right. You saved me a number of unneeded calories. Weightlessness is too easy on the body. I've got to watch it at my age. Now really, how can I be of help?"

Tur pursued the apology no further. "Let's bounce while we talk."

As Car Hom rose from the table, the platter of scraps sank into the gel surface. He walked Tur to the door and out, leaving the odor of dead flesh behind them. The executive officer's growing concern that he had intimidated the young High Commander was short-lived as Tur came promptly to the point.

"It's been four days since we entered the Exodus Corridor," Tur announced. "Loz has correctly located nine of the abandoned colonies. We have a seven-phase Telescien on each of them."

Telesciens, interactive derivative entities, possessed seven levels of artificial intelligence which operated as senses. Each unit maintained the pure energy equivalent of ten pounds of unstable heavy metal. The telekinetic function worked as pseudopodia and could excavate, manipulate, analyze, and even synthesize simple inorganic objects on site from native material. Guided from the safety of the *ReQam* by a skilled Efilu director, a Telescien was a powerful tool for exploration. If there were any dangers, the unit could be sacrificed with no material loss.

Car Hom nodded as he followed Tur's logic. "That dips into our energy reserves a bit, but to end the mission early, it could be worth it."

"Reports have just come in from the last unit," Tur said.

"You don't sound very enthusiastic," Car Hom observed. "No algae?"

"No," Tur answered. He watched Car Hom's shoulders sink. "But there is something else. There are alien traces of organic matter that indicate recent contact."

Car Hom stared in disbelief. "Quatal!"

"No," Tur said impatiently. "Something completely different. We are tracking it now. That's why I need you in the command center. If this is a first encounter with an intelligent species, I'll need a Council member present as ambassadorial support."

Obb, Chief Paleobotanist, was pleased with his quarters. Everyone else so busied themselves setting up their divisions that they had little time to give much thought to personal space. Most apartments were more than adequate, anyway, and no one wanted to draw Car Hom's attention unnecessarily by putting in unusual requests. Obb, however, felt the effort was worth investing.

Obb's selection went unchallenged. His choice drew no attention as the occupants of stratum three were mostly technicians and officers of level 2 and under. The dregs of the crew.

Well, no accounting for taste, he mused. Most of the other senior officers were on the seventh stratum, centrally located and near the staff conference rooms.

Obb's parlor underlooked the tropical gardens on the third stratum. The chamber was open to the glade at pond level. Insects were kept out by a neurodisruptor field. Flying insects occasionally hit the water with tiny splashes as they were stunned in midair by the event horizon. Crawling grubs, approaching more slowly, just avoided the growing discomfort as the diffuse field intensity mounted. The lighting from the overhead ceiling filtered dimly through the thick vegetation—most suitable to Obb, as the Gen Rost were swamp-dwellers by nature.

The humidity almost reached saturation. The plants inside his apartments continued the jungle theme with minimal interruption. Obb swung gently in a hammock as he cracked open a fresh seed-fruit. Large hands extended their articulation from short arms to tip the treat to his beaklike mouth. The thick, creamy fluid trickled down his throat with a tingle. The anesthetic quality of the fruit conferred an icy-cold taste, even at room temperature. Obb crossed stubby legs at the ankles and wiggled his big, flat feet with delight.

The reverberation of the gelport signaled Doh's arrival for his first consultation. Obb stirred enough to trigger the open command with a gesture, but that was all. Gober Dil, his Wilkyz assistant, would escort the guest to the parlor.

As the Kini Tod were themselves facultative amphibians, Doh took in his host's quarters with envy. Doh habitually mired himself in details—even those as trivial as the motif of a colleague's apartments. Obb had finished his fruit by the time Gober Dil completed the grand tour. Sunken den, the work area, sleeping system, and data archives in the remote chambers had entertained the visitor with all the gaiety of an exotic museum. Dil showed signs of impatience as he moved through the dining area, hygiene pools, and his own small, adjacent suite. He thought of *Splitting*, but he would still experience the tedious tour when he reconstituted. Of course, he could always generate a duplicate and have him commit suicide before reconstituting. A silly idea, Gober Dil admitted to himself.

Still, Doh was too preoccupied with the prospective discussion to notice the Wilkyz attaché's pique. There was perceptible relief in Gober Dil's tone as he announced the Chief Paleozoologist's arrival. Doh made himself comfortable as he set up the link to his own database for reference.

"So, do you really think there are still intelligent life-forms on Fitu?" A baiting opening question; Obb liked to start his debates off that way, regardless of whether he agreed or disagreed with the contender.

"I do. I really do!" Oblivious to the form Obb had chosen for the discussion to follow, Doh jumped right in. "It's been over sixty-five million years since the Exodus. Time enough for the heartiest of the surviving life to adapt, regenerate, repopulate, and flourish. Now, I don't expect that they will have developed crystal technology or advanced thermochemical power," Doh tittered, "but I think they will have formed complex social orders, maybe even groups of herds or tribes."

"That requires some degree of complex communication skills, doesn't it?" Obb offered the notion innocently. "I mean, to join several communities together, they would have to be able to share thoughts and ideas."

"Yes, of course," Doh agreed eagerly.

Obb smiled to himself at Doh's response. *This is going to be too easy.*

"There are probably groups of interrelated codes in use," Doh went on. "For example, both land and sea birds communicate with chirps and whistles. These tend to further organize into songs, which are then learned and passed on to later generations. They improvise upon those traditional songs to advance new information and new ideas, don't they?"

Obb felt he could do his opponent in right here and now, but he wanted to enjoy this session a bit more. "Do you think that Fitu is currently inhabited by birds, then?"

"Possibly," Doh began cheerily, "but—"

"*Possibly*? Birds have small brains and high metabolisms. How do you propose that they build delicate devices and tools? The hind talons just can't be adapted that well, and their wings are useless for anything but flying." He paused as Doh floundered a while, then Obb struck again. "And perhaps swimming. Then there is the obvious: where do they get their food? All vegetation was wiped off the face of the planet eons ago. None of the natural flora would have survived the iridium toxicity."

Doh tried to raise an objection, but Obb rolled on relentlessly.

"All right, forget the toxicity for a moment and answer me this: What autotrophs could withstand millennia of cold darkness?" He paused there for effect. "The food chains had to crumble with the basic nutrient elements destroyed."

"Couldn't some autotrophs have survived on geological heat and enzymatically released chemical energy?"

Emboldened, Obb crossed into Doh's specialty for a moment. "And what about the effects of heavy metal poisoning on major organs? How do you explain surviving the universal renal failure and intestinal toxicity, not to mention central nervous system damage, that must have taken place? They'd have needed every precious neuron to survive such a holocaust." Obb was openly laughing at the Kini Tod scientist until Doh retracted his head halfway into his shell.

Peeved, Doh somehow managed to grab on to a little dignity, and he extended his neck in defiance. "Well, I'll admit that the chances of surviving those dark times would have been small, but there are always *some* individuals who manage to survive the demise of their species. Furthermore, they will pass those survival traits on to their progeny."

Still laughing, Obb rejoined, "Oh, that's the other thing: iridium gonadal toxicity is the most common of all deficits. Every sexually reproducing organism on the planet was rendered sterile. Including the Tyen Keepers. But perhaps you're right. Maybe we'll face a world-wide conflict between spiders and insects or something." Obb snickered. "I can imagine, a city of webs woven along the ribs of some saurian fossil looking across a valley toward a beehive empire." He slapped his jiggling belly. "Or even a mound of ants! Haunted by Si Tyen ghosts, no less."

As if suddenly realizing the cruelty he had just piled on his colleague, Obb tried to reduce the humiliation a little. "No doubt the Tyen made some creative adaptations in those final years. We'll certainly see some unique artifacts and dietary changes among their ruins. Vit Na will be fascinated, no doubt."

The implication that Doh's theories were of only archeological value was not lost on the naïve Kini Tod. Gober Dil hid a snicker as he sat quietly in the adjacent room, ostensibly studying ancient civil planning documents.

"I don't know what we'll see, I admit," Doh sulked, the sting of earnest embarrassment finally realized. "I'm not smart enough for that, but I have seen enough surprises in my lifetime to expect the unexpected. Especially where the Si Tyen are concerned."

"Commander, we are now twelve photodymes outside of the Exodus Corridor," Loz announced as he calculated the *ReQam's* position from the Astrophysics station. Moc, the mer who had started the whole Quatal incursion incident, served as navigation director at Loz's side.

Tur acknowledged Loz without turning around. *So, from here we could potentially see images of the Corridor from a hundred and twenty years ago. Preview is a prudent first move,* he reminded himself. *Who really knows what to expect?*

"Hold this position," Tur commanded.

The *ReQam* gauged the alien star system.

"This complicates matters," Tur observed. "Searching for specimens from abandoned settlements is one thing, but here, we are outside our space. Military force cannot be justified if any resistance is offered." *Not even by Meeth's convincing arguments.* Tur added to the command staff, "We don't have time for lengthy negotiations."

"There's no need for either," came Loz's uninvited response.

Tur inhaled deeply, then exhaled without turning around.

Car Hom, taking the cue, ordered Loz, "Just state your suggestion, please."

"We are no longer in the Corridor, but we're still in the Old Dominion," Loz spat out, ego a little deflated.

"Then we still have legitimate jurisdiction," Tur said.

That could have been very difficult, Tur told himself. *He knows his business, that's for sure.* Tur regarded Loz without looking at him. *Flare for the dramatic, though. If I accept roundabout explanations from him, I'll be expected to take them from everyone.*

The benefit of being surrounded by such diversity swayed Tur like the coming of a great storm, at once majestic in its power and awful in its potential for chaos. His attention returned to his astrophysician. Loz's ego exceeded that commonly exhibited by his race, but the Notex scientist sported the species' typical impatience.

High metabolic rates for omnivores. They're even tiring to watch! Tur garnered some appreciation for the trait. *Accounts for their spare, lean physiques, too.*

More than restless, Notex were constantly in motion. Even when they weren't employing *Hyperspeed*, they tended to mobilize their super-joints, presumably to prevent stiffness. Remarkably viscous joint fluid reached a liquid state only when hyperspeed was employed; at rest, the organic lubricant settled to various grades of fluidity spanning semisolid to gelatinous sap.

Tur couldn't resist a private So Wari slight. *That array of hooks and talons on the forearms makes for a great attention-grabber on an otherwise lackluster, midsized species.* To the crew, he projected, "Display current parameters of the Old Dominion, Loz."

Loz relayed a flamboyant command to Moc, assigned as his first assistant. At her gesture, a real-time image of the sector swathed the command center. The entire vista was bathed in a soft purple light up to a distant blue star cluster.

"We're close, but no one can dispute the fact that this civilization arose in the shadows of Efilu space," Loz announced. "Fifty-three worlds with near standard gravity, two hundred and fifty significant worldlets scattered around the system in near orbit about them. The Fituine stone-worlds themselves whirled in wide orbit about seven gas giants. The smallest gas world was the size of Tiest."

Kellis arrived in the command center at Car Hom's behest. Absently, she stated, "I enjoy interesting planetary formations."

The gas giants of the system glowed with the intensity of dim red stars, but in different colors: blue, indigo, red-streaked orange, green with yellow and golden-brown marbling.

"Unnaturally beautiful..." she added when she came to a halt at Car Hom's side.

Tur half turned. "Unnaturally?"

"Of course. You don't think those colors are normal, do you?" Kellis's casual tone could have been taken as impudent by some. "Besides that, those giants aren't nearly massive enough to produce their own luminescence."

"Are you certain?" Car Hom asked sternly, forcing her to shift her attention from the display to him.

More formally, she answered, "I have identified this system from the survey records from fifty million years ago." She awaited the consenting nod before superimposing the archived image on the real-time display. She adjusted for the dyssynchrony of the orbits before explaining.

"These were the planets as they appeared those many eons ago. During the process of Fitu-forming, we utilized the friction of rotation against the contained gasses beneath the inner crust to generate heat and industrial power. If that impossible glow were a natural phenomenon, they should have been brighter then than they are now. As you can see, they simply reflected the combined cosmic radiation that fell upon them at the time of this record."

"This could be an error in the recording. What about the possibility of a 'fade' effect on the visual?" Car Hom asked.

"The records aren't that bad." The wonderment returned to her face. "No. Those beauties are artificially lit."

Car Hom, more practical than scientific, gestured open-handed to the display. "By what power this?"

Loz answered Car Hom's question. "About one hundred and fifty of the smaller solid bodies are mass drivers."

Tur lost his detached affect for a moment. "Are *what*?"

"Mass drivers." Loz projected the thought in a deliberately patronizing tone.

A response to the earlier disciplinary comments, no doubt, Tur noted, but said nothing.

"Those small planetoids are equipped with magnetic feeds which take loose debris and gases from their own fields of gravity—atmospheres, if you will—and 'drive' them through an electromagnetic tunnel, the average being about a hundred times the length of this ship," Loz continued. The astrophysicist formed a tunnel with her hands as the demonstration display appeared, showing the mechanism before them. "The high-velocity 'cloud' strikes a nuclear fusion field in the larger stone-worlds cloud cover. This, in turn, causes a chain reaction to take place, forcing a fountain of high-energy photons to explode outward into the upper atmosphere of the gas giants. The ionizing radiation is the source of the illumination as it disperses into the near-stellar brine."

"Mass to energy. They at least have the first part of Pitkor's unified field equation," Tur observed stoically. "They use the stone worlds as buffers and their own stratospheres to diffuse the power."

"I just haven't figured out how they utilize this as fuel," Loz finished.

"We can't make that determination intelligently until we learn their root anatomy and physiology," Doh said, uncharacteristically somber. "I recommend that Telescien probes scan for life-forms and communication patterns."

"Agreed." Tur sought Car Hom's expectant gaze and said simply, "See to it." Then he exited the command center.

A full day passed before Car Hom appeared in Tur's offices to deliver the progress report.

"As you know, our mysterious cloud-dwellers have decided to come to *us* for a closer look." He sat on a forechair, his tail comfortably supported behind him.

"That should make our investigation of their biology and technology easier." Tur sipped a cool citrus concoction from its bowl as he prepared for his briefing.

"I have Doh, Obb, and Ikara on the task force. Their preliminary conclusions can be summarized quite neatly. It would seem that our friends out there are actually carbon based."

Tur didn't react.

Car Hom continued. "Ikara has named them the Tomet. They are autotrophic organisms that feed directly off the ionized clouds. Structurally, they have vascular membranes that grossly look like petals on flowers. In fact, the arrangement of these append-ages attached to a single spiral trunk is very...well, flowery." He chuckled as he explained the anatomy.

"Are you telling me we're looking at a floral civilization?" Tur asked, also amused.

Sobering some, Car Hom finished, "No. They're actually closer to animal life. If you want to make a comparison, they're closest to some of our native cephalopods. The torso is spun when they want to move." Car Hom crudely demonstrated with his hands as he explained. "The appendages form a helix. As the torso rotates, it cuts through the dense atmosphere with a variable acceleration, pulling the individual with it. Direction is controlled by torsion of the core. The appendages even flap to provide sudden bursts of speed or drastic directional changes."

"The basics are all very interesting," Tur interrupted, "but what I need to know is: how do they manipulate the world around them? Specifically, how did they escape the atmosphere to create those orbiting power stations, for example?"

Car Hom asked the next question for the High Commander. "What you really want to know is: what are they capable of militarily?"

"No." A wry smile preceded the response. "What I want to know is: are we dealing with the most advanced society of its kind, or are they unified into a consolidated power?"

Tur leaned forward on his haunches to get his first officer's response. He had learned to anticipate Car Hom's little games by now.

"Well, the life density seems to be concentrated near the Gray World. The mass supply appears to be the richest, and all the ion trails of comet-like bodies that Loz calls 'transport clouds' lead to or from it." He folded his arms in satisfaction.

Tur, too, seemed satisfied with the anticipated analysis.

"So, we're dealing with a stellar empire—"

"—and the *ReQam* is poised at its hub," Car Hom ended the thought.

Tur turned in the direction of the fore section of the vessel and pointed with his head. "Now to the present situation."

"Their curiosity is giving way to frustration," Car Hom reported. "Their probes are not penetrating our ship's outer layers. They're still in the dark as to what we are and why we're here. I recommend that we let them churn for a while before we make our intentions known. At this rate, one of them is bound to lose its temper and take hostile action." Car Hom shrugged. "Then... we have them."

Tur drummed his fingers a few times on the table as he thought silently. "It seems to me that our interests could best be served by a direct inquiry."

Car Hom gave him a suspicious look.

"I'm very serious," Tur assured him. "Their political structure is sophisticated enough to make direct negotiation feasible."

Car Hom stood and said, "I think you're right. This culture is sufficiently fragile to crumble if thumped in just the right place."

"Let's hope that *they* know that," Tur said.

Car Hom didn't understand the romanticism surrounding alien encounters. Obb and Doh were tacitly envious of Tur, who had decided to go alone. Then there was Ikara. "What do you mean, I can't go? I put two sleepless *weeks* into the research that got us here, and you're trying to cut me out now?"

"Ikara, calm down." Car Hom had been unreasonably patient with his explanation as to why Tur wanted to proceed without a large team.

"One: the energy cost of sending a Telescien through that atmosphere is considerable. More than one unit would be wasteful. Two: a single powerful being threatening the world of the Tomet will seem more like divine intervention. A shallow trick, but scale has a way of compensating for lack of authenticity. Three: Tur is about to bring the Efilu to the brink of war with this unsuspecting race. No one must be responsible for this act but Tur himself."

The hackles on Ikara's neck bristled as she framed her logic when Car Hom tactfully stopped the conversation. "We're done. I've indulged you as much as I'm going to. The next action will be...definitively severe."

Ikara stopped, mid-thought, imposing a Sharu forced composure on her rage. "I'll be monitoring the encounter from my lab, sir." She left with no further argument.

———◖●◗———

Tur remained physically on the *ReQam*, of course. The data integration fields squeezed his body off the floor into midair. They wove an intricate web of force fields around him, each transmitting and/or receiving different types of signals to or from a complementary Telescien generated outside of the ship. The basic form was spherical, but the self-image of the subject—in this case Tur—was usually preserved subconsciously.

This Telescien was powerful. It had ten times the usual power endowment, the capacity of a small security ship—more than enough to do the job. If challenged, or successfully destroyed somehow after a hard-fought battle, the reappearance of Tur as a newly generated Telescien field would demoralize an opponent.

The decision not to descend through the atmosphere, but rather to simply appear, was a risky one. The populace might panic and destroy the ruins of ancient settlements in the pandemonium. Given the ionizing nature of the Tomet physiology, the crew would probably never find the artifacts after such an evacuation, if that happened. The population of the city was estimated at fifty million.

Suddenly materializing, however, might be just the edge he needed to bluff his way through as a deity.

Stagecraft. Tur had decided to gamble on theatrics. Upon arrival, Tur scanned to horizon with his Telescien, recorded and reported.

[*The Tomet empire is ruled by a Pentad; one individual speaks for a group of five equals. This ploy may pay off well. There is no panic, only partially satisfied curiosity, a desire to look at the alien visitors.*]

Tur chuckled as his image was inundated with questions: "Who are you? Where do you come from? Why are you here?"

They kept a respectable distance, unsure whether they were dealing with some sort of hologram or a physical being. Tur had been briefed and well prepared by his communications director. He communicated with the Tomet in their own fashion, thanks to Jeen's deciphering of the signals that comprised their language.

Each of the common gases in the atmosphere could be forced to vibrate at a unique harmonic frequency specific to the individual element. The code was complex but consistent. All expressions followed nineteen basic forms, with no exceptions. Tur had no particular flair for languages, but he managed.

He answered their questions patiently, but briefly. Explaining that this was once Efilu space and still technically under his jurisdiction was simple enough. The term *jurisdiction* was obviously understood, as were its ramifications.

The Tomet Pentad didn't like it.

The first speaker offered a hypothetical response to an unwelcomed expedition onto the worlds of Tomet. Tur sent the potential Tomet response back to the ReQam for careful dissection of nuance. Car Hom and Vit Na confirmed his interpretation of the veiled threat. He nodded at the Efilu intelligence analysis.

The Tomet Pentad awaited Tur's response to violence, also hypothetical in nature...they hoped. The batteries of orbital mass drivers powered up like a small nebula of nuclear cannons, but did not target the ReQam.

Tur recognized the Tomet skepticism of Efilu power. It was but one ship.

They doubt the Telescien has teeth. Tur grimaced. He hated predaceous metaphors.

Tur decided on a remedy for their confidence. He began manipulating several solid objects with his hands and tail, casually at first, all in the course of conversation. When he answered the speaker's question, he affected displeasure. With a wave of his hand, Tur seemingly caused the cities to tremble in an entire quadrant of the capital.

Devit had been the first to realize that the harmonic effect could be scaled up with seismic consequences. He found the Telescien module could transmit the signal quite deftly and to dramatic effect, much like the devastating Vansar Skywake built up kinetic energy to a ground-shattering crest.

Tur apologized. "The problems facing my world represent a Threat to Life. The scenarios you describe are inconceivable. The fact that the Tomet could entertain such notions is deeply disturbing." Tur studied each speaker in turn. "Any interference of that sort could not be tolerated. Whatever steps necessary to correct the situation would be undertaken without hesitation." He then reiterated, "Whatever steps."

Tur's speech achieved the desired outcome.

Vit Na read the So Wari runes to herself from Tur's report.

"The mission went well." She shook her head. *How dry can you get?*

So Wari rarely embellished a story. The document was unacceptably brief.

"We encountered the species known as the Tomet seven weeks into our journey. Apparently, they either evolved or migrated to one of the Fitu-formed worlds in the Exodus Corridor. Upon review of the historical star charts of the area, we ascertain that the species in question lay within Efilu jurisdiction. The necessary steps were taken to accomplish our mission." There. Matter of fact passive voice. That sounded acceptably So Wari, Vit Na thought. "Several options were discussed with the staff. After reasonable research and due diligence on the part of my key staff members the Deity option was exercised."

No flavor of the hunt that Vit Na longed to weave into her report for him.

I'm aware that presentation of oneself as a deity may have ramifications for the duration of these peoples' history, the Quatal precedent notwithstanding. Weighed against the fate of the Realm, the priority was obvious.

MISSION PREPARATION:

Research reports were submitted by: Obb, paleobotanist. Doh, paleontologist. Ikara, xenobiologist. Jeen, communications department head. Car Hom, my chief of staff. Data was assembled and presented to me.

DECISION-MAKING:

1. Energy expenditures. The drain of sending a Telescien through such highly charged intense atmosphere was considerable. Sending more than one would be a waste.

2. Time constraints. The urgency of this mission demanded that the parley be as brief as possible.

3. Diplomatic protocol. As High Commander I'm obliged to accomplish my mission by any necessary means. The discussion with Car Hom is a matter of record. The following sequence of events represents an exercise in brinksmanship. If I have miscalculated my estimate of this race's defensive abilities, I might have plunged the Realm into another war. To minimize the variables, I decided that I would be the sole operative involved.

MISSION DETAILS:

The Pentad replaced the offensive first speaker. It was not heard from for the duration of my visit. No objections were made to the one hundred sites neatly excavated by the *ReQam*.

Efilu ruins had indeed sunk below the Ayqot radius in the worldscapes of the Tomet empire, but eons of ionizing radiation had played havoc on the remnants of any recognizable DNA. The fossilized algae they found were useless.

The *ReQam* telescien probes restored the disturbed surface and overhanging skyscape. The ruins were left as they had been found, as if the Efilu had never even been there.

The Tomet, however, may not forget this visitation. Ever. Their history may be profoundly changed from this moment onward. The beginnings of a burgeoning interstellar civilization may have effectively been extinguished.

The *ReQam* resumed its previous course toward Fitu.

Vit Na finished the report but kept her final thought to herself. *Oblivious to its effect on this alien history.*

Tur hated writing reports. He put down just the bare facts with no juice! She thought he felt a little guilty about dumping the rewrite project on her. As always, a charming Melkyz was happy to help. From Vit Na's standpoint, it was a marvelous opportunity to "create" history. *After all, that's what archeologists do.*

Chapter Nine
— MODUS OPERANDI —

I t was a long way to the outer arm of the Spiral. The trail of worlds abandoned in the Exodus Corridor seemed endless. So many worlds. So many surveys. They all swirled together in her mind's eye.

When did I last eat? Food was but a dream.

A shadow crossed Vit Na's face silently as she slept. It reached the end of her bedding nook before returning to the center of the chamber. She did not stir.

The silhouette of a hand stretched over her shoulder, a dark blot across her throat in the dimmed room. Her eyes opened slowly at the gentle touch of that hand.

"What!" The thought was poorly formed, disorganized in projection. Focusing in the subtly waxing light, she made out a familiar pair of eyes.

"Vit Na?" Gober Dil asked. "I am sorry to disturb you, but you've been asleep for a standard day."

"A whole day!"

"Yes. I was worried and asked Brajay to look you over. The medical report went straight to Car Hom. You showed symptoms that might have represented degradation effects of the substitute nutrition."

"Substitute…?" Vit Na couldn't follow quickly enough to keep up with Gober Dil.

"The substitute for algae-enriched stock?" he prompted. "You know, the substitute they developed to ensure we had a Poison-free food source on this voyage?"

"Oh. Yes. Now I remember." Vit Na scratched at her mane. "I think."

"Tur heard about your collapse and waited for Brajay and Car Hom to make a decision."

"What do you mean, decision?" Vit Na's head was clearing.

"Everyone was afraid that there was a gross foul-up," Dil reported. "Rumor was beginning to spread that some of the food might have been contaminated with the Poison. Loz speculated that we may all be at risk if one mer gets it. No one would voice the logical conclusion."

Vit Na nodded. "That I would have to be eliminated as a source of contagion."

Gober Dil shook his head gravely. "No. That the mission would have to be terminated, the ship itself destroyed with all hands."

"Why would we not simply have to return for mission failure?" Her thoughts became more coherent. "After all, the Poison is already disseminated throughout the Realm, as it is. We are no more dangerous than anyone else."

"That scenario was not as exciting as heroic self-destruction." Gober Dil hummed. "And Loz is getting bored."

Vit Na returned his humor with a smirk of her own. "What other theories were there about my…condition?"

"No one else advanced any. We just kept working." Then, more seriously: "Everyone worried about you."

Vit Na felt a little embarrassed. "I'm sure the commander may have been, but it was the Head of Medicine's responsibility to deal with me. What did Brajay think?"

"His feeling was that you were exhausted and ketotic," Gober Dil said.

"And Car Hom?" she prompted.

"I think he felt guilty about pushing you so hard and ordered that you not be disturbed after you ate," the assistant paleobiologist said.

"After I ate? I don't remember eating. For that matter, I don't even remember retiring to my quarters."

"I brought you here. You were stuporous. Car Hom reassigned me to your service for the duration of the mission."

She remembered Dil now from the International Plaza checkpoint. With a demure gesture of the hand, Vit Na covered her ear. She had been working for nine days since the departure from the Tomet system with no sleep and precious little food. She vaguely remembered a meal ordered by a concerned Brajay.

The chamber brightened gradually. As the light reached twilight intensity, she realized her new assistant, Gober Dil, was not tall enough to reach her sleeping pallet on the upper tier of the chamber. She peered over the edge to see that the Wilkyz had grabbed hold of the ledge and pulled himself up to awaken her.

She looked askance at him. "You haven't been tweaking my ears while I slept, have you?"

"By the Alom, no, Ati Vit Na!" he implored.

Truth, but desire, too, barely kept in check, Vit Na discerned. But she reproached herself. *Ati. I haven't been the object of that Melkyz term for "honored mistress" in years, damn it. I didn't mean to invoke title.*

"You mustn't take everything I say literally, Dil."

Gober Dil shifted his eyes down toward the lower level. Vit Na understood, spotting the Tan Barr mer waiting patiently in the leisure area of the apartment below. She was seated discreetly with her back to the recovering occupant. Gober Dil dropped softly to the floor after the offer to carry his exhausted new superior down was declined. When Vit Na reached the lower level, she paused to groom herself for a moment before addressing Gober Dil.

"Progress report," she ordered, partially for show of discipline.

"We are now in the Fitu star system, tenth shell. Telescien modules are probing the ninth planet for storage receptacles."

"Any success so far?"

"None. The plan is to complete the reconnaissance per your descriptions of the architecture of that era, in conjunction with the geographic data supplied by Kellis." He indicated the waiting Head of Geotechnics with a subtle gesture of his head.

"You don't seem very confident, Dil. What else?" she pressed.

"The geotechnics of the early retexturing technology were less stable than anticipated. Calculation of the Ayqot Radius applied to a uniform sphere, less attention to accommodation of contoured oceans and mountains then. Most of the synthetic continents became unstable. They've been swept away. Loss of cohesion, no chance of recovery." Dil glanced at the officer standing next to him. "According to Kellis, this represents a basic design flaw, not an idiosyncrasy. By extrapolation, the same results can be expected on the other two colonial gas worlds. The theory accounts for the deterioration of the settlement in the Tomet star system, as well."

"The data will be of great use in planning and maintaining structural integrity of retextured gas worlds in the Realm proper," Kellis said, impatiently joining the private conversation. "Still, it casts the shadow of doubt over the likelihood of finding any of the city ruins intact. Examining the other giants will be an optimistic exercise in futility. I'd recommend against it if the goal were any less imperative."

Following the flow of circumstances, Vit Na summarized aloud, "So, Doh gets his dream fulfilled after all."

Kellis and Gober Dil exchanged weary looks before affirming what had just become obvious.

"I suppose we had best start on plans to investigate the Fituine worlds, then," Vit Na declared.

"It's why I'm here," Kellis answered. "I'll start mapping sites of the old cities, starting with regional capitals, if you'll lend me some support staff."

Vit Na responded without a moment's hesitation. "Of course. Just let me conduct a short briefing session on what your people will need. I suggest you appoint a liaison officer, if you haven't already."

The Head of Geotechnics seemed more enthused. "We'll both be there at the appointed time."

After a casual acknowledgment of the courtesy, Kellis turned and left Vit Na's apartments.

The general briefing session was off to a slow start. All department heads were present. The setting and format were formal.

So Wari-formal, to be precise, Vit Na thought. *This is a bad sign.*

The urgent meeting was called too precipitously after Kellis and Vit Na had submitted their report that morning.

It wasn't that she couldn't handle Tur's strict style, it was just that the whole thing smacked of another edict. Another major change of operating procedures for the mission.

I'm sure he's going to pull another tooth from us before sending us out hunting again. The old expression reminded her how much Tur hated predacious metaphors. She reminded herself not to think it publicly. Her staff was becoming disheartened. There had been so many disappointments already.

Tur swept into the room with Car Hom right beside him, instead of the respectful two head lengths behind.

I knew it! Another tirade brewing. Vit Na took a deep breath and settled in with the others. *Let's just wait for the tail to swing.*

"I'm sure that, by now, many of you know that so far, Operation Backtrack has been a failure. The gas worlds are a lost cause. The surviving stone-worlds are of course our last hope." Tur was remarkably calm and open. Out of character, somehow.

Car Hom looked as if his teeth were locked.

What's gone on between them? Vit Na asked herself.

"As you may remember from your studies, the fourth planet was never developed into a fruitful colony. The thin atmosphere, lack of open water, and scant energy resources made it a sinkhole for any meaningful investment. Its limited use as a recreation center may have left some subterranean storage facilities intact." Tur was inscrutable now, his thoughts expressed matter-of-factly, no telltale undertone that Vit Na could detect.

Where's he going with this?

"The second planet, of course, was wrecked by a poorly thought-out fituforming venture."

Why is he dragging us through all of this? Vit Na thought. *Everyone knows that.*

"Neither the first planet nor the rubble of the fifth planet are worth mentioning," Tur announced. "Naturally, the best opportunity for recovering viable algae DNA is on the third planet. The planet of origin: Fitu herself. Now, I know that there is a certain amount of romance, even whimsical fantasy about the fate of Fitu in general, and the Keepers in particular. The purpose of this briefing is to establish an operating procedure for the investigation of this world.

"Number one: Car Hom and I will personally supervise this mission.

"Number two: There will be no digression into nature-loving exploration. We are here to do a job. Nothing else.

"Number three: As we've seen in the Exodus Corridor, alien inhabitants may have visited or taken up residence on this husk of a world. There is a need for caution in any and all questionable encounters. Car Hom will outline the rules of engagement.

"Number four: There are bound to be some extraordinary findings. That fact is inescapable. Vit Na, Ikara, Obb, Doh, Jeen, and Egin will form a committee to customize a Telescien modulation for recording incidental findings. I want results by day's end. I know most of you are tired, and I'm sorry. We don't have much time and

"Finally, we are now over one month into the substitute food source. As Oot Su will explain, there are certain toxic manifestations that will become increasingly apparent." Tur looked briefly at Vit Na as he spoke. "It will be the responsibility of each of the surface scouts to monitor signs of toxicity in his or her comrades.

"Reports are to go jointly to Brajay, Oot Su, and Car Hom. Car Hom will be responsible for action to be taken in the event of impaired competency."

That was it! The reason for the tension between those two. She thought about the conversation with Gober Dil. *What would Tur do if effects of the Poison were to manifest? Tur has charged Car Hom with the disposal of liable staff members! And he doesn't like it one bit. Poor meg,* Vit Na thought. *Car Hom the executioner!*

"Please turn your attention to Loz's image of the Fitu binary system."

An image appeared before them displaying modern-day Fitu and the gray-white worldlet revolving around it.

"The geography looks nearly alien, but at the same time...familiar," Tyot Da projected broadly. The entire staff invoked genetic memories gleaned from their own families' respective Tarns of Animems. This was Fitu, but continental drift had changed its surface since the Exodus.

"Different from historical maps, but almost as we modeled it!" Kellis whispered to Vit Na proudly.

Slowly, as all eyes fixed on the shining blue world before them, the officious masks of detachment melted away.

Weyef raised a question that was several moments late in the asking. "Wait now. Did I hear you correctly, Tur? Are we *physically* going down there?"

Car Hom spoke without waiting for Tur to respond. "We are going down in person because we need to. Telescien are not discriminating enough to separate the current life-form remains from the fossil remains that we need. We have already tried on the outer worlds. Preliminary scans show very subtle changes in microorganisms since the Exodus. This project is going to require delicate, hands-on work."

"Current life-forms?" Doh was almost ecstatic.

"That's right. Preliminary studies show the planet is teeming with life."

Doh asked boldly, "Botanical or animal?"

Car Hom ignored the interruption. "There are masses of organic activity stretching over large areas on the surface. They are intertwined in some areas, but most display indisputable signatures of advanced animal life. The oxygen content is consistent with a huge burden of plant life as well."

"What exactly do you mean by 'advanced animal life?'" Doh prodded further.

Tur intercepted Doh's foray into zoology. "It doesn't matter what form of animal life is there, as we will *all* be avoiding them." He paused, adding, "Unless they get in our way."

Doh began another interrogative, only to be nipped by Tur's restriction. "If we *do* accidentally encounter any indigenous animal life, they will be dealt with in the most expedient manner possible."

He leaned over almost to a crouch to verbally address Doh directly in the ancient common tongue. "You carry out your research on your own time, not mine!" He nodded to Car Hom to resume the briefing.

"The bulk of activity seems to take place during daylight. This leads us to believe that the dominant species is diurnal in nature. We'll send telesciens down at night so as to cause minimal disturbance. They'll appear as silvery spheres, easily explainable as freak reflections of the moon." Car Hom inadvertently looked at Tur for approval of the order.

Vit Na read him to the core. *It's easier to be forgiven than permitted for an undesired order.*

Tur simply looked away.

Car Hom continued, unperturbed. "We will be within optimum range for telemetry survey before day's end. The probe module will be a level one, launched on the dark side of Fitu. The search pattern will be modified by Kellis and Ikara to optimize the yield. We'll know more when the probe data becomes available."

He again turned to Tur, more deliberately this time. A nod from the High Commander signaled the end of the session.

Car Hom announced, "Dismissed."

Vit Na had returned to her rooms to prepare for the surface mission. Her eyes were wide, her down erect, her tail writhed restlessly. The sound of the portal barrier signaling the arrival of a visitor gave her a start. She opened the door, not thinking, only to see Tur enter furtively.

"The Telesciens are back," he said. "Nothing unexpected on the smaller stone-worlds. Fitu, however, is going to be complicated."

Has the hustle and bustle of anticipated landing on Fitu infected even the High Commander? Vit Na looked up at him quizzically.

"Not a threat. Just a lot of questions that beg answers." Tur's brow furrowed deeply. "When it was just Doh, I could ignore it, but now Loz is becoming intrigued by a bunch of derelict mechanical satellites orbiting Fitu."

Vit Na inhaled to voice a response, but Tur cut her off.

"Car Hom is paranoid about disturbing the masses of vermin that have infested the surface. Jeen is fascinated by the electronic echoes reverberating off those metal devices floating in the sky. Now, I hear that you want to investigate these orbiting artifacts for dating purposes?"

By now, Vit Na had ascended to the apartment's upper tier to reach eye level with Tur. She was hopping from the top of one wall shelf to the next in cadence with Tur's pacing.

"I cannot allow this team to get sidetracked, but I also can't be everywhere at once. The expedition may have to be broken up into anywhere from five to seven teams." He paused for a moment. "This world presents too many distractions. Too many variables. I can't see how I can keep everyone in focus and on task."

He had unconsciously resumed pacing. "This mission has already gone on too long! The entire crew could potentially succumb to degenerative nucleotide toxicity—here, countless photodymes from home!"

"And that would be bad," Vit Na canted.

He turned to expound on her naïve reaction to his dilemma, only to find that she was no longer attending him. He whipped his head back and forth, scanning the dim chamber, until he found her sitting on the ledge of her sleeping nook, her feet dangling carelessly.

"Are you listening to me?"

Vit Na said, "That's *all* I've been doing." She flashed a humorous, yet chastising, grin. "Obviously, if you wanted to talk to yourself, you could have done so in your own quarters. I assume you want some friendly and *unofficial* advice?"

Tur answered with a single, curt nod.

"You have a very disciplined and professional staff," she observed, "one that knows the importance of this mission as well as you do. Give them the freedom to use their own good judgement and stop insulting their intelligence."

This was the second time on this mission that Tur had been told to ease up on his subordinates.

He added out loud, "You said stop insulting 'their' intelligence. Why didn't you say 'our' intelligence?" he scoffed.

"You're not smart enough to insult my intelligence," she said coyly.

Cheered by her opinion, Tur brushed her down from the ledge and Vit Na landed softly on her feet.

Poised to leave her quarters, Tur hesitated at the portal. "I don't like this vacillation on my part. It's not...So Wari." He turned to her and surveyed her quarters, then shook his head. "I plan to lead the scouting party myself. You're in that party, too."

Tur's hackle plates quivered. He stroked languid ears past the nape of his neck, momentarily clasping tense hands there to conceal his flight response. The great So Wari brow tilted toward the ceiling, Tur sat on his haunches under what appeared to be an unbearable weight. "May I stay here with you tonight?"

Vit Na took his hand and led him to the widest area of her quarters, shoved the sofa aside, and gently forced first his body, then head supine. Without a thought or word, she lifted his great arm, took in its scent, and snuggled under it against his chest. As he relaxed, she commanded the dim light to darkness.

Tur took the very tip of her ear gently between his teeth and thrilled at the soft hum as her lips brushed his arm. She knew he didn't need the light to feel her smile.

Hours later, the surface team, fifty strong, assembled before the crystal-gel launch spout. Tyot Da gave last-moment instructions.

Less than half the size of So Wari, the So Rikhi represented the only other extant *So* species in the Realm. With no hint of disappointment in his manner, the old meg addressed his audience formally.

"My years limit my usefulness on this trip. I have, however, designed a functional and comfortable crystal gel-core headquarters." The old So Rikhi noted Car Hom's skepticism. Tyot Da added, "The size is deceiving. As you may have noted, Telescien data has ascertained that the land has ample mineral content to supplement the substance of the adventitial support structures."

Tyot Da looked around for questioning faces. He saw none. "May your search be fruitful." Tyot Da flapped small dorsal plates in deference and yielded to Tur.

"Everything that needs to be said has been." Tur gestured for the encapsulation process to begin.

The gel oozed up from the floor to envelop them. All veterans of the process, the team members effortlessly resisted the urge to hold their respective breaths. A giant teardrop squeezed into a silvery thread as it accelerated to pre-photon speed through the tiny port in the vessel's hull.

The strand arced across the night sky. It stretched for three koridymes before disconnecting from the *ReQam*. Once clear of the hull, the thread floated softly, slowly, unwaveringly down through the thin atmosphere.

The Efilu visitors rained down as a single glistening drop, unnoticed, on the cold Egyptian desert. The seemingly endless gel-stream pooled on the northeast arc of the second largest land mass, making a shiny dome on the flat desert floor.

Weyef inhaled ancient air, searching for scents long forgotten by even her ancestors. "I'll schedule reconnaissance rounds."

Tur answered with a single raised finger. "First order of business: set up headquarters as quickly as possible."

"Damn So Wari field manual," Weyef frowned as Tur stalked off, muttering to herself. "Rigid as ice."

Weyef directed a materials detail. They toiled through the night, absorbing the desert sands, fortifying an outer perimeter, and expanding the walls of newly formed compartments.

Still other task team members activated producer subfunctions to raise necessary crystalline and plasticine devices from the main gel core. These generated needed facilities for coordination of the expedition, most importantly the data systems and storage plants for managing reports and specimens, respectively. Tur oversaw these measures personally.

Vit Na helped where she could, but she was ill-equipped for the routine setup and maintenance of the installation. Instead, she interfaced with the com-center and journaled the measures taken by others their first night on a long-abandoned world.

Someone has to do it, she thought. *If Tur does it, he'll make us all miserable.* So, she interscribed:

"Fitu's rising sun licked the sandy mound before grasping it with fiery midday teeth."

Tur wouldn't appreciate classical Melkyz poetry, but he also won't complain about a chore he gets out of, either. It's accurate, anyway.

"Light from this star has not touched Efilu flesh in millions of years. Few of Tur's meren are enthused by our primordial visitor. After an exhausting night's work, most sleep through the brilliant welcome home.

"The gel-complex, now nearly complete, is more comfortable than Tyot Da promised. But Tur does not notice, for he does not sleep. He is driven by demons born from native skies and soil.

"Traffic through the common area ebbs by attrition." Vit Na watched Tur. "He stands atop the storage tower, the energy flow causing gentle vibrations throughout the whole structure. This will be home to our band of weary travelers for the immediate future. Tur is first to divine the essence of our little community. So Wari ritual runs deep. Tur inspects the facility in traditional fashion."

Vit Na knows him so well she writes with abandon.

"Is he thinking already of how good it will be to get off this rock? All chiefs have reported optimal capacity before retiring for the day."

It appears he's decided that he's actually satisfied with his temporary headquarters and its personnel. That expression on his face, it's as if to say, they aren't all So Wari, but perhaps they'll do after all. Vit Na mused. *Can't put that insight into the report.*

"Tur turns his attention to the open desert," she documented. "Heat waves begin to distort the horizon. Peering into the distance, he snaps to a combat stance."

Vit Na followed his gaze and knew immediately what he saw there. She halted the recording.

The warrior in him sees only the apparition of a huge gel-wave crossing the desert directly toward us. Full-speed, with no warning. Vit Na cast her eyes downward. She knew So Wari paranoia. *'Ambush! Someone has beaten us here,' he must think. Uncertainty haunts him.* She pined. *Or is he wrestling with ghosts we have yet to see?*

The heat wave vanished without a trace. Vit Na's features saddened. *He nearly completed the alarm activation gesture.*

She watched Tur recover composure angrily, embarrassed by his reaction. Vit Na *Blended*, then retreated to the lodgings, brooding.

Good that no one else witnessed him panicked by a simple mirage. Vit Na shuddered. *Like all his kind, deliverance of assigned duty is inviolable. There is only one way to relieve a So Wari commander of duty in the field.* The age-old Melkyz adage on So Wari fortitude came to her mind. *May the Alom help he who contests Tur's mantle unaware its cost in blood.* Vit Na closed her journal program and her eyes. *So many ghosts.*

Chapter Ten

— NICHES —

T he conference room would soon be full, and Tur had not rested all day. He clenched blunt teeth at the surge of variables stirred into this mission, misgivings he could not bring himself to share with anyone, not even Vit Na.

An urgency seemed to supersede even the obvious need to replenish the algae supply. He pondered the basis of his distress all day, but by evening he'd found no logical fault. Given the circumstances, he'd react in identical manner.

Could I be the first to fall prey to the neuro-synaptolysis? The very thought of failing at leadership was repugnant to him. *There's no way of checking my health without revealing a potential weakness.*

Car Hom, as expected, was the first to arrive. He took his place, silently, at Tur's right. The others filed in slowly, refreshed after their day-long repose. The oddly shaped auditorium accommodated each in individualized comfort.

As the staff entered, Tur took note of how many department heads were included in the team. He counted nine. Doh numbered among them. His presence was another source of apprehension, but so far, his discipline was exemplary.

Vit Na seems to be doing all right. The thought comforted Tur, but still he worried about her. *This is a hostile world. What if enemies of the Realm have already made their way to Fitu? Quatal would be bad enough, but Efilu traitors could be disastrous.*

Tur wanted Vit Na protected, but he knew he could not afford to be obvious in his assignment of extra security meren to her. Since there were only four or five So Wari other than himself on the surface, discretion had prevented obvious recruitment of Tiest's elite. The next-best thing to assigning one of his meren, Tur reasoned; deploy a Wilkyz.

Not as formidable as an Alkyz or even a Tralkyz, but a super hunter nonetheless. Tur was encouraged. *Dil's more than a match for any animal that walks this planet.*

Gober Dil wasn't in the security detail, but he was at Vit Na's disposal night and day. *Discreet. Dil's young, but he's proving to be an able specialist. And he has taken a liking to his new superior.*

Tur had checked his file. Gober Dil was skilled in *Time-splitting,* that peculiar Wilkyz talent for briefly extrapolating themselves along alternate timelines at will. Depending on one's level of concentration, a Wilkyz could materialize as five to ten individuals of equal strength and intelligence for a few moments. When applied to critical time-sensitive strategy, it made for brilliant creative genius, but now Tur was thankful for the original purpose for the technique: defense.

He thought of the *ReQam* in orbit above them. There was no reason for unnecessary contact, but the ship remained in communications range of the ground team in case of the unforeseen.

Tur had left Ga Win in command. *An able enough officer, I suppose. He, too, is gifted with typical Wilkyz discipline and patience. Thank the Alom for that Wilkyz time-weapon—not So Wari, but makes for excellent emergency response time.* Tur thought about Vit Na's diversity argument for a moment. *Car Hom made a good selection in choosing that one as a senior command officer.*

But his anxiety did not completely resolve. *Loz is a wild dart. Something about him and that preoccupation with those satellites...* The notion of Loz out of sight and unsupervised made Tur uncomfortable.

Loz technically outranked all but Ga Win on the ship now. Nothing could change that, as long as he was Head of Astrophysics. There was no justification for bringing him down to the surface. *His forte is clearly keeping that ship running and everything outside from running into it. I'll speak to Moc privately about keeping eyes on Loz for me.* Recalling Rault's fate, Tur thought, *Maybe she won't muck that assignment up.*

Along with Moc as senior navigator, the ship's remaining support staff included Stihl, the assistant commander; both were competent So Wari tacticians. *Between the three officers, Loz would be kept out of trouble,* Tur expected.

Perhaps Car Hom and Vit Na were right—I do worry too much, Tur thought. *Switching Doh for Loz here on the surface would be sure to keep them both off my mind, though.*

He promptly started his rounds of the facility upon assemblage of the group. Tur and Car Hom would see firsthand what was available for the operation. The assortment of scanners and probes would be the first up for inspection, of course.

"Assembling Telescien probes is possible, commander, but extremely impractical with the resources available," Devit explained. "Mini-Waves are charged and ready for travel."

"Overkill, isn't it?" Tur remarked.

"True, they are more powerful than Telesciens, but not quite as versatile." Devit gestured to the desert outside the compound. "The real advantage we can expect is energy efficiency. Volumes of gel-sol can be augmented with ionized water, which is as abundant on this world as back home." Devit hesitated. "You know what I mean, commander. The present Realm. We can break up a single unit into a phalanx of subunits large enough to accommodate ten to twenty meren."

"I don't like it." Tur shook his head. "The last thing we need is frail derivatives."

"The Mini-Wave can project force fields, deploy offensive weapons, and morph into a limited variety of shapes, including the fluid conglomerate from which the name was derived, all using mostly local resources. Remember, we are not arming against Efilu- or even Tomet-level threats. These are no more than socialized animals." Devit flashed a reproachful look, followed by a grin as he gestured toward the perimeter. "We don't want 'overkill,' do we?"

"Pest control devices only, then," Tur returned Devit's satirical smile and decreed. "No real weapons synthesized for the time being."

Car Hom broke his silence. "Agreed. The outer perimeter is all but impenetrable."

"Nutrition, waste management, and data storage and integration, all in order." The speaker was an ungainly meg under Doh's division whose name Tur didn't recall. "The laboratories are at full capacity."

Tur inspected all with extreme care and asked many questions of Doh and his staff. *All Doh's paleobiology nonsense should keep him busy for the duration.*

Ikara reported, "I've cross-networked all of our genetic databases."

Tur acknowledged her report with a curt nod. *At least, Ikara won't resent being Doh's subordinate for this part of the mission. Total professional, that one.*

Tur watched his people work. The few department heads on the surface were not always project managers. Surrogate chiefs who displayed the most capability naturally fell into leadership positions without resentment from others. There were no rigid hierarchies defining class. The rigors of echelons had their place in society, but here merit transcended rank. Each knew this, in his or her own way.

Do or die. Tur realized, even in absence of So Wari formality, that remarkable efficiency pleased him. He was learning the power of flexibility where strength was not enough.

A warm orange sun set in the west as subspecialist Kira Kesh presided over the first scan. The Mit Kiam mer was small for her kind, barely half a head length taller than Devit. Her analysis accompanied the findings.

"This is a high-density photomagnetic sweep of the grounds directly below us." She pointed to projected images. "As you can see, here and here, there are scattered remains of an Irfonde—or, as we now say, *Ironde*—village." Plumes swept back and forth along her crest as her eyes followed the strata composition displayed.

"Obviously, it was in shambles at the time of its burial." Kira Kesh projected thoughts with typical Mit Kiam detachment. "Undigested bodies everywhere suggest that there was no one left to perform final rites. The scattered plumes, more numerous than can be accounted for by the number of bodies found, further indicate a horrible battle."

"Which they lost," Devit added, with less detachment for his fallen ancestors then he affected.

"So it would seem," Kira Kesh said. "Removal of survivors as slaves would support the fossil record here."

"Is it worth excavating?" Devit asked, his motives to learn the doom of long-dead kin obvious.

Kira Kesh paused, but after searching her memory for data to support the endeavor, she found none. "I don't think so. The food storage buildings have been thoroughly demolished, probably raided beforehand."

Tur looked askance for emotion, but Devit said no more. The only excuse to excavate would have been to search for yellow algae sources.

Kira Kesh swiftly moved along. "The remaining five koridyme sub-iridium radius is basically as barren as the desert above it, for our purposes. Resolution at the microscopic level breaks down at about two koridymes."

Well, that's a vexing limitation to her equipment, Tur griped privately. His discordant hum conveyed more than a public thought would have.

"Low-resolution scans of the entire planetary surface did turn up one other peculiarity; there are large circular burns across all of the land masses, as if from orbital bombardment," Kira Kesh said as she interfaced with the Telescien database. "The odd thing is that they are only about ten million years old."

"Any relevance, with regard to our objectives?" the High Commander asked.

"No, sir," she said.

"Well then," Tur folded arms across his great chest as he spoke, "we obviously can't scan the entire planet for these microbes."

"Nothing's been easy on this mission." Car Hom scowled. "What else is new?"

That seems a bit brusque, Tur noted, *for an Alkyz.*

Sensing the focus of attention shifting to her, she spoke before cue. "We have identified the seven major megacities most likely to contain the goods we're looking for."

She projected a two-dimensional representation of the world above their heads. She nodded to Gober Dil, who smoothly continued the presentation without missing a beat.

"There is a potential complication." Gober Dil expanded the map's orientation as it changed from vertical to horizontal and gave living contours to the face of a modern world. "Several of these sites are now occupied by large populations of animals. Furthermore, there's evidence of towering mounds of metal-fortified stone villages that are growing by the day."

Tur interrupted, "So, what's your point?"

"I would think that finding a way to work around them with minimal disturbance would be the most desirable option, sir."

Vit Na wound her neck in supplication. "Am I not following your own prescribed protocol? If not, we could go for the minimally populated land site and the marine area."

"Wrong!" Car Hom interrupted. "We will not waste time limiting ourselves to a mere two sites this late in the game." He paused to let Tur give the actual order.

"We split up. Five sub-parties of ten meren each." Tur nodded at Car Hom to see to the details. "Assignments are forthcoming."

Fatigue is beginning to tell on him, Vit Na thought, watching the set of Tur's ears. *I know I can't be the only one to notice.*

As if he heard her thoughts, Tur stiffened his ears and rose from his haunches to leave, then hesitated. Realizing he was about to unearth a nest of fur-mites, Tur half turned to Ikara for elaboration. This was unquestionably Doh's department, however. He turned wearily to Doh and asked his question. "Just what do these *new* animals look like? I mean the main ones. 'They who construct?'"

"Oh, I can show you." Doh could not hide his delight at the opportunity. "I mounted a magnetic scanner on a fragment of a Mini-Wave and sent it off that way." He pointed south and tittered. "I haven't seen the recording myself yet."

The entire group gathered round, eager to see the successors of their forsaken home. Tur found himself no less intrigued than the others.

"We modified and programmed the probe to stop and record encounters with animal life of fifty pounds or more."

Tur's weariness melted away as he stepped closer to the holosonographic recording.

"I'm sorry there will be no substance to the images. I didn't see a reason for added detail under the circumstances."

Tur found himself embarrassed by his frustration at not being able to touch these marvelous sights. *Followed orders to the rune, damn him!*

The small audience was astonished not only by the size of these beasts, but even more by their shapes.

"Doh, they look like animals from a hundred and fifty million years ago," Car Hom observed. "How do you explain this?"

Tur watched Doh's chest puff proudly. *I'm sure he wishes Obb was here to see his triumph.* Doh looked to Gober Dil, once subordinate to Obb, perhaps as his surrogate here on the planet: the next best victim.

"Dil, explain, please," Doh demanded.

Gober Dil could only shrug, dumbfounded.

Doh paused long enough for any speculation to surface. None did.

"This is a classic example of analogy," Doh lectured. "The way a mosquito's wings serve the same function as a bird's or even more advanced pterodactyl's wings do. They are derived from completely different organs, but they serve the same function. When we left the mammals and other animals behind during the Exodus, there were innumerable vacant niches to be filled. The need for food presents problems that can only be solved in a finite number of ways."

The recording focused on images of gangly, spotted ruminants stretching tall necks to munch tree top acacia leaves. A single horned pachyderm raised its head to scan the savanna in the near distance. Gasps of awe escaped Efilu onlookers.

"That looks just like a small bolok, but without the frill and forehead horns," Bo Tep observed.

Burly horned ruminants and striped, long-necked mammals with stiff, short manes grazed in the background.

"Though small, those striped animals look a little like stream-lined versions of my own remote ancestors—minus the back plates and tail spikes," Tur added. "Why don't they have tails?"

Doh answered quickly. "They do! They're small, vestigial even, but they are there." He magnified several images and pointed the appendages out to the High Commander. The scene shifted to a pack of mid-sized spotted predators being chased off from a kill by a pride of larger, tan-colored predators.

"The more things change, the more they stay the same," Gren, the Roog botanist, commented from his water-filled corpuscle.

Doh allowed the recording to go on to a pack of small, snub-nosed carnivores bringing down a large ruminant. "That one is reminiscent of a Notex." Tur eyed a gracile predator running down a small forest herbivore. "Look at that speed!" Obb leered at his teammates gleefully before terminating the show.

"Well, you get the gist of it." He knew they all wanted to see more but wouldn't dare ask.

It's like Doh has a shiny new toy, Vit Na mused. *First in the village! He shows it off, then puts it away just as curiosity piques.*

"What about the builders?" Tur asked a second time, a little less patiently.

"Oh, them. I'm sure they're on here somewhere." Doh advanced the recording to a blur, stopping it on the image of bipedal mammals living communally in a primitive village. The villagers were malnourished, but they clearly resembled Efilu meren in their proportions and basic facial features.

"They look like mutated versions of *us*!" a voice in the darkness said. Tur didn't even bother to identify Kellis as the author of that most revolting analogy.

A few emaciated stock animals stood in a wooden corral. Several sun-dried mud and grass huts sheltered two legged mammals with sparse hair limited to the crown of the head. The inhabitants carried crude sticks and dressed in garments woven from cloth scraps.

"They do show basic signs of culture," Vit Na said in passing.

"Please!" Tur cut his eyes in disgust at the sight, rose, and exited without another thought.

Chapter Eleven

— FLIGHT SCHOOL —

Tur awakened to the alert vibration at his portal. He rose slowly to his feet, wincing at the sunlight streaming through the window, then gestured the *open* command for the barrier. The door receded to reveal Weyef.

"You've rested for half a day," she commented. She sat without asking and gazed into Tur's eyes, tracking them as he gathered his thoughts. Presently, he recognized the cause of her scrutiny.

"You really must learn to be more direct, Weyef," he drawled. "It saves time."

If any species had less of a sense of humor than the So Wari, it was the Vansar.

"We need more information about these sites," Weyef ignored his sarcasm. "I've been thinking. Those animals we saw last night certainly didn't build the towering structures we saw, but *someone* did. I think what we saw can be attributed to sampling error."

Tur rubbed his eyes. "What do you suggest?"

She began before he finished the question. "We need personal reconnaissance. Not probes. Not scans. Not Telesciens. Someone has to go out there. Car Hom said it, and you agreed: our technology is not sensitive enough to tell us what we need to know."

Tur found himself nodding thoughtfully. "Have you selected a party yet?"

"No, for this one I think a single mer will do."

"Anyone in this chamber?" Tur said humorlessly and reclined on the pallet again, lacing fingers behind his head.

"I am the ablest aviator in the group, and my size will certainly intimidate anything in the skies of this world," Weyef boasted.

"Not to mention you feel a need to flap your wings a bit," Tur said.

"We don't have personnel to spare on a mission like this. A single strange creature is somewhat less threatening than a squad of them and more likely to be forgotten or incorporated into vague legend, if these creatures have such concepts," Weyef continued, bringing Tur's Tomet strategy to bear in her petition. "Besides, there is no immediate need for security here. If there is a potential threat, which I doubt, it will be in those mound complexes. As Head of Security, I need to assess them firsthand. I can make efficient, immediate decisions that can't be delegated to any subordinate I have here on the surface."

A good argument, Tur thought, rolling her statement over in his mind for flaws. *She probably spent much of the night preparing it. No doubt she's already consulted with Ikara for the behavioral references to myths and legends.*

"Has Ikara heard this proposal yet?" Tur asked without moving a muscle.

Weyef looked as if she were about to boil over with anger. She was born to fly!

"Let's get her in and solicit a few alternative scenarios." *I'd enjoy watching you squirm while she does.* Tur kept that last thought to himself as he let Weyef stew for a moment. Her plumage fluttered nervously.

Useless theater, he admitted to himself. "You're right. We do need good reconnaissance data, and your flying proficiency is beyond question," Tur dismissed her with a wave. "Proceed."

Wings a-quiver, she left before he could change his mind.

Weyef summoned Ju Kol onto a terrace overlooking the desert for a briefing session. The Alkyz meg ranked second among her security officers in the ground unit.

"I'm going to examine the animal herd over the nearest megacity ruins." She indicated an easterly flight path to Ju Kol. The sun was still rising. "I'll be back by mid to late afternoon. The days here seem so long." She ruminated on the timetable for a moment. "Nothing special as far as security measures, except...on that recording last evening, didn't I see some large bird picking over carrion?"

"Yes, I believe so," Ju Kol answered, then laughed. "But they have no teeth!"

His joke drew a polite smirk from her. "I'm probably developing some of Tur's paranoid nature, but I don't want any wildlife wandering in uninvited. Especially not if they come in flocks. I want the shield barriers for this base on standby while I'm gone. I'll stay in communications with you by gel-com link. You and I will review the data I collect this evening. That's all," she said, dismissing him.

Weyef fastened the gel apparatus to her torso and arranged the transducers to maintain 360-degree recording during flight. She had eaten heartily that morning and felt eager to stretch her wings now. Discipline allowed her to function in cramped, close quarters for the weeks the *ReQam* had been in transit, but with that deep, familiar blue sky accented with fluffy white clouds, she could stand being grounded no more.

She took wing and circled the base once, then took off eastward with strong, steady strokes. Weyef waited until the base disappeared over the horizon before engaging in some aerial acrobatics.

How did I tolerate so long a grounding? Continuing on her prescribed flight path, Weyef reveled in wind rushing through the down along her quills as she accelerated. The erector pili muscles vibrated her plumage into a blur of propulsion. She felt the sound waves building up to maximal rarefaction in front of her. The urge to press through it became overwhelming. Skywake.

She waited until she was over a herd of humpbacked quadrupeds watering at an oasis before making her move with anticipated results. The creatures scattered, but there were others on the periphery of the herd. *Those peculiar bipeds again,* she noted. Apparently nearby, but unseen until the commotion started, the creatures were frantically trying to recapture the other animals.

Interesting, but not worth recording. Weyef flew onward.

She enjoyed the cool sea air over the inlet separating the main continent from the eastern peninsula, but the arid heat returned once she soared low over the land again. Supersonic velocity for most of the morning drained many of Weyef's stored calories, and fatigue began to set in. She dropped to gliding speed and took advantage of the thermal updrafts to hold her aloft.

A glint of sunlight off in the desert caught her eye. The structure was too high to be a body of water.

Ice? Perhaps, but an icecap would not sustain solid form in this heat for more than a few weeks at best.

Those peaks are so high and narrow, almost...

Her wings beat now with a newfound fervor at the revelation Vansar eyes spied. She swooped down to collect for the recorder what she had observed from the greater altitude. *A city! A full-fledged city!* More than that, it was occupied. This was more than a finding of interest; this was cause for alarm.

Who could have built this odd habitat? The style is not Si Tyen, by any means. And it's brand-new. Fifty years old, maximum.

She broadcast the alert to headquarters, then zoomed into the towering spires without waiting for acknowledgement.

The avenues were narrow, so she kept to the widest of them, stopping to record gatherings of large numbers of bipeds and quadrupeds here and there. She was mostly intrigued by the network of electrical cables and the abundance of ozone in the air. Weyef added the collection of air samples to her accumulated data. Mechanical conveyances of assorted sizes and functions traveled the broader trails. The air was also heavy with oxidized hydrocarbons. A large stone building caught her attention, not for its exterior, but for its content. She scanned it at length for review by Doh and Vit Na.

A klaxon sounded a loud warning throughout the city and the animals scurried for shelter. Weyef scanned the horizon to the east, north, and south. Nothing of particular interest there, just a small collection of broad, midsized vehicles with smooth cone-shaped fronts resting on a field. The flat projections on either side suggested aerodynamic design, but then why the three wheels? A few low buildings bound by a flimsy metal mesh lay near the crafts, as if serving as storage for them.

Weyef had collected enough data. She beat her wings to regain altitude, then retraced her original route at subsonic speed.

She had already begun to speculate on the origin of that city when she felt the transducers to the gel-com moving on her back. She focused into the lenses and detected two of the three wheeled metal vehicles approaching though the air behind her at super-sonic speed.

Hello, she thought to herself, amused. *What have we here?*

Weyef maintained her present speed to allow them to get close enough that she could shoot a clear image recording. She steadied, recorders on multimodality—and she suddenly faltered as the first projectile seared across her back.

It took several moments before she even realized what had occurred. One of the transducer cores was damaged. The whole assembly nearly fell off her torso. She regained her composure quickly and decided that she had better take the shortest route back to headquarters. Weyef signaled her situation ahead to the Efilu base.

More missiles exploded around her.

Deafening!

Weyef pumped up to supersonic velocity again but found her pursuers matching her speed. Fear welled in her chest as she realized she flew completely unarmed.

Maybe I can't outrun these killing machines, but perhaps I can outfly them.

She scanned the horizon. Nothing but desert and clear sunny skies. No clouds. *This arena is too much to their tactical advantage if I have to take them out by hand and talon.*

She craned her neck to see her approaching adversaries with keen, Vansar vision. *They have impressive speed, but they look somehow…clumsy in the air.*

In a desperate move, she broke, pinned on her wings, and made an immediate turnabout. The two machines zipped right past her and kept going. They sped for more than a finger of a koridyme before making the necessary banking effort to rejoin the chase. Putting her back into it, wing and quill alike danced the wind faster than even Vansar eyes could follow. She performed three more deft aerial maneuvers, evading her pursuers with ease. Weyef almost laughed out loud before the sight of another missile launched in her direction brought her levity to an end.

Those projectiles are not to be taken lightly. She focused on the remaining armament burden of each vehicle. *Still packed. This is no game.*

She knew her maneuverability could compensate for the hunter machines' excessive speed, but not for the missiles. *A Mini-Wave is probably on its way already with reinforcements, but I have to survive long enough to be rescued.*

Weyef needed an equalizer—and fast.

She examined her armpit. Axillary plumes had been singed evading the last missile. *Their aim is improving!*

Weyef spied a mountain range off in the distance. It took her off her home course, but it embodied her best chance to evade certain death. She veered toward it.

She had been analyzing their flight technique for several hundred of her own rapid heartbeats by now, and she'd come to certain conclusions.

They fly faster than their guidance systems can compensate. Weyef realized the projectiles launched were of two types. The small ones were more numerous and came in flurries. Following simple parabolic trajectories, they resulted in nicks and lost plumage. The others were deployed more sparingly, but with devastating results.

The concussion alone bruised bone and sinew, even without making direct contact. The noise was beginning to affect her equilibrium, until she dampened her tympanic network and the hideous racket became tolerable. Weyef reached the mountain maze of cliffs spied from afar. She entered the chasm, her back showered by debris from a missile that impacted the rock face behind her.

That's a good sign! They don't want me to go in there.

She flew another quarter finger or so deeper into the chasm at subsonic speed, all the while looking upward. As expected, the hunters prowled the skies above with no change in velocity. Another tactical peculiarity. The flyers maintained a near-constant distance and orientation with respect to one another. *Perhaps they are automated and have limited programming,* she speculated. *Or they are mentor and pupil on a hunting exercise.*

Both theories had merit, but somehow the thought of an independent artificial intelligence having offspring so nearly identical in shape, size, and coloration was unlikely. "Mechanical construct" was the best hypothesis at this point. *Like our Deathwings. Who built them?*

They disappeared again, only to be followed by a loud crash and a quake that shook loose rubble from the valley walls.

Trying to flush me into reckless flight, she mused to herself. *Conventional, basic tactic.* Weyef waited to test a new hunch.

She picked a recess between two peaks and forcibly steadied her heartbeat. The pair skulked by at exactly matching velocities and that same fixed spacing.

A definite weakness, she noted. *They'll have to bank to reconnoiter.*

Weyef climbed by hand and claw to the underside of a precipice and waited. By Sharu discipline, she quieted her thoughts again and listened to her own heartbeat slow. The blood pounding across her inner ears ebbed, then slowly, inexorably, the rumble of the jet machines returned.

She let the first pursuer pass unmolested. The second was her intended target.

Her body launched from the crevice with ballistic might, hooking talons deep into steel wings. She clutched so tightly to the mass of metal, her legs went numb with centripetal force. The angular momentum threw the combatants apart like a sling suddenly released.

The Efilu recovered her attitude. The machine did not. The spin extinguished the combustion engines and the craft exploded against the chasm wall. The flash was unexpected, but nothing could have added to the stunning effect of that maneuver.

Dazed, Weyef instinctively sniffed for the odor of death. But the stench of the flyer incinerating in its own fuel overwhelmed the scent of burnt flesh.

Nothing, she lamented. *An imitation of life.*

Weyef felt hollow in the absence of the Blood Rush, which she'd so well earned. As a desperate challenge to the remaining fighter, she tried to hoist a rock into the air, but found that her talons had no strength to hurl the projectile.

Panic surged in her throat again as the terrible image of her vengeful foe grew against the blue sky. As Weyef knew it must, the other craft was coming back for her with the recklessness of one who has nothing to lose. Vansar were loathed to underestimate the desperation of either a mate or mentor. The realization followed that this, too, could be to her advantage.

Emboldened, Weyef rose through the air in the glory of the afternoon sun. The light shone off her tightly folded pile like brilliant purple and golden flames. *They have shown no hunting skills so far. Perhaps this one will be stupid enough to become careless.*

"Come, marauder," she shouted in the old common tongue, "you who are so eager for battle—face me, then!"

The flyer banked upward and over Weyef, preparing for a rudimentary power dive. Slowly it rose into the sun, decelerating as its path approached vertical. *A chick's ploy, to hide in the glare of the sun.* Weyef almost found pity for the poor machine as it struggled against its own drag.

Weyef darted up at the flyer's blind belly, marking the gun ports and missile bays on her approach. *All pointed harmlessly skyward.* Her talon strength now recovered, she slashed the structures that most obviously maintained vital integrity.

The pull of gravity would soon bring the pair to a complete midair stop at the zenith. Weyef disemboweled the craft at her leisure, first disabling its engines, then attending to its weapons systems. To gain purchase, she had to climb over the edge of the left wing, both hands grasping the lip of metal; she found her midsection abutting the last explosive projectile the now-flaming fighter carried. Deliberately, Weyef reached a talon up to pry the thing from the jet. The lone remaining missile ripped free, suddenly coughed to life, launching recklessly past Weyef's abdomen. The device detonated at so close a distance as to spray its shrapnel back upon her shoulders and the craft's cockpit. Later she would indulge a shudder, she told herself, as she realized how close to joining her ancestors she'd come at that moment.

Scrambling within the solitary eye of the contraption, something writhed, like a chick helpless in its egg, trying to hatch. As Weyef worked her way around topside, she peered into the broken cockpit with amazement.

Biped. She took it all in at once. *What's it doing? Piloting! Electronics all around.* Weyef retracted her wing plumes to get her fingers under the edge of the shattered canopy.

Before her first tug followed through, the clear covering exploded upward. Weyef barely got her head out of the way in time to avoid the fragmented shell. She looked down into the cockpit to see a tiny device in the animal's hand.

What?

The last thing she thought before the searing pain blinded her was how familiar the little instrument looked. Her right hand clutched an oozing eye in agony as her head and neck reeled backward.

Gravity began to exert its grip now in earnest. The masked pilot dropped its weapon in panic. Weyef suppressed a heave of nausea. She recovered quickly, removing her hand from her right eye to grasp the occupant of the crippled flyer. The small form, now free of its restraints, was slippery in the exuded content of the Vansar's orb. Still alive, the little beast ceased struggling and collapsed. She transferred her limp prize from hand to taloned foot and took flight.

The vermin must not be accustomed to dealing with so much activity in so short a space of time.

Guided by the blurry image of a receding sun, Weyef glided homeward, her muscles nearly exhausted. Behind her, the ruined machine completed a nosedive into an unyielding sea of sand.

Chapter Twelve
— BABBLE —

How are you feeling?" Brajay asked.

"Nauseated!" Weyef responded, first exasperated then in measured locution. "Otherwise, no specific discomfort."

The Sulenz doctor had arrived from the *ReQam* early that evening. He regarded the security chief intently, while Weyef tried to maintain some detachment from the events of the afternoon.

"Any disequilibrium?" Brajay queried, nose crinkled as he assessed her. "Any impairment in judgement? Any confusion?"

"No. No. And *no*," Weyef protested. "I'm telling you, I was attacked by these killer flying machines. I barely escaped with my life. I can show you the exact site—"

"I don't dispute your account, Weyef," Brajay reassured her. "In fact, your injuries and the amount of debris you've acquired cannot be explained in any other way."

Brajay had already reviewed Weyef's log, primarily for an assessment of her injuries. "The record was incomplete—the result of equipment damage from the battle."

Brajay began to deactivate his own probe device when Weyef stared down at his diminutive form and said with obvious irritation, "Well? What about this nausea?"

"Oh, that," he answered. "It's a manifestation of sudden intraocular decompression. Are you experiencing double vision, or is it just blurred in the one eye?"

She closed her right eye for a moment before responding. The image of Brajay was as sharp as ever. "Just blurry on the right," she reported.

Brajay manipulated the probe to scan her right orb. "You were a little slow in closing that one during the attack, huh?"

"No, I wasn't. The little slug threw something in my eye!" Weyef carped.

He probed her eye at the next level of resolution. "Hmmm. This is inconsistent with the other pieces of shrapnel. It's not random." He spun the image around its axis as he analyzed the data on his sensor field. "Hah—constructed to be roughly aerodynamic. Still, that little creature could never have thrown it hard enough to penetrate your cornea. Are you sure it didn't use some sort of launching device?"

Weyef tried to isolate the image in her memory. "I can't be sure, but I think you're right."

"I'll remove it and restore your eye's integrity," Brajay said, raising a thin hand to silence the protest welling up in her throat. He then induced a force field tuned for deep, fine work and raised the power nearly to maximum. Weyef shuddered as the procedure commenced.

Where there had been silence before, a familiar chuckle now came from the shadows. Even Tralkyz laughter carried inherent menace. The softness of the So Wari sigh shook her more. Debriefing would not wait long. Weyef struggled to ignore it. By the time she returned her attention to the procedure at hand, Brajay was done.

"I've placed a pseudo-cellular patch in the puncture wound. It will become permanent as it duplicates the genetic material from the surrounding natural cells, then proliferate normally after that. How are the optics?" he asked.

Weyef looked around the dark chamber. "Normal saccadic movement. A hint of a distortion at close range, but that's all."

Although she dwarfed the concerned medical officer, she regarded him now with newfound respect. Back home, there was little use for medical intervention. The weak and injured either survived and recovered, or died.

"I still don't understand why there's no Blood Rush. Your endorphin levels are extraordinarily high," Brajay observed, his long, delicate fingers flicking through highlights of the battle record. "You were victorious against overwhelming odds, yet you're not the least bit intoxicated."

"It's a predaceous quirk, I suppose, but the Blood never rises fully when the conflict involves an inanimate opponent," she replied. "It's very frustrating to work that hard and not get off." Again, Weyef realized they were not alone. Suddenly embarrassed, she added, "If you know what I mean."

Bo Tep sat beside Tur in the shadows of the room. Other than the ominous venting, they had listened quietly until this point. Waiting.

"Sounds like they pretty much dusted you off," said Bo Tep. The jeering comment was classically Tralkyz. "And I thought you Vansar were supposed to be slick as crest-feathers in the air," he laughed.

Tur placed a hand gently on Bo Tep's arm, ending the derision for the moment. The illumination in the room returned to normal, revealing the intensity of Tur's gaze.

"Where is Car Hom?" Weyef asked, realizing that her debriefing had only been postponed pending medical clearance by Brajay.

"Car Hom is elsewhere," Tur replied.

Typical So Wari economy of thought. His scrutiny, however, was more intrusive than the metal fragments she still carried in her flesh.

The recordings of Weyef's sortie came to life around them. Tur leaned back on his tail, crossed his legs, and commanded, "Fill in the blanks."

Weyef summarily recounted the missing segments and placed the recorded images into proper context. Both Tur and Bo Tep listened with stony expressions and without interruption. Brajay had remained, ostensibly to complete her neuropsychiatric evaluation. Weyef testified in as cool and efficient a manner, as always.

"My impressions: the two machines communicated, I think, by some form of low-frequency EM wave. Some of their navigation was automated, I'm certain, but much of it displayed intelligence," she said.

"Some form of electronic artificial intelligence at work, no doubt. It sounds like the machine was full of those devices," Tur speculated, his gaze distant. "The animal was probably a safeguard in case of insect infestation," he added thoughtfully. "Clever."

Weyef, surprised at his misinterpretation, objected. "Oh, no. That little creature was piloting the machine."

Tur, Bo Tep, and Brajay all snapped to peak attention in unison. Tur looked to Brajay.

He shook his head. "No brain damage."

Weyef, recognizing the question on her interviewers' faces, clarified. "The machines moved as I moved, adapting to my evasive maneuvers. They learned too much, too quickly to be managed by the machines I saw in the control center."

Tur initiated the intercommunication link. "What is the status of the creature, Doh?" he asked.

"It's really fascinating," Doh replied, sounding exuberant. "Did Weyef mention to you that this thing is wearing some form of manufactured respiratory apparatus and an intricately woven garment?"

"Doh's off on a scientific tangent again." Tur scowled to the nearby audience. His fingers danced across the communication console to make the conversation locally public. "Doh, what are your immediate plans for it?"

"Resonance scanning of brain and vital organs, tissue samples, uh, genetic sequencing, then I thought we could just release him into the wild," Doh reported, back on track.

Tur, impressed, muted the transmission to share with Bo Tep and Weyef. "Very goal-oriented." Then, baiting Doh, Tur asked, "Didn't you want to track it after release?"

"I would, but there would be no immediate gain. In my opinion, for this mission, it would be a waste of resources," Doh answered with impressive discipline.

"Don't discard the creature just yet," Tur commanded, suppressing the laugh in his throat. "I want an in-depth study of its intelligence and communications skills. If it can communicate, have it interrogated thoroughly. Report to me by first light. Understood?"

After a brief pause, which Tur could not quite interpret, Doh answered in a simple affirmative.

The mammal looked exhausted as it sat in the middle of the floor. The bright overhead light focused at a radius five of the creature's head lengths wide, with the pilot at its center. Doh approached from the darkness, brimming with excitement. Tur thought he might burst before his demonstration even got started.

Doh carefully and purposefully drew the animal's attention to his lips and spoke in plain English. The tones came out with a hollow, resonant quality.

"How much wood would a woodchuck chuck if a woodchuck could chuck wood?" Doh asked.

"What?" The pilot looked perplexed. "What's this woodchuck crap?"

Doh clapped his hands together in exhilaration. "You see? You see? I projected 'We come in peace,' in the most focused thought possible—right at it—and the only communication it comprehended was that nonsense verbal message. According to our research, that sentence has no substantive meaning, even to its own species."

"That doesn't prove they're solely verbal," Ikara protested from the darkness outside the spotlight.

"No, of course not," Doh agreed. "There is some component of body language that roughly corresponds to our own universal concepts. Perhaps some hint of vestigial telepathic ability, but nothing useful to speak of. No, no. Their communication is almost completely verbal."

"So, what's your point?" Tur asked, trying to cut through the theatrics.

The Kini Tod scientist continued, "There are about five billion of these particular animals living on or near the surface of Fitu. They have developed a rudimentary communications system made up of five or six basic families of languages, each consisting of approximately one hundred thousand to two hundred thousand character clusters. It is this verbal language skill that allows unrelated tribes to coalesce into larger groups and accomplish amazing feats of technical and economic genius through cooperation. From what this creature displays, I would say he is just above average in intelligence."

"Hardly 'genius,'" Tur said, his impatience penetrating the darkness. "I repeat: What is your point?"

"My point is this: This individual and his kind constructed, maintained, and piloted that machine and hundreds more like it.

They transmit verbal codes over long distances via low-frequency EM waves, as Weyef suggested. Large quantities of data are managed through electronic integration networks, many of which are linked to monitor devices and automatons. It's all very sophisticated." Doh was on the verge of giggling. "They never could have developed this technology without help. I believe these Jing were genetically engineered to serve some purpose of the Keepers," Doh concluded.

On a more serious note, he added, "Also, Commander, they do know something about us."

The chamber was filled with thoughtful amazement, and Doh raised a stubby hand to quell conjecture. "Not us on the mission team, specifically," he clarified, then he performed a series of gestures. A display of Weyef's excursion appeared.

"This was recorded inside of one of their buildings." The holograph panned through a building called the Arabian Museum of Natural History.

Assuming the display was a test of its knowledge, the mammal started to chatter in English. "Tyrannosaurus rex, Triceratops, Stegosaurus, Pterodactyl, and Brontosaurus—I think."

Sensing impatience from the group, Doh moved to silence it. At a Sharu touch, the pilot went limp.

"So, they have a few mismatched collections of wildlife fossils. That has nothing to do with us," Tur said, standing now. He ran a finger along a dorsal plate of an enhanced image of the stegosaurus exhibit. "There's nothing there to suggest that they know what we are here for. I see no threat, for now."

Tur crossed his arms, thinking furiously while he looked with disdain at the skeleton identified as "Tyrannosaurus." He shut the holograph off with a single gesture before returning his attention to the briefing session.

"Jeen?" he asked, calling on his communications expert.

The Tal Genj mer's soft antlers bounced gently as she spoke. "I agree with Doh in at least one respect: they have very sophisticated data management capabilities. It's completely binary, though, with data stored on magnetic strips and chips."

"That should be easy enough to access," Tur observed, rubbing his chin. "We should be able to just—"

"I see where you're going with that thought, Commander. But believe me, it's a dead end," Jeen interjected. "The data is not coded in a uniform pattern. A sensor sweep would alter the data almost simultaneously with the scan. What we get would be unreliable at best, but more likely unintelligible." The puzzled expression demanded further explanation. "Look Commander, our gel/crystal probes use quaternary waves pivoting between all four dimensions. Theirs are binary. We can't pare our technology down that much. We haven't for tens of millions of years. I doubt that there's even remnant technology in the rock sediment that could sync with their stuff even if we could dig some up."

"So, a plenary scan of their systems isn't viable." Tur pressed onward. "It might still be worthwhile at some time to access individual databases. Very cumbersome, but feasible. Our own gel/crystal technology can discriminate positive and negative charges. Correlated them to 0s and 1s. We should be able to easily break in on any of these cables or fibrous conduits and monitor, reroute, block, or replace transmitted data. We'll need a small number of selected terminals to experiment on first." He shrugged. "Download the raw data and translate it at our leisure."

Jeen exhaled in exasperation. Her smooth, short pile bristled slightly. "The spoken languages are even more difficult. Again, Doh is correct in stating that there are only five or six basic groups, but there is a myriad of subgroups further divided by dialect and mixed with elements of languages no longer in use. I selected this particular animal's primary language of 'English.' It's a poor language system with many syntactic contradictions, but it's the most widely used among the more dominant groups.

"It took me a while to master it. Amelodic, no disciplined rhythms or cadence..." She shook her head and her antlers danced once again. "Just discordant noises mostly. I spent most of the night teaching it to Doh, Vit Na, and Bo Tep. Because of her Melkyz phono-mimetic ability, Vit Na seems to be most adept at duplicating natural mammalian voices. At some point, that may prove useful."

With nothing further to add, Jeen relinquished the floor to Bo Tep.

"The bipeds are very security-minded, in some respects obsessed," said the Head of Acquisitions, regarding Tur for a moment, "but their security measures are ridiculous. Visual surveillance, barriers of simple metal mesh. Oh, and sentries. Whatever attacked Weyef probably epitomized top-of-the-line technology. What's really interesting is that they have no defensive weapons at all."

Bo Tep paused to let the notion sink in.

"All of their weapons technology is offensive in design. I confirmed this with Devit. They have a deterrent/first strike/retaliation mentality. If we ever have to get past them," Bo Tep made the final statement with the utmost confidence, "we will."

Vit Na presented her perspective in turn. "I have very little to add. Their 'civilization' is very young, but it is a complex of paradoxes. They have extraordinary wealth coexisting alongside abject poverty. Valuable talents are identified in the gifted. Those skills are honed to an artform, coveted, exploited—then those same experts are relegated to supervisors of lesser aptitude. All the while, accumulated resources are squandered by the masters of each industry. The socioeconomic structure is dominated not by the gifted, but by the least inhibited, who are usually of average or below-average intellect. The next tier is composed of above-average subordinates with a variety of useful talents."

"And the commoners are at the bottom of the tree, scrambling for scraps," Tur interrupted. "What's unusual about that?"

"Nothing!" Vit Na explained. "That arrangement would make sense—but it is not the case here. A disproportionate number of gifted individuals are permanently incarcerated or survive in the underworld. It's almost as if they are deliberately excluded from the mainstream."

"That doesn't make sense to me, but there must be some kind of survival value to the arrangement. Do you have anything else?" Tur asked her, as he prepared to adjourn, for the time being.

"I can't explain why they keep a bunch of old bones around, if that's what you're asking," Vit Na said. "An arcane, ritual custom, I guess."

Tur was about to end the session when Vit Na stood again. "Just one more thing." He nodded permission at her expectant frown. "It is a little out of my area, though." She paused again. "Has anyone noticed a certain peculiarity about their anatomy?"

"Yes. No tails!" A soft chuckle propagated through the audience at the anonymous quip.

"Yes, that too, but there's something else even more fundamental." She paused once more, half for effect and half to decide for herself if her theory made sense.

"Their heads are too big," she finally stated. "Proportionately, their brains are larger than ours!"

The dying chuckle turned into a murmur of curiosity.

"Of course they are!" exclaimed Doh, apparently threatened by the inquiry. "Their nervous system is centralized in one place. Evolution has consigned our lower-level neural functions to the caudal center in the tail, and to peripheral neuromuscular plexi. Our diffuse higher nervous system is connected via a more sophisticated spinal–paraspinal cord network. A more advanced arrangement."

Vit Na proceeded cautiously. "Yes, but taking all of that into account, they still should have far more intelligence than any of them display. They clearly have sacrificed strength, speed, endurance, and other sensory advantages to the development of this relatively massive brain. What do they do with it?"

Doh was silent.

"They have no telepathic, prescient, or telekinetic ability," she continued. "It seems from Doh's observations that much of it is inhibitory. At some point during the last sixty-five million years, there must have been a survival advantage to this mutation: the tendency to suppress direct communication in favor of deductive reasoning and their ridiculous babble," she concluded. Her intimate voice began to falter.

Grudgingly, Doh concurred, but didn't interrupt Vit Na.

"It may be that the Keepers pushed these Jing beyond their mental limits by narrowing their receptive abilities, in an effort to override basic instincts and the barrage of superfluous psychic input around them." Aloud, it still sounded good to Vit Na. "Maybe they retained a number of neuropsychiatric mutations long after the last of the Si Tyen died out."

The staff's collective attention meandered back to the newly conscious, nervous subject sitting in the cone of light. Echoes of thought projections rippled through the theater.

Weyef spoke. "Well, this is all very interesting, I'm sure, but we have a serious security problem on our hands. These Jing—or *Jing Pen*, as Vit Na proposes—have gone beyond the level of 'pest.'"

Weyef brought up the lights and spoke again, without asking permission. "If the essential research has been completed, let's get rid of that thing." She signaled to Ju Kol. "Remove its tongue, sedate it, and release it back into the wild."

Predictably, Doh objected. "Why must we maim this animal? Can't we just—"

Weyef reasserted her position without missing a beat: "As I said, it's a matter of mission security—my department." That ended that discussion.

Tur and Car Hom remained silent as she continued. "These creatures tend to babble. You have clearly demonstrated that yourself. I can't have this one telling the whole world we're here. Consider the silencing as an act of mercy. This creature will still be able to eat, excrete, reproduce, and defend itself. What is lost?"

Sensing Doh's sympathetic sentiment, she projected, softly but angrily, "By rights, I should put a talon in its scrawny neck here and now!"

Regaining her composure, she turned to Tur and Car Hom. "I also want a tactical officer with every survey team that leaves this base. With your permission, I'd like to requisition forty or fifty armed meren from my division on the *ReQam*."

Tur looked to Car Hom with a look that was half galled and half amused at Weyef's brazen request. Then he said simply, "Do it."

Chapter Thirteen
— ATTACKED —

I should have opened the little maggot's neck when I had the chance," Weyef muttered. It had been barely more than a day since they released the jet pilot. She stood outside, looking over the heads of Doh and Devit, who in turn were flanked by several of their own subordinates. The light from the exploding missiles illuminated Doh's forehead and cheeks.

Sleek black machines suspended from whirling blades hung in the midday sky, slowly circling the Efilu base. Shots struck harmlessly against the invisible barrier. A few missiles painted bursts of color against the exclusion field embracing the compound, but most just shattered, dully crumbling along the event horizon. Shadows lumbered through the cloud of dust stirred by the swarm of crafts. Ground vehicles launched a continuous hail of incendiary cocktails of their own. All in all, the display proved to be a most spectacular pyrotechnic extravaganza.

Weyef was instructing Ju Kol on situation management when Tur arrived. By this time, the show had drawn quite an audience.

Tur stood with his hands akimbo, watching the muted sparks. "What's all this?"

"The price of mercy," Weyef answered.

Tur restrained a satirical comment. "Just get rid of them," he said jovially.

With her nod, Ju Kol made a series of gestures. The mammalian assault force simply stopped moving. The darkly clad assailants fell silently where they had stood. The flying machines sank gently to the ground, blades whirling to a stop. Dust cleared as the futile attack settled to an abrupt end.

Weyef took pleasure in neutralizing the armada. "This time, no loose ends," she projected, looking directly at Doh.

Doh hung his head, resigned to publicly bearing his obvious judgement error.

Tur and his fellow spectators lost interest as the commotion subsided. Crew meren cleared the terrace and filed casually around a lone figure intently studying a miniature gel-com. Not lifting his own eyes from the handheld device, Devit caught Tur's arm as the commander passed.

"Fourteen bims," Devit stated, still not looking up as he spoke.

Tur looked down at his weapons expert quizzically. "No, you must have miscalculated. Fourteen bims would have ruptured the shield. You know that. Check again, you'll see it comes out to dae bims."

At that point, Devit initiated the display and triggered the repeat cycle. "No mistake, High Commander." He took a formal tone now, his façade grave, as usual. "That pretty display generated fourteen bims of energy. It was low intensity—mostly wasted propelling metal projectiles—but a respectable discharge of power just the same."

He watched Tur's brow furrow as he confirmed the data's accuracy.

Tur activated the comm link. "Car Hom...?" He waited for the response from his number-one, then stated, "We're moving."

Tur drummed his fingers on his knee as he sat waiting. The amphitheater was nearly full; only a security party remained absent. Cleaning up the remnants of the shattered Jing Pen armature had taken longer than expected.

Ju Kol proclaimed, "They were so fragile!"

Weyef sat quietly upfront.

Damn her! She was right from the beginning. Tur looked at Weyef, imagining a smug façade hiding behind her inscrutable expression.

More than an inconvenience, this unexpected guerrilla firepower was developing into a full-blown complication. The phrase "tactical retreat" would never be used to refer to the action he would take here today. *I'll see to that!* Tur pledged.

He commenced speaking as Ju Kol took a seat next to Weyef. The lights dimmed before any of the stragglers had a chance to find seats. Tur displayed an updated three-dimensional holographic globe of Fitu, now complete with the main urban centers.

"There is nothing of interest to us in this region," Tur said, indicating the base's current coordinates. "Today, we will split our forces into seven groups. They will be deployed here, here, and here on this hemisphere," he pointed as he spoke, "and here, here, here, and here on this one. The basic plan remains the same: locate the most likely reserves of yellow algae."

He paused a moment for questions, then went on. "Car Hom will make team assignments. Weyef will assign security personnel. If there are no questions, you're dismissed."

Doh poised to ask a question but was cut off in mid–thought projection.

"If there *are* questions, direct them to Car Hom and Weyef," Tur declared.

Doh was left with his mouth gaping as Tur left the hall.

It was nearly dawn in the western region of the very land mass where Jeen had wished not to be assigned. The Tal Genj had an odd habit of looking tranquil but dissatisfied all the time. Right now, Jeen was anything but tranquil and "dissatisfied" was an understatement.

Car Hom's orders still echoed in her mind: "Be discreet!"

How do you remain discreet when there is no one to hide from? she thought with exasperation.

The desert was awfully big when crossed at ground level, and her Mini-Wave was too small for her party! So what if she didn't have any of the really big meren with her?

Why should I be cooped up with this clod of a Lau Rechin security officer whose knuckles and feet constantly drag on the ground through the bottom of the Wave?

His long legs were leaving tracks in the sand as the Wave flowed.

"Ungh!"

Yet another groan from that grunt, Jeen thought.

"Enough of this!" she exclaimed. She reached down into the nerve center of the amorphous Wave and shifted the control currents. The Mini-Wave engulfed the whole compliment of her team and took on a giant arachnoform configuration. Instead of "flowing," it "walked" with long, smooth strides.

"That's better!" she said aloud, looking back at the security meg with defiance—a look that said, *Report me. Go ahead.*

The going was a little slower, but a lot smoother, with the well-adapted pseudopodia carrying her party easily over the undulating sandy terrain. Overall, it was much more "discreet."

Jeen thought to herself, *Even the Lau Rechin security meg can't argue that point.*

The gel pod allowed visual perception that was apparently keener than that of the mammals they had been ordered to avoid. Twice now, troops of bipeds had come close enough to smell the traces of gel solution evaporating from the pod without spotting the immobile figure in the sands.

Jeen began to consider Weyef's security measures more as a burdensome exercise. She looked back at the security meg with contempt and returned her attention to the changing landscape. They were approaching the site of the ruined city of Meput. There was now more vegetation—and more "Jing Pen" to contend with.

The name with which Vit Na labeled these bipeds had stuck. From the ancient word for "tree mammal," *Jing* was used interchangeably with *pest*. The term *Jing Pen* implied genetic engineering.

What capabilities could be honed in such a clade of species over sixty-five million years? Especially if contrived by the Si Tyen Keepers? Jeen considered the face-off Weyef recounted two days ago. *And the Vansar own the skies.* As she considered that encounter, the team leader suddenly felt her resentment for the Lau Rechin security meg turn to acceptance. She moved on to a different subject. *I wonder how the other search parties are doing.*

Chapter Fourteen
— STAR WARS —

The *ReQam* somehow seemed empty without its strongest personalities exerting their collective presence. Sub-commander Ga Win walked the ship, satisfied with its status.

"Tired, Sub-commander?" Stihl asked.

"My 'cousin' works his staff to the quick." Ga Win projected good-naturedly. "We're used to it. Super hunters, you know." Wilkyz kinship to Alkyz acknowledgement was always an honor. They typically expected more from their own class. Ga Win flashed tranquility through the *ReQam*'s three or four most likely alternative time avenues for the next day.

"Ship's secure, Stihl. Now time for me to rest. Keep your ears up." Ga Win retired to his pallet, leaving Stihl in command. Wilkyz slept deeply when exhausted, nearly hibernating, and Ga Win was no exception.

No sooner had the Wilkyz officer stood down, did Loz check the duty roster. Ga Win and Car Hom had no way of predicting that the Head of Astrophysics would exercise the honorary acting commander rank provision for his own ends. A place-holder title for research department heads, but one-half level up from Stihl's rank of assistant commander.

Loz reveled in command, even if it was only an acting title, still restricted from issuing any martial orders. There were more meren floating in the control center than necessary for the quiet third shift. Loz crouched in the control groove and let it hug his narrow frame.

Comfortable, Stihl read Loz's initial careless reflections as the astrophysicist reveled in that station. *No,* Stihl reassessed. *Powerful! The authority implicit in occupying that chair is not meant for such a meg: undisciplined, untrained.*

Stihl stood obediently, feet and tail clutching the deck left of the command nest. Like many So Wari, Stihl detested the aimless feel of weightlessness. The assistant commander merely observed, silently making mental notes to himself.

Not accustomed to command in any iteration, Stihl thought, eyeing the acting commander. *Preoccupied with power beyond his ken.*

Stihl glanced stoically at Moc. His *synespira* served as Loz's personal assistant. *Perhaps she might impart a measure of So Wari discipline.* But Moc looked helpless to influence her superior. Stihl pitied her this humiliating assignment, even as he admired her discipline. *She shows as great composure under pressure here as she did for Rault. If we survive, we may yet hatch strong cubs for our herd.*

Loz still contemplated the shiny, derelict satellites in orbit below the *ReQam.* "They appear harmless enough."

No reason to step in—yet, Stihl concluded.

"They may actually be mapping devices left by the Keepers, you know," Loz speculated, his thoughts raced as accelerated as his movements. He spoke to his assistant, Moc, but seemed intent on engaging the bigger So Wari for reasons unclear to Stihl. "We may be able to hasten this mission after all, if I'm right."

Stihl did not like games. "What are you asking?"

Loz raised a slick, brown eyebrow.

"Commander," Stihl added.

"I'm asking for your tactical assessment, Stihl," Loz said. "Could any of those metallic constructs represent a threat to the *ReQam* or our landing parties?"

In typical So Wari style, Stihl thought fast, but projected his thoughts slowly and deliberately. "They have neither signaled nor probed us since we arrived six days ago." Before continuing, he brought up the data on pre-Exodus Si Tyen technology. Stihl compared it with the newly accumulated data displayed in the energy scans taken on the derelicts so far. There was no correlation.

"They appear to be machines of various designs. Their structures suggest specialized manufacturing and very little adaptability. Some are clearly made for some form of celestial reconnaissance, but none have focused on us, as of yet. In fact, they don't even appear to have the capability to probe objects this close to their sensors. Most of them are designed for aerial and terrestrial survey." Stihl seemed to address Moc rather than Loz, to the latter's chagrin.

"Project toward me directly when I query you, Stihl," Loz chided.

Redirecting his eyes, Stihl continued his report. "There is definite evidence of subatomic decay, heavy elements in some of them. No doubt they run on a primitive form of long-term power source, probably serving more vital functions. By contrast, some of the others are equipped with solar collectors. The technology is definitely of common origin to that encountered by the surface party." Re-examining his surveillance interface, Stihl squinted. "There is a weird wrinkle in the Pitkor continuum. I've never seen that before."

Moc half turned to Stihl at the observation. "That's supposed to remain a constant sequence. Are you sure—"

"I concur with your analysis, Stihl" Loz drawled, all but ignoring Moc. "We are going to acquire one of those nuclear-powered machines. My calculations show they are most likely to store data for long periods of time, data that may prove invaluable to our mission."

"Wait now!" Stihl protested. "Those machines are sloppily made. Although the radiation they leak represents no hazard to us or to the surface-dwellers from this distance, bringing one on board is an unacceptable risk that I cannot allow."

The Notex's response was accompanied by the usual amount of hand-waving. "I am Head of Astrophysics and Propulsion, as well as acting commander of this vessel. In my opinion, we can easily contain the radiation emanating from ten of those machines. We stand to gain far more than we risk. In fact, we are in far less jeopardy than our intrepid colleagues on Fitu."

The argument was a sound one. Stihl hesitated. *This just...feels wrong, somehow.* He wished Ga Win was not in torpor. Waking him now would be useless—he'd be mentally incompetent for at least a day.

Loz looked at Stihl triumphantly, knowing that he had won a reluctant ally, should his judgement be questioned by Tur or Car Hom.

"I acknowledge that you are in command; however, I have the responsibility of maintaining the ship's safety. That comes directly from High Commander Tur," Stihl said, emphasizing the rank. "I will not allow this mission or this ship to be placed in unnecessary danger. The moment these activities even *look* like they are endangering this ship, I will terminate them and assume command, pending the arousal of Ga Win or the return of Tur or Car Hom."

Loz started to respond, but Stihl cut him off and closed his eyes. "And I will restrain you if necessary," Stihl said. His eyes did not recess to engage *Conflict Vision*, however, the gesture unnerved even the most confident speaker. Stihl confirmed the sincerity of that intent with a glare at Moc, then he resumed his usual stolid vigil without further comment.

Loz didn't have to say more. He knew he had won, but he would have loved to have had the last word.

"Attention, Commander, *Challenger II.* Switch to laser pulse frequency Epsilon."

Chip Rollins closed the door to his cabin and waited a moment after following the initial instructions. He knew what was about to happen, and he felt a shiver run down his spine. This communiqué was security level 1.

The commander floated in the microgravity as he waited for the president to appear on the viewscreen. The first encounter with extraterrestrials mandated presidential attention. Every astronaut had dreamed about it, Chip included, but the reality of the event hit him like a ton of bricks. Chip was nervous. He had not spoken to this new, conservative president yet; the man had earned a reputation as a hard-ass in the space agency.

The head of the Joint Chiefs of Staff appeared instead. The face of Air Force General Michael Chey was alert and intense.

"Major Rollins, you are ordered to proceed with extreme caution. We have been expecting this call from you all week. The administration has reason to believe these aliens are hostile and dangerous. Attempt communication, but at the first sign of trouble, you will mount Operation Bethlehem—and mind you, there will be no command discretion here. You will commence the procedure at the first sign of aggressive intent. This is not to be discussed with the rest of the crew. Chey out."

Rollins stared at the blank screen, absorbing the unsaid ramifications of the communication. "Operation Bethlehem" was the new code phrase for deploying the strategic defense initiative.

The President's maintaining his distance on this one. Why? Rollins wondered. And Chey. *No encouraging "Good luck, Chip"?*

Rollins found himself remembering the fate of the last shuttle named *Challenger.*

Disgust had become a part of Tur's normal disposition since the landing. He had stopped trying to mask his feelings since Geotechnics recommended straining the crude, decayed liquid waste these Jing Pen were dredging up from the bowels of Fitu. Even so, it saved him the energy of having to excavate it himself. There was no arguing over economy for a So Wari.

They had found no golden algae yet, but a good number of microorganisms from that ancient time were being recovered intact.

Kellis commented, "Quite promising!"

Since it was apparently effective practice to harvest ancient Efilu refuse, the other sub-parties were ordered to duplicate the process wherever possible. Tur recalled an old So Wari axiom with a smirk: *When the Dance goes badly, share the pain.*

Nearing time for check-in, Tur thought.

Weyef supplemented the daily ritual with security updates every quarter day. She relayed them to the snowy northwestern peninsula of one of the paired land masses for Tur's review. "In English, the Jing Pen call it North America," she reminded him. "It's easier to cross-check, since we have no historical reference for this continental configuration."

He was really beginning to like Weyef. *She'll make a good So Wari yet,* he chuckled to himself.

Conduits of metal alloy wound in a tangle everywhere in the crude Jing Pen construct. At least the ceiling rose high enough to accommodate his bulk. Tur looked up from the filtration unit for relief from the sickening process, only to notice Devit standing across from him.

It bothered the High Commander more than a little that this one so consistently approached him undetected. *Ironde stealth technique seems even better than I've heard,* he noted. *We'll have to look into this sometime.*

The thought was lost as he spied the little device in his weapons master's hand. Devit offered it to his commander.

"Do you recognize this?"

"Of course." Tur looked at it before taking it from his subordinate. "It's one of the weapons used by that biped pack that attacked our base." He tried to hand it back to Devit but the Ironde refused the offer.

"No, no. Do you recognize the technology?"

Tur still looked puzzled. Devit tipped the weapon on its side in the commander's hand. Tur's eyes shone with a glimmer of recognition.

"It's a handheld Lesad," said Devit, supplying the answer. "Named after the Sulenz inventor."

Tur shook his head slowly in disbelief. "That was invented seventy million years ago. How would they have access to such technology now?"

"Sixty-eight million years ago," Devit corrected. "One might conclude that they had help, Commander," the Ironde offered.

"The Tyen Keepers were nonviolent. Why would they provide these vicious little creatures with even remnant weapons technology?" Tur asked.

"I don't know, Commander, but you have available personnel who are well versed in Tyen psychology. Far more than I am, at least."

Both meren looked uneasy, yoked with this new problem.

A pleasant scent wafted through the space, masking the pervasive, aromatic stench. Kira Kesh, the Mit Kiam technician, had entered the small building. "You two look as if you could use a lifting of the spirit," she said.

Neither Tur nor Devit would admit to how they always welcomed the fragrance heralding the beautifully plumed mer. There was a twinkle in her eye that piqued their curiosity. Following her lead,

Tur and Devit stepped outside into the fresh air and found themselves bathed in a shimmer of the Northern Lights.

Kira Kesh followed a bit behind them as she watched the effect of an old friend on weary travelers.

"*Dragon's Air*," Tur recalled from Animem recollection. "Beautiful as ever."

It was only then that he realized he had come to regard Fitu as an alien world. Just for a brief moment, Tur felt as if he had come home.

His warm moment was interrupted all at once by a burst of something cold and wet on his back. He took a deep breath before turning to face the clumsy aide responsible for flinging snow in his direction.

Vit Na crouched as she assembled another snowball to hurl at her *synespira*. In this environment, her coat was a milky white—an adaptation achieved without true *Blending*. Realizing that she was caught, she tossed the snowball up and down, catching it each time in her bare hand as she addressed her commander.

"Isn't this great?" Vit Na grinned broadly for several moments before she closed her lips. Tur didn't take it as a threat from her, but she concealed her gleaming teeth out of respect. "I haven't played in the snow like this since I was a cub. I love the White Rain."

"Leave it to the super hunters' clade to weaponizing snow." Tur wiped remnants from the back of his head.

"We had to learn to do something with clumsy cubs. Their tell-tale tracks always exposed the hunt." Vit Na said. "At least one adult stayed in the field-nest with a big pile of slush and carried on target practice with the little ones. Just enough to sting. Great for agility training and distraction from meddling with business, though." She stopped tossing the fresh snowball and turned it in her hand, considering it. "Good packing quality."

"I'm disappointed in its failure, this White Rain."

Vit Na arches an eyebrow. "Poetry?" She moved in as she recognized the opening phrase of the So Wari recital.

"Its delicate purity failed to unveil your approach." Taking on the role of troubadour, Tur rendered the ancient verse. "Its fragile silence failed to announce your movement."

Vit Na nodded approval of *The Hunted's Tribute*.

"The White Rain, a flawless layer of presage, uninterrupted as far as the eye can see.

"We So Wari have taken Alom's gift for granted, Vit Na of Kemith. This White Rain.

"But leave it to your super hunters' clade to weaponize snow.

"I failed to remember, I am the hunted!

"You, Vit Na of Kemith, tread like a raptor's shadow and stalked like a Melkyz dream, across this White Rain.

"Its fragile silence failed to announce your movement, this White Rain.

"Its delicate purity failed to unveil your approach.

"So terribly close yet always out of reach, you so skillfully navigate this White Rain.

"Still, Vit Na of Kemith, you came on like lashing wind, battering hail and biting storm all at once... Leaving only this White Rain."

The So Wari have become complacent. Thank you for extracting our weakness.

When next you hunt, Kemithi, you'll face a nemesis, not prey. We'll be stronger, victorious, and without mercy, leaving you broken and silent in this White Rain.

Vit Na flashed black plumage momentarily in contrast to the white drifts around her, the traditional salute to concession. Vit Na all but disappeared when she restored her coat to the bright white.

"Weren't you assigned to Bo Tep's sub-party?" Tur growled. Happy to see her, Tur enjoyed playing this game of feigned irritation. He would never admit to anyone that he liked seeing her teeth.

"I think I was beginning to get on his nerves." Vit Na projected triumphant reticence. "Bo Tep sent me to deliver the soil specimens we recovered this afternoon."

Vit Na coyly projected the half-truth: she disclosed how she delivered the soil samples, but also how she had had to coerce Bo Tep a little to let her do so in person. Tur wouldn't probe Bo Tep's courier choice too deeply, of course.

Who better to share the light show with? Tur thought. As she approached and snuggled against him, he curled his tail around her to break the cold wind and stroked her downy ears as the glow of Dragon's Air flickered across her pelt.

Loz ordered the *ReQam* to reduce its orbital distance from Fitu.

"We are now in orbit closer than the moon," Moc announced, more as a warning to Stihl than to inform her immediate superior.

The new orbit was stable, but now on a deliberate collision course with the slow-moving shuttle. Loz's obvious intention: to "bump" into it.

"Have either of you read Weyef's report?" Loz asked.

Growing more agitated by the moment, Stihl responded with a single nod. He knew he should find a reason to notify Tur, but still he couldn't identify tangible danger to the ship. The *ReQam's* protection screen would deflect the shuttle with ease.

"Moc detected similar lifeforms on that contrivance." Loz slowed the ship once, entering the shuttle's orbital path. "I want to measure their reaction to a little tap."

Moc collected data on the small craft even as it rebounded, shaken yet unharmed, off the force field. The true object of intended study was just ahead. "There. In front of us. That looks interesting." Loz directed Moc. "Ligate the one in focus there and reel it in. Now, let's see how they power these little skyshells of theirs."

As the *ReQam* opened a port and cast a ligand around the nuclear satellite, Stihl found his voice. "Abort. Moc, abort! Close that lateral portal now!"

"Have you lost your mind?" Loz threw his hands up in the air in disbelief. "What do you think you're doing, countermanding my orders? Don't you know who is in command here?"

Loz blinked as the blinding flash caught him by surprise.

Ju Kol reviewed data on the ruins below them. Jeen had supplied each of them with a working knowledge of the local wildlife and the most popular languages in use. The resident Jing Pen called this place Venezuela. So close to the equator, it was exceedingly warm, and the wide river posed significant survey challenges.

"The climate in this region of the planet is different from that of our original landing site," Ju Kol recorded in his report. "The ambient temperature is higher and the air more humid. The soil below us is rich in decaying organic material. The probe readings are less reliable than elsewhere. Too much biological background noise."

Of course, Weyef would not be interested in his excuses, nor would his grand uncle, Car Hom. Ju Kol decided not to accept any from his own subordinates either.

The Alkyz was still berating his aide when Weyef stepped up to investigate the commotion. Almost whining, Ju Kol began, "We need accurate information on this site or this is all a waste of our time. We'll need..."

Just then, he realized that Weyef was not listening to him anymore. She was staring off into the midday sky at a glint of reflected light, barely perceptible to his eyes through the glare of the sun.

"Contact Tur and the other parties, Ju Kol," Weyef spoke with a grave intensity the mundane dilemma at hand did not merit.

"We're in deep trouble."

Chapter Fifteen
— SEIZURE —

Tur paced the floor of the conference room with heavy footfalls, grinding his teeth audibly, even over the hum of the faulty transmission from the *ReQam*.

Car Hom listened calmly as Stihl recounted events leading to the satellite explosion. Loz paced at Notex speed—just a blur in the background—obviously eager to give his side of the tale.

As Stihl's briefing ended, Tur locked eyes with Car Hom. The High Commander had stopped pacing and settled on his haunches, motionless.

Loz took advantage of the momentary silence to interject his explanation. "High Commander, I just thought if I could—"

Without a glance at the image, Tur ended Loz's supplication abruptly with a slam of his fist on the conference table. The communications link was broken.

"Car Hom, it would seem that a few soft meren have gotten into our little fold somehow," Tur said through clenched teeth. He looked away from his chief of staff. "Weakness appears to be rampant around here. I was led to believe you could maintain our strength."

In stating this publicly, Tur invoked an ancient obligation between prey and predator never subject to open criticism in civilized conversation. The historic relationship had evolved to the benefit of both—the Dance of Life. Every kill gratefully removes a weakness from the herd and strengthens the species, and in so doing, challenges the hunting skills of future predacious encounters.

"See to it that the slack is taken in a bit up there, won't you?" Tur finished.

Car Hom stood without ceremony and with no obvious sign of offense. He did not face Tur directly, but silently pointed to three technicians and gestured for them to follow him.

Car Hom half-turned toward Tur as he spoke. "I'll have a damage report for your review before sundown. In the meantime, we'll stabilize the ship's orbit. I'd prepare to send all nonessential gel and crystal equipment up to the *ReQam*, if I were you."

Without further comment, Car Hom's party transferred to the damaged vessel.

With his first officer gone, Tur drummed his fingers thrice on the table before standing. Surrounded by his ground-based department heads in silence, he forgot the northern beauty outside the temporary building he had grudgingly admired earlier that morning. He couldn't even mourn the casualties resulting from the orbiting fiasco. *Not yet.*

"Damn satellites," Tur grumbled. "The danger from these Jing Pen tribes remains unchecked. Bo Tep, coordinate with Weyef. Find out what else they're up to. I want a plan to neutralize this Jing Pen nuisance before sundown. Dismissed."

The staff left him alone in the conference room. Tur reached for the weapon Devit had brought to his attention, placing his smallest fingernail over the trigger mechanism and squeezing a harmless shot into the palm of his free hand without as much as a sting.

"If any of these miserable Keepers are still alive, I'll kill them!" he said aloud. Tur tossed the weapon on the table, then subdued the lights, sat on his haunches, and folded his hands to cradle his aching head.

The *ReQam*'s crew was shaken by the blast: twelve dead including Ga Win and Toyot Da. Twenty-seven seriously injured. Those with minor injuries continued at their posts.

The atmosphere on board was intense, and Car Hom inspected the wreckage in no mood to relieve any of that tension—especially not for Loz. Car Hom thought for a moment about tearing Loz apart at the shoulders after surveying the damage, but refrained; he needed the astrophysicist.

The mission needs him, Car Hom thought, *but not onboard the* ReQam.

Loz already had given his assessment of repair requirements. They were extensive, of course, but could be implemented by maintenance personnel.

"Why do I have to go to the surface?" Loz whined. "My skills are best utilized here!"

Car Hom looked around at the chaos and spread his hands at the pleading meg with a shrug. After a moment, he added, "We'll muddle through up here without you."

"Car Hom, what do I do about Tur?" Loz asked. "I mean, I would imagine he's...a bit upset."

"Just stay out of his way, Loz. You'll probably be all right."

Loz fished for reassurance. "Probably?"

"Well, possibly," Car Hom replied. He could not resist the opportunity to torment the astrophysicist.

"How angry is he?" Loz asked.

Car Hom again looked around at the damage, then back at Loz, and just shrugged.

Loz swallowed a little harder than usual before shuffling slowly down the hall, a pace one rarely observed in a Notex.

Somehow, Car Hom felt better than he had all afternoon.

Car Hom's report was in on time, as always. Tur opened the communiqué from the *ReQam* and read it.

"The situation is salvageable. Please send *all* available gel and crystal tech for support," Car Hom transmitted, his short message reminiscent of So Wari brevity. Tur's culture was losing its monopoly on this stereotype more and more each day.

Tur navigated the halls from his offices to the conference room. He stopped at the door and saw that all key personnel were present for this latest briefing. He strode in, but even before sitting, Tur announced, "It's time to begin."

Bo Tep lifted off his haunches and began the presentation. "As we already knew, most of the Jing Pen assault forces—at least the ones we're interested in right now—are automated."

Because most of their more sophisticated technology had already been relinquished to the *ReQam*, Bo Tep and Kellis had come up with an elegant holographic system that utilized the dust and snow from the artificial cavern floor, its display manipulated by personal field interface. The gestures became mildly tedious for the holofield operator, but they communicated scale and spatial relationships rather well.

"Leave it to Tralkyz ingenuity to employ talents that haven't been necessary in eons," Kellis projected with unabashed admiration.

"Jeen tells me that we can cripple their entire satellite system from either of two strategic centers in the region," Bo Tep said. "My meren had been surveying these centers before the…accident."

No one actually looked in Loz's direction, but he certainly squirmed as if they did.

"They will try to locate us after the hit," Bo Tep warned. "At the same time, they'll be desperate to reestablish control over their systems. We'll need a new base of operations—one that'll afford us access to the same information flow the Jing Pen have. Under the circumstances, it needs to be someplace close to our current location, but not too close."

He paused for a moment. "Here!" The Tralkyz pointed a claw at a dot on the global holograph, and the image expanded to focus on a small community of bipeds. "The military base on one of the icy islands off the shore of the peninsula now known as Alaska we're currently quartered on."

Murmurs rose, only to be silenced by Tur. "Intriguing. How?"

"I took the liberty of catching a few strays wandering around in motorized vehicles. Ikara feels she has a good enough handle on their psyche to emulate appropriate responses to any conceivable inquiry. Vit Na has assembled some of the best mimics in our group to match every Jing Pen voice in this nest. She can already match half of them herself.

"Brajay has been able to dissect one specimen's brain. He's already gotten to the hippocampus and recreated fine details of memory. The crumb-snatcher didn't survive the process, but we learned much of what we have to know." Bo Tep paused, casting a quick glance at Doh. "And there are many more where it came from." He gave Tur a closed-mouth grin.

"With the help of Jeen's mastery of their digital communications web, we can follow their every move, and they'll never even know anything is amiss."

Tur couldn't suppress a smile of satisfaction as he nodded approval. "Do it. Take any personnel you need."

Jeen's research paid off. Schematics pulled from the Pentagon files revealed the remote Eareckson Airforce Base lodged on the

Alaskan archipelago called the Rat Islands. For the past twenty years, the installation had remained a fortified secret against Soviet incursion and hidden from the American public. The ease with which the Jing Pen fortress fell surprised even Bo Tep.

"Most of the sentry animals were spared and taken for special retraining. Surgically," he emphasized. "Fortunately, the four-legged animals were even easier to deal with than the two-legged ones. All alarms were reset, and routine was reestablished to emulate situation normal."

"For the sake of comfort, we set up a control center in a series of connected hangars after the disposal of excess aircraft," Jeen reported. "We have the five top-ranking Jing Pen corralled in the control room for interrogation."

Bo Tep was listening so intently to the report, he missed Tur's entry into the hangar. The High Commander advanced and stood beside Bo Tep in silence.

"There were no specifics on the 'Bethlehem Incident' recorded in their database," Bo Tep said.

Shifting his shoulders suddenly, Bo Tep reached for one of the captives and shoved it off-balance, as if he knew instinctively that one of them knew more than it let on.

"What are your plans for the alien ship that you attacked this morning?" Bo Tep questioned it from a respectable distance. Its garment had been stripped away earlier for examination. The little animal was pale and shaking uncontrollably in the open hangar.

Bo Tep looked to Jeen to confirm he was speaking the correct language to the creature. She nodded, projecting her own confusion at the human responses, perplexed despite her calm, confident exterior.

Bo Tep repeated his question again more deliberately. This time, he stood a little closer. The bipedal mammal, now cringing, still said nothing.

The limits of Tralkyz patience reached, Bo Tep snatched the wretched creature up in his hand, drew it up to his own face, and spoke a third time through clenched teeth. "Where and when is the next attack coming?"

The man stammered, "Ah—ah—ah—" Its shivering gave way to a speechless cold sweat.

"Don't give me that gibberish, I know you—"

"Please, don't eat me, *please!*" the human general begged.

"—understand what I'm—"

Just as the meaning of the general's plea sank in, Bo Tep realized that there was a copious flow of clear, yellow fluid running from the man's legs onto the encircling Tralkyz fist.

Bo Tep dropped him almost involuntarily and unsuccessfully tried to suppress a dry heave.

"Eat it?" Bo Tep stomped at the fleeing animal to encourage its retreat; wholly unnecessary, as the creature scurried as far from the Tralkyz as it could. "How disgusting can you get?" Bo Tep searched his fellow Efilu for empathy. "*Eat it?* Nasty little milk-sucker."

All at once the hangar filled with hearty laughter. Tur slapped his leg in glee.

It was the first time Tur had really laughed since leaving Tiest.

Bo Tep, now embarrassed, found nothing funny in the situation. "Look, that urine could have been infected or poisonous. It could have gotten into my eyes, my mouth—you remember how vicious Weyef said they were." Shaking the noxious excretion from his hand, Bo Tep found a pressured water source and hosed his arm from his elbow down to his fingers.

Weyef and several others had joined in on the laughter. The humor of Bo Tep's predicament finally hit home, but he suppressed his own chuckle. Perhaps they should try a different tactic.

Ikara approached the group of confused humans and repeated each of Bo Tep's questions in a soft, calming voice. The humans were obviously less intimidated by her smaller form and harmless appearance. Still, they said nothing.

Without cracking a smile, she added, "If you don't answer me, you'll have to answer him." She pointed to Tur.

Settled in the shadows, Tur appreciated Ikara's line of thought and stood. Battle mode matched the implied threat best. Eyes retracted, darkening to empty sockets from the prospective of the little mammals. Tur armored up, ears rising and stiffening sideways.

Red. Animem thrust the notion to mind from the depths of the So Wari tarn. *Glowing red. It terrifies Jing.* Tur gazed at the creature, battle vision stirring empty sockets to fiery radiance.

"And we know when you are lying, too," Ikara fomented dread in perfect English. "The price exacted for each untruth will be a limb of your body—at his discretion, of course."

Intimidation fulfilled, answers flowed freely and accurately from all five human officers until dawn.

Chapter Sixteen

— STEALTH TECHNOLOGY —

E stimates from their database indicate dozens of plat-
form-type satellites with scores of fission devices on each
one," said Devit. What he'd learned from the interrogation
affirmed the general Efilu pessimism.

"That's not great news, Devit," Tur chuffed, "but you and
Jeen have done well adapting basic crystal integration modules.
Through the feed of simple binary data streaming between Jing
Pen computer systems, we've been able to stay a few steps ahead
of them."

Devit had taken over as Tur's chief advisor, if not executive
officer. His insights had proven most valuable. At Tur's nod, he
continued his report. "The good news is that none of them can
even match the maneuverability or speed of the shoddily-con-
structed ship the *ReQam* overtook before the 'Incident.'" Devit
indicated the space shuttle *Challenger II*, recovering its prepro-
grammed orbit about the planet. "Now it's simply a matter of how
fast repairs can be made on the *ReQam*."

"Car Hom has requisitioned virtually all high-tech machinery
to effect repairs," Tur said, filling in the smaller meg on the state

of affairs in orbit. "The hull remains intact, but a third of the inner core has to be completely rebuilt. If not for Stihl's actions, the damage would have been much worse."

Tur could feel his blood pressure rising already. He knew he had to get off this subject, and fast.

"Progress reports indicate that the repair process is consuming an exorbitant amount of energy and most of our crew. We have only a minimal complement of the original surface parties left here on Fitu." Tur thumped his tail on the floor to indicate ground level. "At this rate, we may not even have enough power to maintain orbit, much less return home after the essential repair work is done." The High Commander's frustration was almost palpable.

Devit added, "Most of those personnel have been reassigned to the restoration effort and the remainder are engaged in keeping the Jing Pen militia occupied during this vulnerable recess. Of the seven sub-parties on the planet's surface, only Doh's group continues the search for algae. Fortunately, there is minimal biped encroachment into the open oceans. Other mammals, so far, have proven much less troublesome."

As they came to the end of the hall, Tur stopped walking and rubbed his chin. "Doh is on to something quite promising," he said. The High Commander then dismissed Devit and opened the folding door to begin his next meeting with his data integration chief.

"The interlocking computer network is proving more convenient than expected," said Jeen, obviously quite pleased with herself. "Amazing how adaptable even primitive tools are, when you're forced to use them."

The soft antlers covering her protective head frill bounced gently as Jeen looked from the view plane to the High Commander, arms folded in pride.

She has every right to be proud, Tur conceded.

"We've been able not only to follow the plans of our little contenders, but also to confound them. Fortunately, they're still looking for us in 'Northern Africa,' as they call it. Weyef has seen to it that all traces of our presence were completely erased from the Siberia, Venezuela, American Gulf Coast, and Nigeria excavation sites."

"What?"

Jeen clarified. "I'm sorry, Commander. These are the English descriptions for the locations we've occupied. It makes sense to refer to them with these Jing Pen designations, as the pre-Exodus geography is obsolete. I think we discussed this."

"Well, what about the old Sulenz city?" Tur asked.

"They can look all they want in the so-called Arabian Peninsula region. Weyef has adequately probed it from the air. The Sulenz metropolis is sunken so deep they'll only siphon off the light supernatant refuse, clueless to the artifacts underneath it.

"Our takeover of this Eareckson Air Force Base has raised no suspicions so far. These Aleutian Islands are considered remote. In fact, in accordance with orders from their main military head-quarters—a place called the Pentagon—we've launched several squadrons of stealth bombers in search of the 'alien invaders.'"

In anticipation of his next questions, she explained with a giggle, "Flying machines. And, as Bo Tep surmised, 'top-of-the-line,' no less. Ikara plans to have the pilots report nothing back."

Lost in thought for a moment, an expression of concern crept across Tur's face. "No," he finally said. "Let them report nothing *new*. Keep track of reports from the other bases. If our Jing Pen report significantly less than the others, it may raise suspicions."

"Commander, I really think you're giving them too much credit," Ikara protested.

"Maybe. Still, have our pilots report only what they are expected to see—no more, no less. Too much information may prompt a visit from one of their leading officers." After his decree, Tur asked, "Anything else from your perspective?"

Jeen thought for a moment, then replied, "Not at this time, Commander."

Tur acknowledged her report's conclusion with the merest nod of his head.

"Bo Tep?" he prompted. "Peterson Air Force Base?"

"We're ready to go with the infiltration, Tur," Bo Tep answered. "It's the nerve center for their space-based activities, at least military ones, but we can't hold another installation with the personnel we have available. If we spread ourselves any thinner here, we'll start to make mistakes."

Tur nodded, his nascent respect growing into admiration for this meg.

"We need to get in, do some harm, and get out before they know what hit them." The Tralkyz continued. "I'm obviously too big to efficiently navigate those halls. So are my seconds. There are only ten meren small enough to do the job. Of those, only three could do the job right." Bo Tep hesitated a moment. "Loz, Vit Na, and Gober Dil."

"What?" Tur blurted the thought before he caught himself.

"They'll have So Wari backup from Stihl and Moc. They'll be in place already, of course." Bo Tep's briefing allayed Tur's distress and showed surprising diplomatic skill. "Vit Na is best equipped to coordinate the mission."

He chose the order of that roster carefully. First Loz—whose loss everyone could live with, and who has nearly supernatural speed—then Vit Na, followed up closely by the Wilkyz, Gober Dil, Tur realized. Intermediate in size between Tralkyz and Melkyz, Dil will sport overwhelming strength relative to the Jing Pen bipeds. Also, the Wilkyz's special time-splitting talents would not only surge a force multiplier effect, but he'd cause enough confusion to draw attention from Vit Na.

Naturally, Tur had the utmost confidence in Vit Na's own innate talents for survival.

"When will they go?" Tur asked.

"Very shortly," Bo Tep answered solemnly.

"So soon?" Tur's thought bubbled out as an escaped private sentiment.

Bo Tep understood the intended question that Tur tried to reel in. He nodded silently to affirm that there was enough time for Tur to say his goodbyes to Vit Na.

"We have just enough port thread left to get them inside undetected," Bo Tep said.

Before he could finish, Tur demanded, "How do you plan to get them out?"

"Stihl and Moc will launch an attack from the west of the base, using their personal spheres to control a couple of prefabricated force fields I managed to appropriate from a shipment of equipment returning to the *ReQam*."

Bo Tep waited a respectful moment for an admonishment he knew Tur would not voice, then continued. "The incursion team will escape eastward in a similar force field, to a prearranged rendezvous in the marshes that Vit Na discovered while we were filtering the crude waste. We can pick them up later.

"The ones who will be in the most danger, actually, are Moc and Stihl. The Jing Pen are going to throw everything they have at those two. However, with the force fields, some old-style weapons we've fashioned, and their natural armor, they should be all right."

"Well thought out." Tur reviewed the sketchy holographic images laid out before him. "The two So Wari could, of course, burrow to a safe depth under the dry, rocky soil and hide in a prearranged cavern until rescued. Wasn't Stihl reported as injured in the explosion?"

"Why—? Oh...yes." Bo Tep shared the common tendency to overestimate So Wari recuperative powers, a self-perpetuated myth.

"Is he up to this?" the high commander queried.

Bo Tep answered with a noncommittal, "Brajay thinks he is."

"Fine," Tur approved. "Send a summary of your proposal to Car Hom. Let's keep him in the loop."

"We're in," Vit Na announced. The trio had breached the perimeter and entered the base proper undetected. She got no acknowledgment from outside.

What next, team leader? she thought to herself. *I can't lean on tactical advice from the outside on this one.*

Neither Tur nor Bo Tep would fully trust Loz with responsibility for a while yet, not to mention the doubts held by Vit Na or Gober Dil. In all likelihood, had he been chosen, Loz would have come up with some pride-saving excuse not to lead the assault himself.

"Okay. We split up and cover the key areas of the base depicted in the schematics." Intimately connected to Loz and Gober Dil, Vit Na referenced the images scavenged from the Aleutian database. "Go."

The plan called for Vit Na to bring up the rear while Loz and Gober Dil disrupted the base routine and, under cover of invisibility, destroy the computer system during the ensuing chaos. She pried open an air duct, pulled up into it, and closed the lid behind her, then waited, counting one hundred of her own heartbeats.

Rate's a little fast. Her mind reaching through the man-made walls, Vit Na projected, "Loz, report your location."

"Section two, level three." His thought projection was a little faint.

"Level three? Already? You really do move fast," she praised.

"That's why I'm here," Loz projected. "Uh-oh. Something's coming. Talk to you later."

She felt the tension in his last thought. It made her nervous. Sooner or later she, too, would have to face at least one of these Jing Pen. She had never faced wild animals without guards before.

It's time to check in with Gober Dil.

"Dil?" she asked. "What's your situation?"

"I'm fine. Nothing has seen me yet. I think I'm safely out of sight for the moment. I'll just wait for your signal to begin."

I guess it's all on me now, she thought.

Vit Na took a cleansing breath before proceeding out of the air duct. She reviewed the plan for the seventh time.

Step one: Cut off all outside communications. I'll put the routine communication simulator Jeen designed in place first. It looks like a simple crystalline module. She says for a while no one in here will know they've been cut off, and no one out there will know the difference between our relay and their comrades' broadcasts. I hope she knows what she's doing. I sure don't.

Step two: Divert their attention from the weapons control center. That will be up to Dil, with some support from Loz.

Step three: Detonate that orbiting arsenal before it can do any more harm to the ReQam. Yeah. Easy enough.

She didn't dare think about step four: get out of there alive.

Loz had sounded tense, even at this early stage in the operation. *It wouldn't surprise me if Tur had threatened to end his life if he allowed any harm to come to me,* she mused. *I wish he'd quit doing that.* She took some comfort in the thought anyway.

Vit Na proceeded through the well-guarded halls of the installation, invisibly passing sentry after sentry. She *Blended* well in the dim lighting. She had closed all her sebaceous glands to further minimize her already-faint scent. *Probably a wasted effort on these limited creatures, but why take chances?*

She entered the telecommunications center unseen. It buzzed with activity. Her objective sat on the far side of the room, blocked by several alert-looking operators.

Why does the target always have to be on the other side of danger? she lamented.

The tension level in the room was mounting rapidly. Vit Na didn't know why, but she had a feeling that something bad was about to happen. She wanted to confirm Loz and Dil's whereabouts before proceeding and reached for them.

Why can't I read their feelings? Vit Na hadn't noticed before, but in the newly occupied headquarters at Eareckson Air Force Base, Efilu were forced more and more to supplement thought projections with verbal communication and body language.

It dawned on her, *The inhibition factor! Maybe it interferes with our intimate communication, too.* She remembered her theory on the reason for the big brain: inhibition of extraneous intrusive thoughts. She looked around the room again at the group of human beings. *Minds too primitive to cope with the myriad of intimate communications around them could be modified to block them out or suppress them within a given vicinity.*

Vit Na opened her mind wide that she might hear any enlightened thoughts. The silence was deafening.

She tried to relay the information to Loz and Gober Dil. "Loz, report!" she projected. Nothing. "Dil, can you sense me?"

"Yes, but you're very vague," Gober Dil responded, his projection muted. "I'm getting little more than impression. Are you injured?"

"No. The Jing Pen are having an unexpected impact on our communications. I think the interference is related to the number of active Jing Pen minds in the immediate area. I can't reach Loz at all!" She tried hard to keep panic out of that last projection.

"May I suggest we adhere to the original plan for now?" Gober Dil offered. "If Loz is still mobile, he'll do his part on cue. Just remember to try to reach both of us when we're clear of this facility."

The feelings she picked up from Gober Dil were less reassuring than the content of his thought projection.

This really complicates matters, she thought.

It was a small team to begin with. The first such operation she had ever led. *Now, this. If anyone gets into trouble, we won't be able to contact the others or even headquarters. Turtle-spit! Why does Loz have to be the one out of thought range? He's unpredictable enough as it is.*

She didn't know Loz as well as she knew Gober Dil and hoped the rumors about the former were wrong.

Vit Na spotted an opening. The mulling Jing Pen were now settling down. She moved cautiously, but deliberately, toward a panel in the main computer complex. She placed a small piece of resin in her hand and manipulated it as Jeen had instructed. Vit Na worked fast. The resin hardened into the configuration Jeen had described. It fit inconspicuously into the empty parallel port in the central processing unit of the computer, with room to spare. She carefully eased out of the room, weaving between the occasional ambling human. She retreated outside, to a corner of the dark hall, to await her cue.

It wasn't long before a siren went off. Armed men came running down the hall, right past her.

Right on time, Vit Na thought nervously.

She reassured herself that Gober Dil would keep them occupied. *They won't know they're fighting only one being for hours, if at all. If Loz is still on the loose, he'll be cutting as many of the remaining outside cables as possible.*

She checked the volume of incoming electronic messages to evaluate his progress; the number was dropping off quickly.

Good.

The integrating resin would act like a minicomputer, simulating appropriate responses to outgoing messages. At the same time, it would continue the usual routine updates to maintain the illusion of normalcy to the outside world.

That's it, she affirmed as the count reached zero. *The last of the communication cables are out of operation.*

Restlessness, the bane of any stalker's hunt, was her undoing. She moved carelessly, revealing the slightest distortion.

Just then, one of the soldier bipeds stopped, made a quick turn, and began to inspect the corner where Vit Na was hiding. It used a handheld light source to sweep the area. Vit Na could feel herself on the verge of panic.

Go away, go away, go away! She projected the command as hard as she could at the soldier, but there was no change in its behavior. *Why is he still coming? Can he see me or sense me somehow?*

Vit Na could take it no longer. She reached out for the creature's throat and squeezed its larynx, remembering that they could project thoughts no better than they could receive them.

The desperate squirming of the animal continued to heighten Vit Na's anxiety. She instinctively gripped its neck firmly and tilted its head to one side with her thumb until she heard a little crack. The Jing Pen's body instantly went limp on the side opposite the injury. It struggled even more desperately for freedom as she tilted its head the other way with her index finger to achieve total paralysis. Presently, she breathed a sigh of relief as her victim succumbed to asphyxiation.

She tossed the carcass behind her, expanding her *Blend* to hide it, too, from sight. Then Vit Na resumed her vigil in the corridor, as if unperturbed by the encounter, except for a tentative look back at the motionless form followed by a shudder.

Vit Na stirred restlessly. *I may be moving too soon, but I can't abide this rotting fur-mite at my tail a heartbeat longer.* She made her way down the hall toward what the schematic indicated as the War Room. *Dil should have lured or scared the vermin to outer chambers.*

Vit Na had indeed arrived too soon. One of the alter egos of the Wilkyz was still challenging armed guards when she arrived. Carefully *Blended*, she skirted around the activity and moved toward the detonation relays. She activated them in sequence.

One of the armed men in the room noticed the changing display on a transparent polymer screen in the middle of the room. The biped hesitated only a moment, then spun around to confront the intruder it expected to see at the control panel. Seeing nothing, it repositioned to avoid damaging the delicate equipment and sprayed metal pellets in the general direction of the disturbance.

Vit Na made no sound as the stray bullets bit into her flesh. Only Sharu discipline fettered an instinctive shriek of agony. She spied an air duct she knew would lead her to safety and to the end of her portion of the mission.

It was Vit Na's movement that gave her away. As she fled from where she had been injured, her spilled blood became visible. The soldier saw it. He followed the trail from the spatter on the floor to the opened air duct and launched a grenade into it. It exploded, throwing her clear.

As she lost consciousness, Vit Na became visible.

—◖●◗—

Stihl felt as if he had been beaten with a tree. He hadn't realized how badly the explosion on board the *ReQam* had shaken him. As he crouched among the rocks, he felt the stiffness that had insidiously gripped his body. His muscles rebelled against renewed movement.

The sun had set long ago on Peterson Air Force Base as he'd watched. The night remained quiet, lit sporadically by bright lamps that swept surrounding areas with their beams. The sudden eruption of activity signaled the completion of phase two of Bo Tep's strategy. *Hopefully, phases three and four were completed as well,*

Stihl thought. *The alarms are as easy to spot as Bo Tep predicted. It will be pure pandemonium. Our cue.*

Stihl calmed his heart and shut his eyes. Lids warmed up to an almost glowing red, and his *Conflict Vision* scoped the area. His creased pelt smoothed and hardened over engorged muscles. Armored for combat, the difficult part began: waiting.

When the base alarms finally sounded, Stihl signaled to Moc, who lurked some twenty head lengths across the pass from him. They moved out along divergent paths to commence their assault.

Stihl fired the first round of phosphorus grenades. The spread covered the entire compound with spectacular explosions. As the assorted animals ran out to their respective stations, Stihl cut them down with rapid-fire bursts of force, which he released from the storage field that enveloped him.

Amazing! he marveled. *It works perfectly.*

Apparently, these creatures didn't even have a defense from a rudimentary ion-stream assault. Several biped groups seemed to triangulate on the source of the salvo and sought shelter behind a piece of heavy mecha. It only took a few pulses for Stihl to realize he couldn't effectively penetrate the reinforced metal with simple charged particle blasts.

Damn, he thought. He needed to keep Moc out of the fray for a little longer, as reserve firepower. Then it came to him. *The Jing Pen assume they're evading bullets that follow parabolic trajectories.*

It was then a simple matter of directing the high energy ion stream along electromagnetic force lines around and under the vehicle shielding them. The human soldiers were totally committed to their current position, and therefore easy prey.

Stihl launched another round of phosphorus grenades. *It's surprising what one can create from handy natural material,* he thought.

The noise and glare of his assault were effective in maintaining a state of confusion, but Stihl knew they would also attract attention from other dens. *Well, now I've kicked the nest. Heavily-armored vehicles will be more resistant to these weak weapons. An attack force sent in from a fully operational section would be less confused by the distraction tactics.* A low-frequency rumble beneath his feet heralded the Jing response force.

And here they come! Stihl was too far away from the sheltering hills to take cover when the human assault force came in. *Damn! Faster than I thought.*

Armored craft hovered, suspended on whirling metal blades, firing explosive missiles, just as Weyef said they would. Larger aerial vessels clumsily, but quickly, unloaded land-based machines that immediately began tracking the source of the attack against their nest. The direct impact of the missiles missed their mark, but the resulting concussion shook Stihl off balance.

His personal shield held firm. He counted fifteen turtle-like machines to the right and twelve to the left. *The aerial machines have dropped back to continue the attack from what they must have determined to be an optimal distance.* Stihl scanned the area. *Most of the machines remain within my sphere of influence.*

He had an idea. Removing the remaining fifty phosphorus grenades from the folds of his skin, Stihl tossed them into the field bank he had used as the source of his EM ion pulses. Then, marking individual objectives, he preset each pulse to target one machine. He planned to wipe out every war machine in sight in a single sweep. Of course, that would leave him totally without retaliatory capability against heavy weapons. Moc would have to take over to give him an escape route. Certain the Efilu incursion team had done its work by now, he decided to go all out.

Stihl projected the plan to Moc, who waited quietly in the foothills. Just then, a bright flash lit the night sky. Stihl did not have Weyef's acute Vansar vision, but he knew it to be a nuclear explosion in the upper atmosphere. *Vit Na did it!*

The momentary distraction was his undoing. Three of the turtle-like machines charged over the horizon, firing missiles at close range. They caused his little "surprise" to detonate—around *him*. Stihl's personal shield collapsed, overwhelmed by the blasts.

The other war machines intensified their assault, as if they could somehow sense weakening in their unseen opponent. Stihl reeled back in agony from the conflagration, fending off the continuing hail of projectiles with hand and tail.

He had mustered enough concentration to signal Moc to begin her attack when he realized that the bulk of the attacking force had already answered another offensive. Moc had picked up on Stihl's plan and launched a shower of grenades that were each perfectly on target.

One of the little metal turtles continued its approach. Before taking a hit from Moc, it managed to fire an explosive missile at point-blank range into Stihl's unprotected chest.

The impact sent Stihl's heart into spasms. He crumbled to the ground, barely able to move. His peripheral circulatory system had weathered the assault well enough to support protective skin and muscle tone, as well as supply nourishing blood flow to his brain. His thick So Wari down remained fused into the strongest natural armor ever developed on Fitu or anywhere else in the known galaxy. But he knew that soon, even these defenses would not be enough.

He sensed Moc rushing to his aid through the embattled hillside and stopped her with a faint thought projection. "You can't burrow and carry me at the same time, Moc. Rescue was not included in this mission." After a pause that could only equate to a mental gasp, he said, "Tur cannot afford to lose us both. Objective achieved. Follow the plan!"

The logic was inescapable, of course. The fissionable material in those satellites threatening the *ReQam* had been detonated. Moc turned with immeasurable hesitation.

Stihl watched his mer-betrothed disappear into the hillside as the heavy weapons swung back to fire on his now-defenseless form. The bullets ripped through seared flesh even as Stihl crawled defiantly in their direction. He thought of that nuclear explosion and hoped the *ReQam* had escaped destruction.

He glared at the enemy closing in. His final thought filled his consciousness as he took his last breath.

We just can't lose to these vermin.

Moc heard the thought with remarkable clarity and recorded it for debriefing later as she followed Stihl's final orders. The shock of his impending loss triggered an unscheduled ovulation. She quickly buried the excrement under rock and rubble. She felt the fire of his life go out. *Her* synespira's *life*. He who should have become her mate.

Chapter Seventeen

— A RAT IN THE CAGE —

Vit Na awoke in a reinforced concrete cell. Metal mesh stretched across the only opening. Steel bars, three fingers' breadths in diameter, supported the mesh from ceiling to floor at eight-finger intervals. The mesh looked remarkably fragile, until her eyes focused on a faint reflective surface just in front of it. The entirety of the barrier was encased in six-finger-thick, clear, hardened polymer.

There's no obvious opening mechanism on this side of the portal. Vit Na made no attempt to move.

She could make out six figures beyond the barrier. Two were moving; the others were stationary. As one of the blurry silhouettes moved across her field of vision, she identified a portal framed in the same steel as the bars, hinged on the outside.

Vit Na had observed all she could without moving her head, which lay on something soft, exuding an unpleasant odor. A dim light source behind her glowed from some type of whirring electronic mechanism. She lay on a table, a white sheet draped across the length of her body. *The texture suggests a blend of various plant fibers,* she observed. She estimated its weight at ten ounces, based on the average pressure she felt exerted on her chest. *The weave is remarkably uniform for such primitive manufacture.*

Vit Na turned her attention inward. She assessed her volume status and metabolic reserves. *Odd. Metabolic reserves are disproportionately low in comparison to circulating volume—defies the standard ratio. Which is correct?*

She had no idea how much she had bled. *My loss of consciousness may have been simply due to fainting from the pain.* She had no way of being sure. The highborn mer had never been injured before.

Vit Na hesitated in her analysis. *I had better go through this methodically,* she decided, even as she realized her fear to learn the extent of her injuries. *What if I'm permanently crippled?* The notion itself repulsed her. *That line of thought must cease immediately.*

She went on to her neurological review. Without moving a muscle, Vit Na swept her attention up and down her body. Both motor and sensory functions were intact. *I can't find any neurological deficit. Great, but I still don't know what happened to me!*

The wound was deep. A piece of her left lung was missing, along with a cartilaginous segment of the ninth rib. Necrotic tissue had been carefully cut away and bleeding minimized with some kind of cauterization. *Ozone trace.* Breathing hurt a little, but she would manage. All other visceral organs functioned adequately. The chest wound had some sort of complex dressing on it.

I'll have to learn more about these new surroundings first, Vit Na decided. *At least before I deal with my hosts.*

A contraption of metal wires, sheathed in a plastic material that reeked of decay, and thin tubes made of a similar material, carried fluids and gases in and out of her body. For all its associated paraphernalia, the apparatus provided no anesthesia, but it did seem to supplement her fluid deficit and provide a few simple calories. *That explains the discrepancies in my diagnostics.*

Vit Na avoided extending her sphere of influence to scan her "guest room" for fear of revealing her return to consciousness. *Better limit my investigation to passive senses.*

The Melkyz mer listened with super-hunter-born acuity. The sound of fluid rushing through the tiny tube leading into her side could be traced to a source three head-lengths away from her. She shifted her half-shut eyes ever so slightly to her left to see a gleaming silver pole supporting a mechanical pump.

Suddenly, another sound from her right, just out of sight, caught her attention. Vit Na almost reacted instinctively by turning her head but checked the urge. Her peripheral vision detected a vague, furtive movement toward her bed. Long moments of silence followed.

She waited.

She heard a scurrying sound to her right that made her skin crawl. This time, the movement was more distinct—*and there's more than one source!* She inhaled through her nose. *Jing scent. My captors, no doubt.*

She remained still as something tugged at her sheet and then let go. Presently, she felt tiny hands grip the end of her tail hanging over the table's ledge, but she resisted the urge to shake them off. One of the mechanisms attached to the ceiling moved as if tracking movement on the floor wherever she heard sounds.

Surveillance! I knew it.

The scurrying activity in the room increased.

What next? I can't play dead forever. They'll poke and prod me until I have to react, she guessed. *Better to respond to them with the most non-threatening posture possible. I may even learn what happened to the rest of my team—and the ReQam.*

Vit Na drew a deep breath. Pain lanced through her side, but no air leaked from the wound. She sat up.

No restraints—hmm, interesting. They want to see what I'll do. So… what's my next move?

She looked around for her hosts. What she saw were small, hairy, four-legged mammals with tapered snouts, whiskers, and hairless tails. These were like the mammals she remembered from the real world, back home and on Tiest. She waited for one to approach, but they kept their distance.

Apparently, this wheeled apparatus tethered to my side is designed to be mobile. Vit Na swung her legs off the table. *This thing won't encumber my walking, for all the good that will do.* She cringed. *From the looks of this chamber, someone means for me to stay a while.*

A gray animal approached close to her. The largest of the bunch, it bared its teeth aggressively. Its hair was a bit coarser than that of the others, its skin and ears scarred. Most of the others appeared more kempt, almost delicate, and had soft, white hair. These creatures kept to the shadowy corners and huddled together.

A few other unkempt grays lurked under the table. Under the leadership of the big one, they advanced. Sharp, little teeth sank into Vit Na's flesh.

Is this some kind of greeting ritual? she wondered. *Or are they trying to do me harm?*

When the leader's nip drew blood, Vit Na decided she was not going to participate in this custom, no matter what its purpose. She shook them off of her as gently as she could. Then she tried to make contact with the big one. *Maybe some of these smaller creatures retained the ability for direct communication,* she reasoned. *Good selection criteria for first contact.*

The large rat became bold, perhaps sensing helplessness. It climbed onto the table, then into her lap. Vit Na could see it well now. It was male, malnourished, dragging a broken tail. Scars of narrowly won battles, visible in its sparse hair. The rodent breathed concentrated squalor.

She brushed the varmint aside, a bit more vigorously this time. The group of them scrambled and cowered in a dim corner, but the broken-tailed rat still peered at her with that hungry look. Lights flicked on in the outer chamber and a beam shone through the bars, sweeping her cell. Reflexes drove her to *Blend*, but Melkyz guile kept her cool. Her movements had attracted the attention of the larger animals patrolling outside the cell—and, perhaps more importantly, those contraptions on the ceiling.

Great! Now there will be more of the curious pouring in. Invisibility would do no good at this point.

She lifted the tubing and again traced its length to the machine on the pole. The fluid levels in the containers were low. *Whatever they're pumping into me, they're almost done,* she realized. She concentrated on the differences in the content of the blood returning from the damaged area of her body.

Hmm—lipids, carbohydrates, electrolytes, and water. There was something else that she could not quite identify flowing with the nutrients. She made a specific effort to metabolize it at entry to her blood stream. She would take no unnecessary chances.

Vit Na knew her body would need real food soon enough. She drew her knees close to her chest and rested her face between them.

"Perfect!" Tur reviewed Doh's data on the algae specimens. "You say that these—these *Skeewii*, they called themselves—were cooperative with you?"

"Yes," Doh said proudly. "The peoples of the seas. We've collected enough yellow algae to replenish our supplies using cultivation methods—with some help from accelerated maturation technology, of course. Not actually golden algae, but close enough, I think."

Tur decided to let the scientist have this moment of victory. *He's earned it.*

"All the same, I want the genetic code recorded and duplicated for each team leader," Tur said.

"As you wish," Doh said. He excused himself to make preparations. "One more thing, Doh." Tur stopped the Kini Tod at the conference room door. "I want your gel network. We are basically defenseless here, and I've heard nothing from Car Hom since the explosion. Until we know for sure what happened to the *ReQam*, we're on our own. We're going to improvise a bit."

Doh's shoulders seemed to droop past the soft, rounded limits Tur thought they could sink to.

Fun's over, Tur thought, nearly feeling sorry for Doh as he went off to comply with the disheartening command.

"Are you sure about her anatomy?" Dr. Javier Mendez asked as he pressed fast-forward to scan through the video tape.

"Absolutely. Her metabolic rate, eye structure and position, teeth, and general physique all point to a hunting meat-eater," Bruce Stahl responded with confidence.

"I don't know, guys," Robyn Washington objected. "That face...not a maw, not a snout, but a face. Gentle, almost delicate. Certainly, feminine."

"She's a predator, all right. I'd stake my reputation on it," Hollingsworth interjected. "Add to that the fact that she mauled a few dozen armed men at Peterson AFB last week, and I'd say she's pretty good at it," he nodded. "Clinches it in my book."

Max Hollingsworth was the animal trainer/behavioral specialist assigned to Project X. He and Stahl had worked together before, and as far as Max was concerned, when it came to analytic anatomy, Stahl could walk on water.

Their lab was a state-of-the-art affair, arranged in such a fashion that every work cubicle contained equipment tailored to the occupants' needs. Swivel chairs on castors allowed each team member to roll easily out of his or her cubicle for spontaneous discussions. In addition, if all the chairs were turned 180 degrees from their respective workstations, they formed a circle for convenient, impromptu conferences, with minimal interruption of work time.

"We've watched and waited now for three days," Mendez said. "It hasn't killed a single rat. The IV fluids ran out thirty-six hours ago. We're going to watch the first alien in captivity starve before our very eyes if we don't come up with something soon." He scratched his head. "Maybe there are proteins or amino acids that we missed in the screening process, something that it perceives as toxic."

"We were pretty thorough," Stahl answered with bewilderment. "The rats contain everything it needs for survival."

"What about trying to broaden its diet a little? Some predators are taught to eat only certain prey, aren't they?" a shy voice asked nervously.

Mendez, Stahl, and Hollingsworth exchanged an embarrassed glance between them. None of them wanted to admit that the computer geek, Clyde Olsen, had a good point—least of all Mendez.

Without meeting the younger man's gaze, Mendez gave a nod of agreement and said, "We'll take that under advisement. For now, though, we follow our current plan of letting it demonstrate some of its hunting techniques under carefully controlled conditions."

"Chuh!" Robyn Washington blurted over her shoulder as she reviewed the visual analogs of the sounds recorded in the holding cell the previous night. She looked in Olsen's direction and smiled.

"Excuse me, Robyn, is that some language that I don't know? 'Chuh'?" Mendez asked.

"Well, I don't know, Dr. Mendez, do you understand the words 'thank you'? It's English, I believe. Used when someone has helped you out, you know? It seems to me that Mr. Olsen came up with an idea that somehow got overlooked by the mountains of gray matter shared between the three of you guys."

Washington left him and the other two to figure out what "chuh" meant. "Pompous asses," she whispered under her breath and went back to her work with a grin.

Soon, though, the grin faded as frustration crowded the good mood out of her mind. "I just wish she'd make some noise!" she exclaimed.

"You know, I thought only guys made that wish," Stahl jeered. "And usually the morning after, Robbins. Now I guess we have something in common."

He knew the linguist didn't appreciate lewd innuendo, so he enjoyed his joke that much more. Robyn "Baskin Robbins" Washington wouldn't let him get under her skin.

She was unique in many ways, and all jokes aside, the whole team appreciated her importance to the project. Washington had an uncanny flair for languages. Not only was she "fluent in thirty-one different flavors," as colleagues often joked, but she could quickly pick up languages unrelated to any she had ever heard and even duplicate the accents perfectly. She still hated the Baskin Robbins joke, though. Too many other innuendos in it.

Every one of them knew the story of how this African American woman had shocked the Chinese delegation to North Korea a few years ago, when she worked for the Clinton administration. The Chinese translator had taken ill prior to a state dinner. The two camps were struggling to communicate when Washington stepped in and translated for both the Chinese and the Koreans, with nearly perfect accents in both languages. If any human being could communicate with the alien, it would be her.

The final member of the Project X team was arguably the most important. Dr. Hoyt Matthews spoke as he analyzed tissue samples for the twelfth time. "Well, hell! I don't know why it won't eat. I guess it's in a lotta pain from that injury. Intense pain can sometimes cause anorexia. I'll betcha that side of hers is just as sore as a risin'."

Clyde turned to Robyn and whispered, "What's a 'risin'?"

"It's what we call a boil that's ready to bust, back home." The veterinarian scratched his neck as he turned toward Olsen. "Then again, maybe she's just a very finicky eater," Matthews added, his warm smile accenting the laugh lines around his eyes.

With that comment, Mendez could not put it off any further. "We have to arrange to feed her something else!"

I wish it would stop looking at me that way, Vit Na thought as she watched the broken-tailed gray rat watch her.

The big one somehow had taken on the collective mien of the whole pack. They had exchanged places, she and the rat. It stood on its hind legs on top of *her* table. Vit Na sat on her haunches against a wall of the cell. She felt cornered by the rat. She also felt as hungry as the rat looked.

She was light-headed, her eyes glazed. *Properly prepared, I might be able to hide the gamy taste of that little vermin,* she thought.

Revulsion snapped her out of her reverie. A look around the cell again reminded Vit Na of her circumstances. The large gray was looking back at her with a puzzled expression.

I'll never get that hungry, she resolved.

Deep in her heart, she knew she would eventually. Her glycogen stores were already depleted and autodigestion of muscle protein ensued only as a conscious choice—and hard to accomplish, at that. A hundred million years of plenty had reduced her species' fat reserves to a minimum. She needed food, and soon.

A sudden stirring among the guard-animals outside the cage interrupted her fantasies of food. Or were they hallucinations? She wasn't sure anymore.

A large biped approached the door. *One of those glabrous Jing Pen,* she reminded herself: *Human.*

Dressed differently from the others, clad all in white, except for leg and foot coverings, it invaded her cage. The newcomer seemed a bit older than the others and looked extraordinarily overfed as it lumbered into her enclosure.

A notion occurred to her: *Not very intimidating at all.*

It carried something with a white cloth draped over it.

Well, the interrogation at last! she thought. *Maybe I can communicate with them, if I can just hear some more of that babble and watch their reactions. If I'm lucky, they'll speak English like the other Jing Pen we've studied.*

Vit Na moved a body's length away from the door to indicate that she meant no harm and awaited the greeting. To her surprise, the Jing Pen slid his burden just past the door, whipping the drape off as he did. He quickly retreated through the open door, which closed immediately behind him.

Puzzled, Vit Na's nose then eyes soon recognized the raw meat on the tray. Hunger overpowered her. She seized the gift from its place on the floor before her roommates could get at it.

Not only had her desire to parley vanished, but so, too, had her unspoken treaty with the rats. She brushed them off the table with her arm, sending them tumbling across the room.

Vit Na then grabbed the cotton sheet that had covered her body several days before and spread it over the table. She promptly sat on her haunches and surveyed the setting. She placed the tray on the table and set to work preparing her meal.

The meat was lean and thick. She frowned—*not the way I like it, but at this point I really don't care.*

She raked her claws across the steak at an angle, then again at an angle ninety degrees to the first. Turning the meat over, she repeated the procedure. Vit Na sat back and, for a moment, thought she might vomit as she regurgitated stomach juices into her mouth. Then she evenly sprayed them onto her meal. Her patience was rewarded as the digestive enzymes cooked her food right there on the tray. She did the same for the reverse side of the steak, careful to limit the enzyme jet to the meat and avoid the tray.

Satisfied with her culinary effort, Vit Na carefully sliced the now-crispy meat four consecutive times until the pieces were bite-sized. For all her hunger, the consumption of the meal was leisurely, almost dainty.

The observers in the outer room and in the control center watched with fascination. Something seemed very familiar about the process.

"It's like peeking at an aristocrat dining—through a kitchen door, slightly ajar, or an outside window," Matthews whispered.

"Why are you whispering, Hoyt?" Mendez sneered. "She can't hear us."

When finished eating, Vit Na drew a deep breath and exhaled slowly with satisfaction. She rose from the table, carrying the now-empty tray, reached down, and retrieved the small, cloth drape the human had left behind. She covered the tray and replaced it exactly where the man had left it, stood back, and waited.

Shortly, the same overfed biped returned and opened the cell door. As he reached down to fetch the tray, he was frozen by a familiar, but impossible sound.

"Thank you very much. The meal was delicious!"

The biped's complexion went white. He dropped the tray and fled, shutting the door with all his might. Then he nearly collapsed and had to be physically assisted from the anteroom.

Upon seeing this reaction, Vit Na immediately scrambled to the far corner of the room to indicate neutrality.

That experiment could have gone better. Obvious confusion out there, she observed. *In here, too.* She replayed the exchange in her mind. *I hope I didn't get that response all wrong. Hadn't I done something that I was expected to do?*

A delayed notion came to her: *Or maybe I just did something I was not expected to do.*

Chapter Eighteen
— THEY WHO WAIT —

C ar Hom waited, just as everyone else also waited. He had
faith in Vit Na. He had faith in her team. Oddly enough, he
even had faith in Loz.

"Nobody could botch an assignment twice." Car Hom muttered
the thought absently.

"Sir?" Obb responded.

"Huh?" Car Hom became suddenly aware of the awkward
scientist.

The Gen Rost paleontologist was no politician. Obb trembled so
every time he attended to the executive officer. Car Hom noticed
the way he had always warbled with dread in the presence of
super hunters.

The awkward situation couldn't be avoided. Senior staff always
pulled double duty as command and support personnel in times
of crisis. Car Hom had found Obb to be the most qualified of the
remaining team to serve as second-in-command, in the absence of
the designated workforce.

"I asked if you're feeling a thirst to return to the fight," Obb
asked. "Or is something else bothering you?"

"I assure you, I'm too old for the Thirst to draw me in so deep," Car Hom said, but dwelt on the question for a heartbeat or two. "Something else is the bother. It's been nagging at me since before we left the surface." Car Hom balled a fist so tight his forearm plumage stiffened. "But what is it?"

He looked out to the menacing satellites from the vantage of *ReQam's* command center, silently appraising the ship's deteriorating orbit. "We're losing our battle with gravity, despite repairs. There's not enough power to overcome the increasing atmospheric drag."

Obb blinked in confusion.

"We can't generate enough quantum energy to reach the tipping point."

Obb nodded. "Kellis identified the ancient fuel reserves on the fourth planet, but that does us no good. We can't get a landing party there to retrieve it."

Suddenly, Car Hom laughed out loud.

Obb danced nervously back and forth from one foot to the other at the roar.

"I don't know why it didn't occur to me sooner," Car Hom announced.

Obb just looked at him, puzzled.

"There's barely enough time to prepare the command center personnel for what has to be done, let alone to notify Tur." Car Hom regarded Obb with a wry smile. "We really have no choice, anyway."

"What are you thinking, sir?" Obb asked, turning to the gel console.

Car Hom pointed to an image on the tactical display, patted Gen Rost scientist on the shoulder, and said, "Bring that one in closer."

"What a triumph!" Doh swaggered, nearly rocking the boat. "The cycle of life on Fitu is as I theorized, but surprisingly, the seas are populated by a veritable confederation of mammalian species, distant relatives in the clade. The human database classifies them as whales, dolphins, sea lions, otters..."

"Like our own Greater Society?" Tur didn't have to be prescient to anticipate the comparison.

"What a relief to learn that Humankind is not the only intelligent life-form left on the planet!" Doh declared. "Too bad this civilization's collective memory doesn't reach back far enough to reveal what became of the Keepers. The history of the Skeewii, as they call themselves, is nearly as interesting."

"Doh, I don't really care." Tur projected and ended the tail-stroking session. He had praised Doh too much already.

"Of course, sir." Doh sobered. "But this may be relevant."

"Again"—Tur drummed his fingers.—"how?"

"It's just that at one time, they all lived on the land. Those times were dim in the memories of the Skeewii," Doh said. "Somehow, they migrated back to the sea. A guiding force they all called Wholu helped shape them to survive the new environment. Over time, they became aware of one another, first locally, then globally.

"Getting along was difficult at first. Many of the new neighbors in the community were convenient food sources. Eventually certain rules were made to govern behavior in intra- and inter-species encounters. There's been heated debate over the status of their terrestrial cousins. Something important happened among them millions of years ago, but no one in the Skeewii Collective remembers exactly. The only agreement in the history is that there used to be several species of terrestrial biped before a major conflict. When all smoke cleared, the dominant ones were called humans."

Tur had to prod the scientist a bit. "They did not have very good communication skills, those humans," he said, reading from Doh's report. "Men could apparently speak to one another sometimes, but were not always clearly understood. Divergent assortments of that babble again. It seems humans have no concept of interspecies communication."

"Commander, I'm not sure that all the land dwellers were believed to be 'human.' Still, there were those among the Skeewii who felt that humans had a right to at least establish some trade relationship with them." Doh spread stubby hands. "Who knew what riches lay on the land? It was potentially a reservoir of valuable resources. The objects that humans lost or discarded at sea were becoming more interesting by the day."

"The humans seem to rule the land," Tur said, now reading from a dolphin's account, translated as *The Sea Above*. "All other land creatures seem to fear them."

Tur set his gel device down and listened to the firsthand recordings. "...human civilization has always been unstable, however, rising and falling over the centuries in the wake of great wars." A whale spoke, and Tur enjoyed the slow, rich melodious song. "In general, Skeewii policy is to avoid contact with terrestrial animals, with the exception of feeding on the few that stumble into the aquatic domain, the Sea Below. Most of us avoid humans. We can't control the fish, though. Especially those damn sharks."

Doh explained to Tur that the fishlike Jing the humans called dolphins had once been the bipeds' greatest proponents. "They often aided humans who were lost or in trouble at sea. Yet rarely did humans reciprocate with food or other valuable services. Instead, they hunted them."

"It seems the hunting of Skeewii and their protected species has taken its toll," Tur read. "Some species retreated to cities and farms that have been developed in a network of undersea caverns tucked away beneath the continental shelves. There, basic needs, as well as the exchange of ideas, were provided for more than adequately."

"Only a few nomadic tribes and well-trained scientific expeditions go out into open seas these days, and then, mostly at night." Doh finished his report. "Many races were seen so seldom in open seas that mankind had presumed that they were extinct."

Tur was patient with Doh because he conducted the Skeewii meeting virtually. Doh had to hold their attention in confidence; he knew that he had a mission to accomplish. "I described the yellow algae we sought to a host of dolphin scientists. After conferring with a number of manatee colleagues, a group of them took off, presumably to confirm that they had indeed encountered such organisms."

Tur digested the data. "The Skeewii Collective. At least we know where we have to plunder, if we need the trove of algae. That is, if they truly have it."

"As I reflected on the Skeewii situation, I became curious," Doh added. "They built this magnificent culture here, yet they have cut off all contact with the surface-dwellers. The humans could obviously benefit from a lasting relationship."

"And?" Tur asked, already turning to leave the briefing.

"The sea lion I addressed curled his nose a bit and said, 'We are waiting.'" Doh paused.

"Waiting for what?" Tur asked as if on cue.

"The final apocalypse that Mankind will visit upon itself," Doh said, shifting uncomfortably on short legs. "In the end, the Skeewii will survive Man. Then they plan to reclaim the depths and the land between the seas."

Tur found the determination of the Skeewii unsettling. "They've adopted a mission exactly cross purposed to that put forth by the Keepers."

Tur watched with satisfaction as the final entry in Doh's mission log played out. An otter splashed up on the ledge of Doh's vessel, eagerly carrying a seashell full of golden-brown silt. She offered it graciously to Doh. "Will this help?" she asked.

The Kini Todd scientist smiled and expressed the gratitude of the Efilu in the Skeewii language.

"This is what we have come for," Doh said, displaying a specimen. "Living yellow algae." Then he mused, "So close to modern Efilu golden algae that little genetic manipulation will be needed."

A dolphin swam up beside the sealion and offered a brief composition. She spoke to Tur with intimate communication. "This is for you, Elder. That you do not forget us."

Tur read the pearl to himself. "These Skeewii may actually be enlightened." Tur nodded. "Our search is over."

It was now a matter of waiting, and hoping, for the *ReQam*'s repair.

Chapter Nineteen
— SUPERHEROES —

N ow back on the main floor, Hollingsworth vowed to get back on the wagon. Then he remembered he hadn't had a drink in months. The MPs brought him into the observation center, where Washington had forced him into his seat and raised his feet. She then left the room to get him a cool glass of water. Hoyt Matthews, the only team member with medical training, came to his side and took his pulse.

"Look at him!" exclaimed Matthews. "He's sweatin' like a pig an' pantin' like a puppy!"

"Y'all want me to go fetch a cool glass o' lemonade from Aint Bee?" Stahl mocked.

"No, but you can go get me that paper bag on your desk. This ol' boy's gonna pass out if he keeps hyperventilating," Matthews answered. Apparently to show that he too had a sense of humor, he added, "Oh, you might stop to empty it out first, son. Wouldn't want him to choke on that 'London' fried chicken you've got in there."

Stahl scowled as he retrieved the red and white paper bag with the friendly Confederate colonel on it from the nearby desk.

Rebreathing the carbon dioxide from the bag slowed Hollingsworth's respiration to normal. Olsen, however, was still excited.

"We heard it too, Max," he gushed.

Stahl shook Hollingsworth's sweat-soaked shoulder in congratulatory fashion. "She sounded just like Katie Couric on *Good Morning America*, guy." He stepped back and gazed at the monitor to watch Vit Na in fascination, flushed with the joy of the discovery.

Olsen corrected, "Katie's not on *Good Morning America*, she's on *The Today Show*, Bruce."

"Shut up, Clyde!" Mendez snapped as he tried to reestablish order in the room. "Think carefully, Max," he continued when the chatter died down. "Did she say or do anything else we might have missed? Anything hostile?"

Hollingsworth tried to clear his head. "Not that I can think of, Javier. Of course, we'll need to review the tapes to—"

"Been there, done that!" Olsen blurted out. "Her back was to the camera. We couldn't see her face when she spoke." His fingers were already blazing across the keyboard, logging onto the other cameras to see if there was a clean angle somewhere that picked up the momentous event. "The first alien words understandable to humans."

"Well then, we'll just have to ask her to speak to us some more, now won't we?" said Washington, returning with the cup of water. She handed it gently to Hollingsworth.

"Seems to me that someone is out of a job, hon," Stahl teased.

"How so?" Robyn responded.

"If she already speaks English, we don't really need a translator, do we?"

"Fine. We'll send you in next. Then *if* you come back, you can tell us about her language skills. And table manners." Washington seemed to enjoy his apprehension at that last suggestion.

"We've got to inform the president," Hollingsworth said all at once.

"Fuck the president!" Mendez exclaimed. "He'll have his bully boys from Department D down here pumping her full of the truth serum du jour before nightfall. Then we'll have nothing but a corpse from outer space."

Mendez raised his hands for everyone's attention. "This is the discovery of the millennium, folks. No, this base is on radio silence as of right now. I may have been on inactive commission until now, but I still outrank the major who commands this base. No information gets in or out without my say-so."

He looked around for any challenge to his edict. Seeing none, he went on. "I'm going in there next. You all have an hour to prepare. I want a minimum of twenty intelligent questions from each of you for me to ask her. Try to stick to your own disciplines, please."

"Some ego!" Washington said under her breath to Hoyt. "He'll probably claim the credit for inventing Twenty Questions next."

Hoyt chuckled and added in a louder voice, "Can the first question be 'Is it bigger than a bread box,' Javier?"

Everyone, including Mendez, had to laugh at that one.

"And now the disciples of Professor X prepare themselves for the mission of their young lives," Olsen intoned dramatically. "Into the Danger Room go the X-Men, ready to save the world!"

"Will you quit it, Clyde?" Mendez asked, his patience tested.

"Whatever you say, Professor," he answered.

"Don't push me, son, I'm not in the mood. That goes for the rest of you, too!" Mendez panned a glare around the room and everyone sobered.

"Only Olsen could get under Mendez's skin like that." Washington elbowed Matthews and whispered, "Without even trying."

"And that's the beauty of it," the doctor snickered.

Six hours later, Javier Mendez was in the guardroom outside the holding cell. Vit Na watched him interact with the others.

Ah. This one's different, she noted. *He has the same body covering style, but he obviously carries more authority.*

She decided a submissive posture would be most effective. She backed slowly toward the table and sat on her tail and haunches, affecting the facial expression with which they all seemed to greet superiors.

They call it a "smile," don't they? she reminded herself.

Two guards entered with "the chief," a four-legged animal leading a two-legged one by some kind of tether.

Mendez strutted through the door boldly, but he seemed more wary once he, too, was confined by the cage. He pulled up a chair that had been brought in specifically for his comfort and sat.

Vit Na noted that the four-legged guard also sat, while the two-legged guard remained standing. *A pecking order, perhaps?* She watched the seated human produce a sheaf of papers bound at the top by some sort of resin. He looked down at it a few times before speaking.

"My name is Mendez. I'm in command here." Mendez gestured in crude sign language after each syllable, as if to clarify his words. He spoke slowly and loudly. "Do you understand?"

English, she confirmed.

Vit Na noted the flurry of activity the raised voice stirred in the rat pack. They scrambled for the shadows. She waited for the big gray to give some verbal response to "the chief," but there was none. Realizing that he must be addressing her, she cleared her throat and answered the human in clear, soft tones.

"Are you speaking to me or to your friends?" She gestured toward the rats huddling in the shadows.

"Friends?" Mendez looked confused. "Those are only rats. We use them for scientific experiments and sometimes as live fodder for...carnivorous guests. Most of the time, they're just pests. Basically harmless, though. We were very surprised that you failed to catch any of them."

Vit Na was not sure she had mastered the spoken language yet. Puzzled, she asked, "Why would I care to 'catch' one of them?"

"It's obvious from your physiology that you are a predator by nature," he answered. "Study of your anatomy reveals to us that you either were created or evolved to hunt game. Our specialists believe that except for a humanized face and torso, your species is closest to a cross between one of the great cats and a carnivorous kangaroo with that too-long tail and legs, except that you seem to lack some basic features, such as breasts."

Vit Na offered a noncommittal shrug.

"Your hair is so peculiar and light, almost feathery. It's certainly softer than anything we've ever felt. For such rudimentary biology, you're astonishingly complex. Your digestive system is much like ours, but simpler and shorter. This is a tribute to your ancestors' adaptation to a very harsh environment, no doubt. Tell me a little about your planet and life there." The next question was predictable. "Where do you come from?"

Vit Na hesitated. *What can I teach him that he could understand without a year-long prerequisite course?* "Oh, it's much like this place, but warmer." Vit Na waited for his analysis of her answer.

"Go on, please."

She shrugged her shoulders, realizing this was a universal gesture of perplexity. "We...work for food, for ourselves and our families. We try to maintain good health. There are no doctors, as you have here. Most of our medical efforts go into prevention and education. We have no social support for the handicapped or deprived."

"That's too bad," said Mendez sympathetically. "We try to live in peace and harmony with each other and with nature."

"Were there others like myself loose in your facility when I was captured?" Vit Na queried.

"Don't you know?" Mendez asked suspiciously.

"No, I don't. I just remember a great deal of commotion. Then I was attacked."

Vit Na had never lied before. As all Efilu were telepathic, lying was very difficult to accomplish. Being caught in a lie was considered an insult to another's intelligence. *Most embarrassing,* she considered. *Fortunately, this won't be a concern here.*

"What were you doing at Peterson Air Force Base?" Mendez asked.

There was a moment of tension.

"I had orders," Vit Na replied.

"To do what?"

"I'm not sure."

"Did you accomplish your objective before being captured?"

Make him guess a little. "My objective?"

"The explosion."

"There was an explosion?" she asked.

"Yes," Mendez said. "Were you trying to set off those orbiting warheads?"

"Warheads?"

"You mean you didn't know the potential of the devices you detonated?" His questions sounded increasingly incredulous of her ignorance.

Vit Na thought for a moment. *Let's see how far I can take this act.* "I'm sorry, but I don't understand enough of your technology to work any of the equipment I saw."

Javier Mendez thought about her response for a moment.

Vit Na interpreted his expression as doubt. Mendez stroked his chin. *That's a strangely familiar gesture,* she thought to herself with amusement. *Although I doubt that Tur would appreciate the comparison.*

Mendez spoke again. "We have much to teach each other. We would like to learn what travel between the stars is like. It's a pity the starship was destroyed in the blast. What was its relationship to you? Was it chasing your people? Are you a slave, or a worker or something?"

The ReQam—*destroyed.*

Vit Na was stunned by the prospect of never being rescued from this ancient wasteland.

Mendez saw that she could not answer his flurry of questions. He began again. "How do you call yourself?" he asked belatedly.

"I am Vit Na," she answered, distrait.

"You could end much speculation, Vit Na, about alien life forms. There has been much conjecture about alien physiology, but you are not very different from other Earth life forms we know well."

Before she could speak again, the little chief asked, "Just how is it that an alien is so well-suited for life on our world, Vit Na?" He stroked his chin again.

Distracted by the revelation that she might have been one of the only survivors of the expedition and irritated by his tone, she snapped, "Well, it's only natural, as we issued from the Alom and evolved here."

Suddenly, Vit Na felt stupid. *How could I have reacted to such a dangerous question without thinking?* she chastised herself. *There must have been a thousand ways to exploit that opening.*

I'll have to avoid telling them anything they can't get on their own or don't already know. I'll satisfy enough of their curiosity to remain valuable but keep them from figuring out too much more.

"This was once our home, long ago," she began. Before he could ask, she went on. "Millions of years ago, we were forced to leave this place. This world became…inhospitable to us."

Mendez forgot the questions on the page in front of him. "How many millions of years ago?"

She answered his question directly. "Sixty-five."

The guard almost dropped his weapon.

"Then you mean whatever drove your people out was also what killed off the dinosaurs?" Mendez asked, leaning forward in his chair.

Vit Na had heard this word before but did not understand its meaning. "What is a dinosaur?" she asked.

Mendez groped the air in desperation. "Big lizards. Reptiles, like snakes and alligators."

Vit Na floundered for a moment. "I still don't underst—"

She stopped talking when Mendez flipped to a fresh page and began to draw—first a snake, then a crude version of an alligator.

Vit Na said, "But what have these to do with—"

Then, furiously, he drew a picture of a stereotypical Tyrannosaurus rex, with large hind legs, semi-erect posture, short arms, and big, sharp teeth. He turned the tablet to her.

Vit Na stared at it for a moment before slowly taking the pad first, then the pencil. Thinking back to the museum images Weyef captured, Vit Na drew over Mendez's picture, modifying the ears, eyes, mouth, and skin. When she was done, she held the page to face him, offering it back to her host.

Mendez's hands trembled as he took the tablet back and stared in disbelief. Vit Na had sketched a realistic likeness of herself over Mendez's crude drawing.

Mendez's mouth made several contortions before forming the words, "Oh, my dear God."

After a brief recess to collect his composure, Mendez returned to the cage and faced Vit Na. "We have tried to solve the puzzle of how the dinosaurs died out for two centuries. Now you're telling me that they didn't go extinct at all? They just...left?"

Vit Na suppressed a smile. "Something like that."

Skeptical, Mendez asked, "If this is your natural home, then the wildlife here is your natural prey, right?"

"It was," Vit Na agreed.

"Then why didn't you eat the rats when you were hungry? You're certainly capable of catching and killing them. You could have prepared them and eaten them the same way as the other meat."

Shocked, Vit Na glanced at the rats and heaved from her abdomen involuntarily. "What would make you think that I would *ever* eat vermin?" she scoffed.

"We had little information to go on, so we extrapolated from our knowledge of modern predators on Earth. They'd eat anything that moved, if hungry. Especially snakes."

"The long, limbless animals?"

"Exactly!" he said.

Vit Na sought a simple way to clarify the relationship between Efilu and reptiles when she froze. "What kind of meat was it that I ate earlier?"

Mendez said congenially, "That, my dear, was a twenty-ounce porterhouse steak you had."

Vit Na was almost afraid to inquire further, but found she had to. "And... what kind of animal does that come from?"

"The cow. A large grazing animal that lives in herds and is used as a food source."

Vit Na felt relieved. *At least it wasn't pressed rat meat.*

Mendez added, "The cow is a mammal, just as your people must be reptiles of a sort."

He had no way of knowing that just as he had lumped all reptiles and saurian species together, so too had she failed to distinguish between various species of mammals. *I can't believe I ate giant fur-mite meat!* She blenched. *That accounts for that rancid odor.*

"So, how do you like beef?" Mendez asked, misinterpreting her reaction. "It's quite a delicacy for us. How does it compare with the meat you eat at home?"

Vit Na leaned her back against the cool concrete wall. She pressed against it in an effort to relieve waves of nausea. Her facial pallor was invisible behind the soft, black pelt, but nearly all the blood had drained out of her face.

"Can we take a short recess? Perhaps an hour or so? I don't feel very well," Vit Na announced. She saw hesitation.

Desperately, she said in a weak voice, "I need time to more thoroughly assimilate your culture and vernacular language—in order to answer your questions better."

Mendez reluctantly nodded his consent and left the cell with his entourage.

Vit Na closed her eyes and choked back the gastric content threatening to erupt at any moment.

She opened her eyes after regaining control of her stomach. There was a "rat" with two of its friends within an arm's length of her again. They appeared to be sneering at her. Her reaction was like lightning.

Vit Na lashed out with her tail, sweeping all three rodents off-balance, then almost simultaneously crushed them all with a second blow of her tail. She hadn't even looked at her tormentors as she struck.

She brushed the carcasses under the table out of sight and turned away from them with her arms folded across her chest. With as much disdain as she could possibly muster, she muttered to herself, "Vermin!"

"What happened in there?" asked Stahl. "Why did you break off the interview, Javier?" He waited for Mendez at the door to the "lab," as they'd begun to call the observation center. "I can't believe the things that were coming out in that session."

"Why did you stop?" Hollingsworth echoed Stahl's question. "She didn't look like she was in that much pain."

"She became ill, I think, when they began to talk about food," Hoyt said, joining in with a laugh. "Clyde guessed it—she is a finicky eater."

Ignoring everyone in the room, Mendez went directly to his workstation, spouting orders along the way.

"Stahl, I want everything you know or need to know about dinosaurs laid out neatly. Hoyt, help him. Clyde, listen, because I'm only going to say this once. Tap into the Library of Congress and the Smithsonian's archives. Download everything on the evolution of life on Earth from the Triassic Period to the present." He paused briefly. "Also, I want A&P on amphibians, reptiles, birds, and early mammals."

"What's A&P?" Washington whispered to Stahl.

"Anatomy and physiology," Stahl tossed the condescending response back, sotto voce.

Mendez continued issuing his orders to Clyde without interruption. "Pull the files on molecular bio and biochem from my computer in my quarters. They'll be on CD. That should be a good start. Hoyt and Bruce will update you as to any additional requests.

"Robyn, you still have a job," he continued. "Our friend, Vit Na, speaks English fine, but there seems to be some conceptual and maybe some cultural hurdles we'll have to help her over. I think she could be slightly retarded for her kind. She seems to have a lot of trouble answering very simple questions. I want you to get to know her. By her voice, I assume she's female, but we don't know their gender roles for sure. Teach her. Teach her about us, anything she wants to know, but try to keep it simple."

"I know, she's a little *slow*," Washington said, her voice heavy with sarcasm at Mendez's characterization of their guest. "But how do you suggest we all interact with her without falling over one another?"

Mendez's eyebrows tilted out like windshield wipers. It was that silly look he put on that said, "I don't know."

"We could each go into her cell in shifts," Washington offered.

Mendez had not given any thought to that problem yet. If the team was to do its job efficiently, each member would need access to Vit Na. That feat was impossible in such a small cell.

"I'll have to meet with Major Dixon about adapting the gymnasium to accommodate our visitor. Fortunately, we have access to all the Plexiglas one could imagine in Carlsbad, New Mexico. They make the stuff there. The military has been storing the government surplus here at Hennessy Barracks."

Their small army base was not even on the map. It served well as cover for Project X. The compact, state-of-the-art research facility was under the secret authority of retired Lieutenant Colonel Javier Mendez, PhD.

As official commander, Major Dixon was commissioned on the public Air Force duty roster; in actuality, he was directly subordinate to Mendez. The major had wangled this command by proposing, and demonstrating, that waste Plexiglas could be economically recycled. It was quite an accomplishment for an officer with less than a colonel's ranking. Looked great on his resume.

The warehouses were full of Plexiglas scraps. Now their task was just a matter of escape-proofing the gym. Major Dixon's entire battalion would be working all night to finish it. Mendez didn't care. The men could gripe all they wanted; they still reported to the major, and the major reported to Mendez.

Dixon turned out to be a rather eager fellow and very cooperative. *He'll make colonel before forty, yet,* Mendez thought.

Dixon had told Mendez, "These boys can tell their grandkids someday, 'I helped guard the first alien ever captured in history.'"

"Or the first dinosaur." Mendez chuckled, then added, "E. rex, the evolved dinosaur!"

Chapter Twenty
— MOURNING'S SOLACE —

Nothing yet from Car Hom?"
Tur's question had become almost rhetorical by now. He was generally pleased with Bo Tep's intelligence reports, but it had been over two weeks since the *ReQam* was last detected.

"No communications of any kind forthcoming," Bo Tep answered with professional candor.

Tur had long since stopped asking about word on Vit Na.

"We'll recheck the receptor field," Bo Tep said. "It may need recalibrating."

The Efilu ground team had centralized in the northern sanctuary. Eareckson Air Force Base was still secure under Weyef's direction. After acquisition, Bo Tep had turned over the Aleutian base of operations to her.

Tur caught Devit peaking his head out of the conference room. *It's time for the bi-daily staff update.*

"At least our technical support is improving," Devit began. He'd taken stock of the modified equipment. Efilu improvisation at its best. "In spite of the limitations, we've been able to arm and monitor this entire quadrant," the Ironde continued. "Fortunately, the local tribe is routinely monitoring the activity on the rest of the globe and transmitting directly to us at regular intervals. We've been enhancing their signals via simple electromagnetic transducer sensor fields."

"Any new arrivals from beyond the atmosphere, Loz?" Tur's thought projections were solemn. "Even crystal beacons?"

"Not so far," Loz answered, his restless hands constantly in motion. "We're using the most advanced of the orbiting equipment with modifications that Devit and I came up with, but no activity so far, Commander."

Tur looked down the table with concern. On top of this latest news, he noticed that Ikara had been pensive and withdrawn for the past two sessions. "Any reports on U.S. government activity or broadcast news interpretations?" he asked, his ears laid back against his scalp in resignation.

Ikara shook her head without projection or utterance.

Jeen and Kellis exchanged worried glances and looked at Tur in concert. They had both voiced worries about Ikara's coping mechanisms.

Doh broke the silence. "I wish Car Hom would at least signal us with an estimated time of return."

"He's not coming back, you idiot!" Ikara screamed, with searing thought projections landing on Doh like daggers. "He's dead! The *ReQam*'s not coming back because it was destroyed. Who are we kidding? We all saw it go up in a ball of flames!"

She walked over to Tur and began circling him as she shouted hysterically. "We're trapped here! Stuck on a mudhole crawling with hairy monsters!"

Tur approached her deliberately, grabbed her by the shoulders, and shook her thrice. "Ikara, we number only twenty here now: you six department heads and a few technicians. There are only ten or eleven of us that can function as security or combatants, if it comes to that. You are large enough to help in a tough situation, but I need you to maintain control of yourself." He paused, looking her square in the eye. "I can't afford to have one or two of my meren nurse you. *We* can't afford that right now. As much as I need you, I'd be forced to take more *permanent* action." Tur shook her again to drive the point home. "Do you understand?"

Ikara stopped raving. She projected her next thoughts with the utmost clarity. "That famous So Wari efficiency. Eliminate any internal hindrance to the operation. What does the So Wari code of battle say about allowing emotion to interfere with war campaigns?"

Tur's eyes narrowed, and he tilted his head to one side in confusion. "You're losing it, Ikara. We're not in battle."

"Turtle-spit we're not!" she cursed. "We lost thirty meren on the *ReQam*. We lost Stihl in direct battle with these animals. Stihl, a fully trained So Wari warrior!" She beat her fists against Tur's chest. "Now we're hiding from Jing patrols like grubs from a Sulenz pup, while you lament the loss of that Melkyz bitch. Now tell us all again how we are not at war!"

Kellis tried to interject, "They're just fur-mi—"

"Nuk!" Ikara never took her eyes off Tur. "These fur-mites destroyed a class five interstellar Efilu warship. We exterminated the entire Quatal race for less than that. Is this any less a Threat to Life than the Poison itself?"

"How do we know that none of us have been affected by the Poison?" Loz added unhelpfully. "We have no way of scanning for it without the *ReQam*'s equipment."

A group shudder seemed to move through the room. No one wanted to comment on that very real possibility, or its ramifications under these circumstances.

Tur grumbled to himself, *Leave it to Loz to fan the embers of an already-volatile situation.*

The High Commander looked around at his assembled meren. All attended the exchange with intensity, but not even Bo Tep dared wag his tongue the wrong way.

"They're beating us, Tur!" Ikara declared. "These bugs are not only beating a So Wari High Commander, they're intimidating him as well."

Silently, Tur turned his back to them. His expression inscrutable, he walked toward the door.

"*Tur!*" Ikara pleaded.

The warrior half-turned to address the distraught mer. His ears stiffened horizontally, tips turned up and firm. "Ikara. Your point has been made. I trust my point rang equally as clear." Then, to the group as a whole, he said, "We'll reconvene by dark. I want a complete analysis of the enemy's strengths and weaknesses, as well as our opportunities to exploit any natural threats to Jing Pen life.

"Dismissed."

"Are you saying we got them all?" President Rhodes asked skeptically. The ad hoc committee on the alien invasion had joined the meeting well briefed. Jonathan Rhodes would accept nothing less.

"We are not prepared to make that assumption just yet, Mr. President," Secretary of Defense Henry Mason answered. "We haven't seen any sign of disturbance of the wilderness or caverns. Meanwhile, the army has been gassing, then bombing, every cavern within five hundred miles of Peterson AFB. We're now at phase two: searching for bodies. I'm told we've had nominal casualties so far in this operation."

The secretary of defense was an old hand at the word game. This game he seldom lost, as he never chose the wrong words. "From what our reports show, they're too big to hide in anything more crowded than a small rural town. They'd be too conspicuous." He chuckled. "They'd need lots of barns."

In addition to Henry Mason, the president's secret task force included Secretary of State Wilfred Chatham and General Michael Chey, head of the Joint Chiefs of Staff. Major General Dale Schmidt, head of Department D, was a key player in attendance. Attorney General Joseph Ashy, also conspicuously absent, was on Rhodes's "soon to be replaced" hit list. His absence sent the message to those in attendance.

"Mike, what do you make of all this?" the president asked.

"As the secretary says, sir, we're taking it one step at a time. We haven't found any aliens yet, but we haven't stopped looking."

"That's the kind of answer I'm talking about, gentlemen." Rhodes patted the table. "Any word from Major Rollins, Mike?"

"Yes, sir, but all reports are negative for new activity," Chey answered. "*Challenger II* has been in orbit for over two weeks now. We've been feeding the press all kinds of double-talk, but sooner or later, they're going to demand some answers."

"So, we tell them it's a matter of national security and there's no further comment," the president said. "What's so difficult?"

General Chey deferred to Secretary Chatham with a glance. "It's against the law, Mr. President," said the secretary. Without waiting to be asked why, he said, "There is a little-known law that's been on the books for several years. It's known as the Declaration of Principles of Conduct in the Event of Contact with Extraterrestrial Intelligence. This declaration requires sharing any and all information that pertains to alien encounters of any kind."

Rhodes slammed his fist on the studded leather arm of his chair. "What jackass signed *that* bill into law?" he demanded, alluding to the opposing party.

After some hesitation, Chatham volunteered, "It was signed *eight* years ago, sir."

Feeling some mild embarrassment for his own party, the president laughed. "At least it was a kinder, gentler jackass!"

The other men joined in with soft laughter.

"Okay. So, who are the watchdogs we're dealing with nowadays?" Rhodes gazed around the room. "What's the name of that group—SETI?"

"I believe General Schmidt is better prepared to answer that question than I am, Mr. President," Chatham said.

"Dale?" The commander in chief yielded the floor with a nod.

"SETI—a.k.a. Search for Extraterrestrial Intelligence—is defunct, Mr. President," replied Schmidt. "Lack of funds, lack of support, lack of results. Many of SETI's high-profile members have since found other interests." Schmidt looked around the group and smiled wryly. "After all, why spend time and energy searching for the truth when fiction is so much more interesting? Opening the file on Project Blue Book after SETI was terminated was the smartest thing we ever did."

"'We' meaning Department D," Rhodes said. "So, *that's* what I've been signing off on every quarter."

Mason explained, "A small, but extremely well-funded independent subdivision of the CIA. Independence and power might give the United States an edge, if an extraterrestrial dimension were ever to develop."

"As long-term administrative members of this cadre, the Joint Chiefs serve as custodians of the agency," Chatham drawled. "Secretaries of defense, then state, in sequence, act as liaisons to the president, who remains two steps removed from knowledge, in case of Contact."

"Plausible deniability shit again," Rhodes grumbled.

"The rest of the intelligence community would be thrown into a state of chaos," Mason added. "Adaptability and foresight would be the characteristics of the new leaders in espionage. Department D was designed to establish that lead."

"So, Ashy's the fall guy if the shit hits the fan, eh?" Rhodes nodded. "Good. Never liked the sneaky son of a bitch, anyway."

General Schmidt continued. "The fanatics have waded through all the reams of alien abduction accounts, UFO sightings, and crop circle hoaxes. They have actually been of some help in correlating incidents that our personnel never connected. Of course, the Department has been monitoring the Internet for keywords relating to alien encounters. In effect, we have 'volunteer' experts unwittingly working for us around the clock. Only twenty people outside of this room know that Department D has picked up where Blue Book left off.

"The man I have immediately supervising the project, Colonel Doyle, has been doing a great job. If anything significant happened, day or night, I'd hear about it within the hour," Schmidt said.

"And?" asked the president.

"Nothing yet, Mr. President. Doyle and I have a standing meeting three times a week. This morning's report was remarkably underwhelming. I thought he'd find something for sure after the incident at Peterson. Ken interrogated every man on the base. The aliens were either routed or destroyed without a trace. We combed the base from ceiling to floor. Nothing."

"Where's Doyle now?"

"With General Chey's permission, Mr. President, we've assumed command of a small army base in New Mexico as temporary field headquarters. There was a major in command. I don't recall his name. Hennessy Barracks boasts a compliment of some five hundred men and staff."

"What's that, about three companies, General?" asked Chatham.

"Yes, sir." Chey rolled his eyes as the secretary of state played soldier.

With a wave of his hand, the president let it be known that he was not impressed by the secretary of state's rudimentary knowledge of military organization and wanted no further interruptions. He was only interested in what Schmidt had to say.

Schmidt continued. "Hennessy is well equipped, and the staff is excellent, gentlemen. Most of them are assigned to test fiber-optic communications systems and train field support techs for special operations. The tech is state-of-the-art, some of it even experimental."

"So, it's a training base for spies," the president concluded.

General Chey leaned in toward the president and said with subdued pride, "That's why it's not on any map."

"Gentlemen, I don't relish the chore of signing my name to letters for families of dead soldiers," said Rhodes. "And I don't like having to tell them that their sons, husbands, and fathers died as victims of friendly fire in a training exercise. It's a lie, and it makes the US Army look incompetent. Hell, it makes *me* look incompetent! I don't like that. Not one bit." Rhodes paused to make sure his next point was absolutely clear. "I want these monsters. I don't care what you have to do, but I want them. I want them for the lives they cost us, and for the resources they've forced us to waste so far.

"Their ship has been completely destroyed. Nothing could have survived the blast from fifteen nuclear warheads. *Challenger II* confirms no remnants of the intruder. I want to feel equally confident that any aliens deposited on the ground have also been neutralized. The nest of them in Sudan was destroyed at the cost of two hundred fifty American soldiers. Exterminating their murderers will be small consolation for those boys, but I intend to at least give them that."

"So, what have we got?" Tur rested on his haunches as he spoke.

All twenty of the remaining Efilu had assembled in the big hangar next to the conference room.

"We have something special for you, Commander," Devit announced, his doleful eyes smiling for the first time since the landing. Tinkering with scarce materials was his forte, the reason he had been selected for the mission. "How do you like this?"

Tur looked up at the gelatinous mass lurking in the shadows of the hanger. "Is this what it looks like?" he asked in amazement.

Devit beamed. His long plumage seemed to dance around his deep teal face.

"How did you make a Mini-Wave?" Tur asked in genuine astonishment.

"In the Roog corpuscle. It's the basis for the gel synthesizer, anyway. Dru Log let us use his while he swam around in the cove outside for a few hours."

"Devit, this means we now have *producer* equipment!" Tur exclaimed, openly exuberant. "We can make anything we need!"

"Hold on now, Commander. It's not that easy. This is a very limited Mini-Wave. We can't funnel enough energy through it to make anything fancy."

"We don't need fancy," Tur said firmly, more in character now. "All I need is a few more gel consoles for basic equipment production and a Telescien or two."

"That we can manage, Commander."

"Great. Bo Tep, Weyef, we'll meet in an hour. These are the things I'll need from you..."

As the meeting continued, Bo Tep and Weyef reviewed holographic plans and made the appropriate changes and additions.

"There can be no consolation for the comrades we've lost. This entire world doesn't have enough collective soul to repay our losses," Tur said, with passion rare for a So Wari.

Then, almost as if he had become self-conscious about the emotional content of his projection, his demeanor became cold.

"No matter. As we've all grown tired of hiding in the shadows, a more aggressive posture is clearly indicated."

He pointed to a tree diagram, various characters on its branches representing what was known of the United States government. "Ikara, I want you focused now," Tur instructed. "I want to know these individuals better than their own littermates do. The weapons Devit has fashioned are more than equal to any arsenal these varmints can muster. Still, there's no need to waste resources. This culture is sufficiently fragmented to make subjugation a matter of applying strategic pressure to weaknesses." He leaned into the group, projecting such acrimony as to chill a Tralkyz spine. "I'm going to pay their chief a little visit."

Tur met the eyes of each of his meren. To be sure each eagerly took heed, he said, "You see, in the end, it comes down to a battle of wits."

Chapter Twenty-One

— HACKER —

Uniformed men busied themselves all around Vit Na. The odor of hairy, sebaceous secretions assailed her olfactory membranes. She had become accustomed to the melange of scents in the wilderness. She found them a refreshing change from the filtered atmosphere on the *ReQam*. But here, in the company of men, she inhaled gently and gauged the fetor to familiar smells of mammals from the realm. Similar, not unpleasant—musky, but mixed with aromatic additives, some harmonious, others that seemed out of place in this setting. Oddly, she hungered.

Vit Na put in a request with Dr. Matthews for fish, chicken, or domesticated alligator *only* for meals. The look he gave her after that last menu item request told her she probably wouldn't taste any crocodilian meat for a while.

At least he guarantees I will be served no more Jing flesh.

The soldiers modified her cell to annex the anteroom where the guards had been stationed. This gave her a bit more space. The bars and thick polymer sheets had been removed, and the table had been replaced by a bed of soft feathers covered by a cotton afghan. It rested on a king-sized water mattress.

The soldiers working on Vit Na's new quarters had begun to complain bitterly about the rodents getting underfoot and into their lunches. The humans were unbearably clumsy about catching the creatures. The men managed to kill only one of the twelve pests she had counted—and they had made a mess of it, at that.

Vit Na, seeing an opportunity to rid her chambers of the annoyance, asked, "May I be of assistance?"

The GI heading the work detail answered, "Yeah—build a better mouse trap."

Apparently, the novelty of the alien presence had dulled as the soldiers now spoke to Vit Na without affectation or fear. The sergeant, with a look of frustration on his face, held a spring-powered wooden trap in his hand.

Quietly accepting the invitation, Vit Na resolved to exercise at least some of her hunting skills. She had eleven rats neatly executed and piled in a corner for removal before late morning. She decided it was the least she could do.

Her hosts had proposed to modify a larger room to accommodate her needs. The chief, whom she had to struggle to remember to call Mendez, proved very hospitable. Had they better sensitivities, Vit Na would have professed these creatures were acknowledging her proper station, catering to her needs and wishes. Momentarily, she thought of teaching them to address her as *Ati* Vit Na. She knew better than that, though. *This Mendez bears careful scrutiny.*

The intensity of their questions was picking up. *It seems as if these people*—as she had to remind herself to call them—*want to know every detail of the past sixty-five million years, and they desire the information today.*

At the same time, they wanted to know all about space travel and whether there were truly alien civilizations out there. This seemed to be a "hot issue," as Robyn Washington liked to say.

What is this bizarre obsession with alien visitations and abductions? Vit Na thought.

Answering honestly, she explained that she had never personally visited Earth prior to two weeks ago, and she didn't know anyone else who had. The idea of "flying saucers" made Vit Na laugh. Her left side still hurt when she did.

Descriptions of strange lights whisking people away from remote areas seemed familiar. *Stellar Fletts. They really don't need to know about those specters,* she thought to herself. *Harmless, but the poor Jing will lose sleep for months.*

Olsen had used his computer to create a mock-up of the interior design ideas Vit Na described to him, a computer application he called VeriCad. She had to simplify the more elaborate architectural concepts according to the limits of her hosts' engineering skills and resources. Finally, she came up with a livable, practicable arrangement for the gymnasium.

An old oak tree was cut down and defoliated. Raw cotton fibers were woven into a mesh that formed a large tent/hammock, which was stuffed with soft goose down. The bleacher steps were covered with indoor carpeting, the kind that changed hue when something brushed against the weave pattern. Footprints of the clumsy showed easily in the patterns. Vit Na may have been at Jing Pen mercy, but she could still know when they were coming and going.

As she watched Olsen's fingers dance across the keyboard, she memorized each command he entered. She had been testing all her captors individually to ascertain how sensitive they were to increasing variations in her personal field of influence.

Not very! she decided. *This is my opening. These Jing Pen cannot process phenomena they don't know how to measure, so they ignore them. Plus, they blindly rely on these computing machines to interpret and organize data. Their contraptions are only designed to respond to a finite number of algorithms with limited heuristic capacity, and no internal monitoring systems.*

Neither the Jing Pen nor their computers have been able to detect my personal field fluctuations yet. With a little time, I can build my own computer access field right under their little noses, complete with an override system to rewrite their programming. I'll be running this whole complex within a week.

Vit Na maintained an inscrutable facial expression while plotting her coup. When she felt confident enough to elude cyber detection, she decided to verify Jing Pen knowledge through forays on the Internet.

She probed through the circuits and along the nuances of the underused microchips with impunity. Vit Na sensed the stream of data in so-called cyberspace, just beyond the confines of the facility.

Jeen is sure to be monitoring the Internet, she assumed. *Nuk.*

Vit Na stopped as she sensed the safeguards Mendez had put in place to prevent unauthorized external communications from Hennessy Barracks.

Patience, Vit Na, she thought to herself. *Just wait. Their next mistake will come—all in good time.*

—◄●►—

"Now, Vit Na, I'd like you to go through these very carefully." Washington had returned later that afternoon with a bundle of newspapers. "Tell me if any of the pictures or symbols are familiar to you."

The photos she showed Vit Na pictured dolls or mannequins in strange clothing and people in costumes. The captions under the pictures generally said "alien abduction" this or "close encounter" that.

"No. I've never seen any of these characters before," she said. She turned one of the pages casually to hide her recognition of a familiar image. *It's distorted for sure, but the pattern is unquestionable. The Tyelaj!* It had been reduced to its simplest form, a circle bisected by a sine wave. *Half light, half dark. Hard evidence that Si Tyen—the Keepers—are at least partially responsible for the perversion that is now Earth.*

She unfolded the page further and could no longer conceal her shock. There, unmistakably, was an etching of a full-grown Si Tyen!

Robyn questioned, "What's wrong, Vit Na? You look as if you'd seen a ghost." She took the page that lay limp in Vit Na's hand. "That's a dragon. What do you know about dragons, Vit Na?"

Vit Na regained her composure. "I might ask you the same question. How do you come by this name: 'dragon?'" She glared at Robyn. "Are these creatures real, or are they figments of your collective imagination?"

Robyn knew she was on to something, and she secretly signaled to Olsen to record this session in high-resolution video and enhanced sound. "Both, it would appear," she answered.

Damn. Another gaffe. Vit Na realized she had underestimated Robyn. *This is getting to be a habit for me.*

When Vit Na didn't respond, Robyn expounded. "Dragons are known to nearly every civilization on Earth in one form or another. European mythology describes monsters terrorizing the countryside in ancient times. They were kin to devils and gods— usually the former. The legends peaked in the Middle Ages and faded with the advent of scientific thought and the Age of Reason.

"In contrast, many Eastern civilizations regard the dragon as a mystical figure, endowed with great wisdom and strength. Whole philosophies have been based on dragon lore...or is it dragon history?"

Vit Na's peripheral vision revealed Mendez, Matthews, Stahl, and two guards stalking into the immediate area to listen to her tale of dragons. *I didn't give them enough credit. Their communication skills are better than I thought. Maybe there is some latent telepathic ability. Yet…this inhibition factor seems to behave a great deal like the Poison, acting at the synaptic level.*

Did the Keepers…? This last thought frightened Vit Na more than she could admit. The notion of Jing Pen deliberately designed by the Keepers to confound Efilu senses rose like an epic nightmare.

"They were—*are* called Si Tyen," Vit Na said solemnly. "They are of my people."

"Then they do exist!" Mendez exclaimed frantically.

"They did exist here," Vit Na said with candor. "They would have died out millions of years ago, on Earth. Evidently, before their extinction, they made quite an impression on your ancestors."

"But you don't understand," Mendez pressed. "The legends of men fighting dragons are within the span of our recorded history. They must have lived longer than you think. Maybe they *still* do."

"That's unlikely. They could never have survived the holocaust that drove us all out."

Mendez was now standing in front of Vit Na, shouldering Washington to the side as he spoke. "Tell us more about this 'holocaust,' Vit Na," he requested.

"Tell me more about this 'fighting of dragons' first," she countered.

Mendez looked at Hoyt for a second, then shrugged. "In legends of old, men would slay an evil dragon to save a village or a damsel in distress. It was a feat of great strength and courage."

Images of the Tralkyz confrontation with the Si Tyen that she and Tur had witnessed in the Forest of Feelings came to mind.

"What kinds of weapons were used?" Vit Na asked.

"Traditionally, broadsword, lance, crossbow, armor and shield," Robyn volunteered.

Vit Na mentally accessed images of the weapons Robyn described. *There's no way of killing a Tyen with those weapons. There must be more to it than that.*

"No cannons, no bullets or bombs?" Vit Na asked suspiciously.

"Not back then," Robyn explained. "Those weapons were not generally available, and unmanageable by small groups of men when they were."

"Are there any artifacts left of these slayings?" Vit Na asked.

"No real ones. Sometimes precious gems or ivory are referred to as 'dragon's eyes' or 'dragon's teeth.' They were often purported to guard vast treasures."

This Robyn Washington seems to be remarkably knowledgeable about dragon lore, Vit Na observed.

"Usually red crystals and gold?" Vit Na offered.

Mendez looked surprised. "Why, yes. What do you know about such things?" he demanded.

"The Si Tyen often recorded data within crystalline devices. Your ancestors probably stumbled onto those data modules, which were guarded by animated memory sentries. Is the word 'Iku' familiar to any of you?"

Mendez answered question with question. "Should it be?"

"I don't know. I'm just trying to help you. These artificial guardians, or 'Iku,' might have been disrupted by the weapons you described, especially if they were very old and degenerate."

"Vit Na, you said the Tyen were 'of your people.' Are you a baby?" Matthews asked. "Will you mature into a dragon?"

"Or were they the masters you fled?" Bruce chimed in.

"Definitely not!" Vit Na couldn't help laughing. "And no. We are a union of nations with no geographic boundaries. Each is comprised of a sea of individuals who act together for the advancement of a common good. Our philosophy is 'May the All live as One.' The Si Tyen are but a single race among equals." She paused. "They have largely withdrawn from social participation in the last several millennia." Vit Na sighed. "In many ways, they were the best of us."

Subsequent moments of silence seemed like an eternity.

It's as if they have some sort of latent reverence for the Keepers, she observed. *Yet they don't seem to consciously acknowledge the Animem Iku state. Maybe I can use that.*

"Your people are the survivors of an awful accident, an accident of our making. We saved some of your ancestors—as many as could be carried in the time left before the end. Or what we *thought* was the end. Your progenitors grew in the darkness of a ruined planet, a planet that has miraculously healed itself with the help of the Keepers."

"You mentioned the Keepers before. Just who were these Keepers?" Mendez asked.

"A cruel joke. The Keepers of the Faith were the Tyen—I mean, *dragons*—who stayed behind to rehabilitate this marred world and its wildlife from our folly. Your remote ancestors were a part of that wildlife." She paused, noting their intense focus and attention. "The word 'dragon' is strikingly like that of the name of a historical figure of the Si Tyen race. The Keepers could not tolerate the toxins and famine that followed, so they died out. Your kind could not understand the knowledge left in the modules, but I can. I can light the darkness of your past, Javier Mendez," Vit Na lied. It was becoming easier for her.

"We'll need to assemble a group of specialists, Vit Na. We don't have the expertise to take advantage of this opportunity. Give me twelve hours." His face did little to hide his excitement. He turned to Vit Na and asked, "By the way, do you think you could operate one of these computer terminals if Clyde helped you out?"

Mendez sauntered out of the room, triumphant, when Vit Na answered with a simple nod and a smile.

"Okay, these are the rules." Javier Mendez laid them out for his team. "One: no one knows what we have here before they actually arrive at the base. Two: they tell no one where they're going or who called them. Three: they bring any essential equipment or paraphernalia with them. There's no going back until their part of the project is over."

"What if they ask questions? They are very intelligent people, Javier," Max interjected. "They're bound to ask questions."

"Tell them to plan on ten days if they can. Other than that, tell them anything you have to in order to get them here. Wait..." Mendez thought for a moment. "Tell them it's a drill. In the event of First Contact, can we depend on a panel of experts to participate, no questions asked and in the utmost confidence? It'll be an honor."

—◦●◦—

The cover story worked. After the approval of a short list of experts, each was contacted by a familiar face from Project X. Mendez was surprised and a little uncomfortable at Clyde Olsen's popularity with so many of these intellectuals. As it turned out, Olsen was the IT expert for many a scientist on his off time—yet another credit to his abilities.

The list of names read like a Who's Who of the international scientific community. Sometimes, the most highly esteemed individual in a particular field was deliberately omitted if the expert had acquired too much celebrity.

"No one whose absence would attract media attention," Mendez said.

Mendez was good at this. Too good, Robyn Washington decided. He was too sensitive to the needs of security not to have had some covert operations in his background, but she could not figure out how a molecular geneticist could be involved in such operations.

The guests of Project X began arriving within hours, brought in by Army mail planes. Carrying backpacks and computer bags, the majority were dressed merely in jeans and flannel shirts.

Among the first arrivals were the likes of Claude Morgan, the noted Princeton astronomer; Julian Hardacker, physicist extraordinaire; Will Parker, the flamboyant dinosaur fossil hunter; and Saul Pothel, the famous theoretical mathematician. Allister Brumbellow and Neil Cassidy came in the next morning from the UK. Between the two of them, they brought a practical sociological perspective to the table.

All the guests were very inconspicuous, except for Julian Hardacker, the one person in a wheelchair. The lone female in the group, Marisol Estrella, the Nobel prize winning astronomer from Chili, stood a bit taller than most of her companions. That evening, a one-way video link would introduce each specialist to Vit Na's voice, while allowing her to both see and hear her visitor.

Each scientist suspected they were being prepared for a drill to test their readiness for the eventuality of alien contact. Everyone obeyed the rules set forth by Mendez.

Vit Na noted that no one had mentioned the encounters with Efilu so far. *Curious. They seem to take this all in stride. I wonder how much these 'experts' really know. I'll—how does Hoyt say it? "Play it close to the vest," for now,* she decided. *I'll simply answer questions. Let each of them ease into his relationship with me.*

"So, Vit Na, where are you from?" Morgan began, speaking in a patronizing monotone. Vit Na explained the location of the Efilu Realm and indicated the region on a star map displayed on the computer.

"Oh, I see. And how did you get here?"

"By spaceship, of course," she answered.

He's rather casual—as if he receives dignitaries from the Realm every day, Vit Na thought, amused by his tone. *Either that or he doesn't believe the situation. Is he in for a surprise!*

"Where is this spaceship now?" Morgan asked politely, as if anticipating a nebulous answer.

"Either destroyed or damaged beyond repair in an expanded orbit. Didn't you see the explosion?"

"What explosion?" Morgan asked with genuine interest.

"The big one, two weeks ago," Vit Na said.

"You mean the one from the collision between the meteor and that satellite? Yes, that was amazing, but there was no spaceship involved in that. I personally saw the recording taken from Hubble. Try again, now."

There's that smug tone again.

"What about the second explosion? It was larger than the first. How do you explain that?" Vit Na probed.

"It was in all the papers and on television," Morgan said. "CNN did a special on it. The end of the Cold War a few years ago, as well as new trade relations with China, prompted the elimination of orbiting nuclear weapons. It was long overdue."

How interesting. A cover-up. I wonder if I can safely deviate from the official story. Maybe a strategic slip of the tongue might work. "What about the invasion and destruction of Peterson Air Force Ba—"

The audio transmission was interrupted, and the Melkyz was cut off mid-sentence by a voice only she could hear. "Vit Na, we need to maintain a few secrets," Mendez said from a screen in front of her. "At least for today. Try to sidestep those questions if possible. We'll help you whenever necessary."

So, I'm being censored. Okay, for now.

"I'm sorry, I'm not a physicist myself. I'm just an archeologist, and I don't have a very strong background in the hard sciences," Vit Na admitted truthfully.

"Of course not," the human said condescendingly.

Arrogant little garbage-crawler, she thought to herself. Vit Na looked forward to meeting this Claude Morgan face-to-face in the morning.

Her interview with Julian Hardacker was most interesting. Vit Na had done her own research. *A victim of rheumatoid arthritis,*

Hardacker's mobility was limited by deformed hands and wrists. Arthritic destruction of the vertebra destabilized the base of his skull and compromised his spinal cord, and he compensated by using a chair with wheels most of the time.

Vit Na had never before seen an adult with such extreme physical challenges as he. *How has he survived puberty, much less adulthood?* she wondered. *If he was injured as an adult, who would even try to support him?*

But this Hardacker was considered one of the most brilliant scientists on the planet. *He's certainly less pompous than the others,* Vit Na noted. *Somehow, I want to like him, but this urge to put him out of his misery... it's like an itch that won't go away.*

At home, should she have encountered such an individual of her race or one with which her people had diplomatic relations, she would have been required to kill him to strengthen the race. She knew she had no such obligation here, but didn't someone?

She typed out a mathematical equation in answer to his question as to how she arrived here. He made a sound that she could not interpret. He said nothing more that day.

Vit Na made herself as comfortable as possible in her new quarters. She bathed in the warm saltwater of the gymnasium pool out of necessity. The practice, normally enjoyed in leisurely fashion, had to be cut short. Irritation caused by the residual chlorine made the process of bathing more a chore than a pleasure.

Fortunately, there was no detergent in the water that would wash the precious oils from her downy coat. Her ability to *Blend* was her most reliable weapon left to her, even if not currently in use. It would do little good now, anyway. They watched her every breath. A sudden unexplained disappearance would set off alarms everywhere. Vit Na needed more than mere invisibility. She needed a plan.

Vit Na requested that certain musical selections with particular rhythms be piped into her quarters. The humans had no concept of personal fields, spheres of influence, or force fields, at all. Occasional references to personal auras only scratched the surface of what humans called parapsychology. Using Via Sharu rituals, Vit Na siphoned power from the surrounding structure into a force field she constructed from her own sphere of influence.

This is a dangerous gamble, she realized. The power dynamics would have been easily detectable to any Efilu, even the simpler peoples. *The inhibition factor not only prevents intimate communication; apparently, it also prevents the sensing of auras and personal fields,* she observed.

Vit Na wove her secret power source right before her captors' eyes. When guards asked about the arcane Sharu gyrations, she frequently answered, "dancing." She smiled to herself. *And soon, I'll be prepared to attempt an escape.*

The afternoon went quickly for Vit Na. Now that she had regained her strength, she languished, penned in like a zoo captive. If she had just known she could go out of doors, she would have felt more comfortable. Since she could not, she took every opportunity to peruse Animem experiences pertaining to Tyen customs, technology, and culture. Most of these took place under open skies.

Funny—this was one of so many lessons of youth for which I thought I would never have any practical use.

Now her knowledge of Tyen Animems presented a chance to manipulate these beasts called "humans." For the moment, the knowledge was her sanctuary from this madness, and her only way into a peaceful slumber.

Chapter Twenty-Two
— ORACLE —

Vit Na awoke rested, but wary. The warm sunlight streamed across her sleeping pallet through the wide polymer panels. *Plexiglas,* she reminded herself. Welcoming rays audaciously breached those impenetrable windows, the only consolation for such crude surroundings.

The next round of meetings with 'the experts' is scheduled for this morning, she reckoned. *The humans are eager.*

They would be looking into both the future and the past through her eyes. In effect, through the lens of her archeological training, Vit Na would be doing the same. She would explore the age-old question: how does an advanced culture make the transition from savageness to sentience?

Their history, their myths—a two-way window through time, she reminded herself. *This is the opportunity of a career. Finally, the veil of speculation will lift, and the secrets of the Keepers may come to light. Well, this is the day. Mendez's day.*

Her first meeting would be over breakfast. Washington thought it would be a nice "ice-breaker." The victuals were better than usual. Eggs, an unexpected delight that she had forgotten to mention to Dr. Matthews, were plentiful. There was salmon, trout, and catfish—which she had developed a genuine fondness for—and fried geese. Big ones at that, just dripping with grease.

To drink, she had plenty of ice water and a dipping basin of heavy maple syrup at room temperature. She would have to make a note to further investigate this obsession with brown-colored beverages.

All these Jing Pen seem to drink is coffee, cola, and tea, both hot and cold, night and day. Then there's that beer. The latter Vit Na found more distasteful than the rest. *Fermented swill. Looks like urine!*

Vit Na greeted each of her guests graciously before starting to eat. As expected, all but Mendez were dumbfounded. Julian Hardacker was the first to find his voice.

"May I be the first from this assemblage to wish you a good morning, Ms. Vit Na?" He extended a gnarled hand, which she shook gently with no hesitation. Will Parker just stared for long moments, nodding, apparently sizing her up.

He's wondering: "Just how did they accomplish this hoax?" Vit Na smiled triumphantly. *He must have seen all the same newspaper clippings that I did.*

"I'm sure you all must have as many questions for me as I have for you," Vit Na began graciously. "If my eating does not offend you, let us begin."

A very casual and civil meal commenced. Will Parker and Claude, as Professor Morgan insisted that she call him, dominated the conversation.

Claude gestured at her physique. "So are you a professional actress under all of that? Have I seen you in anything on the silver screen, perhaps?"

Vit Na shook the query off. "What?"

"Of course, the Method." He combined the most obnoxious qualities of charm and condescension into five syllables. "We'll play along."

"So, you're both a dinosaur and an extraterrestrial. How long has it been?" asked Parker.

"Approximately sixty-five million years, Will. Give or take a few millennia."

"But the fur—when did you develop the fur?"

"We always had it. Most species did, anyway, in one texture or another. Most of the larger peoples developed dense pelts for protection or camouflage."

"Why haven't we found any fossilized creatures like you?" Parker asked.

"*People* like me. From everything I've seen, you've found less than one percent of the fossil remains of animals from 'our day.' What you have found, you've lumped together—primitive mammals classified together with more advanced animals. It's unlikely that you have found remains of any civilized peoples. The vast majority were disposed of decently, according to our customs. The occasional individual who died while traveling through the wilderness would have been completely devoured by wild animals."

"What about you? Are you a predator or omnivore?" Will asked.

Impulsively, Vit Na shot him a poisonous glare. Will Parker had no way of knowing what an insult he posed with that question. The super hunters tended to be elitists and did not appreciate comparisons to lesser meat eaters—especially not to scavengers!

After a brief hesitation, Vit Na answered, displaying no obvious offense. "We don't hunt for food anymore, so I guess we wouldn't be called predators, but we are strictly eaters of meat—and eggs." She punctuated that last item by hoisting an opened, soft-boiled emu egg to eye level then to her lips. Hollingsworth had them brought in just for the occasion.

"You don't hunt anymore? How do you...eat?" Claude grinned, doodling salaciously with his fingertip on the tablecloth in front of him.

Vit Na swallowed before answering, impressed with the logical line of questioning, the bawdy nature of the action lost on her. "Well, we raise livestock now. We only hunt for sport these days," she clarified.

"Sport hunting." Claude hummed. "How carnal."

"How many different species are there in the Efilu society?" Parker asked.

"Oh, about four hundred or so. That includes avian, terrestrial, and aquatic peoples, but excludes their respective subspecies wards. There are several hundreds of thousands of complex wild species, not to mention millions of species of insects, arachnids, crustaceans, and other simpler animals."

No need to emphasize that we include Jing in the category of vermin, she thought.

"Can any of you tell me how your verbal language developed and diversified?" Vit Na asked, looking first to Washington for an answer.

Allister Brumbellow answered instead. "No one is certain how the various languages came about. The origins of individual words are based in antiquity, probably relating to sounds made by various animals or natural phenomena. The possibilities of reproducing these sounds would naturally be limited by the phonetic constraints of the human voice. This would tend to explain why there have been similarities in languages spoken by cultures that never encountered one another. 'Ps' and 'Bs', 'Gs' and 'Ks' are often interchanged in similar words."

Vit Na was again impressed. "Something of a natural onomatopoeia, in other words?" she offered in summary.

"Why, yes. I've never heard it put that way, but that's quite correct," Brumbellow said.

"You have incorporated into your language a few terms that are very familiar to me. Words for which you people should have no frame of reference. You describe not only dragons, but also the firebird, which you call the phoenix. You also have written in detail about, and even etched, some classes of serpents with which you should never have had direct contact. How do you explain this knowledge?"

Answers are so close I can almost taste them coming. Vit Na salivated as she ate, anticipating her breakfast companions' accounts.

"Vit Na, I think you're taking these coincidences a bit too seriously," Neil Cassidy interjected. "I must admit that I have exaggerated the connection between events for theatrical purposes, but what you propose is incredible. These mythological creatures can have no basis in reality. The powers attributed to them defy all the laws of science as we know them." He paused as he considered the source of the implications she made, then urged her to continue.

Vit Na went on, somewhat frustrated by their lack of ancestral memory. "Your legends tell of magical creatures that are like men yet have the extremities of horses and goats. You describe small, slender men with pointed ears, called elves, and large powerful creatures called ogres. What about them?"

They all looked at one another in wonderment. "Did these creatures really exist?" Neil asked. Even in retirement, the old reporter's knack for asking fundamental interview questions reflected the accolades to his incisive reporting Vit Na had seen in several periodicals. And yet—

"That's what I want you to tell me!" Vit Na exclaimed in frustration. *How could they be so stupid?*

"All right," she continued. "What about references to giants four, often ten times the size of men? Your West African cultures describe a race of giants who became so powerful they were banished from the Earth by your gods. They call these giants by the name of 'Soa,' in some dialects even 'So.' Certainly, this is no accident!"

"We don't understand that reference, Vit Na. What is a 'So?'" Hoyt Matthews asked.

"Who!" Vit Na almost shouted. "*Who* are the So! The So Wari, the So Beni, the So Rikhi—does none of this strike a note of familiarity with any of you?" Vit Na was beginning to lose her temper.

Such stupidity! Using a Sharu technique, she forced relaxation to return before elaborating on her discoveries.

"Among the Efilu, there is a race of exceptionally large, powerful people called the So Wari. In the final days of the Efilu on Earth, they were a fledgling race who rose to power in the shadows of their kin, the So Beni. In studying your civilization, I perused your most ancient history and artwork. West African lore has it that the people who inherited the lands vacated by the So now call themselves the Chi Wari. They were robust, powerful warriors compared to their neighbors." Vit Na closed her eyes and reminded herself of the quote she found in a university database, "'Crafted from fire and iron by the gods.' The word 'Wari' seems to mean 'split' in Japanese. The So Wari subspecies 'split' from the So Beni, supplanting them. The descriptions are too close to be mere chance. You people have a habit of naming yourselves after those you either admire or fear."

Vit Na watched for responses. All she got were more dumb looks.

Better drop this subject, she cautioned herself. *You'll only give them all headaches, not to mention yourself.*

"Vit Na, what did the dinosaurs look like? I mean the ones we do know about?" Will Parker asked with childlike curiosity.

"Well, as you guessed, the bolok—which you have descriptively renamed Triceratops—did look much like a mammalian pachyderm similar to rhinoceroses, elephants, or hippopotami. You're off on many of the other ancient species, though. The Stegosaurus, for example, looked more like a robust horse than the monster you portray. Brontosaurus had colorful, feathery manes that helped them blend into their surroundings."

Careful with the term Blending, *Vit Na,* she told herself. *But again, I give them too much credit. They can't read minds.* She chuckled wryly at the notion.

The questions went on, and Vit Na began to notice a peculiar habit among her hosts. *Why do they keep taking liberties with my coat?* Morgan casually stroked her neck and shoulder as he passed behind her. *Nearly every one of them has either rubbed me or attempted to all morning. I'll have to put a polite stop to this right now.*

"That is a very offensive practice, rubbing another's integument. It is an action reserved for family members only. From anyone else, it is usually taken as a *hostile* act."

A hush fell over the room, and Vit Na began to ask herself if she had gone too far with that warning when she realized none of her guests were looking at her anymore.

Another human had entered the room. He was dressed in military regalia and flanked on both sides by several armed men with weapons drawn.

"Well, Javier," the man greeted Mendez, "it would seem the rumors going around Washington these days are true. We really do have our very own alien." He appraised Vit Na from top to bottom before approaching her.

"Hello." The man stepped up to Vit Na and stroked her chin as one would a familiar kitten. Almost reflexively, she flicked an ear at the newcomer.

"I'm Colonel Kenneth Doyle. From now on, I will be your host." He turned to the persons seated at the table and added, "In fact, I will be host to you all for the next several months. Please finish your meal, everyone. We'll talk later."

His smile seemed to make even Mendez uneasy. "Come, Javier, you and I have a lot to talk about right now," he said, hooking Mendez by the arm as he rose from his chair. "You've been a very bad boy."

Chapter Twenty-Three
— THE HISTORY LESSON —

G oddamn Hoyt Matthews!" Colonel Doyle had taken his feet from their comfortable position on the desk he now called his. "How the hell did he get a former president here so fast? Do he and Jimmy go fishing together, or did Matthews just save the Carter cat?" He threw his hand up in frustration. "Good ol' boys!"

Major Ernie Dixon stood patiently at attention as the Colonel digested the bad news. Former President Carter had been called in as a "humanitarian representative" of the United States of America.

Doyle said, perturbed, "We can't keep a former president holed up here against his will!"

"I didn't hear that, sir." The major jutted his chin forward as he spoke, to emphasize the impropriety.

Doyle became silent and focused on the young major. "And I didn't *say* that, either," he stated. He waited for another comment from Dixon, but got none.

"Shit, you are ambitious. Okay. Damage control now takes priority. Carter has only honorary status nowadays, and with this conservative administration in office, he won't throw that around too much. When does the good president arrive?"

"He already has. About an hour ago," Dixon said.

"Dixon, if you're going to work for me, you're going to have to handle yourself better than this. Why am I just hearing about Carter now?"

"You heard about it exactly four minutes after I first heard about it, sir. Matthews must have had help overriding the communications lockout."

"Olsen! The little schmuck," Doyle cursed.

"My guess, too, sir," said Dixon.

"Well, what are you doing about it, Major?"

"Whatever they did to get President Carter here, they couldn't have given him many details. We'll have to keep it that way. We can completely shut Olsen down, permanently."

"Don't kill him, Major, just break his fingers for me." Doyle chuckled at his new protégé's enthusiasm.

Dixon replied without humor. "I had nothing so dramatic in mind, sir. We can place Olsen in the brig. There will be no more hacking for him this go-round. The Secret Service will keep to themselves, as long as the president is safe and content. They never think; they just follow orders. We can't have Matthews running around telling all our business either. We'll have to keep him in the dark as long as we can and away from our *guest of honor*. I observed the other guests when they first spoke to the alien over the computer phone link. They thought it was some kind of drill. Perhaps we can help Mr. Carter come to the same conclusion."

"Without actually lying to him," Doyle reminded him. "Now, transferring you from your branch of service to mine will be tricky, but I think we can do it, with my connections. Major Dixon, I'd dare say you have a very promising future in my organization."

"Yes, sir. Thank you, sir."

There appears to be a new chief in the village, Vit Na mused. *It's certainly got most of the natives riled up. I wonder if they'll dispose of the deposed chief by execution, imprisonment, or exile. They don't appear civilized enough to simply demote their rivals.*

She looked at the pool and thought how relaxing a swim would be, now that the chlorinated water had been replaced with saline. Things were very tense around Hennessy Barracks, but quiet. There were no more questions. No interviews with the experts. No visits from Mendez's people.

Perhaps this change of leadership will work in my best interests, she thought. *Where there is change, there is confusion. Little things slip. With what I've accomplished so far, chaos can only serve me.*

She continued to fold energy into her personal field for later use. Now and then, her manipulations drew quizzical looks. When human music played, she moved to the rhythms with perfect timing. Her dances were endless entertainment to the men. When no music was playing, she simply smiled and said, "I just can't get this tune out of my head, you know?" and continued her work.

Vit Na had been waiting for Matthews to visit all day, so they could update her menu. She had some new ideas on food preparation that she thought human technology could handle.

As she waited, she noticed that her guards' uniforms had changed subtly. Their color had changed from green to tan and the little insignias were altered. *How significant is this change?* Vit Na wondered.

One of the new guards came into the gymnasium uninvited. "How are you feeling today?" he asked. "Ya feeling all right?"

She looked at the name tag over his breast pocket from across the room. "I'm just fine, Sergeant McCray," she answered.

He continued to approach her. She noticed the other guards of lesser rank were standing at the open door with weapons drawn.

"Can I help you, Sergeant?" she queried.

He was close now.

"How's your side, Vit?"

"Vit Na," she corrected with more apprehension than pique. "You can say it as a single word, if that's easier for you."

"Whatever." McCray glared at her for a beat, then asked, "You don't recognize me, do you?" He grinned hungrily. "I'm the guy who shot you at Peterson AFB. Sloppy aim, but not bad against an invisible target, huh? How did you do that, anyway?"

This is too clumsy for an assassination attempt—this is more like some kind of provocation. Maybe they're trying to learn more about the Blending *process.* She shivered inwardly.

"They say that you never forget the face of death. The face of someone who almost killed you," he taunted. "Do you remember this face?"

Vit Na remained silent.

"No, obviously not. Will you remember it in the future?" He shrugged, then extended his index finger in her direction, cocked his thumb up, and jerked his hand as if firing a gun. "Sure you will. I'll be watching you, Vit."

Vit Na watched the sergeant exit her gymnasium.

Great! Just what I need—a new ripple in the stream of my life. At least he didn't follow up on that question about invisibility. Yet she knew that if he now oversaw security, the subject would come up again. *I had better have answers for him next time,* she decided.

Fortunately, he seemed even duller than average, and filled with pure hate. She felt this emotion spilling through the inhibition field. *Easy to twist.* There was something else Vit Na recognized nearly submerged beneath the hatred.

Fear!

Vit Na paddled around in the pool for a while, the saline additive making the experience more comfortable. She surfaced after a few moments to see Robyn Washington squatting at the edge of the pool.

"Good afternoon, Vit Na. You must be confused about all the sudden changes around here," Washington said.

"Change is a part of life, Robyn. When you can't direct the stream, you just have to go with the flow."

Washington smiled at the witticism.

Vit Na climbed out of the pool and regarded the woman. She realized the ancient proverb was lost on Washington. The archeologist shook most of the water out of her down.

"I admire your serenity, Vit Na. You're very accepting of the situation. You're very interesting in many ways, I'd say."

"Oh?" Vit Na was curious now. "How is that, Robyn?"

She moved closer to Washington and lounged comfortably on the indoor/outdoor carpeting.

"Well, for one thing, that coat of yours reminds me most of a black leopard, but soft as a mink. Yet you seem to enjoy the water so much."

She's stalling, Vit Na thought. *Both leopards and minks like water. Either she doesn't know it, she doesn't know that I know it, or she's making small talk. I'll wait for her to come to the point in her own time.*

"Your people—did they go through the same changes we're going through?" Washington asked.

"Specifically?" Vit Na prompted.

"Greed, prejudice, selfishness, short-sightedness. These are problems my people face today. We think we root them out and make laws to protect ourselves from crimes, and yet they keep coming back to haunt us."

Vit Na still sensed hesitation. "These are very general things that any species must overcome on the path to civilization. There is something else more specific troubling you, Robyn. What's wrong?"

"Do you understand the concept of genocide, Vit Na?" Washington asked.

Vit Na rolled off her back and propped her head up on her hand to look directly at the linguist. *Now this is interesting. Does she know something about the Poison situation?*

"I know the definition of the word, but like many words, it is inadequate in and of itself. Context adds another dimension to give the word true meaning."

"We are in danger," Washington let out.

"We are?" Vit Na responded, not sure how the pronoun in question linked her with her inquisitor.

"No, not you. Us! Not just this country, but probably the entire human race. We exploit anyone or anything that has what we want, without conscience. We're out of control. I don't know if this means anything to you, but this is not the first time we have encountered aliens."

Vit Na didn't move, but she regarded Washington with greater intensity. "It's not?"

"No," Washington said gravely.

"You don't mean those ridiculous fakes in your newspapers?"

Washington shook her head before answering, "No, but they are close to the truth. An alien spacecraft did crash onto Earth fifty years ago. The creatures on board were dead or dying when we found them." Washington looked around furtively. "This is highly classified information. The kind for which people disappear for divulging."

"Go on, Robyn," Vit Na reassured her. "Nothing could be more classified than me. And I doubt that there are any more secure settings than this base."

"Well, the military came in then, as it has now, and dissected the lot of them," Robyn whispered. "Then they analyzed the technology retrieved from the ship."

Vit Na's ears prickled with intrigue. "So, what did they learn from that encounter?"

"Nothing then, but the data was stored. I think some agency, I don't know which, has been making slow but steady headway on those secrets for the past fifty years. There must have been a breakthrough. Recently we've gained a considerable edge on our competitors in weapons and electronics technology. In fact, we've basically eliminated the competition over the past ten years."

Vit Na interrupted. "You mean Russia and the Chinese Republic?"

Washington nodded. "I think my government has been deploying some of that technology in covert operations and counterespionage."

"And you think they may use some of it on me?"

"It wouldn't be the first time. They moved this site from Roswell to Carlsbad, but the intention is still the same."

Washington again looked nervous. Vit Na appreciated the risk she was taking, but she also realized that Washington was at least as cautious as any human being she had met so far. "Robyn, you've done something to the surveillance systems, haven't you?"

The sharp look she returned rendered all the confession unnecessary.

"How long do we have?" Vit Na asked.

"Ten more minutes. Fifteen at the most," came the answer.

Vit Na hesitated for just a moment as she assessed Washington's veracity. Then she said, "The aliens that you describe are unknowns. They sound primitive, but of course I don't know the circumstances of their visit." She whispered the next few words. "I do have a theory about your mysterious abductions, though."

Washington looked stunned. "But you said no Efilu has been to Earth since the extinc—the migration."

"Very true," Vit Na said, "but this world has regular *local* visitors."

Before Robyn Washington could organize a question, Vit Na decided to take a chance. She might never leave this world. If she were trapped here, she would need something with which to barter. *These people do value information, even if they can't use it,* she surmised.

"They are known as Stellar Fletts. Normally, they're docile and avoid larger concentrations of biological life forms. They feed mostly at night, when the Earth's magnetic fountains peak.

"Some humans and their domesticated mammals must be oblivious to the proximity of a magnetic fountain. Perhaps they occasionally stray into the reach of a Flett in the process of browsing. Mammals just get sucked into the funnel. Their unprotected minds are disrupted by the vibrations of Flett EM fields and subject to major defects in memory, like confabulation. Extensive DNA damage would certainly lend credence to reports of abduction and experimentation."

After a brief moment of reflection on Vit Na's revelation and a glance at her watch, Washington steered the conversation back to her original point.

"The U.S. government—at least, certain factions of it—is engaging in various forms of biological warfare. At first, these activities included modifying natural diseases. Then, they began developing artificial viruses."

"You mean HIV."

Vit Na was not in the least impressed with her own conclusion, but Washington was. "How did you come to that—?"

"Robyn. A virus that is nearly one hundred percent lethal to a single species, that appears abruptly in a single community that the larger society deems undesirable, can be nothing but an artificial weapon. That's painfully obvious."

"Are there any precedents from your time?"

"My time is now, Robyn."

"Sorry. I still tend to think of dinosaurs as creatures of the past."

"People, Robyn." Vit Na took the opportunity to plant the seed of empathy in this fertile emotional soil. "Like you, we're just people."

Washington said, "I am sorry. I really meant no offense. I'm just wondering if there are similar examples from your history—and solutions."

I've got to think carefully about this, Vit Na deliberated. *If this is a setup, this conversation is bound to be monitored. I can't afford to align myself with a weak faction of this culture. Still, there may be a way, if Washington is bright enough to think this through.*

"Do you know this symbol, Robyn?" Vit Na drew a circle with a wave through it and colored half of it in with a pencil.

"Of course—the yin and yang," Washington answered.

Vit Na nodded approval at this new knowledge. "The meaning of this symbol is universal, and it governs the Dance of Life everywhere."

She saw confusion in Washington's face. She knew that directly explaining the statement could be considered subversive, if overheard or recorded; that, she reasoned, could weaken her negotiating position, if she ever had to deal with the U.S. intelligence community. Vit Na formulated a way to encrypt the answer into a fable that might seem innocuous.

"There is a tale that has long been told among my people. It has its origin deep in our antiquity, some one hundred million years ago—before we were truly Efilu." Robyn took a breath as if to couch a question when Vit Na held an open-palmed hand up. "Our cultural origins are complex and not pertinent to this discussion, but suffice it to say the times were wild and in many ways savage.

Intelligence was our greatest weapon against the protomammals and reptiles."

"But I thought—"

The shake of Vit Na's head, nearly imperceptible, silenced the human again. "At the time, there was yet no high-yield food source. We lived on domesticated animals and harvested wild grains. There were only two hundred and fifty enlightened species then. International law was young, rigid, and naïve."

She pointed directly downward. "A certain expanse of terrain, right here, if memory serves me, was of interest to a race called the Kalkin. They were, for the sake of comparison, much like large ground squirrel people. This particular species was exiled from their genus for developing different cultural practices and beliefs.

"They were few in number, perhaps one hundred or one hundred and fifty thousand strong. There were not enough of them to develop this land into what they needed it to become. Their plight was not a unique one, they discovered, so they struck a bargain with a tribe of—well, again, for the sake of reference, a species of powerful antelope people known as the Tal Lurd.

"A contingent within the Tal Lurd community was eager to explore new frontiers and curious about the strange Kalkin. The Tal Lurd were adventurous and strong—natural explorers. The leader of the Kalkin surveyed the new country alongside the Tal Lurd chief, and plans were agreed upon. The clearing process opened flat highlands for burrowing new Kalkin towns while Tal Lurd village construction took place above ground.

"The arrangement worked out quite well for decades, until the Tal Lurd became too comfortable. There were no predators for them to flee, so the young Tal Lurd spent much of their days engaged in mock battles for dominance and mating rights—mostly 'roughhousing,' as you might say, but it did get a bit noisy sometimes. Worst of all, they were certainly nonproductive.

"The Kalkin flourished and developed an aristocracy of sorts. Their industry was limited only by the availability of wages to pay their workers, and of viable land on which to raise crops and livestock.

"The Tal Lurd ranged over large tracts of land in seminomadic fashion. Kalkin nobles began to covet the open territory grazed by their neighbors. Disturbing rumors about the overwhelming strength of the Tal Lurd and their unstable temperament spread. The Kalkin workers began to regard Tal Lurd as dangerous. Kalkin working class, living marginally on the allowances of their lords, came to hate the Tal Lurd.

"This came to be troublesome to the Kalkin merchant lords, so they created herbs designed to enhance the Tal Lurd's natural abilities. Young Tal finding themselves attacked by Kalkin mobs soon had the means to challenge the threat.

"A new contingent of strong, aggressive, undisciplined Tal Lurd arose. They not only fought Kalkin vigilantes, but they pillaged and killed brothers, elders—any Tal Lurd who stood in their way. Divorced from tradition, they lost their 'Way.' They became culturally isolated from their heritage.

"Emboldened Kalkin merchants began to develop strength-enhancing potions—effective, but at the cost of Tal Lurd sterility and susceptibility to Kalkin telepathy. Tal Lurd populations dwindled. Kalkin merchants, furthering their perversion, created the salt pits to spawn Tal Pen, Tal Lurd clones. The result was a class of biological robots, to use your terminology, whose only purpose in life was to serve their masters. The virile Tal Lurd were slaughtered by Tal Pen rape gangs, causing the extinction of the parent race.

"Kalkin working class began to question the hierarchy within their own culture, demanding extermination of the Tal Pen and more of the profits gained from their own toil. The merchant lords had grown rich on the ruthlessness of their new Tal Pen, but their kindred workers began to arm themselves with lethal weapons."

Vit Na paused for Washington to absorb the subtleties of her tale, then continued. "As slave labor, bodyguards, and suicidal warrior hordes, the Tal Pen wiped out any threat to their Kalkin masters—including the Kalkin working class."

"So, the Kalkin won," Washington concluded.

"Hardly," Vit Na huffed. "The Kalkin took advantage of a weakness. The Tal Lurd elders ignored a festering problem: an ever-growing and increasingly disenfranchised population. The Kalkin did not create the depravity; they simply took advantage of an opportunity that was already there."

Washington scratched her neck uncomfortably. "Weren't there any laws to protect innocents from such predatory atrocities?"

"You must understand, the law applied to many species then. It had to be adhered to quite strictly, yet it had to be flexible enough to accommodate a wide spectrum of customs. 'Each race shall have its freedom, as long as it does no harm to another race.' A naïve axiom. You see, the Kalkin found—how do you say it? A 'loophole.' The Tal Lurd youth took these potions of their own accord. In fact, they actually petitioned for their *right* to take the drugs. Because the resulting damage and devastation was visited on their own kind, the Tal Lurd incurred no violation of international law. It was, by definition, an internal Tal Lurd affair—one their Elders would not admit existed until it was too late."

"But you said the international community would step in if there was a violation of one race against another," Washington protested.

"So it would," Vit Na conceded. "However, the Kalkin had thought their actions through carefully. Since the Tal Pen were grown from cloned embryos, and not born of Tal Lurd mer, they could no longer be recognized as an independent species. They were property of the Kalkin. As always, the rich got richer.

"The problem for the Kalkin was that they failed to recognize their own fatal flaw: they never learned how important their own working class was to their survival. Kalkin sold the surplus resources available after elimination of the lower class they replaced with the Tal Pen pseudo-life.

"Neighboring peoples, however, did not tolerate unchecked Kalkin expansion and trading customs. They cooperated to undermine the Kalkin economy. Eventually, the Kalkin merchants began to squabble and feud over their shrinking markets. They used Tal Pen gangs to attack each other as the Kalkin republic crumbled around them. Finally bankrupt, their food supply exhausted, and the population unsustainable, Kalkin civilization fell. The few Kalkin survivors fled back to their parent nation and those refugees were reabsorbed. We suspect that their descendants rose again as the Sulenz people, but no one is certain."

"The Four Horsemen of the Apocalypse rode even then," Washington murmured.

Biblical references, Vit Na observed. She smiled. *Now for the useless information she really wants.*

"To answer your question specifically: yes. Following the Kalkin-Tal Lurd conflagration, a law was enacted to prevent the development of sentient weapons and slaves. However, in the ages to follow, some Efilu found yet other ambiguities in the law. That is how those monsters you know as Tyrannosaurus rex came to exist. Of course, we dealt with that problem permanently."

Maybe someday, when she repeats the story, it will dawn on her that the tale has more than one moral, Vit Na contemplated. *There must always be a struggle. The Dance of Life must play on with its ever-shifting balance of force. It's not easy, but it does provide both stability and passion—a reason to live that strengthens its participants. A spring of fire and water, the Alom.*

The fable had always been an interesting bedtime story for cubs, designed to amuse and teach. Under these circumstances, it wasn't so amusing to Vit Na.

Washington eyed the camera on the ceiling. The red light was still dark.

"We are in danger of perverting our own so-called undesirables into monsters so that some bastard's unthinkable dirty work will get done safely." Washington paused, then asked, "How does a society ensure the rights of the individuals?"

Vit Na's shoulders shrugged. "A people must move beyond mere intelligence to enlightenment."

Humbly, the linguist asked, "How?"

Vit Na acknowledged her candor and said simply, "The usual way. First, learn the difference between what you *want* and what you *need*. The path becomes easy after that."

"Where to begin?" Washington asked, shoulders sagging.

"I don't know, Robyn. The current carries you to the same place no matter where you enter a river, so it really doesn't matter."

Vit Na smiled and thought silently, *It didn't matter then and it doesn't matter now. The Alom flows from what they call yin and yang like a mighty river. One day, they will recognize what is obvious; that the symbol is no more than a cross section of the DNA molecule. And the Dance of Life can NEVER be contained. We don't steer it, we follow it. They'll learn that what can happen once, can happen again...or before.*

Chapter Twenty-Four
— LA COSA NOSTRA —

A re we getting all of this?" Colonel Doyle asked his assistant as he watched the monitor screen intensely.

"Yes, sir." Dixon answered with a little rush, "Every interview has been recorded from three angles. Editing will be done at your discretion."

"Good, good," Doyle said absently, transfixed by the series of answers Vit Na offered the interviewers. He made notes on a pad as he listened.

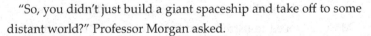

"So, you didn't just build a giant spaceship and take off to some distant world?" Professor Morgan asked.

"Of course not, Claude. We established a number of colonies on the way to our present home," Vit Na said.

"What I still don't understand is how you could have done that. There are certain limitations that even your people would have been forced to observe. For example, there are only a few Earth-sized planets in this solar system. We have investigated Mars,

Venus, and several moons of the outer planets. We haven't found a trace of life, much less intelligence, anywhere."

"I suspect you're looking in the wrong places, Claude. You see—"

"Underground! You built settlements under the icy surfaces of the moons. That's why we haven't seen any of your ancient colonies."

"No. Not exactly. Again, I don't have all the details, but my ancestors did colonize the gas giants."

Morgan had already asked the obvious question: how? Vit Na answered vaguely. "A physicist would be better suited to discuss the particulars, but as I understand it, retexturing the gas worlds had to do with establishing a platform at a distance from the gaseous body sufficient to reduce the effective gravity field to match that of Fi—of Earth. We call it the Ayqot radius. Don't ask me how it's calculated. Large platforms were woven of polymers derived from waste material. They floated on the gaseous atmospheres to form a firm surface. There's more to it than that, but that's the gist of it."

Marisol Estrella spoke for the first time. "I don't have time for this. We've been invited here to indulge this exercise. I've been quietly protesting the farce of alien visitation for years. But if this is even to be remotely realistic, convince me of believable space travel." She leaned in to the table between them. "Intrigue me."

Vit Na smiled and turned to the mirror behind her interviewers.

Morgan looked to Estrella and back to Vit Na. "To say that I'm intrigued would be an understatement. You must tell me more about it..."

Morgan droned on about the technicalities of space colonization, but Vit Na no longer listened. She looked to the reflecting wall again. *Come on, little chief. I know you're watching me. Come get me! I have what you want. The power you crave.*

She tracked the monitoring cameras as they followed her every gesture around the gymnasium. He was up there, this Doyle. She could *feel* it—not with her personal field, but with something else. Something more basic. Her ears twitched. It was as if she had another sense she hadn't previously known about, but the knowledge seemed perfectly natural.

She instinctively fed Morgan coils of uninformative answers. Vit Na spoke in riddles, with never-ending *I-don't-know*s and *that's-not-my-forte*s. She made it plain that she would not let the new chief get anything cheaply. What he wanted, he would have to come after himself.

How deep is your patience, little chief? Do you even know you're being tested? Somehow Vit Na knew he did.

"The little bitch is being evasive," Doyle said.

"Sir?" Major Dixon asked.

"Huh? Oh, I was just thinking out loud, Dixon. That lizard is feeding this guy crap by the shovel. She knows much more than she's telling him. Any idiot could see it. Mendez and these assholes he's hired have been treating her with kid gloves. No wonder they haven't learned shit."

Dixon didn't answer. The new "Old Man" had risen to his feet, pacing. Doyle didn't want to debate interrogation tactics, and Dixon knew it. He was deciding how much info he could get out of the alien before he had to kill her. Dixon had seen this look before on the faces of other men—men of power, hungry for more. Ernie Dixon had even seen this same look in the mirror of late.

This look could kill, and before long, likely would.

Major Dixon had been up all night. There had still been no official promotion to executive officer. That didn't matter. He was now Colonel Ken Doyle's de facto right hand. He felt like Doyle had plunged that hand to the bottom of a cesspool and asked him to pull the stopper.

"Sir, we have everything we need on order. We can have it within the week."

The colonel shot him a cross glance. "Within *this* week, soldier. It's Friday already."

"But sir, the cost. We've already spent more money than we had in our budget, plus that chest of cash you brought with you."

Doyle spoke without turning. "In this matter, Uncle Sam has given us carte blanche. Understood?" He didn't wait for a reply. "Now, run down the inventory I ordered."

Dixon had sunken in over his head, and he felt like he couldn't breathe as he rattled off the items on the list: "Inner Vision's next-generation MR scanner. The Sensidyne 6000 biochem analyzer. The Bull's-Eye laser probe. The Hermes One containment isolation system. And the Crick's Stepladder nucleotide sequencer. That's the bulk of it, sir. Most of this stuff I've never even heard of before, and my dad worked for GE."

Doyle looked at the young major dubiously. "Of course you haven't. They're mostly prototypes. We don't even know if they'll work. We're sort of…testing them for these folks."

Major Dixon still looked uncomfortable.

"We do it all the time," Doyle finished.

"Then there's the $1.2 million in conventional equipment and civilian support staff you asked for, sir." Doyle just glared impassively at the major. Dixon knew he was treading on thin ice. He decided to drop the subject and pivot to a safer topic. "We can get the inventory delivered, but the question is: where to put it all? Hennessy Barracks can't even accommodate storage of all that equipment, much less deploy and utilize it."

"It's not coming to Hennessy Barracks, Major. It's going to San Francisco."

Major Dixon was dumbfounded. "Sir?"

"We're going to need more operating funds. Are you up to it, Major?"

Vit Na found herself in a cell that was even smaller than the original one and more heavily fortified.

So, he wants to meet me on his own terms. Now I know something else about this Colonel Doyle, she mused. *Not only is he bold and ambitious, but he is cautious as well.*

Vit Na's feet and hands were bound firmly by steel bands to the arms and legs of a makeshift forechair. Even her tail had been restrained.

How strange, she thought. *I really find myself looking forward to this interrogation.*

Colonel Kenneth Doyle entered the cell without reservation. He spun a chair around and sat in it backwards, resting his arms on top of the back of the chair. When he tipped the chair forward as he sat, it too resembled a forechair. Flanked by two personal guards, one of whom she recognized as Sergeant Jerry McCray, Doyle looked confident. McCray stood silently behind Doyle and made that threatening gesture with his fingers again. Vit Na wasn't sure if Doyle knew it or not.

"So, Vit Na, how's tricks? Are you enjoying the hospitality?" Doyle asked with a smile.

She noticed that this one had a different kind of smile. It conveyed no comfort, no warmth. Just a hunger. It brought to mind that broken-tailed rat trapped with her in the first cage. Reminiscence of that Jing's fate brought a smile to Vit Na's face as well. Her smile was almost a reflection of Doyle's.

"I've been very comfortable. Thank you for asking. Your sergeant there has made me feel so safe in the confines of my quarters." Then she asked smoothly, "Now, how can I help you?" *Let's see how he handles that.*

Oddly, his smile broadened, yet seemed to fade at the same time.

"I'm glad you asked. I've been listening to your conversations with the other—"

"Oh, Colonel? I was under the impression that eavesdropping was considered impolite, even in this culture." Vit Na interrupted with an exaggerated twitch of one ear. Again, she smiled. A pretty, disarming smile.

Doyle's expression faded further. "Yes. Well, survival sometimes supersedes etiquette, my dear. As I was saying, I've been watching you very closely. I think you know that. I also think you know more about your friends and their technology than you will admit." He waited for a response. Doyle received only another smile accompanied by a vacuous gaze.

"You may not realize this, but we did get one of your compadres." The shock value of that statement hit her with obvious effect. "Didn't anyone tell you?" After a beat, Doyle continued. "I guess not. Oh, don't get excited. And don't get your hopes up for rescue, either. It's dead."

The calm quickly returned to her face, but as team leader, Vit Na roiled. *Who did I lose?*

"Whatever it was, it put up a hell of a fight. It was no match for our weaponry, though. Maybe you're not all so high and mighty after all."

Vit Na answered him smoothly, "Then why am I here, Colonel?" Tilting her head back but still restrained, she managed to look downward on him.

"I'm glad you asked," Doyle replied. He snapped his finger for the third man in the room to hand him a yellow paper tablet. "Just how did they make you invisible?"

Vit Na tensed imperceptibly. *I thought I had drawn them off that subject. He's like a Tralkyz with a bone!*

"As I told Dr. Mendez, I don't understand the technology used to do that," she said.

"I know. You're just an archeologist," Doyle said. He leaned forward in the chair again. "But I'm not Mendez. So, tell me again. This time with feeling." The other guard had handed him some kind of mechanical device that Doyle sadistically switched to life. Instantly, electric current lanced through Vit Na's body.

Fortunately, it was a surprise, to which Vit Na responded with a natural twitch. She noted the reaction her initial response drew from the men watching her and decided to duplicate the same twitch each time the current flowed. She initiated a Sharu exercise to increase the impedance of her skin. In so doing, Vit Na controlled her anguish to the point that a hundredfold increase in current would cause no significant discomfort.

If they believe they are doing me harm, manipulating the situation may become all the easier.

"Please don't make me hurt you again, Vit Na. That's really not my goal. Just answer my questions as truthfully as possible and let's all just get along. Okay?" That deviant grin returned with as much sparkle as ever. "Now. One more time. Why were you at Peterson AFB?"

She hesitated just long enough to affect the resignation the circumstance called for, then answered just before Doyle hit the buzzer again.

"We were a reconnaissance team. Our leader wanted to know just what we were up against. I was sent to guard the team leader's back. I guess I didn't do such a good job of it, though."

Doyle didn't swallow that as readily as she had hoped. "How were you selected for the mission in the first place?" he asked suspiciously.

"I was not a volunteer, that's for sure. As nearly as I can guess—and that's all I can really do—he selected me on the basis of my size."

Doyle leveled his chair with all four legs on the floor and said, "Explain."

"Many of my people are too large to stealthily negotiate your corridors and stairways," she said.

Vit Na recognized their hesitation as the colonel and his men decided whether to believe the lie or not. She added, "I was the wrong size, at the wrong time in the wrong place. So, I got drafted for a suicide mission. After all, who needs an archeologist when you're at war?" She waited for the response.

"That's a good question," Doyle asked. "Why did your mission require an archeologist, Vit Na? I assume you weren't picked at random."

Damn! He's better at this than I thought he'd be. His thinking embodies real military training. I must watch what I say.

"This started out as a scientific expedition," she said.

"And what was the nature of this mission?" Doyle asked.

Vit Na thought through possible interpretations and misinterpretations of her most likely answers before replying. "We were searching for fossilized microbes. They were a missing piece of an important puzzle on my world."

"And your job, specifically?" Doyle prompted.

She smiled inwardly. *Fascinating.* From an archeological perspective, Vit Na had wondered how this culture was driven without the pressures exerted by a predator class.

This Doyle is the missing link, Vit Na gathered. *They breed predators from within! Doyle is as focused as any hunter I've seen. He has already devoured Mendez and has probably undercut his superiors in the Jing Pen military machine. This may prove an interesting contest. Modern intellect against primitive pack cunning.*

Doyle cleared his throat to remind her of the electrical stimulator. Ignoring the threat, Vit Na smiled pleasantly. "I'm sorry. I was distracted for a moment."

"Sorry if we're boring you," Doyle said, feigning offense. "We'll try to be a little more entertaining." He fingered the controls of his torture device.

Vit Na spoke, appropriately rushed, "My job was to locate sites of major city ruins in the remains of the continents we left behind."

"Ruined cities?" Doyle's interest was piqued. "What ruined cities?" He then raised a hand and rephrased. "A better question would be, *where* are these ruins?"

"The ruins were a myth. Any remnant of our civilization is mired deep in fossilized excrement—what you call oil reservoirs. There's no way to get to them, even with your greatest technology. Sorry." She sounded convincingly sincere.

"What about those treasures you mentioned?" Doyle looked down at his notepad to remind himself of the details. "Dragon treasures? You told Mendez that the dragons used some kind of crystal devices to store data. Where would be the most likely place to find such gems?"

She looked trapped for only a moment before starting to answer, but Doyle cut her off.

"And don't give me any of that 'I don't know' crap. As you've pointed out, you're 'just an archeologist.' No one could know where to find sixty-five-million-year-old artifacts better than you."

He has me there. There could be no convincing reason to the human mind for bringing an archeologist countless light-years into outer space unless she was assigned to locate valuable artifacts. Vit Na knew it.

"You mentioned that there was another one of us captured. And killed. May I see him?" Vit Na asked, staring the colonel down.

"Why? What good will it do you?" Doyle considered the request for a moment, then consented. He nodded to the corporal to his left. "Tingley? Bring in the specimen." The corporal took off to fetch the item.

Doyle pressed on with his interrogation. "So, tell us about your military strength here. Your friends may have been able to hide from those boobs in Washington, but I know we didn't get you all. In fact, I know we didn't get anybody who isn't expendable to him."

Efficient, Vit Na noted. Then she cocked an eyebrow. "Who is 'him?'" she asked.

"Why, your leader, of course," Doyle answered. "I know he must be out there somewhere, reconnoitering, biding his time."

She regarded him carefully for a long moment.

He just smiled back at her, waiting.

"You have a remarkable sense of military strategy, Colonel," Vit Na asked, almost angrily. "How ever do you come by it?"

His smile broadened. "Easily."

This is a true predator, she decided, *and at least for right now, he has the sharpest teeth.*

"That was an interesting conversation you had with Ms. Washington yesterday," Doyle said. "How does your society view the mixing of the races?"

The question's probably not as facetious as it sounded, Vit Na decided. She sensed that this particular Jing Pen did not waste words often. *Washington was probably duped into believing we were unmonitored.*

"Do you root for the underdog?" Doyle looked toward Corporal Tingley reentering the cell and then locked his gaze on Vit Na once again. "Or is it survival of the fittest?"

Vit Na almost laughed as she answered, "A little of both, actually."

Corporal Tingley returned to his position, nervously carrying the "specimen" draped in a small, white sheet.

"Ah. Here's your friend now." He reached up, took the package from his subordinate, and held it in his lap. Doyle ripped the sheet off a charred, dismembered forearm and hand.

"Now, I hope you two weren't very close."

Vit Na couldn't help but recoil at the sight of the So Wari limb. She didn't even hear herself gasp in horror, "Tur!"

"Who is Tur?" Doyle asked intensely.

Vit Na hesitated for just a heartbeat. Then she answered, with resignation, "Tur is the one you seek. He is the leader."

"Too bad he went headfirst into the fray. Looks like he's one dino who is permanently extinct," Doyle clucked.

Vit Na strained against her restraints in anguish.

"Vit Na, just who was this Tur to you, anyway?" Doyle became cruel, almost taunting now. "Your boyfriend?"

She countered with restored calm and an unexpected weapon: candor. "No, he isn't my *boyfriend*. He is my *best* friend. I understand your tactics and your intentions as well. You want to know if you can crossbreed me or the nucleic material from this bone tissue with an animal you can control."

Doyle was momentarily taken aback by her keen insight.

She sighed. "I'm never going to see him again!"

Doyle's levity returned. "Sure you will. You'll both live happily ever after in dino heaven."

Vit Na shook her head. "You vicious little beast. You think your bungling band of ruffians can stand against So Wari power?" Her eyes closed tightly. "You'll feel the cold shadow of death before he does."

Still laughing, Doyle said, "That'll be some trick, considering his condition and all." He shook the seared hand in mockery.

"So Wari 'power' doesn't look that tough to me," McCray added from his post at the door.

"You asked about our military strength," Vit Na said. "A war is first won in the heart, then in the mind, then in reality. What lays in your lap is an example of a warrior's heart. To fight against all odds so that others may triumph. Sacrifice is too weak a word for this phenomenon." Then, nodding to the severed limb, she stated, "The one who made this sacrifice wasn't Tur. The remains are too small."

"So, we're supposed to get scared because you've got a bigger T. rex up your sleeve? We'll burn the next one down just as easily. You see, now that we're ready for you," Doyle said with confidence.

Time to shake him up a bit. She tried to smile once again, but what she produced was a bone-chilling sneer. "The meg you so proudly mock was severely wounded. Notice the irregularities of the finger bones? They've all been broken. This warrior survived that first explosion in space. Healing took place within hours. Not only did he survive your worst, he stood head-to-head with your combined armed forces. Moreover, he did it unarmed. He single-handedly decimated your pitiful militia. This one," she added with reverence. "Stihl was his name."

The humans were silent for a moment. Doyle handled the "specimen" with newfound respect. The other two men showed more fear than anything else.

Trying to rally courage in his men, Doyle taunted her again. "You make these So Wari sound like Jedi Knights or something!"

Vit Na responded solemnly. "Or something."

"So, what—are we going to have to fight the champion now, or what?" His demeanor became more serious.

"Now you will face Tur." Vit Na's tone had become grave. "He is like nothing you've ever imagined. The So Wari, as a people, have not lost a war in the sixty-five million years of their history. They represent the vanguard of the most successful coalition of species this galaxy has ever known. No intelligent race in the stars would ever consider challenging a So Wari head-to-head. They are the ultimate martial artists, on *every* level. You should take pride in the death of this one."

Again, she gestured toward the arm in Doyle's lap. "You've seen nothing. Tur has been working his way around you creatures as one would to avoid getting the pulp of crushed insects on one's foot," she spat. "Until now."

"Earlier, you mentioned war. Are we at war with him, Vit Na?" Colonel Doyle asked formally.

She answered in deliberate tones, "No, not war. You've made the mistake of placing yourselves in harm's way. And now, you have Tur's undivided attention. There's no place for you to hide—not even in this military underworld you've created, Doyle." She used his name, instead of rank, for the first time in the interrogation.

Evidently, Doyle didn't notice.

"You know nothing of war. You play games of dominance with your kin and call it 'war.' You don't even have your Si Tyen bene-factors to guide you anymore." She added, "You've slain all the dragons, you see?"

"This Tur can't be all that," Doyle searched her eyes for hints of a bluff. "He'd have made his move already."

Vit Na's tenor was sympathetic now. "By the time you see him, it will be far too late."

Doyle faltered. "You make this Tur sound like some kind of super God-fucking-zilla."

"No," Vit Na smiled thinly. "More like your Satan."

A hush fell over the room. Even Doyle could find no words.

Vit Na's voice cut through the silence like a razor. "You started this game, Doyle. Now you're alone on the field with him, and you don't even know the rules."

— PART 3 —

EFILU REX

— GUIDEPOSTS IN THE DUST —

Trudge we, trios three, Earthbound in perpetual misery.
Too great for crania of men, we endure the Thunder of the Mind.
An affliction so mundane, with so simple a remedy.
Yet, bound by a promise are we. To watch, to preserve.
We mold the tools that shape tomorrow.
Once our work is done, and our Toy chest clean,
We must sweep Mother's face of all blemishes we wreak.
With the depth of its channel, the wilds of its pace and the breadth
of its gap, let the eternal Alom bathe her wounds.

— Interlude —

THE LORD, THE CRONE, THE SAILOR, AND THE JING

Dank fog rolled in, bidden by an otherworldly summons, shrouding the castle in a thick gray haze. The three Keepers mulled restively about the familiar high-ceilinged drawing room.

"This doom is epic," the crone murmured and pulled a drag on the stem of a long theater-style cigarette holder. "A five-soul *synesprit* is unheard of. No wonder we could not anticipate the effects of the Melkyz on our scheme." She blew her words out with the smoke.

"The involvement of the Jing blinded us with our own inhibition device." The sailor stood by the fireplace, chewing one end of his cigar between puffs. "We, too, underestimated them."

The aristocrat retired to his wing chair, stuffed his pipe, and crossed his legs in apparent relaxation that belied his perturbation. "Like a claw, Fate rends anything it catches: friend or foe."

"The deed is done," the sailor groaned, more lament than declaration. "We cannot interfere so long as our Efilu kin are world-side."

The lord of the manor bit his pipe's stem and clasped his hands in his lap. "Our plans must remain in play to whatever end the Alom deems. Even if it heralds Dies Irae."

"Be of bright cheer, my friends," the Chinese spinster smiled, extending anemic hands toward the waning fire. "Remember, this is 1996, is it not? The Year of the Rat!"

Chapter Twenty-Five
— THE ART OF WAR —

President Jonathan Rhodes stood on the veranda over-looking a calm meadow. The morning was cool. The six-foot-four, 260-pound mass of muscle sitting by the door sipped on a mug of hot coffee. Mike Palmer, Rhodes's personal bodyguard, led the Secret Service detail and epitomized a most formidable sentinel. The president's own cup sat half finished.

President Rhodes was grateful for the solitude Camp David afforded him. The First Lady and children were visiting family this weekend. He had the cottage all to himself, except of course for twenty-five marines. The other Secret Servicemen were stationed at various checkpoints. Inconspicuous, but ever vigilant.

The president nodded to the agent on the porch and retired to the library. There, he looked for the pair of glasses he had left on the bookcase. Upon locating them, he shut the door behind him. He reached the bookcase in two strides, snatched the glasses from the shelf, then settled at his desk and proceeded to catch up on some work he had brought with him.

"There appears to have been a misunderstanding, Jonathan Rhodes," intoned an unexpected visitor. "One that should be cleared up forthwith."

The president looked up to see a towering, armored figure addressing him from the center of the room.

Telescien technology allowed Tur any conceivable metamorphosis, but his most recent self-image served as default. The dimensions of the room limited his current height to two meters. Assuming such a diminutive size made him uneasy, so he stood with an unusually formal posture. This Telescien projection was not as elaborate as the one he had used in the Tomet encounter, but it would serve Tur's purposes today.

Though he seemed startled by the intrusion, the human leader still managed to keep his wits about him. He looked past Tur to check if the door was open. It was not. Tur wondered if the man was trying to recall seeing or hearing it open.

"Who are you and what are you supposed to be dressed up as?" Rhodes asked indignantly. His fingers palmed a button under his desk—probably a secret alarm—as he spoke, intending subtlety, Tur assumed, though he found the movement obvious. "Furthermore, how did you get in here?"

"I am Tur, High Commander of the *ReQam*. Here, I represent the Efilu Realm." The verbal announcement was uncomfortable for Tur to utter, but he delivered precise English in a deep baritone. "I have been monitoring you people since our hostilities began. You seem to have a number of misconceptions about us."

Just then, the doorknob turned. Before the door could begin to open, Tur thrust his tail against it, holding it shut. "This is a private conversation, and I don't like to repeat myself." He raised an eyebrow. "You can't afford to miss anything I say. So, let's dispense with any distractions, shall we?"

Tur waited a moment for President Rhodes to absorb the meaning of his words. Seeing that his message had failed, Tur clarified, "Dismiss your guards. They can't protect you from me anyway. If I wanted to harm you, the deed already would have been done."

Rhodes looked his guest in the eye as he pondered his options. With no more than a nod to Tur, he crossed the room and opened the door. Tur made no move to stop him.

"Mike, I have an unexpected guest. I accidentally touched the alarm. Settle the men down for me. There's no need for alarm. There's no danger. Do you understand?" he said.

The monologue was well rehearsed, and Mike Palmer understood perfectly. The president was in no immediate danger, but the small force of Secret Servicemen was to surround the library from every conceivable exit. The marines were on alert for unseen intruders.

Palmer could not see the second party in the room and made no effort to try. Someone else *was* in there. No one but the president was to get out without being apprehended or killed.

Rhodes closed the door and returned to his desk. Tur watched him carefully as he sat. He made a mental note of the human commander in chief's clumsy attempt at trapping him before continuing his own remarks.

"You have been acting on the assumption that we are alien invaders, coming to this world to subjugate your people."

Rhodes folded his hands on the desk in front of him and said, "And you're not aliens?"

"No."

"Then what are you?"

Tur was becoming impatient, but he knew some basic information was necessary if these animals were to keep out of his way. After all, they had never encountered superior beings before. They didn't know how to act.

"We are the originals." Tur let the words hang for a moment. "Our races left this world long ago—about sixty-five million years ago, actually. An accident threatened to render this world uninhabitable. Our ancestors chose to migrate to safer worlds where we had more opportunity to expand.

"We took representative specimens of every species with us to keep our new worlds viable and similar to Fitu." Tur grimaced. "Which you call Earth. Some of our people stayed behind to resurrect this dying planet—animal rights, environmental preservation, and such nonsense." Tur waved his hand dismissively, "Obviously, they were successful in getting the process started before dying out from the toxins our previous salvage efforts failed to eliminate."

Rhodes nodded as he considered the story. "So, in other words, this world was once yours."

"No." Tur calmed himself. "I mean this world is *still* ours. By Efilu law, soil that has spawned any Efilu is the demesne of the Greater Society, to manage as it sees fit. There is no statute of limitations on this canon. The fact that you yourselves have a similar tenet should make the matter simple enough for you to understand."

Rhodes raised an eyebrow before responding. "Are you referring to our practice of eminent domain?"

"It would seem most applicable," Tur said with approval at the president's grasp of the situation.

"Just how many of you are there on Earth now, Commander?"

Tur was puzzled by the question. *What possible difference could that make to him?* "Twenty, all told," he answered.

"And your ship?" Rhodes asked.

It became clear to Tur that this vermin was preparing to bargain with him. Tur decided to watch as the Jing Pen chieftain played out his options.

"We presume it was destroyed in your second assault, along with the majority of our equipment and company."

"I take it your people have certain...special needs?"

"Of course," Tur conceded.

The president nodded again, as he did when making important decisions, and casually swung his chair around to look out the window behind his desk.

Tur found this odd behavior amusing.

"I can't promise you anything on the spot," said Rhodes. "Our government doesn't work that way."

Tur interrupted him. "Your title is commander in chief, is it not?"

"Yes, but I answer to other parties empowered to place certain checks on my authority. May I suggest that we set aside a reservation of terrain suited to your special needs in exchange for the benefit of some of your extensive knowledge?"

He assumes we seek asylum. Funny. Tur sat on his haunches now and folded his arms. "And you expect to bargain with us for advanced technology?"

Rhodes shrugged. "You can't expect us to put ourselves out on a limb simply out of the goodness of our hearts, can you?"

Tur didn't smile, although he was more entertained than threatened by this attempt at extortion.

"You, personally, don't have very many choices," the president continued. "You're not leaving. Oh, and you can attack me, but they'll kill you." The president gestured toward the men on the other side of the door. "I'll be replaced by the vice president, and your people will still have the same problem, but then they'll be down by one. With a total number of twenty—I'm sorry, nineteen—and no way home, that's not a choice you can afford to make."

President Rhodes played sincerity well. He waited for Tur's response.

Tur stood and walked past the doorway. "Rhodes, is it? You don't know what I can or cannot do," he stated.

"Where are the rest of your people hiding?" Rhodes asked.

Tur thought about it. He guessed Rhodes figured he had nothing to lose by asking. Tur had nothing to lose by answering. "We took over one of your bases. The one in the Aleutian Islands. You call it Eareckson Air Force Base. It served us well."

Rhodes gawked, "You can't be serious. That's impossible. We've been getting regular, accurate reports from that base for weeks. That facility is among the most heavily guarded in the country."

"Yes." Tur answered slowly and deliberately. "We've virtually mastered your language—and your routines."

Then, with astonishing speed, Tur turned, flung a closet door open, and dashed through it.

The president heard the door latch upon closing behind the creature. He immediately went for the hall door. He opened it and beckoned the guards, directing them to the closet.

There was a jagged hole torn through the floor. The wood looked as if it had disintegrated from rot. Rhodes watched a heavily armed man drop down through the hole while another shone a flashlight down on him. The man in the hole looked around at ground level, then up at the president and Mike Palmer. He shook his head.

Jonathan Rhodes slammed his fist against the closet doorframe. "Damn!"

Tur recounted his meeting with President Rhodes in good-natured fashion.

"So why did you tear the hole in the floor?" Bo Tep asked.

"They have no concept of Telescien technology," he answered. "Given this one's ambition, I'd like to keep it that way."

Suddenly, the humor left Tur's voice. "Something unexpected, though. I think this fur-mite's actually going to challenge us. I told him about our utilization of that base we just abandoned."

The new Efilu headquarters was nestled under undisturbed cornfields in Iowa. A benefit of Mini-Wave technology: excavation with *in situ* construction. No exhaust, waste, or noise; completely undetected. "If I'm right, they'll attack that base with everything they have," Tur said, then hesitated.

"But there's something else?" Jeen prompted.

"This 'government.' It's not a true republic as we were led to believe. It's more of an administrative bureaucracy. Perhaps a simpler version of our own. We need to know who this commander in chief answers to and what unseen influences control his administration. I'll have another meeting with him in the morning."

Tur stood and indicated for Bo Tep, Jeen, and Ikara to follow him into the monitor room of the newly fabricated Efilu headquarters. "We have a lot of work to do," he said.

The next morning, President Rhodes was up early again, this time, back in the Oval Office reviewing security measures for the White House. His Secret Service contingent had tripled, complemented by two Navy SEAL teams inside the building and Marine Special Forces on the roof and grounds. All were armed to the teeth.

He would *not* have a repeat of the Camp David fiasco today. With the best electronic surveillance technology sequestered in the infrastructure of the subbasement and catacombs beneath the White House, while E-3 AWACs canvassed the airspace around the capital, Rhodes felt assured of three-dimensional security. If this

Tur had the balls to return, and somehow Rhodes feared he did, the President of the United States would not be caught unawares.

The president's special committee had hardly seated themselves when Rhodes entered the Situation Room. Even before taking a seat himself, he started chewing out General Chey, as the chairman of the Joint Chiefs, for the military's incompetence.

"Mike, what the hell am I paying you for, anyway? You tell me about this glory-boy...what's his name? Doyle?" Then, pointing to Schmidt, he said, "And you assure me that everything possible is being done to find these aliens—correction, dinosaurs—and yet one shows up at Camp David of all places?" He pounded the table for emphasis. "You call that security?"

Rhodes stopped to take a cleansing breath, then continued. "Check the security of the phone lines, and not just for tapping. I have reason to believe someone may be fooling around with our data systems. I've brought in someone who has some interesting ideas you gentlemen should think about," he said, pointing to a visitor seated at the table.

"I'd like to introduce Dr. Derrick Barnhill from the University of Toronto. Our top paleontologist, Will Parker, is nowhere to be found. It's as if he and his colleagues just dropped off the face of the Earth. None of our other paleontologists have Dr. Barnhill's credentials or discretion."

He waited while his team looked wordlessly at the unassuming scientist. "Dr. Barnhill was kind enough to join us at a moment's notice," the president continued. "Maybe we can combine resources to get some leverage against these monsters. They must have some weakness, or else why would they have left when things got rough on Earth millions of years ago?"

Dr. Barnhill added, "And more importantly, why have they returned?"

"Another potential weakness. Good point, Professor. I want to know exactly what we're dealing with. I want you and your—"

The room went silent.

Tur stood at the opposite end of the table as if he had been there all along.

"You have some gall coming here!" Rhodes exclaimed.

The creature paced casually around the table in silence, seemingly taking note of the oddities to be found there. Incredulous gawkers followed Tur around as if they expected a chorus of "April fools!" at any moment.

Rhodes went on as if continuing an interrupted argument. "You break off negotiations begun in good faith, including a generous off—"

Tur cut him off. "We were not in the midst of negotiation. I was explaining the facts of life to you to save time and energy." Tur circled back to the opposite end of the table and met the president's glare. "Obviously, it was an exercise in futility. Now we are going to have to do this the hard way."

Jonathan Rhodes stepped on the hidden alarm button in the floor before responding. "So, I guess you're going to disintegrate us with a death ray from your ship. Oh, I forgot—your ship has been destroyed. Pity. Then I guess you'll have to send your vast armies to punish us. Oops, that's right—there are only twenty of you, aren't there? Well, what are you going to do now, beat us up one at a time?"

He expected to see Mike Palmer come charging in with a SEAL team at any moment.

It didn't happen.

"No interruptions today, Rhodes. I need your full attention. Your subordinates may stay if you wish."

The president quickly calmed himself and, without taking his eyes off his unwanted guest, addressed his staff. "Gentlemen, I'd like to introduce High Commander Tur of the Efilu Empire."

Tur said nothing, but continued to stare into the president's eyes.

Rhodes paused, then asked, "Commander, I'd like my staff to stay. They can learn a lot from this encounter."

"With such limited powers of retention, I can't see where they'll be of much help to you," Tur said blandly.

Rhodes ignored the jibe. "Now, I presume you're here because you have a counterproposal?"

"There's no need for proposals," Tur said. He slid the upholstered chair aside, sat on his haunches and made himself comfortable at the end of the table. "You took hostile action against a facility you thought we occupied. That was a premature act."

Rhodes blurted out, "You could never have escaped that attack—if you were there at all!" The realization of Tur's tactic slowly took root in his consciousness. "You—you were lying, weren't you? You wanted to throw us off your trail. Have us waste resources!"

"First lesson: I have no reason to lie to you. It's a waste of thought. Second lesson: I like brevity. Your future responses are to be more to the point. There's no need to embellish; my decisions do not waver with details or excuses. Third: since you were aware of our presence there, that attack represented a declaration of hostilities on the Efilu Realm. Claims of ignorance can no longer apply."

The committee members turned to the president for the counterpoint… and to see if he would blink.

"Tur, no matter how powerful you may be, you have no resources here. Even if you have lasers or blasters or whatever, they will someday run out. You don't know the terrain, you have only a handful of men, and you are trapped here. You'll have to deal with us eventually. This is our world now. You *have* to negotiate—if not with me, then with my successor. We are not going to just go away," Rhodes said.

Then the president added, with manufactured confidence, "He who knows when to fight and when not to fight will be victorious. Your kind has had its time in the sun. Make way for the new."

Tur pursed his lips with disappointment. "I expected you to be briefed earlier. It seems your species has limited organizational powers as well. You should know why I'm here today."

"And why is that, exactly?" the president asked.

Tur responded coolly, "Damage control."

A hush fell over the room.

Tur said, "Your tribal bylaws proclaim these United States as a democracy headed by an elected commander in chief. However, we spent the better part of yesterday afternoon learning otherwise."

The air in the room became heavy for Jonathan Rhodes. The other men seemed tense as well.

"This republic is run by a few economic factions. Major decisions simply represent compromises between them. We had to change our entire approach," Tur said.

Genuinely curious, Rhodes asked, "Your approach to what?"

"Management, of course. We have identified each faction and come to terms with them. Nelson Dithers was the last holdout. He took a little coaxing to come around, but eventually, he did. The others fell into line with much less persuasion."

"What?" Rhodes babbled, then, barely above a whisper, "What have you done?"

Seeing the confusion in the human faces, Tur added, aggravation dripping from his every word. "We've brought them all to the same side of the table."

Chatham broke the silence of the senior staffers. "And what side of the table is that?"

An expression that was nearly a smile crossed Tur's face. "My side."

"What makes you think *we* will keep quiet?" asked the secretary of state. "Tur, we have access to a telecommunications network that can broadcast information to virtually every corner of the globe. What do you think will be the response to an alien invasion?

The armies of the world will pursue you relentlessly until you are cornered and finally destroyed."

Tur inhaled and exhaled slowly in exasperation. "I'm rarely guilty of being too subtle. I see now that subtlety is a relative concept, so I'll speak plainly. You have no armies, no media, no following. I do. Try to expose me, and I'll have your own friends remove you. Permanently."

Rhodes seethed for a moment, then said, "Americans have much more integrity than you credit them with. This isn't over yet."

The So Wari was losing patience. "You are clearly a little dense. The point is: this conflict is over. It was finished while you slept. Your entire power base has been co-opted in a bloodless coup. I now control the economics, politics, communications, and trade in the nation you call your *United States*. To control the military effectively, I need this office as well."

Rhodes wasted no time in responding to the offer. "You'll never have my cooperation in selling out the American people. I'll fight you tooth and nail."

Tur eyed him calmly. "Be careful. There are those in my camp who feel that the entire human species should be eradicated. That would be a potentially time-consuming course of action, but it's feasible, if it comes to that."

Body language was clearly universal. Rhodes's allies were all distancing themselves from the president. He was scared now. He didn't know how or why, but he believed that Tur could and would kill every human being on the planet.

"The very fact that you mention an option so drastic tells me that you can't do it." Rhodes swallowed hard. "I'm sure there is some law—some limitation—that prevents you from committing genocide, even if you are capable of it."

Tur replied with a cold, deep stare.

"In fact, if you could do it, you would have done so by now and dispensed with the theatrics." President Rhodes felt that he had regained some ground with that statement, until the phone on the table rang.

Tur gestured for the man to answer it. The president did, then switched on the speakerphone.

"Rhodes?" The assemblage heard a voice that needed no introduction. "This is Dithers."

The board chairman of the world's largest telecommunication company never made direct calls to the president. The president picked up the receiver.

Nelson Dithers sounded scared. "Jonathan, I don't know what's going on here, but I had a visit last night from someone who asked to remain nameless. No one saw him but me. I've told this story once before, and my confidantes thought I was crazy. This... 'individual' said you would know what was going on.

"He touched my nine-year-old grandson, Joshua. Just touched him! Now Josh's been admitted to Georgetown Hospital. He's in intensive care with unbearable agony, and the cause is unknown. The doctors have tried everything they know to break it." Nelson Dithers sounded unhinged. "Nothing is working! They can't even ease it with general anesthesia. The child has been medically paralyzed and placed on a ventilator. The doctors say his EEG shows no change in brain activity. He's still awake and writhing with that excruciating pain. This creature said He's willing to release His hold on Josh if He gets His way, but if He gets any more opposition from your administration, He'll touch the rest of my family. Jon, I have thirty-two grandchildren."

The air in the room felt thick with the fear spreading from man to man.

"I'm an old man, but if this happens to another one of my family, you never will be. Give Him what He wants, or I'll destroy you myself!" The voice was replaced by a dial tone.

Rhodes stared at the receiver blankly then replaced it. He sat to recover from what he had just heard, but then the phone rang again. Hesitantly, he opened the line.

"Mr. President?" It was another familiar voice.

Chey said, "That's Admiral Healy, commander of the Pacific fleet."

Healy's voice was controlled, but terrified. "Mr. President, why are we on yellow alert, sir?"

"What are you talking about, Healy?" the president asked.

"I've spoken to every nuclear sub commander in the Pacific, sir. Every ship is on yellow alert. Only your password can do that, and only when used with that of the secretary of defense and the chairman of the Joint Chiefs of Staff. We thought it was a malfunction, but it won't respond to any override command on our end, Mr. President. Please tell me if we're about to go to war and with whom."

The president looked at Secretary Mason for support. He found none. "Rest assured, we are not *at* war and we're not *going* to war with anyone. Stand down all weapons immediately. That's a direct executive order, Admiral. Do whatever it takes to follow it. Rhodes out."

He avoided Tur's gaze for a moment. Then he looked up after what seemed like an eternity.

"What are you trying to prove with these threats?" President Rhodes asked, trembling. His aides could almost feel the table shake as he did so.

It was said, Jonathan Rhodes had nearly supernatural intuition when it came to reading an opponent. He'd always supported those comments. But his instincts told him that he didn't want to read this one any further, and that no mortal man ever should. He also knew it was already too late to yield to the Efilu.

"If you need my help, you had better negotiate a little more amicably, Tur," said Rhodes.

"I did not say I needed *you*, Rhodes. I just need this office. The vice president will do nicely if I am forced to remove you." Again, Tur spoke, voice ominous and resolute. "I have no interest in compromising."

"There must be some middle ground," the president said, almost begging.

Tur delivered surreal truth with little emotion. "You will cooperate because you're a politician. You have no real loyalties. This is all an endless game to your kind. It's more important to you than eating, breathing, or procreating. You'll do anything necessary to remain 'in the game,' no matter who suffers for it. Now that you realize 'the game' is not over, you'll play by the new rules. Or not at all."

Every man in the room realized that the United States of America had, as Tur described, been the victim of a quiet takeover. Now they were just fighting for personal survival. The eternal unsaid law of politics is simple: only fight to the death when there is no tomorrow. Otherwise, go with the flow and fight another day.

"This is the essence of war," Tur said. "I don't need your mythical 'death rays' to subjugate this world. What I am capable of wreaking is beyond your ken." Tur raised a heavy eyebrow at the small audience. "You have translated winning as ruling, losing as being vanquished. The truth is, winning means surviving and losing means not. Challenging me means losing."

The knowing, fearful look on each man's face confirmed his comprehension of Tur's message.

The president found his voice. It came out as a hoarse rasp. "You can't just come in here and treat us like pawns in some chess match. We are men!"

Tur looked at him as if Rhodes spoke an unintelligible language. "What's the difference?" Tur waited honestly for an answer to his question before clarifying their respective positions. "Your species has always played its little games. I am merely changing the rules a little."

"So, now we play your game, is that it?" Rhodes asked in frustration.

"So Wari don't *play*," Tur chuffed, a nearly subsonic tone. "You have no choice except between cooperation and destruction. I can go through your entire line of succession and your public would never know the difference. Plausible reasons for the changes can always be manufactured. Every one of you knows that, or you wouldn't be here," Tur explained. "I will leave the details to the survivors."

Tur stood and walked away from the table. His image began to glow a little as he armored up, assumed battle vision, and prepared to dematerialize. Before he faded, he turned to the president. As Tur spoke, the mixture of light and shadows made his stiffened, long ears, tips curled up, look vaguely like horns. His deep-set eyes shone crimson. His spiked tail wrapped around before his feet, completing the unintentionally sinister image.

"You need to understand this: there will be order on this planet. My order. I only need a few of you to restore it. It doesn't matter to me which of you I use. Overall, nothing need change. You will still answer to the powers that be. From now on, though, *they* will all answer to me."

Chapter Twenty-Six

— ESCAPE FROM ALCATRAZ —

E YES ONLY" was stenciled in red across the document. Colonel Ken Doyle scanned down to the middle of the first paragraph in search of a single word.

"T.U.R."

He said the name aloud, and a cold sweat broke out along his spine. It was an acronym: Transcontinental Unrest Resolution. Doyle read the rest of the communiqué. The content was chilling, in light of Vit Na's warning.

FROM: THE OFFICE OF THE CHAIRMAN OF THE JOINT CHIEFS OF STAFF
To: ALL FIELD COMMANDERS
SUBJECT: OPERATION T.U.R.: TRANSCONTINENTAL UNREST RESOLUTION

1. ANY SUSPECTED ALIEN ACTIVITY WILL BE IGNORED. THIS IS FALSE INFORMATION PROPAGATED BY A FOREIGN ADVERSARIAL GOVERNMENT DESIGNED TO PANIC THE PUBLIC WITH APOCALYPTIC NOTIONS. SUCH ACTIVITY WILL NOT BE INVESTIGATED ON ANY LEVEL. ANY SEARCH OPERATIONS OR INVESTIGATIONS CURRENTLY BEING CONDUCTED WILL BE TERMINATED IMMEDIATELY.

2. The adversary's secondary intent is distract and unmask our foreign and domestic covert operations. All lines of communication with JCS will remain open. Any and all files on suspected alien activity will be sent to JCS office at the Pentagon.

3. The rising public hysteria resulting from the "Apocalypse Syndrome" has increased the already present concerns of this advisory council. By Executive Order, POTUS invoked martial law as of 16:00 today.

4. Major General Dale Schmidt has been assigned as Task Force Commander. His orders supersede all local authority. Any insubordination by commissioned or non-commissioned personnel constitutes a breach of Executive Order, the punishment for which is detention and special court-martial. Civilian noncompliance is to be met with immediate incarceration and enhanced interrogation.

5. All media outlets have agreed to systematically reduce the amount of "alien-related" information they disseminate, in support of martial law. Violators of this plan will be in noncompliance with the Executive Order and Operation T.U.R. will be implemented accordingly.

6. This memo supersedes all previous orders. All follow-on orders will be issued by the President and JCS.

The document was signed by General Michael Chey and countersigned by the president himself. All signatures were accompanied by the appropriate seals.

"Even the president?" Doyle said aloud. He resumed hand-written entries into his own command log:

This could mean a major shake-up in the government. No, not just a shake-up. Not just a conspiracy. This has all the earmarks of a takeover. By whom?

Wishful thinking had Doyle in hopes of a human extremist faction takeover.

The local television news was on mute as he mulled over the memo. He clicked past CNN, CNBC, and C-SPAN. All the familiar talking heads were on the air. Not a hint of trouble. He switched over to the Armed Forces Network. Again, not a hint—not even a break in the scheduled programming. Then, at the end, there was a clue—almost as a footnote.

Reassignments.

Doyle wrote furiously: *Major General Dale Schmidt has been assigned as the assistant to the Joint Chiefs and stationed at Pentagon City. Ostensibly a promotion under any other circumstances, but why now? And who would be replacing him?*

Major Dixon walked in while Doyle pondered ramifications of this new command structure.

"Sir?"

"Huh? Oh, it's you." A startled Doyle vaulted out of his reverie and stopped writing. "Come in. What's our status?"

"Fort Alcatraz was completely operational as of twenty-one hundred hours, right on schedule. I just stopped by to make sure your office was satisfactory and to see if you needed anything." Dixon looked concerned. "Anything wrong, sir? You look upset."

Doyle hadn't realized his mood was so obvious. "I'm just a little tired. I had to make a few log entries for the official record. What's the status of Hennessy Barracks?"

Dixon was caught off-guard by the question. "Lieutenant Colonel Lyle Hampton officially relieved me at fifteen hundred hours today, sir." A subtle tone of "who the hell cares" underlay the major's response. Dixon went on, giving what seemed more like a formal debriefing than a casual answer. "Our guests were escorted over at or about thirteen hundred hours, including Matthews and Olsen. The captive was transported at fourteen hundred hours. All traces of its presence have been eliminated. As of twenty-one hundred hours, Alcatraz Island stands completely secured."

Alcatraz had been a tourist attraction in the San Francisco Bay area for years. A colorful history surrounded it. The Native American protest of the early seventies bore late fruit. The federal government finally capitulated and agreed to renovate the facility as a joint Native American administrative headquarters.

The renovation was to be completed by the Army Corps of Engineers over a ten-year span at a cost of one hundred million dollars. That was dirt cheap, all things considered. Then-Senator Henry Mason had chaired the oversight committee. The trade-off was that the armed forces would have access to the facility while it was under construction, or until the renovation costs were paid in full.

The colonel had pulled a few favors out of his hat and rattled a few skeletons in some tightly shut closets in order to gain the run of the island. Now Doyle realized that his shenanigans might just backfire on him.

Doyle also knew that Dixon was too sharp a soldier from whom to keep a development like Operation T.U.R.

"Ernie, we've got a little problem here." Doyle didn't even notice when the major came to full attention. "What do you make of that?" he said as he handed Dixon the memo.

Dixon's brow furrowed as he read. "It sounds like we should have taken Vit Na's warning a little more seriously, sir."

Doyle lunged up from his chair and ripped the memo out of the other man's hand. "No shit, Sherlock!" He sat down and hoped his shaking was less apparent from the seated position. "He's trying to send her a fucking message. The question is, how much time do we have to accomplish our goal?"

"Well, sir, all the hardware is in place and running. Reassigning personnel is going to be a problem from now on." Dixon tapped the document lying on the desk. "We have about half the technical staff we're going to need. Even taking into account the talents of Mendez and his people, we're still short about eight essential men for what needs to be done."

Doyle drummed his fingers impatiently on the desk. "We'll use civilians."

"Sir?"

"Civilians, damn it! I have files on five ex-naval officers who serve on the faculty at the UCSF hospital and zoology department. Then there's you and me, Ernie. We'll have to make do with that."

Ernie Dixon inhaled, ready to voice a metaphor about the difficulties of steering a ship and rowing it too, but he caught himself. He knew Doyle was aware of it. The colonel was just in too deep.

They were both in too deep. So, it was either sink or swim.

Vit Na wasn't fully awake yet. She felt different somehow. It wasn't just the overwhelming effect of the ether. There was something else. She lay on the cold metal table with a feeling a human might have described as *déjà vu*.

This table was smaller and colder than the previous ones, although by objective measurement, it was almost identical to the one she'd awoken on weeks ago, in Hennessy Barracks. It was a moment later before she realized she was strapped to it. She tried to scan the area with her personal field and almost choked from a dry throat as she gasped.

It's gone! She double-checked. *Nothing.*

Loss of consciousness should not affect a personal sphere of influence. Have I been found out? All hope of escape was gone. Without the energy she had sequestered in her personal field, she had no chance of bypassing the security networks.

Vit Na had not cried tears of despair in over fifty years. She shut her eyelids tightly now against the indignity, which only served to force the soft, gentle droplets out of the corners like a cascade of pearls. No Sharu trick could prevail against emotions as intense as what she felt.

A hand appeared from nowhere to brush the tears away.

Who...? She looked up.

The face was familiar even through the tears, and she enjoyed the slightest moment of relief. Had Clyde Olsen come to rescue her?

Then her flesh went cold. Her first impression had been either hallucination or wishful thinking, for it was not Olsen at all.

Sergeant McCray stared down into her big, dark eyes. "This is your new home, Vit," he snickered. "I know. I know. No need to thank me. Those tears of joy are enough." He stopped laughing and sneered, "Better get used to it. No one ever gets out of here. This is the Rock." He turned to go, but then faced her again.

"You know, I never noticed how pretty you were until I saw those tears. I'd have to say, you're damn gorgeous!" He touched her face, then gave her a surprisingly gentle caress. "I've never felt skin so soft. Not even on a newborn. Tingley, come feel." McCray groped her torso, gliding his palm across jet black pelt. He beckoned to Corporal Tingley.

The man came closer, but did not touch her coat.

"Tingley, you're such a wuss!" He rubbed her head. "She can't hurt you. Look." Before either companion or captive could respond, he bent over and kissed Vit Na deeply on the mouth. He smiled as she spat his saliva out of her mouth with disgust.

"See? No harm done. The eggheads say this thing's biologically compatible with us or something. It's like letting a dog lick your face. It's perfectly safe! Loosen up and take over. I'm off duty as of twenty-two hundred hours. I have a poker game with the army boys tonight, and do I feel lucky!" He rubbed his hands together, looked at Vit Na, and laughed.

"Don't worry about Tingley kissin' on you, Vit. He doesn't like girls much. Oh, that's right—you're not really a girl, are ya?" He affected a terrified look and went out the door, the echoes of his laughter fading slowly down the hall.

"He's a real jackass," Tingley said after the laughing had died into the distance. "Are you all right, M—Miss?"

Vit Na barely heard him. She sobbed softly. Tearlessly.

How dare he? How DARE he?

Corporal Tingley shook her gently.

"DON'T TOUCH ME!" she snapped. "Don't you ever touch me." Vit Na regained her composure. She endured one final shudder, then looked coldly at Tingley as he spoke.

"He had no business taking liberties with you that way. He has no right to belittle everyone the way he does."

He paused thoughtfully for a moment.

"Do you have—people who like their own kind—where you come from, Miss?"

Vit Na didn't blink when she responded. "Again, Corporal?"

"Homosexuals. Gays. That's what he meant. When he said, I don't like *girls*." The corporal looked agitated. "They say we screw thousands of men a year, but I only had one friend, and he's gone now."

Vit Na allowed the distraction. "What are you talking about?"

"My sexual preference is men. Males," he said reassuringly. "But even if you were a man, I would never make such an assumption. To touch someone without invitation is off-limits. Who does that? What about your people? They're an advanced race. How do you live with those among your people who have other tastes?"

Vit Na looked puzzled for a moment, then thought to herself, *Ah.*

"We don't tolerate them," she replied.

She watched his reaction. "You can't mean that you're as backward as these Neanderthals," Tingley retorted in dismay.

Vit Na said in her most soothing voice, "You don't understand. We don't tolerate homosexuality because it's a waste, not out of moral judgement. The only way your kind knows to express intimacy is through sexual intercourse. We do have intimate relationships, but they are nonsexual. We delineate a difference between intimacy and sexuality. We mate only for a short time each year. Those encounters are for procreation and the advancement of the species, not for whimsical and frivolous reasons."

Tingley looked at her skeptically. "Come on—are you telling me you don't enjoy sex?"

"Of course not. I love it! We all do. That's not the point. It has its time, it has its place, and it really is not so important what your mate looks like. We have our mates, and we have our friends. With very few differences, one male's organ feels pretty much like any other's when it's inside you. From what I'm told, the reverse is also true. We just enjoy the moment to its fullest and cherish the memories."

Tingley looked disappointed. "And then?"

Vit Na said, "And then we look forward to the next one! Homosexuality only serves our purposes during times of over-population or pestilence, when the urge is uncontrollable, but fecundity is undesirable. Even then, there are more constructive ways of using that energy than wasting precious seed."

The corporal thought about it and nodded. "Interesting philosophy."

Vit Na took advantage of his receptive mental state to probe his knowledge. "What happened while I was unconscious, Corporal?"

Tingley was caught off guard. "Oh, they etherized you. I'm sorry. I've never seen that done intravenously before. I always thought IV ether was lethal."

Vit Na prompted him. "I have a strong constitution."

Tingley caught the hint. "Yes, well...they did an MRI on you. You know, that magnetic resonance thing. They had some problems with it, I hear."

So that's what happened to my personal field! Vit Na thought. *It was stripped by the magnetic scan. My sphere must have distorted the image beyond recognition. I'll just have to convince them to run me through it again, so I can reconstruct it. It's my only way out of here.*

"I think I can help you with that. The ether is very toxic." *But it won't be next time!* "My body went into a kind of generalized seizure activity that scrambled your image. A clearer picture can be obtained while I'm awake."

Tingley squinted one eye at her and asked, "Why are you being so helpful with our study of you?"

Go with a plausible lie. "The alternative to getting noninvasive data from me is not appealing."

Again, Tingley nodded in understanding. "I'll let 'em know."

He draped the sheet back over her restrained body and left the cell, and Vit Na breathed a quiet sigh of relief.

———◦◉◦———

Mendez sat in one of two chairs in front of Doyle's desk. He rubbed his fingers together absently. Matthews sat in the other chair. They had been granted a reluctant extension on their progress report. The cumulative data led to more questions than answers.

"No wonder these people ruled the Earth," Mendez muttered.

Matthews came out of a dazed reverie and said, "What?" He looked at his watch. "I know. Doyle's late."

"No. Not that. Look at the resources we've poured into this project so far, and what have we come up with that Vit Na hasn't already told us?" Mendez asked. "Nothing."

Matthews commented, "Kind of nice to work with such fancy equipment, though."

Mendez conceded his point grudgingly. "Doyle's a real patron of the sciences."

The scanning electron microscope Doyle had "acquired" for use on this project was but one of the technical toys that filled the cubicles and halls that formerly comprised Alcatraz Penitentiary. The cells made very pleasant, if monotonous, office space. The mess halls, offices, rec rooms and laundries had been converted into auditoriums, labs, conference rooms and computer server centers. The good colonel planned to get the most out of his prize captive. He had spared no expense.

"What kind of man is this Doyle, anyhow?" Matthews asked.

Mendez considered the question for a moment. "The worst kind."

Matthews pushed the issue. "What business did you have with him that you got to know him so well?"

Mendez looked up in thought, wincing at the halo that surrounded the fluorescent ceiling light. The answer that Matthews had so casually asked for had eluded Javier Mendez a thousand times.

"I wouldn't know where to begin. Most of our activities were sanctioned by the government. Many more weren't. He has a way of getting your mouth to make promises your conscience can't fulfill. Most of our work is still classified, but you wouldn't believe some of the—"

The door opened behind them and they both turned to greet the new arrival.

"Speak of the devil," Matthews said.

"And I'll make you a deal, doctor," Colonel Doyle sneered as he entered the room.

"Why are we here?" Mendez asked coldly.

"Your progress reports. You and Andy Griffith here are overdue for one."

"When we have something to report, we'll tell you," Mendez said. Then he admitted, "So far, we have nothing but new questions. What did the MRI show, anyway?"

Doyle looked peeved for a moment. Then he said, honestly, "Nothing."

Mendez looked at Doyle quizzically, then glanced at Matthews to see if he had any insight into the response. Hoyt just shrugged.

Mendez asked, "You mean there was nothing unexpected?"

"No, I mean we literally saw nothing that made sense. Just a jumble of static and noise. No image. We tried to reconfigure the data four times. Nothing. The man guarding her on the last watch says she said she had some kind of seizure from the ether, but I'm not sure that I buy that either." Doyle scowled. "At any rate, she says we may have better luck if we repeat the procedure while she's awake. That's fair. She knows the next step is dissection, and she wants to delay that as long as possible. So do I.

"I had an idea about an electromagnetic aura surrounding her. It would explain some of the MRI readings," Doyle reasoned. "We went old-school. Took some Kirlian photographs of her."

Mendez was at the edge of his seat. "And?"

"Stone-cold normal. We compared them with some control photos we took of the staff. No difference." He crossed to the comfortable chair behind the desk and sat. "We went ahead with the repeat scan. Technically adequate, they tell me. The radiologists are reading it now."

Mendez scrutinized Doyle as he sat there with a furrowed brow. "There's something else eating you, Ken. What is it?"

Doyle squeezed the bridge of his nose between his thumb and forefinger. "I had to release two members of your team today. Robyn Washington and Clyde Olsen." Before being asked, he expounded more freely than Mendez had ever known him to. "The big brass wanted to know why Project X is still intact after that memo from the Pentagon. I don't so much mind turning

Washington loose. She's harmless. Olsen worries me, though. I just know that son of a bitch is going to pull some bullshit stunt."

The colonel stopped talking for a moment as he watched Mendez, then asked, "Why do you keep rubbing your fingers together like that?"

Mendez stopped, self-conscious. "Oil from Vit Na's skin. Very smooth. Very light. It feels good. Really good! I guess I've been doing this for hours." He noticed Doyle's concerned look. "Is there a problem I should know about?"

"One of my men was found dead in the john tonight—Sergeant Jerry McCray. He had been playing cards with some of the other noncoms. There was some drinking and maybe a little light drug use. I don't know. All I do know is that a perfectly healthy thirty-five-year-old soldier just keeled over and died."

"Why, Ken, I didn't think you cared." Mendez said.

"I don't. No more than I care for your snide remarks." Doyle cut him a derisive look. "What bothers me is that he was the second-to-last man to have contact with Vit Na!"

Mendez's jaw dropped.

"Yeah, not so funny anymore, is it?" Doyle asked.

"Does this other soldier remember anything out of the ordinary going on between your dead man and Vit Na?"

"Nothing at all," Doyle said in resignation. "He says she was completely restrained the whole time. Funny thing, though—he was surprised, but not too broken up about McCray's demise."

Dr. Matthews speculated out loud. "Still, no one else has suffered any ill effects from contact with Vit Na. It could be just a coincidence."

The colonel added his usual skepticism to the dialogue. "There's an old saying in the intelligence game, Doctor. 'Coincidence is a conclusion of exclusion.'"

Mendez placed a hand on Matthews's arm to silence any further discussion. "We'll check all the specimens from McCray and Vit Na for any matching traces of toxins."

The colonel nodded. "Go to it. In the meantime, I can't risk any more men. Stahl and Hollingsworth have a little surprise in store for our guest."

I've got to get out of here while I can, Vit Na thought. *It's only a matter of time before they figure out what I'm doing. That stupid sergeant hadn't made things any easier.* She bristled. *That disgusting saliva-drinking ritual. They'll never find the traces of venom in him or in my normal secretions, but they'll suspect, and I just can't afford that.*

She occupied an old solitary confinement cell. The overhead light was very bright in the small space. The fortified steel door was electronically controlled from the outside only. A small square opening was enclosed by steel bars. The legacy of Alcatraz haunted the recent renovation.

The new guards were like living nightmares—monstrously huge and grotesque. They rivaled Tralkyz in size, but their build was bulkier. There was something else unnatural about them, too. But Vit Na had no time to think about it. She had to concentrate.

One of the beasts jammed its snout in between the bars in the small opening in the door and bared its teeth. Some Jing used the 'smile' for a more familiar sentiment.

The portal is obviously designed for communication with prisoners, she surmised. *It effectively prevents harassment of visitors from the occupant. Glad it works both ways.*

She wove her newly restored fortified personal field in and out of the maze of computer circuitry that made the new Alcatraz facility manageable. She smiled as she overcame one system after another. She needed no modems or accessories to conquer cyberspace. She just needed to get past those infernal security measures. She had been at it for hours now.

Music played gently in the background. Hollingsworth intended for it to soothe the strange animals left to guard her.

Bears! Vit Na realized. *I knew I had seen references to such creatures. But that size can't be natural. Growth enhancers of some kind must have been employed. And all that metal hardware they're wearing doesn't look very friendly.*

Just then, a number of familiar faces entered the outer room: Hollingsworth, Stahl, Mendez, and Matthews, led by a grinning Colonel Doyle.

"It looks like your assessment of your friend's talents was accurate. He's taken over the central government and imposed a loose version of martial law. We underestimated him."

"*You* underestimated him," Vit Na said, gyrating rhythmically to the music. "You were the only independent human who knew anything about him. I assume you are plotting some kind of countermeasures?"

I won't underestimate this Jing again, she promised herself.

"Nothing you can do anything about," Doyle said. "I don't know what happened to my man, McCray, and I don't care. What I do care about is that you remain safe and secure in my custody. Some of your friend's orders are actually working to my benefit. I've been able to justify the restoration of Alcatraz Island, under the guise of preparing a short-term, high-security detention facility. Everyone knows that California is full of radical dissidents. That little stereotype also gave me a free hand to have Air Force personnel and equipment reassigned to me for security purposes. It works out nicely."

Doyle pointed to the two bears in the room. "Even these little pets were easy acquisitions under the T.U.R. mandate. I like them," Doyle said. "They follow orders without question, and I never have to worry about security breaches. Kodiak bears are naturally the largest land carnivores on the planet. Stahl, Mendez, and Hollingsworth developed them for use in battle. A judicious use of growth hormone at the right stage of development increased their size by over thirty percent. They are trained to use an array of surveillance and telemetry equipment in conjunction with an impressive arsenal of heavy weapons no three men could hope to carry and operate. Not one elite soldier in the world stands a chance against one of these 'teddy bears' in hand-to-hand or even knife-to-hand combat. I've got a dozen of them ready to go. It'll be interesting to see them go up against your So Wari. It'd even make a cool video game."

Stahl stepped up behind Doyle and said, "We used a similar process to produce Akita dogs the size of ponies."

"The two species work very effectively as a team," Doyle said, petting the animal's snow-white coat. "They're the ultimate combination of speed, strength, ferocity, and endurance—coupled with expendability." Doyle fanged a lupine smile. "We can always breed more."

Stahl worked an electronic control device that seemed to direct the bears' behavior.

Hmm. If I can get into that control algorithm, I could make this exit short and simple—and cripple their command chain in the process. She continued her interface with the security system, expanding her efforts to include the control mechanism for the Kodiaks.

"We've learned a lot from you, Vit Na. I intend to learn much more," Doyle said. He grinned that horrible grin he often used before doing the unthinkable. "You like music, I see."

"I like to dance." Vit Na smiled prettily. "I told you that before."

"I'm glad you're happy. You're going to be my trump card. If worse comes to worst, I can use you as a bargaining chip with Tur."

"No, you can't," Vit Na quipped. "Even if he discovers I'm alive, he'd never negotiate my release. As far as he is concerned, I am a casualty of war. My final duty to him is to do as much damage to the enemy as possible with what remains of my life."

Almost there—got it! Vit Na allowed herself a moment of internal celebration at having gained control of the entire system, but there was still a slight glitch. *Why can't I activate the weapons system? Nuk! There's an activation override switch.* Exerting her will to push Stahl bore no fruit. *It operates manually. Damn that inhibition field. This will be tricky, but I think...*

"Vit Na, tell me something. I know why I'm smiling. Everything's going my way," Doyle said. "I have a little trouble understanding the reason you're smiling, though."

She stopped dancing. "I'm smiling because I know something you don't know," she purred.

Go ahead. Jump, Doyle.

The colonel motioned for the bears to come closer to the cell door, their guard up. He hesitated.

Why is he so damned cautious? she fretted. *Well, looks like he needs another little nudge.*

The lock to the cell door clanked, and the door suddenly swung open. The bears growled a warning and then fell silent.

Instinctively, Bruce Stahl flipped on the weapons system activation switch.

Vit Na smiled broadly. She turned a bear toward the shaking Bruce Stahl via the remote communicator in the beast's middle ear. The bear's machine guns blazed to life, cutting Stahl's own short. The bullets destroyed the control box. Humans scattered. Bullets ricocheted of concrete block walls and poured cement floors, piercing tiled ceilings and bouncing off the cement of the underside of the floor above them back into the room.

She activated another bear. Their two heavy machine guns crisscrossed the small room with three hundred rounds of pure chaos. She saw Doyle remove his sidearm from its holster and tip over a heavy steel table for cover. Hollingsworth and Mendez joined him. A wounded Hoyt Matthews was dragged to safety, bleeding profusely. Stahl's body looked like a mound of ground beef.

An armed Colonel Doyle still blocked Vit Na from the exit. He fired futilely at the bears. She commanded the Kodiaks to aim their machine guns at the lights and fire. When they stopped sparkling, the windowless room turned pitch-black.

Now or never!

Perfectly at ease in utter darkness, Vit Na smoothly negotiated the fallen bodies and debris in the room and leapt silently over the table. She evaded Doyle's blind aim effortlessly. Vit Na commanded the bears to face one another before making them fire their weapons again.

She opened the outer door and slipped out before the humans had a chance to turn around and adjust to the bright light from the hall. By the time Doyle recognized that the sliver of light heralded no reinforcements, Vit Na was gone. The door slammed shut behind her and locked electronically.

I'm not free and clear yet, she reminded herself, not allowing the joy of the maneuver to cloud her thinking. *I think I can create holographic illusions in the surveillance network. Minimize use of Blending, save some strength—I hope. Once I'm out, I'll crash the whole system. By the time they sort everything out, I'll be miles away.*

She made her way through the complex, evading confused soldiers and staff. She *Blended* sparingly, limiting the integral ruse to evade direct encounters with armed men. The security center was near the main exit. She counted eight guards.

All this commotion and they're still here? Then it occurred to her: *The alarm—they're confused because there's no alarm. Well, we'll just remedy that situation.*

At Vit Na's command, the klaxon sounded. The guards ran to the magazine, broke out the automatic weapons and grenades, and filed out of the room along their preassigned routes. One individual remained: a woman, still monitoring camera displays that showed only static. Vit Na crept in behind her, hooked her tail around the woman's lean neck, and slammed her head against the nearest wall. Her skull cracked. Life slipped away before her limp body slid to the floor.

Vit Na's eyes found the exit from the building less than ten feet away—sweet escape!

The door to the lavatory swung open. "Hey, Susan, what's going on out h—" The big sergeant stopped short, seeing the dead body on the floor. Vit Na—caught by surprise, and so focused on the freedom nearly within arm's reach—didn't have time to *Blend*.

The man was dark-skinned with straight hair. The name tag on his khaki jacket read "Juarez." Motionless, Vit Na locked gazes with the new adversary and measured the threat. Both pairs of eyes darted to the sidearm lying on the table between them. With her tail, Vit Na flipped it and the table out of reach of the soldier. The man turned back to the intruder and smiled as he reached down into his combat boot to draw his knife.

"I don't know what you are, but you're fucking with the wrong guy today," he warned. He flipped the blade into readiness with the dexterity of one who had done great harm many times—and with pleasure. He assumed a combat stance and moved within lunging reach of Vit Na as she observed the knife, wide-eyed.

After months of captivity, she knew how these soldiers were normally armed. This one was nastier. *That weapon's not government issue. A personal weapon of choice?*

He feinted several thrusts to the chest and throat, then smiled more broadly at the unarmed Melkyz.

This one looks like he knows what he's doing, too, Vit Na surmised.

With a frightened, desperate look, she half-extended her finger-claws. His attention went to them, and he backed off a foot or so.

A distinct clicking sound crisply broke the silence in the room. Juarez looked down at the source. He only caught a glimpse of the sickle-shaped claw on her toe before it blurred into motion. He looked up to see Vit Na backing away before he realized she had slit his throat.

His last act in life brought desperate hands to his throat to stanch the bleeding. The assault knife dropped between quivering knees to land on the floor with a *clink.*

Juarez never fully appreciated the elegance of her cut. She had cleaved all the way back to the vertebra in one stroke and pulled the razor-sharp claw through the soft flesh.

Odd. Vit Na watched Juarez until he stopped moving. *He was a trained soldier. Why would he deliberately draw attention to his deadliest weapon instead of away from it?*

There were no further complications in her escape. She breached the final barrier of razor wired fencing to the outside world.

The February air smelled cool and sweet in her nostrils. Ruffling her down upon contact with the frigid San Francisco Bay water, Vit Na swam with alacrity to the shore and climbed toward the tree line. From her new vantage in the woods, she looked back at the island, still visible in the moonlight. She breathed in the night and exclaimed, "Free!"

Chapter Twenty-Seven
— BATTLE LINES —

Devit reported to Tur after inspecting the new core of Pentagon City. It was secure from the world of man. Officers from three of the armed service branches stood at each door interfacing with the old structure. No human with less than the rank of colonel or Navy captain was permitted entry. The sentries had the glazed look that indicated the new Volition Override in effect, a clever device Devit had developed to make the most of available Jing Pen personnel.

Dropping an electromagnetic static field into the frontal lobe and limbic system to cut away and replace the intrinsic neural activity was quick and easy. Jeen had wasted no time in encoding telecommand receptor engrams into the fields. The system operated like any gel-com and responded to focused Efilu thoughts. It solved the problem of human resistance to telepathic command.

"We are secure, Commander," proclaimed Devit. "Exterior to this gel core, the building called the Pentagon shows no trace of disturbance. The top-ranking officers are all inside. Out there"—he gestured with his head—"we control everyone down to the rank of lieutenant. The rest will follow our orders through them."

Tur nodded absently as he read through the most recent reports from the U.S. military network. The data was thick and monotonous, but this was no deterrent to So Wari diligence.

Jeen watched him for a while before asking, "Why are you spending so much time on those routine reports? I've already read them all. There's nothing of consequence there."

Tur didn't respond.

Jeen tried a different approach. "Maybe I can help," she said, reaching an open hand toward the sheaves of paper.

"You wouldn't see it," Tur answered with little more than a glance to meet her inquiring eyes.

"Wouldn't see what?" she pressed.

"The clue."

She felt her frustration rising. "What clue?"

Jeen had been doing well since Ikara's outburst. They had all felt relief at the return of Tur's aggressive style, but now he seemed distracted again. Jeen refused to retreat.

Tur realized that she asked a fair question and lowered the tiny pages from his face. "These Jing Pen know more than they're telling. Not all of them, but enough of them to be dangerous. This intelligence community is fragmented; they each have their own agendas. One group doesn't know what the others are doing. Add to that the fact that they receive more binary electronic data from their satellite facilities than they can correlate under normal circumstances. Now that every one of them is transmitting everything, these idiots are completely inundated."

"Your point, Commander?" Jeen asked.

"There are records of a project called Blue Book responsible for collecting data on extraterrestrial sightings, abductions, invasions…" Tur returned to his reading.

Jeen shrugged, dissatisfied with the response. "Any validity to the project's reports?"

"None. It's mostly trash. Hoaxes, rare natural phenomena, occasional Solar Fletts that get temporarily trapped in the atmosphere and feed on random magnetic fountains until they can break loose of the planet."

Intrigued by the last mention, Jeen pursued it. "Solar Fletts?"

"Sorry—an archaic term. *Stellar* Fletts," he corrected. "We haven't bothered with them in millions of years. They're harmless to us."

"So?"

"So, the Jing Pen leaders have spent millions of dollars on monitoring these vague events, and they've hidden it well from the public. How do you think such a paranoid mindset would react to an actual attack?"

Jeen's eyes widened. "Then you think Stihl and Vit Na are alive?"

"No. Not really. I saw Moc's report. Stihl couldn't have survived, but they may try to exploit his remains. They're heavily into recombinant DNA and cloning research. Vit Na, on the other hand, may still be alive. If so, I feel personally obliged to retrieve her." He paused. "Or her remains."

In a respectfully caring tone, Jeen asked, "How will you know?"

"There will be...an inconsistency in the status reports. Something very small, downplayed."

As he spoke, he noticed something unusual in the command roster. "Hennessy Barracks," Tur read aloud. "It has changed command three times in the last few weeks. Dixon, Major, Army. Doyle, Colonel, Air Force. Hampton, Lieutenant Colonel, Army."

He laid the stack of papers down on a ledge of the six-story chamber. "Jeen, pull up the tactical map of U.S. bases," he instructed.

She activated the gel console and complied in silence. Her eyes darted rapidly back and forth over the four hundred installations on display. She finally said, "It's not on the map."

"Bring up everything we have on Hennessy Barracks," Tur said. "I want Chey in here immediately."

"Search completed, sir," Major Dixon reported upon entering the lab. "She's not on the island."

Colonel Doyle sat on a lab stool, deep in thought. "Okay, we go to plan B."

"What's plan B, Colonel?" Hollingsworth asked.

Both Doyle and Dixon looked at him with contempt.

Doyle said shortly, "Find the subject, Hollingsworth. Wherever she is."

Hollingsworth pressed, "Is this to be a 'search and destroy' mission, sir? She still has the fail-safe device in her chest." Hollingworth's words were heavy with venom.

Doyle thought of the plastic explosive wired to a micro transponder that had been placed in Vit Na's chest wound during her initial recovery.

Doyle answered Hollingsworth with more sympathy than anyone thought possible. "No, I want her retrieved alive if possible. The detonation receiver has a range of about four hundred yards. She's beyond that for sure. And the plastique won't leave very much anatomy behind. I want more than just some tissue recovered intact."

"She didn't leave much of Stahl intact," Hollingsworth said.

Doyle had already chosen to ignore that subject when Mendez and Matthews burst in.

"I got something you need to see, Ken." A winded Javier Mendez dashed his report on the table and flipped several pages. "Here!" He stabbed at the center of the page with his finger.

Doyle looked at the graph, puzzled. "What the hell does this mean?"

Mendez had almost caught his breath. "This is a spectroscopic analysis of the oil I was rubbing between my fingers yesterday. After you implied that it might be lethal, I scraped as much of it together as I could for analysis. It's innocuous to us, but its index of refraction is identical with that of air. That's why it feels so slippery but looks so thin."

Completely in the dark, Dixon asked, "What does that mean exactly, Doctor?"

Doyle answered the question for him. "It means that she can become invisible at will! Damn it, why didn't you know about this sooner?"

"To find something, you have to know what you're looking for," Matthews interjected. "This discovery was pure serendipity. She hadn't used this power in front of any of us."

"We assumed that her disappearing act at Eareckson was managed by means of a sophisticated electronic device." On his feet and beside himself, Doyle paced the floor. "I don't think her success has been all luck."

"Think she's gotten help, sir?" Dixon asked, then in little more than a whisper, "Think she's made contact with...Tur?"

"Shit!" Doyle bristled. "Luck or not, she now has four advantages: the power of invisibility, superior strength, superior intelligence, and the freedom to use them all."

"You left one out, Ken." Mendez had long since stopped acknowledging rank when addressing Doyle. "She has the ability to control animals. We may not be able to depend on canine trackers to find her."

"Not necessarily," Dixon interrupted. "She went directly for Stahl in the confinement area. Why?" There was a collective pause as everyone tried to catch up with Dixon's train of thought. "He controlled the bears! She achieved some kind of override, all right, but to do that, she had to knock out the primary control box."

"It makes sense," Doyle pondered. "No one else was so specifically targeted." He nodded, still thinking it through. "So, we may have limited use of conventional police dogs—which she could rip to pieces if they caught her anyway," Doyle said in frustration.

"I can fix it." Everyone in the room turned to look at Hollingsworth. "Bruce and I worked on this years ago. I know the system better than anyone…alive. Give me some technical support, and I'll set up a random radio signal receiver in the headgear. She'll never be able to get a fix on the frequency in order to override our control again."

Doyle clapped his hands once with genuine enthusiasm. "You have carte blanche, Mr. Hollingsworth. Let's go, people!"

The Northern California woods were cold. A light snow covered the frozen ground. Vit Na circumvented every broad patch of virgin snow or took to trees, leaping trunk to trunk. In the distance, a pack of dogs barked, their voracious howls nearing.

They have systematically cut me off. Doyle anticipated my attempts to access any computers or telephone lines. I should have gone toward the city instead of running for the forest. Vit Na raged inwardly. *Stupid! I let that damn tower light sweeping the forest influence my decision.*

I have to find some way to signal Tur and the others. She paused. *I sense more of those bears and dogs, but no men. I wonder why?* Doyle's words echoed in her mind. *Expendability.*

She worked her way up the heavily wooded hill and saw her answer. A hundred yards away, a handful of men lay in ambush. Equipped with night vision goggles, listening devices, and automatic weapons with silencers, they awaited their quarry.

They're going out of their way to keep this little chase quiet. Why not just squeeze me between the beasts and soldiers? Vit Na vacillated for a moment, deciding which force to confront. She had tried to order the dogs and bears in another direction, but to no avail. Something had changed. They didn't respond to her signals anymore. She didn't look forward to having to face those savage Jing Pen on even terms. The men were easier targets, and the darkness, her ally.

A red light flickered to life on an adjacent tree. *Infrared motion detectors*, she noted. Muted shots zipped through the cold night air, ending in an inhuman death cry.

A deer—a ten-point buck—had triggered the device. Vit Na looked up. There was a similar device on the tree behind which she hid, but it hadn't been activated yet. Irises wide, she turned her ears forward to capture every sound in anticipation of their next move.

A light split the darkness and stopped at the fallen animal. "It's just a deer." The holder of the flashlight appeared to be the ranking officer and said, "Stein and Johnson, go get it and drag it out of the line of fire. We don't want it distracting the bears and dogs—or warning the subject."

Two men ran furtively through the woods to the rapidly-cooling corpse.

Obviously, they'll have to deactivate the detection chain to move that carcass.

Vit Na *Blended* and took advantage of the opening in the perimeter, following the soldiers so closely she could feel the warmth of their breath. They lashed the hooves with rope, each taking an end, and towed the limp animal. Vit Na hid her footprints in the drag-path of the deer. The threesome disposed of the deer remains and trekked back to the fortified position. Vit Na evaded the movements within the little camp, all the while listening to clandestine plans unfold.

"The major says that we lay low after the detection grid is done. The nerve gas ready?"

"Yeah, Sarge. I can start launching the grenades at the first signal."

Vit Na looked at the crate behind her, one with "Toxic" stenciled across its face. *They want to flush me into that gully ahead—where they can gas me, with those beasts at my heels all the way. I guess they really are expendable.* She planned her next move. *I'd better listen a bit longer, learn their strength and position before moving out of the area. Maybe I'll do a little sabotage before I go.*

A lower-ranking soldier inventoried the gas masks piled on a rack in front of her. "These have all checked out, Sergeant. I put the rejects in the can to avoid confusion. They say this stuff causes permanent brain damage."

"Nice work, Smitty," his superior said. "Let's take no chances. When things pop off, we'll be in the thick of it."

Seizing the opportunity, Vit Na used her smallest finger claw to make tiny triangular tears in the masks, at the seams. Against positive pressure, they would appear intact. The negative pressure resulting from inhalation within the mask would suck outside air in like a one-way valve. The gas was stored in canisters stacked on their sides.

Hmm. Metal.

Laying her hands on the crate, Vit Na managed to build up a low-grade magnetic force field. She used the total mass of the containers for leverage and made small punctures in several of the bottom canisters. The gas concentration wouldn't build up to toxic levels for hours, but when the top canisters were removed, the rate of gas flow would increase exponentially within the camouflaged tent.

Six fewer animals to contend with, she thought with satisfaction.

Vit Na learned what she needed to know, identified the scent of what the Jing Pen considered "odorless" gas for future reference, and then disappeared back into the darkness.

Doh couldn't have been happier. He not only had the opportunity to observe the Jing Pen in their natural habitat, but moreover, he could actually discuss their behavior with them.

"What do you know about the theory of analogy, Doctor?" he asked.

Doh imagined his own distant ancestors at the same stage of evolution as this Jing Pen scientist. Fascinating!

"Biologically?" asked General Schallek.

Doh identified General Schallek as the army's chief investigator in the biological defense division.

The general intoned, "The principle of convergent evolution holds that two given organisms of different phylogenetic origin and stages of development can arrive at similar solutions to the same environmental problem. The best-known example is flight. Birds, insects, and bats all fly with the benefit of wings."

The doctor was seated at his desk facing Doh, who had perched himself against the fourth-floor railing overlooking the central atrium. Weyef stood below on the floor of the atrium, her head reaching the middle of the third floor. She glanced up briefly at the mention of wings. Apparently choosing to ignore them, she continued to monitor satellite communications on the console in front of her.

"Of course, the respective structures have different origins," Dr. Schallek pontificated. "The bird has feathers that fan out from its upper limbs to assume aerodynamic perfection, whereas the common fly takes advantage of outgrowths of its exoskeleton. The less efficient bat uses modified hands to fly."

Doh listened, thoroughly entertained.

"Humans, by contrast, have taken lessons from Mother Nature and combined the greatest features of all three to create flying machines that are superior to any nature has devised so far," Schallek continued.

Out of the general's line of sight, Weyef also listened, her eyes following him as he went on, oblivious to her attention.

"Our technology more than makes up for what we humans lack in physical prowess." A look of consternation crossed his face. "I still can't understand how your people survived the climatic upheavals of sixty-five million years ago. Granted you have accomplished some real miracles, but we would have surpassed you, had we started on a level track. The fact is, the complex mammalian brain is capable of more cognitive functions and is faster than any other in nature.

"First we dream, then we comprehend, then we create," Schallek bragged with impunity. Enthralled, with keen interest and amazing tolerance, Doh allowed the human to believe he posed no threat. "For example, a mere forty years ago, the microwave oven, cellular phone, and space shuttle were science fiction. Today, they are reality. If your people had this kind of capacity, you would never have been cast out."

Doh was confused for a moment, then actually offended. "What do you mean, 'cast out?'"

"In biblical terms, the serpent—i.e., you people—were cast out of Eden. We never took the Genesis story literally until now. This attempt to take over our world is doomed to failure."

Doh interrupted him. "You have either heard or told too many of your fireside stories. You're beginning to believe in your own myths." Doh had never encountered a species so...so *arrogant* as to espouse superiority to Efilu society. Doh found his liberal, objective mind-set crumbling. "If anything, humans were made in *our* image. Mankind has been the interim custodian of this world, and look what you've done." Doh spoke with atypically brutal candor. "Pollution, mayhem, disorder everywhere!"

Schallek was startled by the intensity of Doh's response. He recovered his composure and countered, "We will learn your strengths, your weaknesses, and finally your technology. We will win in the end. Oh, not me personally, but mankind. The laws of nature favor us, even with all of our flaws."

"Your species really suffers from delusions of grandeur, doesn't it?" asked Doh. "You are expecting some version of your *War of the Worlds* mythos, in which you'll win by discovering some miraculous weakness we've overlooked. Humanity's worst fears are only born of the familiar. Your most hideous nightmares are mere combinations of actual experiences. Such dramatic assaults are too crude. Subliminal weapons are so much more effective. It's no wonder you have anticipated our influence over your species erroneously."

Doh interpreted the absent look on Dr. Schallek's face to indicate feigned humility, so he continued. "Natural forces are always terrifying when they're beyond your control. Yet a virus need not be as lethal as HIV or Ebola to incapacitate billions. To be effective, it simply has to leave them chronically dysfunctional. Then the survivors become a drain on the target society." Doh chuckled wickedly, unable to control himself. "You vermin barely hold your own against the forces of chaos. Unrelenting winters, decades of drought and fires, civil war? Just think about it. What chance could you have against us?"

"Divine law," the general blared, his retort nearly desperate. "The will of God."

Weyef had never seen Doh angry before. *Refreshing,* she thought and joined the discussion, which was developing into a heated debate.

"You speak of law, fur-mite?" Weyef asked. "Two things make a law work. The first is its acceptance. The second, and more important, is its enforceability. The most natural of laws dictates who wins and who loses: *the law of survival.* On this world, in this time, *we* are the ultimate force. Therefore, *we* are the law.

"Your ancestors contended with mine in an environment where protomammals had all the advantages," Weyef declared. "You still lost! We were small and weaker, but smarter. Here we are again in conflict, two hundred and twenty million years later, and it looks as if the outcome will be the same. As Doh suggested, we have surveyed your popular entertainment media. Sun Tzu's wisdom indeed!" Weyef's eyes narrowed at the little man. "You quote ancient So Beni battle philosophy as if it were your own."

She had risen on her toes in order to catch him with the intensity of her scowl.

"You must have learned something about war. Do you think you have learned enough to compete with me?" she asked with a smile. Weyef opened her hand as if to allow some invisible object to alight on it. "We have crushed challengers that could reduce this planet to cinders."

She clenched that hand into a fist.

After a pensive pause, Weyef looked almost sympathetic. "In all honesty, we should never have come into conflict. We are on... *different* orders of existence. You don't even realize that you never had a chance."

A radio was playing music softly in the background. A show tune was in full swing when Weyef speared her elongated fifth finger through the speaker.

"You may have us now," General Schallek boasted, "but when the combined armed forces of the United States of America realize this alien conspiracy—"

"They'll what? Show us some real destructive power? We already have your top officers and executives. What good do you think a few lackeys who were effectively trained never to question authority will do for you?" Weyef settled down, flat-footed.

The doctor looked frantic. "Well, what about lasers?" Schallek neared tears. "We have secret weapons, you know?"

Weyef glanced upward over the railing without moving her head to give a terse, verbal response. "Don't make me hurt you."

"Do you have one of my people in custody? Yes or no, General?" Tur was like an avalanche momentarily poised at the brink of a cliff.

Sweat beaded on General Chey's forehead as he lined up for the interrogation along with his lieutenants.

"What's going on at Hennessy Barracks?" Tur demanded evenly. "I won't ask again."

Chey swallowed hard in a dry throat.

Jeen and Ikara had discovered that there was an entire level of consciousness they could not directly access through their machinations. Pain, they soon learned, was an unreliable incentive for truth-telling. Tur had devised a more direct form of persuasion.

Tur hesitated for the briefest moment before clenching the force field he had woven round the human's nervous system. The eviscerated mush of General Russo's brains smacked the wall between General Chey and General Schmidt, then dribbled down to the floor.

General Russo had been responsible for the entire southwestern sector for the U.S. Army. He didn't have the necessary answers. Tur's inquisitorial eyes turned to the next in rank.

Angry and frustrated, Tur gripped Dale Schmidt by the torso, with his thumb pressed firmly against the fragile Jing sternum. "Schmidt, you are the immediate superior for this Colonel Doyle. Are you going to tell me what I want to know, or is this going to be a short year for senior officers?"

Schmidt, unlike Russo, did have the answers, but he had just been too slow in giving them up. The mangled mess from Schmidt's failure to communicate was more than General Chey's stomach could stand. His lunch made a sharp contrast on the floor next to Dale Schmidt's viscera. While on his knees, scrambling to maintain balance in his own excrement, Michael Chey simply could not stop babbling to the Efilu commander about Hennessy Barracks.

The Groove Gourd. A quiet little café, typical of the San Francisco night scene, drew a genial gathering with its subdued, smoky intimacy. Its headliner, Carla Shedrick, was hot tonight, and the room loved her. Not the expected site for intel exchange.

Robyn Washington cast a furtive eye through the crowd from the coat check desk, looking first for Doyle's men. Surely, she had eluded them. Turning her scrutiny to finding her contact among the guests, Robyn relaxed for the first time since her exit from the Rock.

"Looking for someone?" A pretty hostess asked. "Can I help?"

"No, thanks," Robyn spoke over the music and applause. "I see him. There in the front row."

The handsome smile ensnared her even from the door. Robyn cut through the audience toward the stage and the man who instigated the standing ovation at the end of Carla's song. Even after the crowd joined him on their feet, the man still stood at a six- or seven-inch advantage over them.

Robyn took a deep, reminiscent breath and drank in a smile which grew more disarming as she moved closer to him. "You'll never be the next Woodward or Bernstein with meet ups like this." She whispered in the ear of one Adrian Dunbar.

"Robyn!" he shouted, before the applause of the last number ended.

At the sound of her name, Washington became wary. "Not the best choice of seating for a clandestine exchange of information."

He reached down and hugged her, then took her hand. They threaded through the throng to the bar. He looked into her liquid eyes, raised both her hands in his, and kissed them gently.

"Wow," he said, looking her up and down. "You're no longer that naïve eighteen-year-old college sophomore, that's for sure."

"Some things can never go back to the way they were," she said to him, "but congratulations on the TransWorld News anchor spot."

Seeing him there in the club setting, Robyn remembered him in the warm glow of their history. Goose bumps rose in the wake of strong fingers gently stroking her forearm.

"So, how are you?"

"I don't know yet." Washington said, self-conscious. "Hey, can we sit somewhere less conspicuous?"

"Where?"

She searched the dimmest corners of the room and spotted a booth that had just been abandoned by jubilant fans. "There," she pointed.

Adrian led her across the club toward a couple of empty stools at the far end of the bar. "No, not here. That booth there." She took him by the hand and directed him around the bar impatiently. The pair slid into the booth and faced each other across the table.

"What's with this cloak-and-dagger bit, Robyn?"

"Look, A.D., you know I don't go in for theatrics, so just believe me when I tell you this is some serious stuff we're into here. Both of our lives are in danger if I've been followed."

He sobered. "Okay, so stop wasting time and spill it."

She paused for a moment, not sure where to begin. "First of all, I have no evidence to support what I say, but you know me well enough to know that I'm telling you the God's honest truth."

He said nothing, but returned an intent stare as she told her tale.

"Aliens and dinosaurs rolled into one?" Adrian said when she finished, after several moments of careful listening. "Am I looking to be Bernstein or Scully?"

Robyn permitted herself a laugh. "You obviously didn't watch the show. Mulder's the guy, Scully's a woman."

"I caught enough of it to know Scully was the skeptic and Mulder was the true believer." He stared across at her thoughtfully, "So how did you get out alive? That's the kind of info that people disappear for having."

"It's complicated, but I think they control part of the government somehow."

His mouth dropped opened. "Dinosaurs. In the White House?" Adrian said incredulously. He thought for a second more, then added humorously, "Now, wait a minute. Maybe that's not so far-fetched."

"I'm serious now, A.D.," Robyn said. "Someone *made* Doyle release the whole team. Of course, he's had us followed as discreetly as possible. I hope I lost them. They can't be that good."

"Look at this attitude!" Dunbar chuckled. "So, they're not smart enough to keep up with you, either?"

Recalling their final date, she caught his meaning. "That's not what I meant. I just mean they aren't FBI or CIA. They're not trained in espionage and covert surveillance techniques."

"Well, let's hope not."

Their coffee arrived. It was the best she had smelled in weeks.

Dunbar sipped from his cup and seemed to ponder his next move. "Any chance we can get an interview out of someone who can confirm—"

Robyn shook her head. "No way. No one involved in the military is going to cross Doyle. In obedience, they *are* well-trained."

"You mean in loyalty?"

"No, I mean obedience." She looked deeply into her black coffee. "Do you think you can get it on the air?"

"I don't know," he said. Adrian had always been honest with her. "Maybe if you actually came on the air."

She drew a deep breath. She had known in her heart it would come to this. She absently drummed her fingers on the mug as she estimated how long she'd live in freedom after revealing the capture of an alien visitor. Or how long she'd live, period.

"What's she like?"

Robyn snapped out of her reverie. "Huh?"

Adrian repeated his question. "I said, what is she like, this... alien?"

Robyn scrambled to catch up with his line of thought. "Vit Na? I guess she's remarkably like many women I know. Stronger, more confident, though. She seems like she's accustomed to having her way in many matters, but she's amazingly adaptable to strange circumstances. Mostly, she seems...alone."

She thought about her choice of words for a moment, appreciating the irony of a linguist unsure of verbal expression in her native tongue. Then she affirmed, "Yeah. Alone, but not lonely. There is someone just for her that she keeps in her heart, I'd say. Someone named Tur."

"What does she look like?" he asked. "Is she green, or gray?"

"Actually, she's black," Robyn said.

"Really?" He chuckled. "So, the first alien is one of us?"

"No. Not dark brown." Robyn smiled as she corrected his quip to her reality. "She's actually *black*. Beautiful face. I'd say she's glamorous; tall, with an elegant neck, lithe arms, long, graceful legs. You'd like her."

As she pondered Vit Na's fate, she felt embarrassed about how trivial her own danger was by comparison. Robyn followed the familiar lyrics the songstress elegantly wove through the air by tapping out the rhythm on her own coffee cup. The finale in that rich contralto that echoed as Ms. Shedrick's hallmark resonated through the café: "...*Just get here if you can.*"

The piano tinkled in the background through the applause as Robyn thought aloud. "I was just thinking about how powerful this song is. You know, Adrian?"

The last time she called A.D. by his first name, he'd ended up making her breakfast.

"I want a Mini-Wave fully armed and six meren ready to go, Devit." Then Tur faced the remaining Efilu contingent. "You know who you are."

As he prepared for the assault ahead, he tried to diffuse the tension. He hadn't thought about the odd mix of Efilu meren in weeks. Bo Tep, his two aids, Moc, Devit, and Loz stepped forward.

"We have a new assignment: following the former commanders of Hennessy Barracks. They have commandeered a facility called Alcatraz Island in the western most reaches of the continent. We'll transport the Mini-Wave across the continent in Air Force One," Tur added.

"The Mini-Wave would move faster under its own power," Bo Tep offered.

Tur didn't even look up as he answered, "We are talking about a patchwork Mini-Wave imitation. We can't push it. The plane will attract less attention, and no one will question the squadron of fighter jets escorting it. We need to conserve our energies any way we can."

Tur directed his attention immediately back to the weapons master, his plans solidifying. "Devit, you will arm the jets—US standard-issue, nothing fancy. You might as well utilize them to the fullest. We will be completely armed and ready upon arrival. I will lead the recovery maneuver. You all will maintain maximal dispersal of any counteroffensive efforts."

The main body of the remaining Efilu numbered a paltry thirteen meren to be left under Weyef's command. Tur turned to look at her. "Weyef, you will carry out the mission in case of any... delays," he said. "The sooner the algae specimen gets home, the better off the Realm will be. If the *ReQam* is...unavailable, see what you can salvage from some of the pre-Exodus Fitu relics. There is still enough gel core to assure complete invulnerability. Maybe some restoration work as well. Any questions?"

Tur looked around briefly, not really expecting any queries. "Then I—"

"What provisions have you made for air cover after the Jing Pen escort is exhausted?" Weyef asked smoothly.

"None. We can handle anything they throw at us from the ground."

"Like Stihl?" She knew that the issue was like a raw nerve to both Tur and Moc.

"Stihl faced them unarmed and unsupported. There is no similarity between the two situations."

Weyef pressed her argument. "Still, the loss of any of you seven could seriously jeopardize the completion of *my* mission."

"You will be the only senior staff member with any military experience left here." Tur vocalized patiently, only because he knew she was right. "Without you, the mission *will* be over. You stay here. End of discussion."

When a So Wari felt it necessary to actually "say" it, it really was the end of all peaceful discussion.

Weyef crossed slender arms and said no more, but the set of her jaw expressed an understanding of the ages-old axiom, "There's only one way to remove a So Wari who's lost his way."

Chapter Twenty-Eight

— ARMAGEDDON —

H e must be responsible," Doyle seethed. "No one else would have the know-how. The question is, why?"

"You've got to calm down, Colonel," Hollingsworth implored.

"That's all we need now: a human traitor!"

Mendez objected. "Ken, you don't know that Clyde sabotaged the system. This Vit Na has shown inhuman brilliance and ingenuity."

"Bullshit. All the alien's tricks were software related. She had no access to the mainframe downstairs. That room remained secure throughout the entire escape. Someone else had to have done it. Hell! Even *my* men aren't savvy enough to wreck the system this badly—present company included. I want Olsen arrested, Dixon!"

"I'm on it, sir." Ernie Dixon had been furiously working one of the few PCs not connected to the house mainframe. "Here it is. Olsen, Clyde. Born Rochester, Minnesota, April 4, 1968. Graduated MIT 1990, twenty-third in his class. Never held a regular job for more than nine months. Political organizations: none. Social orga-nizations: Greenpeace, SETI, Society for the Preservation of Sacred

Native American Burial Grounds. Save the Whales campaign, '87. Participated in a number of animal rights demonstrations."

"That proves nothing." Matthews found his voice in the fray. "The boy has no history of subversive behavior. How do you know he's helping her?"

"Here, here!" Dixon snapped his fingers for attention. "Thrown out of ROTC for unauthorized experiments with explosives. He also qualified with automatic weapons."

"That's it!" Doyle spat. "I want Olsen picked up, if possible—but really, I just want him taken out of this equation. There are enough variables in it already. We still have no location on Vit Na."

A sergeant entered, handed Major Dixon a printout, and left.

"Sir? The inventory reports," the sergeant said. "An M60 with grenade launcher, six hundred rounds of ammo, and a forty-five automatic with three magazines are missing. The depot door was forced."

"Olsen," Dixon concluded.

"Ernie, I want that renegade dead!" Doyle looked around the room for any opposition to the decree.

There was none.

They aren't taking any chances. Vit Na bristled. *Troop formation in five layers. The little chief didn't expect me to strike first. Now he'll be even more cautious. More ruthless.*

The barking in the distance grew closer, setting her nape plumage on end. She knew the spotlights shining through the darkness meant more bears, too. Lots of them. No way to avoid a confrontation. Bloody bodies lay strewn about the dark forest floor, victims of her nocturnal prowl.

Clumsy humans. She preened. *Such easy targets.*

A small alcove in the face of the mountain served as a temporary refuge from both chase and cold. She dared not utilize any of the small caves for fear of booby traps. Vit Na watched as the assault bears climbed the hill toward her position. If they didn't already sense her presence, they were sure to stumble over her on their way through. She *Blended* then steeled herself against their impending foray.

The slope allowed her to clear more distance with the leap downward than she could have on level ground. Her trajectory landed her in the midst of the lumbering squadron. Immediately, she crippled the lead bear and proceeded to take the others out in the same brutal fashion. A tail to the throat, a toe claw to eye or midriff, and a straight punch to ursine spine took out the majority of the party before they knew what hit them.

The three bears that could still defend themselves circled Vit Na. Vit Na also circled, executing each crippled bear where they lay as she passed. Despite the remains strewn around her, she knew the odds were not in her favor. Success so far had been the result of surprise and bluff.

At her feet, she spotted an equalizer. She hefted the heavy weapon from a fallen bear, aimed at the comm links, and fired. She hit two before the remote human controller began returning fire.

What was it Bo Tep said? Line-of-sight, parabolic trajectory. Those laser-targeting beams may work in my favor—if I can just stay one step ahead of their movements.

Her reflexes were so much faster than the primitive mammals that she evaded nearly all attacks. Then a paw caught her full in the face. Claws that barely broke her skin were quite effective at breaking her rhythm. The red beam crossed Vit Na's torso. She nearly cleared the beam before two rounds tore through her flesh.

She rolled, barreling between the legs of the last of the disarmed bears. It took the remaining fire in the spine. Rage overwhelmed the beast holding the machine gun and it charged Vit Na. Its movement made aiming the automatic weaponry it carried impossible.

Ignoring the pain in her hip, she rolled backward, allowing the bear's momentum to carry it up and over. Its claws dug deeply into her flesh before she managed the tight tail grip necessary to snap its neck. She spun the limp body to one side and rose shakily to her feet.

By now the dogs had doubled back, waiting for an opening to attack. Vit Na emptied three hundred rounds from two salvaged weapons. She wiped out the entire pack before the overheated weapons jammed.

Vit Na's unsteadiness marched into bone-wrenching convulsions. She dropped the smoldering guns and sat among the dead. She took a cleansing breath in the foul, flesh-burnt haze of the clearing. She made a brief assessment of her injuries and staggered off over the next hill as the echo of barking grew in the distance.

"What is the closest Jing Pen threat to Alcatraz Island?"

Devit checked the map before responding to Tur's query. "The naval base at Alameda. Six battleships and one aircraft carrier are stationed there."

Tur paused for the briefest moment, then commanded, "Take it out. Jets only. When they run out of ammunition, order them to crash into any military hardware that remains intact." He pointed. "Set us down in San Francisco Bay." The gel console generated a topographical image. "There, we'll split the Mini-Wave into three sections, as planned."

Tur drummed his fingers on his knee in the cramped Air Force One. "Let's do this quietly. If Vit Na is alive in there, I don't want the Jing Pen alerted until the last possible minute."

"'Quiet' takes time." Bo Tep rubbed his chin. "Just how long do you plan to spend on this operation?"

Tur raised his head slowly. "As long as it takes."

"Casualties are proportional to the duration of a strike, but I'm sure you realize that," Bo Tep continued. "There are only seven of us. How many of us can you afford to lose?"

Tur didn't respond.

"Do you have any ideas on minimizing this raid?" Devit asked, addressing his question to no one in particular.

Bo Tep looked at him. "Not yet, but I'm sure I'll think of something."

Devit smiled, an expression most unusual for Ironde. "I already have a plan."

The watchtower was still manned. Guards crisscrossed each other's paths, never letting themselves out of one another's sight. Alcatraz Island was tranquil, but not the abandoned facility the U.S. federal records indicated. In Bo Tep's estimation, it looked like a military installation expecting company.

Devit's plan was ludicrous. Just crazy enough to work.

"Watch. If the profile of the human patrolman holds, curiosity will do the job for us. If not, well, we can still do it your way," Devit said.

He nodded to Bo Tep. Devit then plucked a feather from his coat and dropped it from the Mini-Wave the three meren piloted through the night. It twirled downward to the guard tower and landed gently in the north corner station. The Efilu trio waited.

The first guard looked at the plume from a distance. He tipped his head quizzically and lifted his eyes toward the night sky, searching for the great bird that had lost the feather. The Mini-Wave exploited the darkness quite effectively. The soldier took two steps closer and paused. He looked around suspiciously, then crossed the catwalk to the resting quill.

"Wow!" he mouthed.

Devit smiled as the man stroked the long, white plume. It was luxuriously soft and delicate.

"Hey, guys!" the guard whispered as loud as he could. "Come here!"

They all converged on the north tower. Devit nudged Tur gently in the ribs and said, "Time to go to work."

With that, he slinked across the blackness by way of a Mini-Wave bridge, then caught hold of the tower, below the position of unsuspecting humans. He climbed into position and silently counted.

"Check it out. Have you ever seen a feather this big?"

"Nah, man! I'd hate to see the buzzard this fell off," a newcomer said. "Hey Weiss, you know about birds, don't you?"

"Yeah. A little. I was in the Audubon Society in high school, but I'm not a real birder. Let me see that." After an intense, but brief examination, the soldier said, "I've never seen a feather like this. Even ostriches don't grow feathers this big. And it's more than just big; the pattern is weird." He drew his finger along the length of the plume. "Soft!" He repeated the action several times. "It just flows."

The four guards marveled around the plume.

As Devit had suggested he would, the Jing Pen called Weiss drew his fingers down the quill against the acute angle of fibers, expecting them to give way with the same yielding softness. Before his hand had reached the stem, Corporal Weiss lost two fingertips and a thumb. The other men watched in mute horror as the digits dropped to the ground.

Devit took the opening to silence three before they could draw another breath. Two well-thrown rigid quills to the throat of each flanking guard sent them gurgling and sputtering blood as they fell to their knees. An opened palm to a chin thrust the neck of a third man beyond the breaking point in yet another silent death.

Only the fingerless one was left. Alone, in shock, Weiss's life ended with a chest full of penetrating spines from Devit's back, when their struggle pinned the guard against a handrail.

"Well," Devit said as Tur and Bo Tep joined him on the parapet. "That's that. Nice, quick, and quiet."

"Quit showing off," Tur said, unimpressed. "You could have taken them out just as easily without the theatrics. Let's go."

Bo Tep caught up with Devit and whispered a comforting thought. "I thought it was great—more fun than anything else we've done so far." Cautious to avoid the sharp angles of Devit's quills, Bo Tep fanned the Ironde's shoulder. "Good work."

Tur was kneeling at a communication cable. "Devit!" he called. "Can you access this system from here?"

The weapons master jaunted up to the cable and manipulated fiber optic strands skillfully exposed already by a surprisingly nimble Tur.

"I don't know," Devit answered. He reached deep into the gel core of the Mini-Wave and pulled out a handful of goop, then swiftly configured it into a gel console. He attached it to the mass of glass threads. "I can access some of the main system from here, but it looks like somebody is expecting trouble. The thing is loaded with safeguards."

"Jing Pen safeguards?" Tur turned a wry smile. "You're kidding me!"

"Don't laugh, sir. Within the parameters of their technology, they can be very resourceful. The lockout is configured to keep out a rogue program of their own design. I can bypass some of the programmed barriers, but most of them are physical. We'll have to take them out accordingly."

Tur slammed his fist into his own thigh. "I'm tired of this tiptoeing around. I'm not built for this kind of turtle-spit. Disable as much as you can, then we go in and kill anything non-Efilu we meet."

That was a general order, and everyone in the expanded group heard it. The High Commander took the lead. He had to crouch and crawl through many of the corridors leading to the main hall. Devit made better time through the narrow passages and quickly found the main engineering section.

His assimilation of the data was nearly instantaneous. The most efficient method of securing the island was to use the Mini-Wave. Upon convergence, the three teams relinquished the fragmented Wave to Devit, who discharged it forthwith. Like a tide of death and destruction, the apparatus rushed ahead of the infiltrators, softly neutralizing every Jing Pen it washed over. Along the way, the Mini-Wave achieved its secondary directive as it widened the necessary passages to allow the larger Efilu to follow.

Moc was the first to report in.

"She was here, sir."

Tur felt himself rocked emotionally. He hid the reaction by pretending to catch an overhanging pipe for balance. "Any... remains?"

Moc was nothing if not discreet with her superiors. "I should have been clearer, High Commander. She *was* here, but she left. There are signs of a violent escape and a desperate pursuit. Which explains the scant troops and lack of resistance."

Tur was all steel. "How long?"

"Two hours, maybe a bit more," Moc answered without hesitation.

Already moving toward an exit, Tur called over his shoulder. "Track them." He then whipped his hand in a circular gesture indicating the building in general. "Burn it down."

Vit Na felt cold, that deathly cold one feels after acute blood loss. Her spleen did auto-transfuse enough blood to keep her conscious and mobile, but efficient combat was out of the question. Her mind was exhausted and unfocused. She would have to rely on instinct alone to get past her malefactors.

Remember, I am the hunter! she drilled herself. *I will pick them off one at a time.* In a moment of clarity, she thought of the ship. *I have to signal the* ReQam. *Sphere of influence depleted. I'll need a power source…and just hope I don't burn myself up in the process.*

Vit Na listened and heard barking nearby. *Those stupid canines again.*

She clutched the oak tree with her claws and rested. In her best state of health, she could have pulled a body four times her own weight into the highest branches, but she now struggled to scale every inch. She hung upside down from a branch, twenty-seven feet off the ground.

The inverted position set gravity to work in her favor. Her head began to clear. Vit Na *Blended* into the snow-covered branches, her coat marbled white and black to match her perch. She inspected the effect. Unbidden, memory of her coach pilot on Tiest came to mind, *Put Ri. Put Ri of the spotted pelt. Why did his name not register when he told me?*

Dogs whisked by below her, the slower bears following their lead. One of the bears hesitated beneath her. The action caught the attention of one of its companions. They both raised their noses to sniff the wind for the faintest scent.

Now!

She grabbed one beast by the head and wrenched it 180 degrees with all her might. The other watched its partner fall for no apparent reason just before an invisible claw raked out both its eyes in one swoop.

The bear, too, had instincts. It lashed out with its own great might, now completely blind and in terrible agony. It struck Vit Na solidly. Too weak and tired to effectively dodge, the dangling Melkyz plunged to the snow-blanketed ground.

The bear howled in agony and wandered blindly into the night. The sound of the dogs grew louder.

Highest Mother! They're coming back!

Lungs heaving, Vit Na had no strength and left bloodstained footprints with every agonizing step. She felt like a cornered animal. In truth, the Melkyz huntress fled, little more than game for the pack. She heard automatic gunfire in the distance, the dogs barking and howling in pursuit. Now survival demanded the unthinkable.

I've been burning calories with impunity. My nutrient reserves are exhausted.

She remembered the rat back in the cage. She had known that at some time, somehow, this decision would have to be made.

I'll have to consume some of the fallen bear.

Her stomach too empty to vomit at the thought of eating raw mammal flesh again, survival overruled all etiquette. Vit Na tore into the flesh. No aristocratic niceties, just savage, urgent hunger. She finished the liver, heart, and most of the fat underlying the waist-level skin. Then she braced herself for the fight of her life.

Dead pinecones crackled somewhere in the dark. The dogs still could be heard barking in the distance—but the clumsy footfalls, slipping and sliding nearby on the ice, belonged to a biped Jing Pen.

A man.

She sprung at the lone human, pinning him to the ground. An involuntarily wave of nausea repulsed her.

"Vit Na, wait! It's me. Don't you know me? It's Clyde. Clyde Olsen! I've come to help."

In her frenzy, Vit Na could neither recognize nor hear the man. She also could not bring herself to take another bite of mammalian flesh.

Out of desperation, she began ripping at his mind with all her own. His soul screamed a long, silent scream that only she could enjoy. Vit Na devoured his memories, his beliefs, even the very pillars of his spirit. She left the psychic carcass that was Clyde Olsen lying, bereft of all will, in the void of his life's essence. His body, fully intact, rested motionlessly on the frosted ground.

She took his weapon, her head clearing again. Digesting his thoughts and memories, Vit Na came to a realization: *Mendez's artificial intel specialist. He came to help. Too bad. I need no Jing Pen assistance. Like all the rest of them, he is my prey!*

Her mind took advantage of Olsen's most recent memories as the rush of calories from the bear's flesh revitalized her brain. *Power condenser, just over that ridge. I've got to get to it!*

San Francisco Bay was ablaze with naval fuel. Under Efilu command, the F-16 escort jets had completed their final sortie against their own navy. Tur's contingent caught the rear guard of ground troops on Vit Na's trail unawares. In all, the seven Efilu took out three of the eight human companies on the search and destroy mission for their fugitive companion. Before the soldiers ever knew they were under assault, Efilu forces ended them.

Even Tur didn't expect to see what lay over the hill. Twenty Kodiak bears, all an average height of eighteen feet. All armed to the hilt. All ready to kill.

It didn't take Tur long to respond, even to an unbelievable foe. Lids shut, Tur's eyes receded into their sockets as he armored up. *Conflict Vision* took over and radial thinking began. He skewered the first bear to charge his way with his spiked tail and slung the flailing body back at the rest of them.

Bo Tep, flanked by his two bodyguards, went after the crazed bears that broke ranks. He cleared a path for the smaller meren to spear through the crowded hill unmolested.

Moc, having experienced human combat technique firsthand, was prepared for artillery fire. Her body armor was solid and fortified with a contact force field. She disabled the artillery and allowed Loz and Devit to mop up the scattering humans and Akitas. Loz slashed the animals left and right with his forearm blades, running past them at speeds they couldn't hope to match or evade. Devit simply threw his natural projectiles with lethal accuracy.

Tur, too, engaged the Jing in mostly hand-to-hand combat. The mini-Wave operated at its peak capacity, configured to repulse air-to-ground weapons at Moc's suggestion. Tur saw flashes of light moving away from the battle, led by gun and artillery fire.

"Vit Na!" he gasped.

Tur collapsed the Mini-Wave, engulfed his assault party in it, and carried them over the hill. The suspension field charged to disrupt the metabolic hydrogen ion transfer. As the Mini-Wave passed overhead, its field of influence worked as effectively on the Jing Pen as cyanide gas. They dropped one by one.

——⫷●⫸——

Vit Na had made her way to the electrical transformer. She used the energy to fashion a force field by means of her personal sphere of influence, but it wasn't enough. A focused, intense multiphasic laser pulse would serve as beacon to the *ReQam*. The arrival of more firepower than she had seen so far interrupted her plan. Now she was trapped. It was all she could do to deflect the bullets and light artillery shells reverberating against her failing shield.

They'll send reinforcements soon. I can't stay in here forever! Vit Na knew she had less than a minute left. She had to take a chance. *With any luck at all, my pursuers will be momentarily stunned by the light and cease fire for a second. A moment's quarter,* she prayed. *Just a second or two, that's all I'll need!*

The sound of gunfire slowed to random reports in the darkness. It was as if their focus had momentarily shifted from her to another target. A helicopter spotted Vit Na near the transformer on the hill and circled about. Guns went hot in a pylon turn just as she made her decision.

The barrage had driven her to her knees. Vit Na readied herself, raised her hands straight up over head, focused a blinding purple-white beacon which lanced through the night sky.

The gunship caught the beam full in its belly. The explosion made a distracting display as all weapons fire came to halt.

Chapter Twenty-Nine

— SALVATION AND RUIN —

The brief artificial daylight faded in seconds. Confusion ruled as the color of night returned. Soldiers groped and stumbled with the pain inflicted by the blinding flash through their night vision goggles. Major Dixon's back was to the window of the mobile command center.

A split second after the burst, Colonel Doyle was on his feet. "Who authorized nukes?" he shouted, bracing for the aftershock that never came.

"No one, sir." An unnamed lieutenant checked his computer. "Geiger sensors indicate no radiation. No nukes, sir."

The helicopter gunship explosion registered as a vanishing blip on the officer's tactical display screen.

"Okay, so what the hell *was* that?" Doyle asked, but his attention was drawn to the random small arms fire on the hillside. "How did she get ahold of incendiary grenades? Ernie, confirm that blast came from our quarry, and that there are no other high-yield weapons missing from the armory that you didn't catch. In the meantime, have those men fall back."

Doyle pulled nervously at his stubbled chin. "Where are those bears, anyway?"

"They're firing from the bay!" Devit exclaimed as he watched the incoming missiles streaking hundreds of yards overhead.

It was true. The plan to cripple the San Francisco-based naval fleet with a sneak attack had backfired. Reinforcements already en route had arrived from the Pacific, ten warships strong. They concentrated fire on the skirmish in Muir Woods.

"She's unprotected up there." Tur's thoughts were almost a murmur. Then, more firmly, he projected, "Wave shield up. I want the entire hillside blocked off."

Bo Tep stepped up to Tur with uncharacteristic discretion. "This makeshift Mini-Wave can't handle the demands you're about to put on it. If it collapses, we'll be out here all alone and unprotected. Just like Stihl."

Tur turned fully to face him. "She's out there all alone, Bo. I know I'm placing all of us at risk, but I can't help it. I brought her to this Alom-forsaken planet. I can't just leave her in the hands of these savages."

Pleading eyes in a So Wari face were even more incongruous than Tralkyz compassion.

"All right, Tur, I'll drop it," Bo Tep said with a submissive nod. "Let's clean up this mob, though. I don't like all these stray animals running wild."

Jeen was running, Gober Dil two steps behind her. She couldn't believe the operation had gone as wrong as the reports indicated. "Weyef. You've got to see them NOW!"

Jeen rushed into the central atrium where Weyef stirred in her usual place, brooding over the fact that she, the former Head of Council Security, had been left out of the action.

"We've got problems, Weyef."

Jeen acknowledged Ikara and Doh at the commander's side, explaining some human peculiarity to Weyef before she interjected. "Activity in the southwest region is escalating."

"No kidding." The new mission commander emphasized understatement with her own style of sarcasm.

"Have you seen this yet?" Jeen asked, handing Weyef the satellite photos and local California news broadcasts.

Weyef checked the photographs twice, her Vansar eyes enhancing the images. "These photographs have a diffracted quality about them. Normally, I would attribute the phenomenon to poor lens quality, but, as I recall, we saw the same type of pattern when the animals attacked the first headquarters."

She beckoned the other Efilu to come closer. "Notice here and here," she instructed, pointing as she spoke. "Warships. The heaviest armament in the US arsenal. And they are firing weapons."

Fear tinged Jeen's thoughts. "You realize that if Tur reveals our position to the Jing Pen at large, it will be all out war with these people. We'll exhaust our remaining resources in a matter of months. If the *ReQam* has been destroyed, we're stuck on this rock without supplies, without reinforcements, without a way to communicate with the Realm. There may be remnants of ancient technology buried who knows how deeply underground, but it could take us decades to restore enough integrity to even get off this planet."

"Let alone get us all home." Frustration painted Weyef's features dark. Then, suddenly, a wry expression crossed her face. "Tur mentioned cloning, did he not?"

Ikara nodded slowly.

"And the Mini-Wave shielding shows signs of failing?" Weyef asked. After a nod from Jeen, she concluded, "We cannot allow Efilu genes or technology to fall into Jing Pen hands."

"Of course not," Doh added. "But what can we do? Tur gave specific orders that the safety of the algae was to take top priority."

Weyef waited patiently for the paleontologist to make his beleaguered point, then said, "Precisely. We can't leave this ball of mud for several months, yet we cannot afford a compromise of our tactical edge."

"But—" Doh stammered.

"This is now an issue of security," Weyef stated with So Wari finality. Only Doh still looked uncomfortable with her position.

One of the human generals stopped his assigned task to try to investigate the commotion among the Efilu and caught Gober Dil's eye. "What do we do about them?" Gober Dil asked, nodding his head toward the human.

Weyef looked at the little general with a smile that seemed to chill the man's bones. "Nothing," she said. "But the others, the ones that Jeen fixed, we burn."

Ikara protested, "You can't just leave—"

Weyef put a hand on her shoulder to silence her objection. "It's all right. We will command them to hold the others here indefinitely, but set the cortical field intensity on maximum. The overload will burn out every synapse serving higher functions in their fat little heads within two days. It will look like meningoencephalitis, but their diagnostics will turn up nothing familiar. They'll conclude the cause was a biological weapon gone wrong. The others will be quarantined, especially after telling the story of the Pentagon being taken over by 'alien dinosaurs.' It doesn't matter, anyway. This society is already dead." Weyef smiled again. "These people just don't know it yet."

Ikara's puzzled look found an answer from the Vansar mer. "Good government is a matter of empathic rapport and response, just as good security is a matter of alertness and habit," Weyef explained. "You can't compromise on fundamental principles and hope your mistakes get forgotten or compensated for by 'the system.' This entire bloated economy is running out of resources. It's concentrating the wealth in the top one percent. They're reducing the workforce to save capital, at the same time pushing the remaining workers beyond reasonable limits. They still have to support the growing ranks of the poor and unemployed with health care, food, shelter, and infrastructure." She shook her head slowly. "The minions, empowered by desperation, will bring leaders to task and bring down one staple institution after another: health care, education, law enforcement, finance, entertainment, the legal system, even the politicians themselves, in time. The leaders have become complacent in the mistaken belief that the trends simply represent a cycle that will run a limited course and return to an acceptable status quo. I see chaos destroying them in no more than fifty years."

Weyef looked around at the humans working at their assigned tasks, narrowing her eyes in contempt. "Remember, we've seen these signs before. We don't need to do another thing here," Weyef became grave. "But I still have to deal with Tur. Let's go."

Devit's coat had thinned visibly from throwing quills at attacking dogs and men. Loz had reached the crest of the hill. "Over here!" he shouted. "They got—" An explosion rocked the top of the hill. Suddenly, Loz was nowhere to be seen.

Tur ignored the loss and didn't even look for the body when he reached the high point.

At the foot of the hill, he saw the mobile command center, guarded by two bears. When the others caught up to him, Tur just gestured instructions as he led them toward it. Bo Tep silently ordered his left-hand meg to work his way around the battlefield.

One of the ursine sentries growled in confusion at the charging Efilu force. Colonel Doyle came to the window. Instinct recognized the antagonist before intellect did.

"Tur," he breathed almost inaudibly. "Lieutenant! Turn the turret a hundred fifty degrees," he shouted. Noting the confusion on the young man's face, he barked, "Now!"

The officer complied.

Doyle nearly tripped getting to the gunnery controls and began firing at will. To his horror, Tur took the brunt of the antitank weaponry in stride.

"Ernie, raise Bravo Company," Doyle commanded. "Tell them to forget Vit Na. Redeploy them here. If those monsters get to us, we're all done."

Major Dixon carried out the order, but he imagined he already felt the icy grip of death closing around his soul.

The major had no sooner completed his instructions when the rear wall of the vehicle peeled open. Rig Ejen, Bo Tep's right-hand meg, barreled through the view port, just as a gash in the back wall revealed his left-hand companion, Di Otz. Every human in the room froze and simultaneously lost sphincter control. Until now, humans had not known what every Efilu cub knows: Tralkyz always attack in pairs!

The command center rocked for a while, quivering with inhuman screams that issued from human victims overwrought with terror.

Then there was silence.

The Tralkyz pair emerged, not even winded, looking for fresh adversaries. The meren trampled the remains of humans and guard bears Rig Ejen had dispatched on the way in.

A rain of shrapnel signaled the ruin of the Mini-Wave shield.

"We're on our own now," Devit murmured under his breath.

Tur crouched, too far away from Devit to hear over his own roar. He scooped ice and mud, crushing the muck into a wad the size of a small car. With the ugliest snowball ever molded cocked for action, he engaged the tank brigade responding to the distress call. Two tanks vaporized before he could move toward them.

Tur gazed skyward.

Weyef hovered above the battle site in full regalia. Gel-enhanced field compression made her virtually invulnerable. The *Translation Horizon* she generated allowed her to maneuver far beyond the physical limits of a body with her mass.

"It looked like you needed a little help," she called to Tur defiantly.

An unexpected smile greeted her. "I'm glad you're here. Get that missile fire off us. We'll handle the rest."

The complement of smaller Efilu provided ground support, sporting Mini-Wave mass drivers designed to spew high-energy free radicals. Configured for supersonic flight and designed right out of traditional Vansar arsenals, the unpiloted gel-mecha fell neatly into Weyef's *Skywake*, prepared to rain aerial destruction on mammalian targets. She signaled the synthetic Deathwings to deploy against the tanks and warships in the harbor.

Weyef's orders: "Spare no one."

"Wait!" Tur called to her before she got into the thick of it. "Drop a bit of gel down here. Vit Na is hurt. I don't know how badly yet."

Weyef could see Vit Na lying still on the ground near the smoldering transformer. Tur, too far away to make out the Vansar's grave expression, waited as Weyef complied with his futile request.

Tur met little resistance as he took the hillside.

The only light in the early morning sky came from naval jets, burning as they fell victim to Weyef's vengeful fury. Devit came up beside Tur, already silently bent over Vit Na and obscuring the Ironde's view of the Melkyz mer lying so still. As he came around to face the High Commander, he saw a grievous sight: So Wari tears washing over a broken figure.

Agonal breathing wracked Vit Na's chest, and her eyes glazed. Steam rose from a battle-frayed form that could no longer contain precious body heat in the chilled night air.

Devit seemed helpless. His medical training was so limited. He couldn't do anything.

No one could do anything.

Weyef came about after finishing off the bulk of the human air assault force and closed rapidly on the retreating survivors. She slowed just enough to build up a lethal charge in the rarefied air mounting a *Skywake* in front of her. She then plotted the optimal course to spread the energy through the formation of planes and zoomed through it. The explosions were deafening. Blinding.

Somehow, the effect seemed to last too long. Then Weyef realized the light was coming from above her. Pulsating silently. The evening sky shone as midday. The source was an oddly familiar spiral shape. The *ReQam*'s stasis field suppressed vibration, draping the countryside in an eerie, unnatural silence.

Weyef watched the human confusion with glee. Soldiers screamed futile instructions to each other at the tops of their lungs. Distraught dogs howled mutely at the light for mercy, to no avail.

The Efilu, communicating telepathically, were unaffected. Most by now had gathered around Vit Na's still form. None of them noticed as muted mammals, running wildly about the hillside below them, simply began winking out of existence. When it was over, wisps of ash were the only Jing legacy from the conflict.

A silver thread dropped from the *ReQam*'s underside and pooled on the ground a few yards from the group. Car Hom rose out of it and approached his companions somberly, knowing already via the ship's sensors what most of them were just learning: Vit Na was dead.

Chapter Thirty

— PHOENIX —

"We must prepare," Tur said. He displayed no emotion, but his thought projection contained an overwhelming intensity.

"Of course," Car Hom responded in a solemn tone.

After a moment, Tur added, "Surprised to see you again alive, old friend."

Car Hom didn't know how to take that comment under the circumstances, yet he noted a touch of warmth in the statement.

"Friend?" Car Hom asked. "Since when did you count me among your friends?"

Tur smiled, closed-lipped. "I suppose friends are like fingers: lose one and you begin to keep count of the rest." The High Commander turned to face his first officer. "I've always considered you a friend." After another pause, he added, "I just never said so."

Sensing discomfort, Car Hom changed the subject. "I had the hardest time finding you all. When I saw the devastation at the Aleutian base, I surmised that you must have gotten into some trouble. Normally, I wouldn't have been so pessimistic, but knowing that you were all under the influence, I couldn't be sure. Naturally, we monitored the air waves for distress calls, but—"

"Wait. Hold on," Tur demanded. "Under the influence of what?"

"Oh. I'm sorry. I should have told you immediately. I must have been distracted," Car Hom said, realizing the source of Tur's confusion. "The Jing Pen inhibition field. We discovered that not only have the Jing Pen evolved these inhibitory centers in their brains that block telepathic communication and coercion, but they can actually generate a field of psychic inhibition. It's amazing you conducted any intimate communication at all with that static. We discovered that it also interferes with the radial thought process. Basically, it reduced you almost to their level." Car Hom gestured down the hill toward the human camp. "Glad to see you were up to the challenge."

Tur looked distressed. "If we are at risk for psychic interference—"

Car Hom interrupted him with a gently raised hand. "It's no longer a problem. The stasis field the ship is generating nullifies the inhibitory effect. The mute quality was just a flourish."

"You super hunters and your *flourishes*." Tur gave him an approving shake of the head. "Nice work, Car."

"Don't get carried away with praising staff, now," Car Hom said. "I'd have to become the disciplinarian, and I'm too old to play 'bad commander.'"

He looked over Tur's shoulder. Brajay was there now.

"They found Loz. Looks as if he might survive." Car Hom frowned. "I'd wager he'll be crippled, though. What does a Notex do without full use of his legs?"

"A long, slow death I wouldn't wish on a Jing," Tur said, nodding as Weyef landed and approached the swiftly-constructed shrine.

They were ready. A congregation of comrades and friends now encircled Vit Na's motionless form. Tur joined them, followed by Car Hom.

No commander ever wanted to perform the traditional death ceremony. Vit Na had no kin aboard, and she and Tur were acknowledged *synesprit*. Someone handed Tur a sharp pair of ritual wrist shears. He accepted them absently, ignoring their significance for as long as he could.

Tur caressed her fingers gently, lovingly as he performed the Sharu Touch ceremony. In unison, all in attendance followed Tur's lead and they breathed life into that spiritual void. Their thoughts reached deep into the stillness that was Vit Na's mind. Slowly she rose from the cold darkness of the beyond.

The specter briefly looked down at the cooling remains but could not yet fathom remorse at the knowledge of her own death. Instinctively, the avatar stroked the hands intertwined between Tur and Vit Na's body. In so doing, she focused the group, aiding them in funneling some of their life force through the corpse, extracting every iota of memory, feeling, and intention—in essence, the very soul of the mer that was once Vit Na of Kemith—into astral form.

The configuration process, private and intimate, lasted only moments. When it was done, the Vit Na Animem materialized and again reached for the fingertips of her corporeal form, but suddenly turned away. It reached out instead for Tur. The High Commander and the Animem enjoyed a warm hug without shame—a relationship that survived even her mortality.

Vit Na Iku, as she had now become, ordered a gel console and proceeded to catalogue the information gained while she was held captive. Doh's findings needed correlation with archives from the archeology department. The Animem was helpful in organizing information, but limited in its ability to analyze the new data brought in by Doh. Preliminary debriefing would take place once on board the *ReQam*. Then, Vit Na Iku would rest sequestered in the disembodied hands of her progenitor.

"The *ReQam* is fully armed and at seventy percent of full power. How much of this world would you like to eradicate, Commander?" Car Hom asked. Absolute formality filled the old Alkyz's obligatory request.

The decision fell to Tur alone. Weyef observed him for weakness, ready to take the final step when opportunity presented itself. The gel-cannon wrapped her wing powered to kill. Bo Tep appeared at her flank, clasping her shoulder with a firmness that left no room for doubt. If she moved to dispose of Tur, the Tralkyz would crush her shoulder to pulp. With the return of Car Hom, Weyef would not become mission commander in any event, but Bo Tep would see to it that she would never fly again if she attacked Tur.

Never leaving Weyef's side, Bo Tep asked Car Hom, "How did you repair the ship, anyway?"

The first officer assessed the Vansar/Tralkyz situation with appreciative curiosity before answering. "Remember when we came into this star system, and we bypassed the binary dwarf planets?" Car Hom asked. "Ages ago, the larger of the two was our sentry station at the edge of the solar system. It was equipped with supplies and armaments. Relics of a little archeologic interest, although no algae. It was of no use to us when we approached, of course, but we were able to dock and repair the ship adequately without dealing with a significant gravity well. We did a tight perihelion to recharge the core, and here we are. Of course, there is no way of achieving full power from a yellow star without a singularity for energy compression—"

"But it's enough to get us home," Tur concluded. "When you were last in contact, the *ReQam*'s orbit was rapidly deteriorating. Even fully deploying the photo-net, you couldn't have powered escape velocity. How did you even get out of the atmosphere?"

"That was the embarrassing thing," Car Hom explained with corrugated brow. "My head cleared once I escaped the inhibition field, and it was obvious. The damn thing works a lot like the Poison. The only reason the *ReQam* sustained any damage at all was because that pompous idiot," he nodded toward Loz, "brought the nuclear device *into* the ship! The majority of the hull was intact. We were in danger of crashing to the surface of Fitu, suffering even more damage and casualties, but that was all. The ship would not have suffered irreparable damage, even if we had crashed on rocky land—but we'd have been trapped."

Bo Tep and Tur then finished the explanation for him in unison: "The second blast."

Tur offered, "You used the force of a nuclear explosion to propel you out of orbit."

Car Hom glibly bowed in affirmation. "Employing a modest economy of motion, we made for the nether regions at low speed. Simple." Then, becoming more serious, he asked, "So, Tur, about your orders—do we wipe them out, or don't we?"

The High Commander shook his head. "What's the point? I just came here for a bucket of algae, and these rats had to start all this turtle-spit. Razing the planet won't undo anything, and they really don't represent a significant threat anymore."

Without another word, Tur walked deliberately to the hill.

He returned to Vit Na's corpse. Tur took the shears he held in his hand and neatly snipped off Vit Na's hands at the wrists.

Custom usually dictated that the following act be done by the departed's next of kin, if present, but circumstances demanded that the final part of the ceremony fall to the mission commander during a loss in combat. For the first time since he met Vit Na, Tur viewed their special relationship as a burden he was unsure he could bear.

He slicked his ears back and held his right hand high. The air around it began to glow red. He then began to manipulate one hand around another in a careful, complex maneuver, never touching one with the other. The red glow became an intense white, radiant sphere encompassing both hands. He extended his hands toward Vit Na's body, but hesitated.

Tur swore he would not humiliate himself again with tears. He squeezed his eyes shut, jerked his head away from the group, snorted once, and unleashed a searing white beam. Vit Na's remains, minus the all-important hands, incinerated under the burst. The heat, though hardly felt by Tur, was sufficient to dry the lone tear that had escaped from beneath his eyelid before it could fall.

He returned to the lift point where now only Car Hom waited. As the So Wari stood, his arms looked as though they had become too heavy to carry on his shoulders.

"Just take us home, Car." Tur's head hung low. He tried to lift a hand to Car Hom's shoulder, but couldn't manage the effort somehow. "I'm so tired."

He cradled the limp, dismembered Melkyz hands in his own. "I just want to go home."

Clyde Olsen lay writhing on the cold forest floor until the sun rose. Visions of small fuzzy creatures with big, pointed ears and twisting tails crawling all over his body haunted him. He remembered seeing alien hieroglyphs and, somehow, now understood their meaning.

He had an overwhelming compulsion: *I must get to Tur! He needs me. Needs to know I'm safe, at least.*

He stood and felt off-balance. He fell forward more than once. Something was wrong. *Something's missing.*

When he tried to envision home, his thoughts raced between two drastically different images. His mind reeled. Too many voices spoke at once—*Stop that noise! Let me out! Don't tie my tail that way! Quit touching me! Leave me alone!* And there was no way to answer.

Leaves blew wildly. To his horror, he saw—and recognized—the *ReQam* lifting off in the distance. He screamed in distress, "Don't leave me!" Then as the ship vanished into the sky, he sat back down on the damp leaves and sobbed uncontrollably.

Through tears, Olsen muttered, "How can anyone hope to live like this?" The sunrise brought little warmth, but by its light, almost more than he could bear, revealed a form most alien to him. He looked at his hands in disgust, seeing pale skin sparsely covered with hair stretched across a clumsy physique.

His first coherent thought came quick. *Damned to a living hell in my own body.*

Then, his sobbing ceased as if a switch had been thrown. A single desperate notion came to him.

The Keepers.

Chapter Thirty-One
— THE DIET OF TIEST —

T ur rested casually in the ancient forechair reserved for the
Sentry at Arms. His field promotion to High Commander
was now official upon completion of the Retrieval, as the
mission was now known. He sat quietly during the remaining
interviews.

*Why does everything have to have a grand name in our culture?
The Exodus. The Return. The Keepers. I'm getting sick of all of this
"uniqueness."*

The Council in session had the full Diet of Tiest in attendance,
and Tur had to keep all 400 meren in line. There would probably
be jubilation when they informed the public of a mission they had
been told so little about. Crisis resolution at hand, most of *ReQam*'s
crew had been debriefed and dismissed. Acquisitions—Bo Tep's
department—was slated for last on the agenda.

The chair-meg announced a break in the proceedings. The
Round Table chamber had been opened to the large anteroom,
which was usually subdivided into offices in order to accommodate the recess staff. This unrestricted configuration, often
reserved for High Society galas, now arranged for exchange of

momentous thoughts following the retrieval and disposition of the algae.

"Very compelling testimony," someone projected a thought to Tur without identifying himself.

Tur turned to where Thea had been resting on his haunches in a dim corner, listening. "You do realize that 'intelligent mammal' is a contradiction in terms, don't you?" the Ironde leader asked, attempting debate with the So Wari least interested in engaging. "What is this Doh trying to prove? The common Efilu will never believe this story. Now, mind you, I don't suggest that you are fabricating the report, but we all know the Kini Tod are prone to… shall we say, *exaggeration*."

Tur looked at him coldly. "You weren't there."

The tone conveyed the danger of offending a So Wari well enough. Thea stood and took a step toward the light and out of reach of Tur's tail.

"We will see," Thea said, looking back over his shoulder as he walked away from the High Commander.

Murmuring meren filled the gallery, sharing opinions on what they'd learned of the adventure so far. When the Council reconvened, each delegate reclaimed her seat at the table. The *ReQam's* senior staff was accounted for, save one: Bo Tep was nowhere to be seen.

"Engage the Melkyz Animem sequence," Yaw Daor ordered, looking to Meeth for approval. "With your leave, of course," he added. As First Impressor, Yaw Daor needed no one's permission. The courtesy was born of friendship, not duty.

Meeth nodded curtly. Vit Na Iku began her humble salutations before recounting for the assembled dignitaries the details of the trek back to Fitu.

Memories flooded back as Vit Na referred to the private sequence. The whole affair had a surreal quality to it. Tur closed his eyes. Straining, erect ears tilted and scanned, but yielded nothing. *Still she treads like a shadow.* Shifting eyes opened their lids to enjoy the flow of the familiar visage. *But she strides like a dream.* Again, Tur reflected upon the delivered testimony. *All my dreams.* He had lived them as well. Tur wasn't sure he wanted to relive those feelings by viewing the coded sequence of the Vit Na Iku Animem. Certainly not that final tear shed in remorse. *So not So Wari.* Tur stilled his mind so that his feelings could not be heard. Sharu discipline was not his forte, but he was So Wari. He watched on without further emotional entanglement.

—◖●◗—

The Council experienced Vit Na's six-month ordeal like the fascinating fury of a storm during what was left of the evening. The doubts that initially permeated the chamber melted away as the extraordinary trek became a facet of each Council member's present experience. When Vit Na Iku finished telling her tale, a long silence suffused the chamber before any thoughts were shared.

"What a noble sacrifice. The Melkyz community should feel exalted," said Slijay with the elegant oration for which the Sulenz were so well-known. "She has done us all honor."

"Yes, but be that as it may, we still do not know from whence this plague has come to us. As Vit Na Iku has shown us, this inhibition field the Jing Pen generate is, in effect, strikingly similar to the Poison itself. This is too strange to be coincidence. We may still have a deadly enemy amongst us," Meeth said.

"Meeth, we've been through this," replied Slijay. "The Quatal made a bold move against us, gambling everything on one clutch. They missed the mark. We all feel terrible about this ugly affair, but it's over. Give it a rest."

Car Hom stepped up to Slijay deliberately. The move, intentional and disconcerting, reminded all gathered that Slijay's last statement could easily be interpreted as a challenge to the Head of Council.

"I apologize, Meeth," the Sulenz offered. "The pain of Rault's loss, the humiliation of impeachment. You must be aghast with the chain of events. I meant no ill will."

Slijay yielded the floor back to Meeth, who never formally accepted the Sulenz contrition and continued his statement as if he had never been interrupted.

"We have taken the liberty of purging the entire algae population." A general wave of surprised thought projections rippled through the chamber. Meeth showed no reaction. Someone would be more outraged than surprised. He asked, "Any objections?"

Thea spoke up, boldly. "Don't you think that's a bit excessive? I mean, the threat is gone—why waste the resources? The healthy algae will just supplant the bad, won't they?"

He shows annoyance, but no more, Meeth thought. *Someone here must be feeling more.*

"Meeth, I'm sorry, but I, for one, agree with Thea. You had no right to commit those resources to such a large-scale and useless project," said Slijay, choosing his words with relish. "We have been watching you. My intelligence on you suggests a string of irrational decisions on your part. This mission, for example: what an incredible discovery. But the logic for launching it in the first place? Flawed. There was never a need to send so much expensive hardware into the unknown. We could have solved our problems from this end."

Meeth allowed Slijay to ramble on uninterrupted and circled the room as the smaller meg spoke. The Sulenz loved attention, and they so seldom got such an audience. This one now, unknowingly, held Meeth's attention most closely.

"It's a wonderful find," Slijay continued. "The legacy of the Keepers at last comes back to the fold. Let us speak plainly here today. We have been drifting apart for ages, each of us seeking our own destiny. Subtle friction between our societies is tolerable, but in recent years, indifference has become the norm."

Enjoying the limelight and feeling poetic, Slijay's thoughts became stronger and more eloquent.

"Whatever happened to the days when we cared about each other? When we shared our cousins' glory as well as our cousins' woes? We have become selfish and cold. These Jing represent a rekindling of the fires that forged our Realm."

Yaw Daor eyed Meeth, pacing restlessly as the Sulenz spoke. "What do you mean a 'rekindling,' Slijay?" the Alkyz asked.

"An opportunity, brother. When was the last time someone outside of your clan called you brother? I'd guess more than a lifetime. We have an opportunity to welcome a new society to the fold."

Slijay looked around the Council, wide-eyed and alive with anticipation. "Alone, scared, confused in a hostile world, the Jing survive and grow, but at a snail's pace. They live, brothers, in our cold shadow, with no one to protect them. They exist at the mercy of those who envy us and our Realm.

"The Quatal tried to get at us through something as simple as the algae our livestock consume." Slijay lectured on, "What if some desperate foe—or, as Meeth has suggested, some deranged faction of our own society—were to exploit these Jing? Those who would might seek to destroy us through them."

Meeth kept his pace constant, all the while keeping a pulse on the emotional temperature of the room as Slijay held the floor.

"These fledgling Jing need guidance," Slijay projected lovingly. "Our guidance."

Slijay momentarily stopped pacing and paused for dramatic effect. "I refer you all to the Pact we swore to uphold so many eons ago: 'No child of Fitu, upon achieving sentience, shall be denied audience to petition for admittance to the Greater Society.'"

Hushed murmurs followed as the ramifications of Slijay's observation sank in. "By definition, whether they have been engineered so or not, they do meet the minimal criteria for claiming Efilu heritage. The enlightened children of Fitu shall be welcomed!"

The Melkyz delegate, Yhm Vel, spoke mockingly. "There is a veritable chasm between simple sentience and enlightenment. They seem more like stepchildren than *actual* heirs, by my reckoning."

Slijay's response was immediate and smooth. "On the whole, the Efilu are traditionally a matrilineal society, Ati Yhm Vel. It doesn't matter how they were fathered."

The argument was all too neat. Consternation and distaste typified most of the participants in the room—all save two.

Chybon, the High Tyen, sat at his station, ostensibly devoid of any opinions at all.

The other was Meeth.

I still don't know for sure who is responsible for this duplicity, Meeth thought. *But Slijay seems to voice a lone opinion. He is persuasive and knowledgeable, but no one is buying what he is selling—not so far. Still, if what this Melkyz Animem says is true, Jing Pen entry into our ranks could prove disastrous. This Sulenz must be silenced.*

"Many of us have grown testy," Tur interjected, apparently judging the restive dynamics in the room, and Meeth nodded in satisfaction. He'd been right about Tur. The officially minted High Commander's intimate mind-voice rose above the projected murmurs and rampant queries amidst the Council. "The neurologic strain of the substitute food source for so many months has made us all irritable. May I recommend that we all table this discussion, for now, and resume at a later date?"

As the new Sentry at Arms, Tur was responsible for peacekeeping during session. Weyef's old job.

"That Animem has some Jing psychic components. The chance to learn from them could prove invaluable," continued Slijay, unresponsive to the rationale behind Tur's suggestion. "They *do* make references to our images as 'gods.' It would be quite beneficial to them if we could reverse this inhibition factor with which they are burdened. Open their minds as it were. On behalf of the Sulenz people, I volunteer our resources to voyage back to Fitu to begin the transfer."

"I forbid it!" Meeth decreed.

"We do not recognize your authority to forbid the return to Fitu," Slijay said. The Sulenz watched Meeth sigh in resignation and droned on. "It is within our right..."

Has Slijay become bold or desperate? Meeth steeled himself. *The spirit of the law...* His father's haunting words echoed in Meeth's mind.

Action! Slijay didn't see the deadly So Wari tail whip at him at lightning speed.

"I can point out—" Slijay's elegant thought projection ceased abruptly.

The Sulenz leader's last vision was of his peers' horrified looks as his body was cleft in two by the lethal spikes. Meeth deftly followed through with the wheeling movement, obvious satisfaction on his face, as if he had ground an unseen Jing into expensive floor cover with a careless misstep. Then, he feigned just the right amount of remorse when he noted Slijay's hewn body at both ends of his station.

"I forgave his transgression once," Meeth said, referring to the slight Slijay had delivered moments earlier. "Twice, I am loath to grant. I say now that the Jing Pen race is a potential Threat to Life. I don't know what could happen if they were brought here to the Realm, but we all have experienced the results of Sulenz biologic experimentation."

He shook his head as if to uncloud his thoughts. "Until we can all clear the neurotoxins built up from utilizing the substitute food source, I don't want any complications from Jing Pen psychic contamination. I hereby move that we seal off the Fitu star system until we can sort this thing out."

Meeth sat down and noted that many of those assembled were still staring at Slijay's remains. Tur came forth, motioning to a contingent of So Wari guards to quell the volatile situation.

Meeth hung his head for several heartbeats, then projected for all to hear. "Undoubtedly, my pique may have led to tetchy impulses here today. Until I have recovered enough to carry out my responsibilities, I will step down as Head of Council."

Tur took Meeth by the arm, only to be relieved of his charge by two Tyen security meren. Weyef's old job had apparently been broken into two new ones, with the Si Tyen taking on the clandestine aspects of the position.

As Meeth was led away in Si Tyen custody, he thought, *Since when did the Tyen concern themselves with the intelligence community?*

The absent Tralkyz contingent addressed private matters, separate from the Great Council Diet, paramount to the transfer of power in the Tralkyz Alliance. Bo Tep found himself at the heart of those matters.

"Ol Ygar died two months ago, Bo," the Tralkyz emissary, Tee Spuun, informed Bo Tep. "You have been named his successor."

Tee Spuun looked as if he had more to say but was tentative about saying it. The small conference chamber lay adjacent to the main Council room, door opened, while Bo Tep and the emissary spoke within.

"Two Si Tyen security meren have detained me for a 'preliminary' debriefing in private," Bo Tep whispered his thought.

"Not just Tyen," Tee Spuun corrected with a wry smirk. "The Children of Dragon stand guard at your door."

"So," Bo Tep reasoned, "the Council supports a change in leadership—and the populace thinks we're due for a tour of duty."

"You don't look surprised," the younger meg observed.

"The Tralkyz haven't led the Council in three hundred thousand years." Bo Tep winked. "When you've been through what I've been through over the past seven months, there aren't many surprises left."

"Well, here's one for you," Tee Spuun said. "You got the go-ahead from the Si Tyen quarter. Most of the minor societies cheered the decision on after the nomination. The high societies were outvoted in the election."

More than surprised, Bo Tep was shocked. "The Tyen? Are you sure?" He peered over in the direction of two guards outside the half-open door.

"Positively. They actively swayed the lower societies to bid in our favor—" Tee Spuun tapped Bo Tep on the chest. "In *your* favor, my liege."

Bo Tep raised an eyebrow at the note of sarcasm. The meg was also a pack leader and nearly eye to eye with Bo Tep.

"Watch that, Tee. I'm not bound by Round Table etiquette yet. I can still take you out and wipe you down."

Tee Spuun flinched at the warning. A smile from Bo Tep took the edge off the threat.

Tee Spuun seems very diffident for a chief, Bo Tep thought. *He wouldn't last long in the trials of leadership.*

"Anyway, we can finally get a few things changed around here, you think?" a humbled Tee Spuun said.

"I don't know," Bo Tep answered slowly in whispered tones, more to himself than to his dull informant. "Why would the Si Tyen, of all peoples, manipulate *us* into a position of power? *Me*, in particular? After all, I just led the most recent Tyge in the Forest of Feelings. It doesn't make sense." He tugged at his chin.

"They are very righteous by nature," Tee Spuun offered.

"Yeah, maybe." Bo Tep hesitated. "Maybe."

He closed the door to the room.

"I don't think anyone's that righteous," Bo Tep whispered harshly in the ancient Tralkyz tongue. "Even if they were, this is more than righteous; it's disruptive. That's never been in Tyen nature." No accompanying projection. "Anyway, it won't matter for years. Meeth is old, but I'm sure he'll be around for a good long time."

That prospect rendered Bo Tep's installation as Premier Apparent to the Head of Council no more than a ceremonial affair, downplayed by the Tralkyz. For now, he would serve only as High Chief of the Alliance of Tralkyz Lesser Societies.

Bo Tep reentered the Round Table chamber just in time to see Meeth being led out by two Tyen guards. Something about the set of their shoulders troubled him.

Super-hunter attitude.

Tur shot him a cautioning look accompanying a tight thought summary projection of what the Tralkyz missed in Council.

Bo Tep eyed the arrest warily. *I expected the Sulenz to whine a bit about Slijay's death, but they wouldn't dare charge Meeth, under the circumstances. Slijay publicly offended Meeth. The fact that Meeth did not give him a pass was a matter of record.* Bo Tep surveyed the chamber. *There sure are a lot of Tyen around here these days.*

No one expected the Si Tyen to press for an ethics investigation. It seemed societally out of character. As the acting head of Council Intelligence and Security, Timon had Meeth arrested. *And with Meeth in custody and me only newly anointed Premier Apparent, Council leadership fell to...the Si Tyen,* Bo Tep concluded. *Turtle-spit!*

Bo Tep entered to the Council's formal and cool welcome—all except for the High Tyen's smile. That one warm, almost friendly.

He's the one! Bo Tep recognized him in an instant. *From the Forest! I'd recognize that smug look anywhere.*

It all makes sense now. Bo Tep's mind raced as he processed this new information. *The Tyen have been playing us from the beginning. Me, Tur, Meeth, the Council—even Vit Na. And now everyone will think I'm in on this whole thing!*

Bo Tep reached his seat at the traditional foot of the table. The Si Tyen sat at the opposite seat vacated by Meeth. The inauguration was casual in its simplicity. Timon, the Si Tyen Council Intelligence chief, stood, obviously ready to decline the official position as Regent Custodian of Council. Bo Tep was installed as Premier Actual.

It's too pat, Bo Tep decided. *I have to break this up somehow. They've installed me here for their own reasons. I don't know what they've got on me, but if one of them also gets the top security position, too...*

He glanced at Tur, So Wari steady. Bo Tep now knew him well enough to detect concealed uncertainty.

The new Tralkyz High Chief thought fast. He knew the people he could absolutely trust and rely on were few. More important now than basic competence was loyalty.

"Timon, may the Tralkyz be the first to thank you as acting Head of Council," Bo Tep said. "As newly appointed Premier Actual of the Council, my first duty is to select a new Head of Intelligence and Security. As of now, you are relieved of all duties as head of Council Security. Effective immediately, I name Tur to that position."

The Si Tyen stiffened, their collective countenance statuesque. In the history of the Efilu, never were Si Tyen so visibly shaken by the unexpected.

Bo Tep suppressed a wry smile. "I've come to know this meg better than I know my Seconds on our little outing, and I can't think of anyone the Council could trust more than he. As for the Jing Pen and the remainder of Fitu, from this moment on, the planet will be off-limits. Completely quarantined. No visitation, in or out. No one communicates with them, and no one sends any little 'care packages' to them."

Bo Tep eyed the Sulenz, Ironde, and Si Tyen carefully with that statement, hoping to detect a tell.

"We can reexamine Doh's records at our leisure." Bo Tep nodded to Jeen. "See to it that the information is made available to all interested parties. Weyef, as you are now unemployed, you will head the official study of the Jing, alleged Jing Pen, and their right to claim Efilu heritage. This session of the Council is here by adjourned."

Bo Tep left the room with regal bearing none had seen before on a Tralkyz.

Weyef exchanged glances with Tur. As the chamber emptied, she asked, "What do you think?"

"Short and to the point," Tur said. "I think I'm going to like this new Council."

"Do you want to tell me what this is all about, Sedon? You're not regular security," Meeth said casually to his Si Tyen escort.

"And you're not crazy either, Meeth," replied the Tyen. "You deliberately killed Slijay because he threatened to bring our Jing Pen into the bosom of Greater Society." He tightened his grip on Meeth's arm. "We may have lost our hold on Council Intelligence for now, but Timon, our *ear*, still sits on the Council."

Sedon pushed Meeth in front of him, forcing him further and further down a seldom-used hallway. He was joined by two more Tyen guards before continuing to speak.

"These catacombs are crawling with Jing," Meeth observed. "Both tree and sewer varieties I see. Loathsome creatures." He read the runes on the wall. They became less erratic as Meeth and his unwelcome entourage rove through the restrictive conduit.

"We've been exploring new avenues of thought and new alliances," Sedon verbalized in the old tongue. "We believe there's a swell in the Alom ahead, one that may carry more souls to greater heights. You don't win a war by fighting every battle tooth and claw. Skirmishes don't count for much in the course of the Alom." Sedon smiled, "Ripples in a river. What does matter is that to survive, any Lesser Society must take responsibility for its members or the Greater Society will do it instead. When our peoples truly understand the difference between simple sentience and enlightenment, the remaining answers will become obvious. We've already primed Bo Tep to lead the Council."

Sedon and his companions led Meeth deeper into the winding corridors that ran the length of the catacombs beneath the Round Table. Meeth noted a pair of Melkyz hands dangling at Sedon's side.

"You were hoping to get at the data on the fate of the Keepers," Meeth said, trying not to struggle. "That's why you supported the Sulenz motion to admit the Jing Pen to the Greater Society."

Sedon urged Meeth, "Consider, we may have come to a level of arrogance that will lead to ruin. Such power, such knowledge. As we've bent time and space to our will, we assume that we can change the tide of the Alom instead of following its course. The Jing have changed the game. Guiding them may remind us all that we need to return to the humility of yielding to the flow of our destiny."

Don't alert them to your next move, Meeth thought.

"You still don't understand, do you, Meeth?" Sedon paused in the isolated hallway. In hushed tones, he projected, "We aren't looking for the Keepers. We, the Children of Dragon, *are* the Keepers."

Meeth looked at him with both disbelief and horror.

"That's right. The Children of Dragon cult discovered millions of years ago how to travel, via astral displacement, to distant worlds,"

Chybon, the other Si Tyen escort, said. "Unfortunately, it requires a combined group effort. We can only send one or two at a time. The drain on our life force leaves many of us sterile. We discovered that too late. Needless to say, our reproduction has dropped off. Thank the Alom that we can count a few Wilkyz among our order. Their *Time-splitting* talents have proven extremely helpful to our cause. Collectively, *diversity* used to be our strength. Remember? Yes, we boast Wilkyz, Melkyz—even a few So Wari among our ranks." He laughed.

"We've had a very weak presence on Fitu for the last five hundred thousand years—since the Great Revolt there. There were complications, you know. A few Animem Tyen were left to guide the surviving Jing." The Tyen meg shrugged. "It was the best we could do. We have been completely out of contact for the last thousand years. We needed you to expose the existence of the human race, to see what the Jing have done in our absence. Humankind belongs to Fitu and therefore to us."

Sedon now took on a more persuasive tone. "We have become stagnant, Meeth. The Efilu have not admitted an independent, new species to the Greater Society in nearly sixty million years. We have to broaden our definition of intelligence to include new species of Fituine origin, even if they are quasi-artificial. The Greater Society is becoming spiritually barren." Sedon nodded earnestly. "A sterility of the soul. Both the human tribes and the Efilu Realm will collapse if we don't bring new blood into our communities. The Jing will probably end up killing themselves if we don't guide them. *They* need our help," Sedon coaxed. "*We* need a dose of their... innocence. We need each other, whether you realize it or not."

"We So Wari, at least, are doing just fine on our own," Meeth growled. "We don't need some fur-mites coming in here and getting into everything. And we certainly don't need mystical guidance in making our decisions. We are not impressed with level-four psychic tricks."

"Actually, level six. With that level of control, the Kini Tod became the perfect pawns to direct our efforts on Fitu." Chybon snickered. "And none became the wiser."

Meeth's mind raced through the possibilities of what a level-six psychic could do. He had never heard of such a thing in any Efilu records, just the legends. The revelation came to him like the shock of ice water suddenly coursing through his veins.

"Tyen! You got to Vit Na somehow, conditioned her before the Return. You maneuvered Doh onto the *ReQam* roster, too. *You* were the architects of the Poison!" Meeth declared. "The nuances involved in meddling with golden algae—only level five or better could have engineered such a mechanism."

A chorus of rushing water intruded upon the quiet conversation. A massive root system filtered sewage of pollutants, the drainage collected into a clear stream under the ancient tree that cradled the Round Table.

The third Tyen mer had remained silent, until now. "We can never admit it. For hundreds of thousands of years, we have tried to teach these Jing Pen how to Dance Life."

Meeth heard a splash. The distraction marked his move.

"They're slow learners." The mer said, returning her attention to Meeth, too late. "We only wanted to show all Efilu what it is like to—"

Meeth suddenly broke free of the grips that he had been subtly loosening from his arms since they started down the hall. He was able to trap one of his captors against the wall. He crushed Chybon's spine. The other dealt Meeth a crippling blow to the chest. An undulating silhouette bobbed in the waterway beside them. Not a Tyen exactly, but something...older. Meeth couldn't tell if he was seeing double or if another Tyen had joined the ruckus.

"Sorry I'm late. Level seven travel takes so much out of us these days." The nameless Si Tyen mer spoke placidly over Meeth's heaving body. She had but one eye. "All three triads have convened on Fitu. We are in agreement; there was no other choice. I told you we could not reason with him. It is said, 'There is only one way to relieve a lead So Wari who's lost his way.'"

Meeth's armor grew soft and ashen, and his breath came shallow with great labor.

"We've learned that Fitu yet retains some remnant of Vit Na the Kemithi. And more than an Animem, too. But he and his *synespia* Jing mer will need help. Guidance we dare not provide."

Solemnly, the Fituine Tyen watched the So Wari soul before her slipping away. "When he is done, we must take the hands of Meeth."

Meeth knew he was dying after the second blow to his head. "Help!" With his last iota of concentration, he projected, "Bo Tep—*someone*—don't let them into the Council's inner circle. The Tyen are mad, all of them! They ruin everything they touch! They *are* the Poison! They'll destroy us all! Fight them, Bo. You must fight!"

— EPILOGUE —

Martial law in California had been rescinded weeks earlier. Still, after a winter of cleanup, business as usual had not quite returned to San Francisco. Whispers on the street about aliens and monster-bear carcasses lingered. Rumors of dire wolves roaming Muir Woods endured for months.

At the corner of Post and Taylor stood a little oddity shop with a lone figure working behind the counter. A radio broadcast of TransWorld News anchor Adrian Dunbar lampooning accounts of aliens in the woods drew a "chuh" from the black woman.

An elderly gentleman ambled in, cane in hand. The cashier, a tall black woman, looked up from the yellowing pages of a weathered book. "Hello, sir. Can I help you?"

"'The Dragon's Heir.' What an interesting name for a store," he said.

"Thank you." Robyn Washington had been absorbed in translating a druidic text. She closed the volume to greet him warmly.

The elderly man was bald with a trimmed, white beard and wire-rimmed spectacles. He sported a well-worn tweed jacket with oversized pockets and suede elbow patches. Washington smiled at him and glanced at the ornate umbrella in his hand, which she first took for a cane.

"Best to be prepared." He hiked a thumb over his shoulder. "Looks like there's going to be quite a blow."

"Glad I'm in for the day," she said, patting the bound edition beneath her fingers and smiling. "Me and my books."

"Do you also fix the computers?" he asked, pointing to the sign with his umbrella: Computer Repairs. Payment Only for Reparable Damage. Free Diagnostics.

"No." She smiled more broadly. "My fiancé does that."

The man wrinkled his brow. "He must be very good to make such a bold offer."

"You have to leave it overnight for the diagnostic," Clyde Olsen said, parting the curtains that separated the back room from the main storefront.

The older man didn't even raise an eyebrow at the sight of the white man emerging from the workshop. Clyde Olsen noticed that the old man's left eye did not track along with his right eye when he shifted his gaze.

"Well," the patron said. "I have been having some trouble with my desktop computer. It's a little old, but then, so is any technology over six months of age these days!" He laughed at his own joke.

Olsen smiled politely.

"What's your name, son?" the man asked.

"I am called Ol Sen."

"Nordic heritage." The man nodded. "Good stock. I'll bring my CPU in tomorrow. I came in from the street expecting the usual paperbacks, comic books, sci-fi and fantasy magazines." He grinned. "I'm pleased to have found what appear to be fellow seekers of forgotten truth. Your collection of books, maps, and curios here could be the envy of any shop in New England or the UK."

"Do I detect a northern New England accent, sir?" Robyn ventured. "Maine, perhaps?"

"You have a good ear, missy." The old sailor had cleaned up nicely. "Quite the assemblage of arcane material!" He fingered a faded copy of *Encyclopedia of Occultism and Parapsychology.* "I've spent some years at sea. Still working on my land legs. One collects a thing or two on those journeys. I'll bring some very old books you may find interesting, young lady—and maybe a dragon or two!" he said with a wink of his good eye.

"We'd be very happy to see them," Ol Sen said cheerfully. The bell over the door tinkled upon opening. A disheveled Chinese spinster shuffled in, creased face bracketing a senseless smile. She began rummaging aimlessly through the piles of used books on the shelves. She chanted a strange song:

"Same heart, same spirit; ill- fated,
never depart, but never fear it, soul sated.
Found; Dragon's lair,
breath; a fiery air,
death defying heir,
safe, but ever-hated."

The old woman caroled, *la-di-da*s, to fill in the rest.

Robyn and Ol Sen redirected their gazes to the Asian woman as her pleasant confusion turned to disruptive agitation. Presently a well-dressed gentleman entered the shop, apparently in search of the demented fugitive.

"She's quite a wanderer, I fear," he chuckled. "A better explorer than a songstress."

The clean-shaven man claimed the crone and gently led her away by the arm. As he offered his apologies on her behalf, the British accent charmed and soothed proprietor and escapee alike.

"Her family owns the Panda Antique Shop across the street. She loves these old books. Can't read a word of them," the newcomer explained. "I'm hard-pressed to place that tune she sings." He laughed and panned an affable gaze around the shop. "Can any of you?"

Thunder cracked as the sky broke open, and sheets of rain hurtled sideways, spewing the dark of night before its time. Caught off guard by the suddenness of the squall, Ol Sen draped a comforting arm around his woman. She whispered urgently in his ear, "Efilu could control the weather you say?"

Ol Sen spoke sotto voce. "We could, but we seldom did. Efilu did not fear nature, we simply stood against the storms when they came." He patted her on the shoulder, spoke more audibly, and nodded. "There's a certain beauty in nature's strength, though."

Backs to their customers, Robyn and Ol Sen admired the ferocity of the weather through the shop window. Unseen by the couple, the wealthy man extended his arms, pressing his hands down and the gale ceased. In turn, the aged sailor pointed his umbrella skyward, and the rain drizzled to a mist. The old woman, confusion vanquished, reached toward heaven, drawing in clenched fists to her chest. Brilliant sunshine split the cloudy umbra, bathing the shop in a golden halo.

"Wow!" Robyn exclaimed. Perplexed by the sudden storm break, Ol Sen and Robyn returned their attentions to their guests.

"Stay dry, you two." The sailor said, inclined his head, and left, merrily humming the crone's little ditty, umbrella hanging from his forearm. The eccentric couple calmly followed the first patron's exit in short order.

When the store was again empty, Ol Sen asked, "Find anything new, Robyn?"

"Not much. Most of this is the same as the others—just vague references to dragon hordes—but there is a section in here that actually contains a map."

Ol Sen stroked his hair backward and frowned. "If it looks promising, we'll check it out."

Robyn looked at him with a little concern. "How are our finances, Vit—" She chuckled as they shared a smile. "I mean, Ol Sen?"

"You should call me Clyde in public, Robyn." Ol Sen's smile faded gently as he rubbed his eye. "Don't worry. The stock market has been very good to us this month. We have about thirty-eight thousand dollars after expenses." He breathed in and sighed slowly.

"Headaches again? Maybe it's the weather." Robyn regarded him until he shook his head and returned to his work. "Something else is bothering you then."

"I didn't know your linguistic skills extended to intimate acuity," Ol Sen said, returning his attention to her.

"We have another word for it, smart aleck." She stood with fists akimbo. "*Intuition.*"

"I could use some of that. I'm getting nowhere fast screening keywords from hard drives. Not even scouring random computers brought in for repair does us any good." Ol Sen had already lost focus on the conversation. "There's a word I just can't remember that I feel I should know. Less a word than a familiar notion, anyway. I can't find it in any database."

"On the tip of your tongue, huh?" Robyn crossed to his desk where he studied an old text. He poured over memorable images Robyn hadn't given much thought to since childhood.

"Why are you stressing out over elves and dwarves?" she asked.

"I don't know," Ol Sen said, frowning. "And that also bothers me. There's something about these combinations of features... they're disturbingly familiar. Remnants of something in the deepest recesses of my memories. Wish I had a Tarn of Animems to reference."

"Did they really exist?" Robyn asked in wonder.

"No. Not exactly. Nightmares." Ol Sen shrugged. "Specters of freakish Jing-creatures that parents conjured to frighten cubs. You know, to encourage hygiene and cleanliness to keep fur-mi— mammals out of the food stores."

She arched an eyebrow and tousled his hair. "Remember, you have fur now, too."

"Yes, I get it," he said, grinning. "I'm part of your tribe now. I'll yield to your health practices." Ol Sen shook his head. "Hard to get used to the physical disabilities you tolerate."

"Vision care is very limited in other places, it seems," Robyn observed as she tidied the countertop. "Did you notice that each of the last three visitors had only one eye?" She hummed a few bars of the little old lady's tune. "Funny, huh?"

— SHEPHERDS OF LOST HISTORY —

So much of Fitu's history has slipped through time, buried under
the soil and rock.
A saga unremembered, uninterpreted.
She who finds and reclaims those lost days owns them, writes
them...
Pages that define every chapter that follows in the Book of Jing.
The coming of Efilu pilgrims has long been foreseen by The One.
We, the Children of Dragon, are ubiquitous.
Our destiny, to shepherd His heirs, at the cost of our lives if need
be.
—And the lives of all the Toys in heaven.
We'll remain as Guideposts along that long, winding way...
For, it is written, "Even in the wilderness, there must be order."
So say we, The Keepers of the Faith!

THE ABRIDGED JING PEN TRANSLATOR

STANDARDS AND MEASURES

AYQOT RADIUS - The distance from a celestial body's center at which the gravity matches Earth's standard surface gravity. This calculation is the guiding principle in Fitu-forming gas giants for Efilu habitation. A simple Ayqot radius defines a perfect sphere with 1 G surface gravity, but a world with mountains and oceans is more nuanced and requires a more complex adjusted Ayqot calculus.

BIM - Measure of energy equal to the radiant energy that strikes a plane the area of a square dyme in 1/1000 of a day at a distance of 50,000 dymes. Modern humans would measure bims in terms of kilojoules.

DAEBIM - One tenth of a bim. See BIM.

DAEDYME - One tenth of a dyme, or about 1800 miles. See DYME.

DYME - One tenth the distance traveled by sound in 24 hours. About 18,000 miles.

KORIBIM - One hundredth of a bim. See BIM.

KORIDYME - One hundredth of a dyme, or about 180 miles. See DYME.

INTIMATE COMMUNICATION -Telepathy.

Level 0 - Sensitivity to the presence of other minds.

Level 1 – The ability to read another's projected thoughts.

Level 2 - The ability to precisely project thought content.

Level 3 - The ability to psychically operate advanced technology beyond one's sphere of influence without physical contact (gel technology, Telesciens, etc.)

Level 4 - The ability to control another's thoughts.

Level 5 - The ability to project one's mind and senses beyond one's sphere of influence.

Level 6 - The ability to possess the body and memories of another sentient being.

Level 7 - The ability to transport one's physical being to a distant location without the benefit of advanced technology. Considered legend, no one in known Efilu history has been able to perform at this psychic level.

PHOTODYME - The distance traveled by light in ten years.

PITKOR'S TIPPING POINT - The precise phase when/where matter has no mass but has not yet transitioned to pure energy.

SEKWOY REACTION - Type 1, 2, and 3 equations via which matter is pushed to Pitkor's tipping point, where matter has no mass but has not yet transitioned to pure energy. In type 1, the state is volatile and is used to power and arm weapons. Type 2 reactions are used on a larger scale for storage of energy and maintain organic matter in that transitional state for extended periods. Type 3 reactions power mass/energy/mass transmutation;

folding space for precision conveyance of large masses over quantum distance, creation of complex force fields, and gel devices which interface with the Efilu's personal spheres of influence.

COMMON TERMS

ALOM (also ALUM) -The inescapable Current or River of Fate. The Alom is represented by a temporal double helix, one strand of water and the other of fire. Life is the bond of fire by water. It both leads and follows one everywhere. The Efilu personalize their particular branch of this stream of time and space.

ANIMEM - Animated memory used for interactive storage of an individual's life experiences, mind, soul, and body image. Animems may take tangible form but are limited to deductive reasoning. An animem can process data submitted according to its experience but cannot internalize new knowledge.

BOLOK - Livestock used much as cattle are used today. These were the ceratopsia of the Cretaceous period.

THE CHILDREN OF DRAGON - popularly used to describe Efilu who were exposed to the Tyelaj or the arctic Yin and Yang symbol. The term actually denotes a cult that includes the Keepers, as well as Si Tyen mystics still operating in the Efilu Realm.

EFILU - Enlightened children of Fitu. Intelligent peoples who originated on Fitu. All are telepathic to some degree. All are descended from what we have come to know as dinosaurs. (See EFILU: THE PEOPLES OF THE REALM.)

EXODUS - The escape and migration from Fitu after the catastrophe 65 million years ago.

EXODUS CORRIDOR - The pathway through space traveled by the Efilu when they abandoned Fitu.

FITU - The Efilu name for Earth.

FORECHAIR - Because the anatomy of most Efilu includes a sizable tail, few people of the Realm are comfortable sitting in a chair with a back. The forechair has a vertical supporting structure in the front for the torso and a horizontal extension in the rear for the tail to rest on. Arms are either absent altogether from forechairs or are located as a shelf on the front of the chair, over which clasped arms may rest.

FUR-MITE - Efilu slang term for a mammal. Usually derogatory.

GEL APPARATUS - A variety of crystal integration machines used for managing, storing, and transmitting data. They are coupled with a solution of electromagnetically active particles that act as nanoscale construction devices or building blocks to form a macroscopic tool or structure (e.g. gelconsole, gelcore, gelcraft, gel-decor, gelfactory). Also, See WAVE.

JING - A broad term referring to mammals. The Efilu make no distinction between Jing, with reference to size or species. More formal than fur-mite, but still a term of derision.

JING PEN- Artificially engineered mammals. In high times of Fitu, "Jing Pen" was synonymous with "toy."

KAS PEN - Snakes. Genetically engineered reptiles designed to control mammalian (Jing) infestations. The absence of limbs was a genetically engineered adaptation for pursuing their smaller quarry deep into burrows and crevices. This increased reach of the Kas Pen fangs and venom completed a combination of weapons against which the primitive mammals had no defense.

MEG - Any male Efilu.

MER – (pronounced *mare*) Any female Efilu.

MEREN - More than one individual Efilu of either or both genders.

MINI-WAVE - A powerful gel apparatus that is one thousandth the mass of a Wave. See WAVE.

PEN - The modifier used to denote genetic engineering of a natural organism to suit Efilu needs. The name of the natural base organism always precedes the word Pen.

PERSONAL SPHERE OF INFLUENCE - Derived from the natural electromagnetic aura that is generated by all living things. The Efilu generate a more intense field than most lower life-forms, owing to the formers' high metabolism and tissue density. Furthermore, by means of extra-sensory perception, the field is partially visible to Efilu. To one degree or another, the Efilu have been able to fold and convolute the field into more complex and versatile psychic appendages (e.g. astral sensory probes, electromagnetic emitters, telekinetic pseudopods).

QUATAL - A defeated enemy race. They were dendritic shape shifters who unsuccessfully challenged the Efilu in battle.

SKYWAKE- As in flocks of modern birds, air currents form a "V" pattern and thin the air density immediately behind an apex flight-leader in formation. The lower air density affords less resistance to subordinate wings, but the multiplier effect by supersonic avians build-up skirts of kinetic energy that crest into Skywake with explosive intensity. Especially effective when weaponized to targeted impact by Vansar in legion.

TECTONIC PLATFORMS – Larger versions of *Wave* technology, Tectonic Platforms are patches of simple biosynthetic mesh deployed above uninhabitable gas giants. Spreading organically over the outer atmosphere, the continent-sized masses are adhesive at the edges and coalesce into one layer a few miles thick (much like Earth's tectonic plates float on magma). These carefully engineered Tectonic Platforms eventually form a closed sphere at the Ayqot radius (see AYQOT RADIUS definition in Standards and Measures.) The low intrinsic gravity of the platforms gradually attracts debris and dust from the trapped portion of the native atmosphere, building a bedrock stratum across a vast inner surface. Compost seeding the outer surface, with organic refuse, microbes and mold spores contributes to formation of soil on the outer crust. An outer atmosphere selectively released for the gases below the surface mixes to achieve the elemental content and terminal velocity of the native Efilu atmosphere. The end result creates a fertile Fitu-like biome, and the foundation for making a terrestrial giant world ideal for colonization.

TYELAJ - The holographic symbol of the Dragon alternating with the traditional Yin and Yang sign. There is a mystical Si Tyen aspect to this planetary shrine as well as the end-on image of the DNA double helix molecule.

THE ROUND TABLE - Hosting an elite, limited population of one million politicians and administrative support personnel, the city was carved from a single hardwood tree and established as the seat of Efilu power. Still living, the tree is fed and powered by nutrients channeled from its ancient roots and carbohydrates, lipids, and proteins supplied from a network of saprophytic plants drawing from the surrounding soil and grafted to the tree's circulatory system. Sekwoy generators supplement the city's power with organic nuclear energy. The center piece of this structure is the Round Table itself: an elaborate edifice with a grand council chamber, and an advanced integrated data processing system. The whole structure is the handiwork of extinct So Beni engineers and has remained intact for over seventy million years. It was salvaged from Fitu fifty years after being left behind during the Exodus.

SENORI - Known by the current fossil record as the Allosaurus. Smaller than Tyrannosaurus, with proportionately longer, stronger arms. Wild Senori hunted in packs like lions.

SENORI PEN - Genetically engineered by the Sulenz to act as guardians against marauding therapods, Senori Pen were derived from the Allosaurus. The arms were genetically shortened to limit their ability to fend for themselves. Known by their skeletal remains as the Tyrannosaurus rex, they all but drove their natural counterparts to extinction in the wild in the last days of the Efilu on Fitu. They were virtually unstoppable without the use of advanced weapons. Eventually they became like mad dogs, prone to intimidate, accost, and ravage. The Efilu exterminated them during the Exodus.

MINOR SUBSPECIES - Many of the dominant Efilu served as sponsors to subspecies of their genetic lines. These close relatives were usually fertile and often cross bred with Higher Societies. Some became independent (Lower Societies) but were never potent participants in Efilu politics.

SHARU DISCIPLINE - Neurologic manipulation technique to relieve pain, anxiety, or involuntary movement (shivers, seizure, itchiness). In terminal circumstances, it may be invoked to read the mind and soul of the dead. This is the basis of creating an Animem as more than a simple recording or clone.

SYNESPRIT - A romantic or philosophical description indicating "as one of spirit." The term describes lovers, great artists, and thinkers who harmonize with one another, often sharing a common fate in the stream of the Alom. Synesprit partners refer to each other as synespira.

TELESCIEN - A pure energy machine with no mass. One of a variety of Sekwoy type 3 reaction-powered External Field Appendages (EFA) used by the Efilu for remote manipulation. The compound force field unit is controlled through a telepathy-sensitive interface with its Efilu pilot. It functions instantaneously, even at great distances. Effectively, it's a temporary, god-like automaton with artificial intelligence beyond that of any computer known to man.

TOMET - A peaceful alien race doomed by settling a star system once inhabited by the Efilu.

WAVE - Large gel apparatus used for extensive planetary or orbital tasks, (engineering or military). Very versatile, it can assume many configurations, such as space labs, bases, factories, or surface cities, but not the nearly infinite metamorphic options offered by the Telescien. Its potential energy output is greater than a Telescien's since it has mass. A Wave is more durable than a Telescien and can carry massive amounts of cargo, a myriad of passengers, or whole armies as it is derivative of similar, but more complex technology than the Tectonic Platform.

EFILU (THE PEOPLES OF THE REALM)

THE GREATER SOCIETY - The governing body of all enlightened species of the Efilu realm. This is unofficially divided into the more influential Higher Societies and the participatory Lesser Societies and a variety of subspecies with less formal and hence, insecure status.

THE HIGHER SOCIETIES

THE SUPER HUNTERS

ALKYZ - The largest of the class. Golden brown with ruby red highlights. The fur-like pile is mostly short, except at the back of the head, neck, forearms, and calves. The ears are relatively small and inconspicuous, and rounded rather than pointed. Size: 25 to 30 feet, 5,000 to 10,000 pounds. The largest and strongest of the super hunters. Previously ALKZ, the name evolved into Alkyz after the Exodus. They are well known for their administrative and diplomatic skills.

NELKY (Obsolete) - Over the 65 million years since the migration known as the Exodus, the name has evolved to adhere to the nomenclature of super hunters (-lkyz suffix) by changing to Melkyz. They are among the most brilliant strategists.

MELKYZ - Small therapodian people of the class of super hunters descended from a distant ancestor similar to the Velociraptor. Jet black to black and white marbled coat. The fur-like down has the consistency of mink or ermine, only softer, with a delicate, lightly oiled sheen. They have the ability to *Blend* into any surroundings. The large, pointed ears and long lean tails overall give the Melkyz an appearance much like a cross between a human upper body (including human facial features and hands) and a predatory kangaroo (kangaroo-like lower body with retractable claws). Size: 6 to 8 feet from head to toe when standing, 5 to 6 feet when sitting on haunches, 300 to 600 pounds of dense muscle.

SULENZ - Small, (6-8 feet tall, 300-400 pounds), almost tailless omnivores with soft, slick, pewter-gray pelts. These weaselly people primarily eat mollusks and insects they raise on ranches or farms in order to exploit their meat and honey. Sporting tiny tails, they are reminiscent of large prairie dogs. They are among the most gifted telepaths, but not very popular among Higher Society. The Sulen adapted the "z" at the end of their name to insinuate themselves into the super hunter class. They were never accepted as such among the Efilu. Because their population failed to keep pace with other higher societies, many in the Realm relegated the Sulen(z) to the lesser societies.

TRALKYZ - Charcoal gray/black coats with dull, fur-like, sound-absorbent plumage. Blue-gray highlights. Second largest of the Super Hunter races, they are heavily muscled, with thick, powerful tails. Ears are proportionally smaller than those of Melkyz and have tufts of feathers that fan out from behind the ears and glow red as a warning or when prepared to attack. Size: 15 to 18 feet tall, 2,000 to 3,000 pounds (Chiefs are bigger, at 22 to 25 feet tall and 4,500 to 7,000 pounds). They are unpredictable in every respect, except for their viciousness. They are known to always attack in pairs. Pound for pound, they are the fiercest of the Super Hunter class.

WILKYZ - Tan, auburn, brown, and burnt orange striped coats. Structurally similar to the Melkyz with rounded ears, but a little bulkier in the chest and shoulders. Long and lean with more substantial tails, they stand 12 to 15 feet from head to toe and weigh 1,000 to 2,000 pounds. Smaller than the Tralkyz, these Super Hunters usually travel alone or in small groups. They possess the ability to merge divergent time-lines temporarily, *Time-splitting*. The effect produces the illusion of greater numbers, for the purpose of briefly confusing an enemy, or attacking with overwhelming force. For short periods, parallel persona can collaborate on intellectual projects.

VANSAR - Avian people. Tall and slender, with wings that are powerfully muscled. Super joints allow for conversion from wings to effective arms and hands, almost instantaneously. Brilliantly colored, the plumage is a neat mixture of wide bands of golden yellow, orange, and iridescent purple. The bones are hollow and lightweight. The Vansar are disproportionately strong for their mass. Size: 800 to 1,000 pounds, 25 to 32 feet tall. It is widely believed that the Vansar race is the origin of the Phoenix legend. Vansar are among the largest avian species in the Efilu Realm. They rival the So Wari and Tyen in length, if not in mass.

PACHYDERM PEOPLES

SO WARI - Brown suede-like hides of various shades. The dorsal plates are hunter green but become marbled with age. The pointed, rabbit-like ears are long and move from flat against the head to stiffen sideways in a horizontal rather than vertical position, nearly straight out from the head when on alert or alarmed. Subtle changes in orientation focus on the source of sound without revealing alert status. So Wari are bulky, nearly muscle-bound in appearance, but incredibly fast and agile. They are the largest extant So species and are among the biggest of the land-dwelling Efilu. Size: 25 to 30 feet tall, 10,000 to 20,000 pounds.

SO BENI - Extinct *So* species. The average specimen was smaller than the extant So Wari. Tan, with yellow and green dorsal plates. Size: 23 to 28 feet tall and 7,500 to 14,000 pounds. Large saurian people; among the most influential and physically powerful. Their ancestors were herbivores, similar to the Stegosaurus. They and their successors were known for their military and engineering skills. They were eventually supplanted by the So Wari.

SO RIKHI - Smallest of the extant So species. Bulky and fierce, with permanent patches of armor fused from sections of their pelts during adolescence. Size: 8-10 feet tall, 800-2,000 pounds.

SI TYEN - Evolved from the typical European winged dragon physique. They have short, gun-metal gray mixed pile, with long silvery plumage. The build is intermediate, between that of the Alkyz and the So Wari. They stand 28 to 33 feet tall and weigh 8,000 to 14,000 pounds. Often referred to as TYEN; technically, Si Tyen is correct. They are distant relatives of the So species. These people have developed a pair of oversized dorsal plates that function as wings. A few stayed behind to try to salvage the Earth from the catastrophe caused by the Sulenz. The Efilu called them "The Keepers" short for "Keepers of the Faith." We know them from our distant memories as Dragons; Dragon was the proper name of the leader of the original Keepers who stayed behind.

ROOGS - Marine dwellers. Roogs are large aquatic people who raise fresh produce and develop biologic power sources, as well as designing most large complex space craft like the *ReQam*. Deep blue-green matted pile with moss green patches. Broad, powerful jaws are set in a humanoid face that sits atop a long neck. They resemble giant manatees. They have short, powerful limbs with oversized five-fingered hands and fin-like webbed feet. Size: 40 feet long. 18,000 to 30,000 pounds. Although amphibian, on land they travel in large water-filled corpuscles— sacks shaped like gigantic red blood cells that float on force fields.

MINOR or LOWER SOCIETIES

DENAR – Medium-sized fishers, they eat small game and occasionally supplement their diets with fruits and nuts. They are easily irritated. Their coats are an unassuming brown, with reddish patches around the eyes. They are 12 to 14 feet tall and weigh from 1,000 to 1,200 pounds.

GEN ROST - A cross between an owl and a penguin in appearance, Gen Rost are awkward when walking and possess limited flight capabilities. They have loose, short brown feathers with a few white accents. They live in humid, swampy climates. Size: 6 to 7 feet tall, 200 to 300 pounds.

IRONDE - Nomadic by nature, the Ironde are also omnivorous. Large, nearly rotund, they have short, thick tails and are covered from head to toe with long, luxurious, snow-white plumes that become deadly when stiffened. They resemble a cross between a giant porcupine and a badger. The face is a deep teal green.

Size: 12 to 14 feet tall, 1,200 to 1,500 pounds. Formerly IRFONDE, theses omnivorous people have a loose nomadic trading culture and are well-known for their adaptive skill using very little raw material. They are power producers and hardware suppliers for many of the lesser societies.

KINI TOD - Turtle-like appearance. Red-orange armor with green borders and bellies. Short, thick club-like tail. Size: 5 to 6 feet tall, 400 to 800 pounds.

MIT KIAM - Graceful and muscular, the Mit Kiam wear long, fur-like feathers and are shaped like ermine or chinchilla. The coat is a blend of golden tan, brown and red-brown hues. Serene, even tempered, difficult to rile. The plumage about the head is particularly spectacular, with contrasting highlights and dark tips. They stand 14 to 16 feet tall and weigh 1,200 to 1,600 pounds.

NOTEX - This species shows another example of super joint development. Lean, with disproportionately long legs, Notex have hyper-speed capabilities. They can achieve and sustain speeds as fast as 200 miles an hour, almost instantaneously. They alternately manipulate the coefficients of friction from 0 to 100% along the soles of their feet with each stride in a skating like motion. Darkly-colored indigo blue, with hints of violet, obliquely striped plumage throughout the body with razor sharp, blade like quills along the forearms. The tail is rigid and moves as a counter-balance. They are 8 to 10 feet tall and weigh 800 to 1,100 pounds.

TAL GENJ- A herbivorous people, they bear coats of rich brown, sporting short plumage with black accents—think of our deer markings. They have a frill or upper facial ridge above the forehead anchored to an array of flexible antlers. The effect is that of a neat, complex display of gleaming curls in females or dreadlocks in males. They are slender-to-medium in build and graceful. Size: 12 to 14 feet tall. 1,400 to 1,700 pounds.

TAN BARR- These herbivores have fluffy gray down with stripes and patches of purple-to-mauve plumage. They are medium-sized, stocky Efilu shaped like humanized koala bears. Size: 10 to 12 feet, about 1,000 pounds.

The Unabridged Translator... to be continued.

ABOUT THE AUTHOR

Glenn Parris writes in the genres of sci-fi, fantasy, and medical mystery. Considered by some an expert in Afrofuturism, he is a self-described lifelong sci-fi nerd. His interest in the topic began as a tween before the term Afrofuturism was even coined. As a graduate of The Bronx High School of Science, as were Samuel R. Delany, Jon Favreau, and Neil de Grasse Tyson, he was in good company to have his interests cultivated.

Parris encompasses his own dichotomy: physician by day, his scientific outlook informs his creative work. As one of the too few African-American men practicing medicine, his unique perspective makes his writing compelling and makes him an engaging speaker.